THE GIFT OF A CHILD

BY
SUE MacKAY

HOW TO RESIST A HEARTBREAKER

BY
LOUISA GEORGE

MILLS &
BOON

Dear Reader

When my editor suggested that Louisa George and I write a duet with an over-arching story I had no idea where it would lead. Fortunately Louisa and I know each other well and have critiqued each other's stories often, so we knew we'd be able to work together. That's about all we knew. But many e-mails and phone calls later, and after a few nudges from our editors, here is my half of *The Infamous Maitland Brothers* duet.

Right from the start I loved Mitchell and Jodi. I so wanted to sort out their lives—interfering, that's me—and give them their happy ending. But with the drama of their very ill little boy going on it wasn't easy. I hope you enjoy reading how these two reach out to each other for the special love they need to get them through a harrowing time.

Cheers

Sue MacKay

www.suemackay.co.nz
sue.mackay56@yahoo.com

Dear Reader

There are two reasons I particularly enjoyed writing this book. Firstly, I had the opportunity to work with good friend and wonderful writer Sue MacKay on the over-arching theme linking the two stories in *The Infamous Maitland Brothers* duet. With suggestions from our editors and lots of brainstorming we took a germ of an idea about feuding twin brothers and developed two intensely emotional stories.

The second reason I enjoyed writing this linked story is because it is set in a busy hospital, which is a new departure for me. The hospital is a fictional one, based in the centre of Auckland—New Zealand's largest city. Writing about twin brother doctors who are equally successful and important members of this hospital community was fun and challenging. Mitchell and Max have reputations as heartbreakers and neither of them is looking for commitment.

Transplant surgeon Max has had enough of people walking out of his life, so is reluctant to lose his heart to new nurse in town, Gabby. After a difficult past Gabby has moved to Auckland to reinvent herself, but she is not prepared for a life that involves falling in love… These two are so perfect for each other, but neither wants to admit it, so of course I had lots of fun helping them along a little!

I hope you enjoy Max and Gabby's story.

Warm regards

Louisa x

The Infamous Maitland Brothers duet
is also available in eBook format from www.millsandboon.co.uk

THE GIFT
OF A CHILD

BY
SUE MacKAY

First published in Great Britain 2013
by Mills & Boon, an imprint of Harlequin (UK) Limited.
Harlequin (UK) Limited, Eton House, 18-24 Paradise Road,
Richmond, Surrey TW9 1SR

© Sue MacKay 2013

ISBN: 978 0 263 89902 3

Printed and bound in Spain
by Blackprint CPI, Barcelona

With a background of working in medical laboratories and a love of the romance genre, it is no surprise that **Sue MacKay** writes Mills & Boon® Medical Romance™ stories. An avid reader all her life, she wrote her first story at age eight—about a prince, of course. She lives with her own hero in the beautiful Marlborough Sounds, at the top of New Zealand's South Island, where she indulges her passions for the outdoors, the sea and cycling.

Also by Sue MacKay:

YOU, ME AND A FAMILY
CHRISTMAS WITH DR DELICIOUS
EVERY BOY'S DREAM DAD
THE DANGERS OF DATING YOUR BOSS
SURGEON IN A WEDDING DRESS
RETURN OF THE MAVERICK
PLAYBOY DOCTOR TO DOTING DAD
THEIR MARRIAGE MIRACLE

**These books are also available in eBook format
from www.millsandboon.co.uk**

This one's for my friend, Anne Roper,
who is always so cheerful and fun to be with.
Thanks to her lovely daughter-in-law, Michelle,
for her help on YOU, ME AND A FAMILY.

And for Leslie, number one fan.

Also a big thank you
to Melanie Milburne and Fiona Lowe
for way back in the beginning.
This might be late but you've never been forgotten.

CHAPTER ONE

JODI HAWKE SWUNG the budget rental car against the kerb and hauled the handbrake on hard. Her heart was in her mouth as she peered through the grease-smeared windscreen towards the small, neat semi-attached town house she'd finally found after an hour of driving around, through and over Parnell. Auckland was not her usual playground. But that was about to change—for a time at least. No matter what the outcome of this meeting.

A chill lifted goosebumps on her skin. 'I can't do this.'

Brushing her too-long fringe out of her eyes, she turned to glare at her guilt-ridden reflection in the rear-vision mirror, and snapped, 'You have to.'

Think what's at stake. 'Jamie's life depends on you doing this. And doing it right. This day has always been hovering in the background, waiting for show time.'

Before she could overthink the situation for the trillionth time Jodi elbowed the door open and slid out onto the road. The unassuming brick town house sat back from the road, a path zeroing in on the front door with the precision of a ruled line. The lawn had been mown to within a millimetre of its life, and the gardens were bare of anything other than some white flowering ground cover.

'So Mitch's still too busy working to put time or effort

into anything else.' It followed that he'd still not be taking care of any relationships either.

'Some things never change.' Which was unfortunate because, like it or not, big changes were on Mitch's horizon. She was about to tip his world upside down, inside out. For ever.

Whatever his reaction he would never be able to forget what she was about to tell him. Mitchell Maitland, the man who'd stolen her heart more than three years ago, was about to get the shock of his life. The man she'd walked away from in a moment of pure desperation when it had finally hit home that he was never, ever going to change. Not for anyone, and especially not for her.

Unfortunately she'd needed his total commitment, not just the few hours he'd given her in a week. Growing up, she'd learned that when people were busy getting ahead they didn't have time for others, not to mention handing out love and affection. Except, silly woman that she'd been, she'd thought, hoped, Mitch might've been different despite all the warning signs to the contrary. She'd believed her love for him would overcome anything.

Lately she'd learned the hard way that there was more to a relationship than love and affection. There was responsibility, honesty and integrity. Things she'd overlooked in Mitch. Because of that, Mitch wouldn't forgive her in a hurry—if at all. And now it was payback time for what she'd omitted to tell him in the weeks and years since she'd told him to go.

Stepping up the path, she ignored the butterflies flapping in her belly, and went for bravado. 'Hello, Mitchell. Remember me? I'm the one who got away still mostly intact. Left you when it became apparent you had no more time for me than it took to have a good bonk.'

At the very moment her palm pressed hard on the doorbell she noted the open windows, the curtains moving in the light breeze, heard music inside somewhere. Not Mitchell's preferred heavy rock but a country tune.

She closed her eyes and hauled a lungful. What if he's got a wife now? Or a live-in partner? But the answers to the few questions she'd felt safe asking of a colleague from Otago Hospital, Mitch's old stomping ground, had reassured her he was still single and playing the field as hard as ever. But what if the information was incorrect? Maybe she should ask around some more before dropping her bombshell. Maybe she should go and hide from the truth—again. That would help heaps. Not.

In truth, she didn't want to hurt Mitchell—at all. *Too late. You already have. He just doesn't know it. Yet.* But if there had been another way around the problem she'd have found it.

'I need to do this,' she said under her breath. 'It's life or death. Jamie's life—or death.' Bracing her shoulders, she pressed the bell again. And gaped at the waif-like woman who tugged the door wide.

An open face with a beautiful smile, long black hair falling down her back, big brown eyes filled with friendliness. 'Hello?'

Jodi's fingers combed her own straggly tufts that looked as though she'd taken the wool clippers to them. No time or money to spend on caring for inessentials such as hair. A twist of envy wound through her as she studied this woman. She'd been fooling herself. Mitch wouldn't be alone. Good-looking, highly sexed, streetwise men like him never were. 'Hello, I'm Dr Jodi Hawke. Is Mitchell at home?'

The woman smiled easily, apparently not at all concerned with a strange female's sudden appearance on the doorstep. 'Sorry, but he's at work, even though it is Saturday. I'd say come back later but who knows what time he'll get home. He puts in long hours, always doing extra shifts.'

I know. That was the problem. One of the problems, she corrected herself. 'He works at Auckland General Hospital, right?' Just checking she had *that* fact correct.

'Isn't he wonderful? Helping all those sick kids? He's got such a lovely way with them. When our Lilly broke her arm Mitch fixed her up as easy as, and even made her laugh while he was doing it.'

Our Lilly. Mitchell had a daughter? The guy who'd sworn off having his own kids for ever? Jodi's head spun and she groped for the wall to gain some stability as darkness crashed down over her eyes. This was turning out an even bigger nightmare than she'd believed possible.

'Hey, careful. You're going to fall in a heap.' A hand gripped her elbow firmly, propelling her over the doorstep and into a small entranceway. 'What's the matter? You look like you've seen a ghost. Or as our Lilly would say, seen a vampire. Here…' The woman pushed her onto a chair. She was surprisingly strong for such a small woman. 'Sit and put your head between your knees while I get you a glass of cold water.'

'I—I'm s-sorry,' Jodi whispered to the departing woman. 'I never faint. Must be something in the air.' Yeah, something called cowardice. 'Toughen up. You're a mother and mothers do anything for their children. Anything.'

A shadow crossed the floor in front of Jodi. Carefully lifting her head, her eyes met a sympathetic gaze.

'Here, drink this. My name's Claire, by the way.' The woman knelt beside the chair and held the glass to Jodi's lips. 'What happened? Gee, one minute you're asking about Mitch, the next you're dropping like a sack of spuds.'

'I'm not sure. Must be the heat.' Heat? In autumn? 'Or something I ate earlier.' Her voice dwindled off as she sucked in her lie. The half piece of toast at six that morning would hardly do this. Taking the glass from Claire, she sipped the refreshing water, and met the perplexed gaze of this kind woman. 'I'm sorry, truly. I'll get out of your way.' Suddenly in a hurry to leave, she stood up, and swayed on her feet. Once more Claire grabbed at her, pushed her down on the chair.

'Not so fast. You can't walk outside like this. You'll fall and hurt yourself.'

Embarrassed at her unusual situation, Jodi drained the water and forced her brain to clear away the furry edges brought on by her near faint. In an attempt to divert her mind she looked around the entryway, then, through an open door into the lounge. Something wasn't right. Too neat and tidy, impersonal. No toys or children's books. Nothing to show a child resided here. 'Your daughter doesn't live with you?'

'Of course she does.' Then understanding dawned in Claire's eyes. 'I don't live here.' She chuckled. 'I'm Mitch's cleaning lady. Not his girlfriend.' She went off into peals of laughter, crossing her arms over her stomach. 'As if. I'm married to Dave, a long-haul truckie. We're saving to buy our own house.'

Relief poured through Jodi. 'I've got it all wrong, haven't I?' Thank goodness, because she really didn't want to upset this woman who'd been so kind to her. 'I'd better get going. No point in waiting for Mitch.' Back to the motel and Jamie. Mum would be busy working on her latest financial report, hoping Jamie stayed asleep while Jodi was out. But at least she'd come up with them to help out over the first few days until Jodi knew what would happen. Totally unlike her hardworking mother to be away from her corner grocery store for even a day, let alone a whole week.

Concern clouded Claire's eyes. 'Hey, I wouldn't let you stay here without Mitch's say-so. He doesn't know you're visiting, does he?'

How had she figured that out? 'No. I, we, flew up from Dunedin today. It's a surprise.' Surprise? If what she had to tell Mitch was a surprise then she'd hate to think what a stealth bomber was.

Claire headed for the front door and waved her through. 'That's all right, then. I like the guy. He's kind and always pays me more money than I ask for, and never leaves a huge mess to clean up. I wouldn't want to muck up what I've got going here.'

Once a charmer, always a charmer. Jodi squeezed past her. 'Thank you for the water.' The path wavered before her and she concentrated on putting one foot in front of the other as she headed for the car.

'Excuse me. Jodi, wasn't it?' Claire called after her.

She paused, glanced over her shoulder. 'Yes.'

'In case you want to know, as far as I can see, Mitch hasn't got a woman in his life at the moment. When he's here he only uses the bathroom, one half of his bed and the kitchen.'

Relief made Jodi feel wobbly again but she kept focused on that footpath and finally made it back to the stuffy car. Inside she rolled down the window to let some cooler air float across her face. Phew. The fact she'd all but fainted showed how much of a pickle she'd got herself into. The prospect of facing up to Mitch had given her endless sleepless nights. And now, after getting mentally prepared, her moment of reckoning had been delayed. It was killing her.

Nothing compared to what's happening to Jamie.

She reached for the ignition. Glanced at the house. Saw Claire wave before she closed the front door. Claire, the cleaning lady. Not the wife or girlfriend. Mitch really was single.

Something akin to excitement bubbled through her, warmed her from the inside out. Mitch was single. So what? He was toast, had been since the night he'd done his usual no-show. Except that time she'd been sitting in the swanky restaurant, at the table he'd booked for her birthday, drinking the champagne he'd pre-ordered, tossing up between roast salmon on fennel or venison steak when she'd seen his brother come in with his current glamorous toss. The brother she'd previously gone out with, and who'd never let her down. But who'd also never made her skin ache with need or her hormones dance the tango at the thought of him touching her. Only Mitch had ever done that.

Max had seen her, seated his date, then crossed to say in a satisfied tone, 'So Mitchell's let you down yet again, has he?'

And that had been the moment she'd known she was done with the Maitland twins. For ever. She'd taken her bottle of champagne and what was left in it, bought another, and headed home, stopping only to get a burger and chips on the way. She'd got thoroughly drunk all by herself. And in the morning she'd called in sick—not hard to do with the hangover she'd had—and had spent the hours packing. When Mitch had raced in about midday full of apologies she'd pointed to his bags and asked for her key back. 'I won't be treated as an afterthought. Last night was the final time you do that to me. I'm worthy of more than what you're prepared to give me.' Pride had kept back the words 'I love you', instead replaced with, 'We're over. I'm sorry.'

And she had been very sorry, and broken-hearted, but she'd known if she hadn't stood up for herself she'd eventually have been worn down to become a needy woman waiting and begging for a few minutes of Mitch's attention. Like her mother had with Dad. She'd done her share of begging her father for some attention too. Dad had spent every day and night charming people into handing over their hard-earned savings for him to invest. He'd missed her birthdays, too.

So Jodi Hawke didn't do needy. Not now, not ever. She stood up for herself. Had learned the hard way at ten years old when she'd been humiliated and harassed at school for her father's crimes that when you needed friends onside they let you down. When he'd ended up in jail there'd been an endless stream of kids to taunt her. Turning to her mother for solace had been a mistake. Dealing with her own problems and working every hour she could to climb out of the debt-laden hole Dad had left them in, Mum had had very little time for her too.

Withdrawing from everyone, Jodi had learned to fight back. If anyone wanted to be her friend they'd had to prove their worth. Two girls had stood by her, and were still there for her, as she was for them. But not one of the trio was needy, just sometimes requiring friendship and a shoulder to soak with tears. Entirely different.

Driving away from the house, Jodi wondered what Mitch would be like now. One thing was for sure, he'd still be a hunk with a sculpted body that he worked on in the gym. And those hands. Her tongue lapped her lips. The hands that knew unbelievable things about a woman's body, had incredibly exciting ways of ramping up the desire that was always waiting just under her skin whenever he was near. Then there were those mesmerising blue eyes that had reminded her of summer, even on the bleakest of days. Until the end of their relationship, that was. That had been a grey day.

'It will be winter glittering out at me today, though. Mitch is so going to hate me.'

Being dunked in an ice bucket couldn't have chilled her as much. Her skin lifted, her spine shuddered, and her fingers clenched.

'Remember how quickly he replaced you. Two weeks? Or was it three?'

That did not alleviate the chill gripping her body. At the end of the day there was no denying she'd done a bad thing. The fact they'd broken up wasn't an excuse. But everything else that had happened might have been. Would Mitch understand her actions back then? Forgive her?

She already knew the answer, and yet still pleaded, 'Please, please, Mitchell, remember one of the good moments we shared and go easy on me. I know I did wrong, but I need you onside now.'

Five hours later the digital clock in the rental car clicked over to eight-thirty.

Jodi grunted. 'He's not coming home any time soon.' She'd returned to his house to find it in darkness, the curtains not drawn. As far as she could make out, Mitchell hadn't been back in the time since her previous visit.

Still obsessed with putting in the hours at hospital. That man was driven. He never wanted to come second in anything. To anybody. Especially not to his twin brother. Their one-upmanship battles had been legendary at Otago Med School. Probably still were here at Auckland General.

She shivered. The temperature had dropped when the sun had gone down. And her memories of long, lonely nights waiting until Mitch had deigned to come home and see her sprang out of the dark place she'd forced them into a long time ago. Not so surprising when she sat outside his house, in his city, the closest she'd been to him in three years.

'Back to the motel, and Jamie.' Her darling boy would be tucked up in bed, hopefully sleeping easily. Earlier she'd kissed him goodnight after a meal of chicken bites and chips, a treat that remarkably Mum had forked out for. Breathing in his little-boy smell, stroking his head, tickling his tummy, a huge lump had blocked her throat. Rapid blinking had kept the tears at bay. Just. Even now they hovered, ready to spill down her cheeks in a moment's weakness. *Toughen up. There's no room for weakness.*

What if Mitchell didn't agree to her request? There was no 'what if'. He had to agree. He might be a self-focused man but he also knew the right thing to do. So Jamie should be safe.

She couldn't, wouldn't, imagine life without Jamie in it. He was so sweet, wickedly cute, and totally uncomplaining even when the pain struck. He didn't know what it was like to be full of energy, to be able to run around the lawn shouting at the world, or to ride a bike, or to go a whole day without having to take at least two naps. And yet he still had an impish grin that twisted her heart and made her hug him tight, trying to ward off the inevitable.

A tired smile lifted one corner of her mouth. Even now her mother would be hooked into the internet, reading the stocks and shares figures from the other side of the world, impervious to anything else. Another workaholic who hadn't learned to stop or even just slow down and, as the saying had it, smell the roses.

She took a right turn to head back to the grotty, dank motel room. Back to another night tossing and turning as she argued and pleaded with Mitch inside her head, as she argued with herself. Back to check up on her darling little boy, her horrendously ill little boy, who'd been dealt a black card in the stakes of life.

A car zoomed past in the opposite direction, headlights on full, and temporarily blinded her. Her foot lifted off the accelerator as she twisted the steering wheel sideways. 'Idiot,' she yelled at the unseen driver whizzing past, narrowly missing her rental vehicle.

'Delinquent. Look where you're going.' She vented some of her pent-up anger and fear. 'You could've killed me.'

Then who would talk to Mitchell about Jamie? Maybe leaving this until tomorrow wasn't such a great idea. Who knew what might happen in the intervening hours? She hadn't tried to find him anywhere else but at home. Which was fairly silly. The Mitch she'd known would always be at the hospital. Which meant he'd be very busy. Saturday night in ED was never a picnic. She had to wait until the morning.

'No.' Her fist crunched down on her thigh. 'No. I'm done with waiting. Done with planning the arguments for and against my case. Done, done, done.' Her palm slapped the steering wheel. She had to see Mitch. Now. The time had come. No more avoidance. No more lying to herself, saying she'd done the right thing. Because being right or wrong wasn't going to change a thing. It wasn't going to alter the fact she should've told Mitch about Jamie a long time ago.

The hurt she'd known of waiting up for Dad to come home and read her a story, or to say she was his princess, had been behind her decision in not telling Mitch about Jamie. Yes, Mitch, love him or not, would act the same as her father had. He'd never be there for his child because there'd always be one more patient to help, one more urgent case to deal wtih before hanging up his white coat and heading home.

If Mitch kicked her butt hard and fast when she told him why she was here, and why she hadn't come knocking three years ago, so be it. If he sent her packing, refusing to believe her—which was her expectation—she'd deal with that too. She'd argue till she was all out of breath. If he refused categorically to meet Jamie, to help him…then she'd tie him up and pour boiling oil over his beautiful body.

Doing a U-turn, she headed into the city centre and Auckland General, the hospital with New Zealand's best renal specialists and the most modern equipment available for what ailed Jamie. The hospital where Mitch was head of the emergency department. Where he looked out for patients, including other people's little boys and girls. Would he look out for her boy? Of course he would. He wasn't an ogre.

Over the coming days she would ask him to consider doing something he'd never, ever have contemplated. Who would, unless faced with it?

She was also about to grovel before the man she'd once loved, the man she'd never shown a moment of weakness to in the months they'd lived together.

She was about to give away her soul.

It was far too easy to find a parking space outside the ED. But despite the pounding in her chest Jodi didn't linger anymore. The time had come. Having once worked briefly in the ED, she knew the ropes and within moments she was inside the emergency department asking for Dr Maitland.

'I think he took a break.' A young nurse answered her enquiries. 'Though he was talking about going to a party tonight so you might be out of luck.'

She'd been out of luck for years. Just not tonight, please.

'Where's the staff kitchen?' she asked the next person. 'I'm looking for Mitch Maitland.'

'Mitch headed towards his office,' a harried junior doctor told her as he raced past.

'Which is where?' Jodi asked the disappearing back of the doctor.

'Down the corridor, turn right, left, left, and then try the third door on your right,' another nurse told her.

Okey-dokey. Showtime. Jodi's footsteps slowed as she took the last left. They stopped entirely outside the third door on the right. Her knuckles rapped on the door. No reply. Her hand shook as her fingers gripped the doorknob. Shoving the door wide, she stepped into hell.

'Hello, Mitchell. Long time no see.'

The reply was a snore.

She felt like a balloon that'd just been pricked. 'Oh, great. Wonderful to see you, too.' All her over-tightened muscles cramped further. Her tongue licked her dry lips. And once again her legs threatened to drop her in a heap on the floor.

Another snore.

Jodi closed the door quietly, leaned back against it, desperate for support. Her breasts rose on a slow intake of air, and she studied the view. Definitely still hunky. Those hands she remembered so well were hidden behind his head as he sprawled in his chair with his feet crossed neatly at the ankles on his desk. But those muscular thighs under the fabric of his trousers cranked up some hot memories. Dragging her gaze upwards, she studied his face.

His head was tipped back slightly, the sparkling blue eyes invisible behind closed eyelids. But his long black eyelashes lay softly on his upper cheeks, twisting her heart. Oh so sexy stubble darkened his chin, his jaw.

The air whooshed out of her lungs.

How had she ever found the strength to leave him?

Worse, where was the strength to break his world into a million little pieces?

Think of Jamie. That was the only thing she could do. Anything else and she'd fall apart at the seams.

Clearing her throat she pitched her voice higher. 'Mitch. Wake up.'

CHAPTER TWO

MITCH KNEW HE was hallucinating. Too many strong coffees. Had to be. Nothing else would explain why he thought he saw Jodi Hawke standing here in his office. He shut his eyes tight, concentrated on removing that unnerving image from his brain. Slowly raised his eyelids. There. Leaning against his door. Jodi Hawke. No, not leaning. More like melting into the door, becoming a part of it. As in an attempt to remain upright.

A Jodi lookalike, then. The Jodi he'd known had had more confidence than a one-hundred-metre sprinter. Through narrowed eyes, he studied this apparition. Worn jeans hung loosely off her hips. A shapeless, faded cotton jersey bagged from her breasts and over her tummy, while scuffed trainers on her feet completed the strange picture.

The Jodi he remembered had been a fashionista. She'd certainly never gone for the ragdoll effect. And she'd definitely never been quiet, let alone silent.

God, what had been in those coffees? Definitely something weird and potent. His eyes drooped shut as the need to continue sleeping washed over him. It had been a big day made huge after a multi-car pile-up on the motorway. He'd attended to five seriously injured people, not to mention the usual number of patients continuously filing through the department. No wonder he was exhausted and seeing things. Then a nag set up in his skull. Wasn't he supposed to be going somewhere?

'Mitchell,' squeaked the lookalike.

Jodi never squeaked. Through sheer willpower he did not move, not even an eyelid. Until his mouth let him down, demanding, 'Tell me this is a joke.' A very sick joke. But there'd be no reply. He *was* hallucinating.

'Mitch, damn you. Look at me.'

He snapped forward so fast his neck clicked and his eyes opened into a wide stare. His feet hit the floor with a thump. 'You're real.' He knew *that* voice, had heard it against his chest in the heat of passion, had felt it lash him in anger.

'What else would I be?' Her eyes bored into him, unrelenting in their determination to get his attention.

She certainly had that in spades. What was she doing here? Should he be worried? Nah, couldn't see any reason for that. But after three years she just waltzes in through his door and tells him what to do? No way, sunshine. 'A bad dream.'

She winced, and a whole ton of emotions blinked out at him from those unnerving eyes. Anger, hurt, shock, caution. But the overriding one appeared to be fear. Jodi was afraid of him? That had him standing upright faster than a bullet train. Nothing was making any sense. They hadn't seen or spoken to each other for so long there was nothing between them now; not good or bad. Yet now she looked as though she wanted to be anywhere but here with him. Odd since she had been the one to walk in unannounced.

Even in the deep quiet of night, when nothing stirred except his memory, he'd never believed Jodi would want him back. *Jumping the gun a bit, aren't you? She's probably passing through and decided to look you up for old times' sake. As if.* It had hurt beyond comprehension when she'd kicked him out and before he'd left Dunedin he'd often started towards her place to beg for a second chance, only to back off, knowing Jodi would give him most things but never that.

So why was she here? She didn't do casual. Whatever had brought her through his door must be serious.

Apprehension crawled up his back. Somehow he managed to drawl with feigned nonchalance, 'Jodi, long time no see.' Three years five months, to be nearly exact. Tension overlaid tension in his weary body. And he'd thought he'd forgotten all about her. Forgotten making love with her in the long grass above the beach in summer. Forgotten how her laugh always made him feel he could slay dragons. But he'd been kidding himself. Big time.

Now his gaze was back to cruising, checking out that wacky, totally unstylish hair, the eyes that weren't bordered with a pail of war paint, the non-lipsticked lips bruised where she must've nibbled for hours. So she still did that.

What had happened to this woman? He struggled to recognise her for who she'd been. A bright, sparkly woman with a figure any model would die for and the accessories to match. An intern adored by patients and staff alike. The only woman he'd even considered doing something way out with—as in settling down and buying the picket fence with. Everything he remembered about her had disappeared. All gone. Replaced by a stranger. Or so it seemed.

'What brings you to Auckland? I presume you're still living down south.'

'Yes, I am.' She still leaned against the door. 'At least, I did until today.'

'You're on the move? Anywhere exciting?' *What the hell's this got to do with me?*

'I don't know about exciting. But I'm shifting to Auckland for a while.' She choked over that last word. Tears glittered on her eyelashes.

Oh, God, she hadn't taken a job in ED? Here? In his department? No, don't be daft. Who would've sanctioned that if not him? Think about it. She wasn't trained to work in an emergency department. The tension in his belly backed off a notch. So, what was her visit about? Had she really turned up for a chat about old times? Nah, not at this hour of the night.

He stamped on the flare of sympathy that drawn face caused, and parked his backside back on his chair. Stretching his legs under the desk, he started at the beginning. 'You arrived today and already you're knocking on my door? Do you need a job? Because I'm sorry to disappoint you but I'm overstaffed as it is.'

'No, I don't need a job.' She swallowed. 'Actually, I will do at some point but that's not why I'm here.'

There was a relief. But the tension gripping his muscles didn't relax at all. 'So this is a social call?'

Another swallow. Then her tongue moistened her lips. And that fear in her eyes grew. 'No,' she croaked.

Mitch studied her carefully as a sense of falling over the edge of a cliff began expanding deep inside him. Jodi hadn't spoken more than two sentences to him—and, yes, he remembered what they'd been, word for word—from the day she'd put his packed bags on the front doorstep of the flat they'd shared and said goodbye. Even his explanations about helping seriously injured people hadn't softened her stance. Neither had telling her he needed just another year of putting in long hours and then he'd be set for life, would have the career he wanted and a whole lot more time for her. In the end he'd swallowed the hurt, sucked up his pride, and got on with his life. Like he did with most things. Except his brother.

But Jodi's departure from his life had hurt far more than he could've ever imagined. What had started out as fun had turned into something deeper but, being him, he'd realised that far too late. After he'd lost her. So really she'd done him a favour, saved him from himself. It had been his only foray into something resembling a proper relationship and he'd sucked at it. As he'd known he would. But he'd have liked the opportunity to rectify his mistakes.

But Jodi Hawke didn't do second chances.

Besides, he knew all about the fickleness of relationships. All relationships, not just the boyfriend/girlfriend ones. Hell, Jodi was just one in a line of people who'd hurt him by disappearing out of his life. Which was why he did the moving on, usually quite quickly. Easier to protect himself that way. But he'd been in love with Jodi—as close to being in love as he'd ever been before or since—and had hung around too long, thinking it might work out. That she might be the one to see past his disillusionment. Of course he hadn't done anything to try to keep her.

The break-up had been behind his speedy move up to Auckland. He couldn't stand the thought of bumping into her at any corner within the hospital, in any bar or nightclub in town. Shifting cities had turned into a wise career move that had helped him clear his horrendous student loan and buy himself a modest house. And he'd shown his brother he was also capable of having an outstanding career.

Damn it. Jodi did this to him in a matter of minutes. Brought back the heartache, the guilt and doubts.

Someone knocked on the door and Jodi shot across the room looking completely flustered. Mitch shook his head at her. What the hell was wrong? This timidity was so not Jodi. Something terrible must've happened to her in the intervening years. His heart rolled. He might be wary about seeing her again, but if anyone had hurt her they'd better watch out, be prepared to answer to him.

'Hey, Mitch—oh, sorry, I didn't realise you had company. I'll catch you some other time.' Aaron might be talking to him but his eyes were fixed on Jodi.

Mitch shook his head again, and focused on the guy who ran the night shift in ED. 'Is everything all right in the department?' Hopefully it was ripping busy and he could get out of here, go to work and forget his unwanted visitor. Problem or no problem.

Aaron waved a hand through the air. 'All good, no worries. I was going to read over the terms of the TV company's visit next week, nothing important.'

How was that for an understatement? None of his staff, including Aaron, were happy about the documentary a national television company was making about life in a busy emergency department, and it fell to him to make it work, even when he agreed with his staff. Visitors in the unit, especially ones the board forced on them, were a pain in the butt, getting in the way, asking crazy questions, upsetting staff and patients. 'I'll catch up with you tomorrow sometime.'

'Sure.' Aaron took one more appraising look at Jodi before glancing at his watch. 'You should've clocked off hours ago, Mitch. We don't need you hanging around taking up space.'

Mitch grimaced. Thanks, pal. Go ahead and make Jodi welcome while you're at it, why don't you? 'I've got other things to attend to first.'

Aaron raised his eyebrows. 'Yeah, sure. Weren't you going to Samantha's party?'

The party. That's what had been niggling at his half-baked brain about the time he'd seen Jodi slumped against his door. 'I'll be on my way in a moment.'

'You won't have missed much. Sam's parties don't usually crank up until near midnight.' Aaron glanced at Jodi, back to him, fixing him with a not-your-usual-type look before slipping out of the office and closing the door noisily.

Closing Jodi in with Mitch. Again. He sucked air, steadied that shaky feeling in his stomach and tried for normal. 'Want to tell me why you're here? Because, as you heard, I am busy. I'm meant to be somewhere else.'

She didn't even say, 'When aren't you?' Which he admitted she had every right to do, that having been the crux of their break-up way back then. Instead, she surprised him. 'Mitch, can we go somewhere to talk?' Her gaze clashed with his and she didn't back off. Something resembling the strength he'd always associated with her slipped into her gaze, pushing that fear sideways. 'Somewhere quiet where no one will interrupt us.'

There was a warning in her voice that gave him the impression that something terrible was coming. Yet for the life of him he couldn't imagine what. Whatever it was obviously wouldn't wait. Which made him want to stall her for as long as possible. He didn't want to hear her out. Opening his mouth to say no, he said, 'Just give me a minute while I grab some coffees and tell the night staff to leave us alone. We'll be undisturbed in here. I see no need to leave the hospital.' Except those gathering clouds in her eyes.

'I think you'd prefer to hear what I have to say somewhere else, neutral territory if you like.' Her bottom lip trembled. 'With no one you know likely to burst in on us.'

'As you heard, I'm going out tonight.' He nodded at his overnight bag against the far wall. 'I need to shower and change so I'd prefer to get this over right here. Whatever this is.' Why did he feel such a heel? Could it be the pain darkening those toffee-coloured orbs? Did he have some

lingering feelings for her? No, definitely not. Crazy idea.
But he should cut her some slack, at least until he'd heard
her out. They'd lived together for six months so he owed
her that much. 'So, do you want coffee?'

'No, thanks. Nothing.' She dropped onto the spare chair.
The fingers she interlaced were white. She looked so tiny,
all shrunk in on herself, and when she lifted her head to
face him he gasped.

'Jodi?' Her eyes stood out like snooker balls against her
colourless cheeks. Was she ill? Please, not that. Anything
but that. His heart lurched and he had to fight the urge to
wrap her up in his arms. Shelter her from whatever was
troubling her so much. 'What's wrong?'

She swallowed, opened her mouth, and whispered, 'We
have a son. You have a son.'

Wrong, wrong, wrong. That was not how she had meant
to inform him. What had happened to easing into telling
him about Jamie? She'd been going to explain the situation
carefully, one thing at a time, not hit him over the head
with a baseball bat. Now he'd never hear her through. The
arguments were already building in his eyes.

Nausea roiled up and she gripped the sides of the chair,
forcing her stomach to behave. Her teeth bit down hard
on her lip, creating pain to focus on. There was nothing
she could do to take the words back. There would be no
starting again. No second chance. So get on with it, tell
him the rest.

He was staring at her as though she'd gone crazy, his
head moving from side to side in denial. 'I don't think so.'

'It's true.' Again nausea threatened, stronger this time.
She had to get this over, tell him everything. But he was
already saying something.

'Jodi, Jodi. I don't know what's behind this but your outrageous idea won't get you anywhere.' When she opened her mouth to reply he talked right over her. 'It's been done before.'

'What?'

'You're not the first woman to try using her child to get me to set her up in a lifestyle she thought was her right.'

'What?'

'Last year a nurse from the surgical ward insisted I was the father of her unborn child. Wanted to get married in a hurry before everyone noticed. What she really wanted was the wedding, my wage packet and the supposed fancy house. She played me for a fool. She lied, she lost.'

Where was the rubbish bin? Every office had one somewhere. Her hand over her mouth, Jodi frantically looked around as her stomach threatened to evict the few chicken nuggets she'd eaten earlier.

'Hey, Jodi? Oh, hell. Here.' A plastic receptacle appeared under her nose. A hand pressed between her shoulder blades, forcing her over the bin.

Don't be sick. Don't. Swallowing the bile in her mouth, she slowly counted to ten, fighting her stomach. Sweat broke out on her forehead. Her hands were clammy Breathe. In, out. In, out. The nausea began to recede. But she daren't pull back from that bin just yet. 'I'm sorry.'

Why was she apologising? And for what? Feeling ill? Because another woman had done the dirty on him? For giving him the news no man liked to hear? She'd hardly started. He hadn't heard the worst yet. He still didn't know about Jamie's illness. That's when he'd take her seriously. And really hate her. Because he'd understand what she wanted from him.

She lost the argument with her stomach.

CHAPTER THREE

MITCHELL PUT THE rubbish bin in the far corner and covered it with the hand towel hanging beside the basin. Who knew when Jodi might need it again? She looked terrible, pale and shaky, the fingers she gripped some tissues with trembling non-stop. Half the water in the glass he handed her splashed over her jeans.

Returning to his desk, he parked his butt on the edge and folded his arms across his chest. He studied her carefully as she sipped and rinsed her mouth. Looked hard for the Jodi he used to know. Impossible to find behind the unhappiness in those eyes. Not easy to see in her bedraggled appearance. Hadn't she been looking after herself? If he'd thought she'd been white before, he'd been totally wrong.

A tiny knot of fear formed in his gut. What if she was telling him the truth? Jodi never dodged bullets; always told it like she saw it. So wouldn't she have told him about a baby right from the get-go? Wouldn't she? Maybe not. She'd always been fiercely independent.

Not to mention the memory now flashing across his brain of how she'd called him the most unreliable man on the planet when it came to devoting time to her or anyone not involved in his work. Had even gone so far as to call him selfish. So she'd expect the same of him when it came to their child. At the time, her frank appraisal had stung. Honest to the point of being brutal. That was Jodi. And right now he'd swear that same honesty was blinking out at him.

He tried to dampen the sarcasm. He really did. 'You turn up here after all this time to tell me I'm a father. Do you honestly think I'm about to believe you without knowing more? Come on, I might not be top of your favourite people list but you also know I'm not stupid. If you were pregnant, why did you kick me out? I'd have been the gravy train.'

He stood up and headed for the door. He couldn't do this. He didn't want to do it.

You're running away, big boy.

Yeah, well, it hurt to think she'd even consider him fool enough to believe her. Hadn't she got it? Way back? Got that he didn't do commitment or that for ever stuff?

Wake up. That's probably why she never told you she was pregnant. 'What took you so long to tell me?' He ground the words out.

'I tried to tell you.'

'How come I missed that?'

Her finger picked at her jeans. 'I phoned the flat you moved to a few times but you were never there, night or day. I didn't want to spring it on you in front of your colleagues in the ED. But finally I gave up thinking like that and tracked you down at work.'

The hairs rose on the back of his neck. He knew what was coming. Hell, damn, double damn. Once again he'd blown it—big time.

'You were well and truly absorbed in a nurse. That was some steamy kiss going on in the sluice room. Her arms must've taken a month to unwind from around you.' Anger and hurt blended to turn her voice sad and low.

'You'd got over me so fast I wondered if you'd even re-membered my name.'

Embarrassment made him squirm. 'It was deliberate. To make you think I didn't care. I saw you come into the department.' He sounded like a fifteen-year-old. Actually, that was insulting all teens.

Jodi gaped at him. 'You did what?'

'Yes, well, it kind of upset me when you kicked me out but I had no intention of showing you that.' If only he'd known why Jodi had come looking for him that day. Would it have made any difference? He'd like to think he'd have stepped up to the mark.

She was shaking her head at him. 'Do you know what that stupid act did? The anguish it caused?' She splut-tered to a stop, twisted her fingers around each other and stared at her feet.

'For what it's worth, I'm sorry. But be fair, I had no idea why you were there. You still could've insisted on talking to me.'

'I went away to think it all through. That took a lot lon-ger than I'd expected.' Did she mutter 'Months longer' under her breath?

He felt beyond terrible. Despite everything he'd heard, that knot of fear hadn't evaporated at all. But what hap-pened now? What did he say? Do?

Jodi's voice wobbled but her words were loud and clear. 'Trust me, I wouldn't be telling you now if I could avoid it.'

Stopping in mid-stride, he spun back to her. 'Hey, I certainly didn't ask for this. I'm not the one making you spill the beans.' *But I am the one behaving badly. Hear her out before showing her the door. It might be quicker and easier that way.* And if there was something he could do for her then he'd do it just to show there were no hard feelings. *Sure you're not remembering how much you liked*

*Jodi before she sent you packing? Sure you don't want to
make amends just a little bit for treating her so offhand-
edly back then? For kissing that dazzling blonde whose
name you can't recall?*

I was looking out for myself.

Excuses, excuses.

Jodi pulled herself upright and still looked small. But
fighting hard. Like she wasn't about to give up on this in
a hurry. A mother protecting her child?

That twist of fear grew bigger.

'Mitchell, we can go the DNA route if you want proof
Jamie is yours. But I think I can persuade you with this.'

His gaze was glued to her as she slid her hand inside
the back pocket of her jeans. As she began withdrawing
a cellphone, a sudden landslide of emotion engulfed him.
He knew without seeing whatever she was about to show
him that finally everything he'd ever done, all the deliberate plans to remain unattached to anyone for ever had
just come completely undone.

He did know Jodi. Knew she'd never pull a stunt like
this on anyone. Knew how she would not have hesitated
to bring a child up on her own. Knew that she'd love that
child more than life itself. All the arguing in his head
couldn't change that.

Her hand shook violently as she held the opened phone
out, a photo shining at him. 'This is Jamie. Your boy.'

He stared and stared at that phone, unable to reach for it
because the moment he did he was finished. Life had come
full circle on him. He'd spent years perfecting avoidance
of commitment. Even his town house was just a building
to sleep and shower in. His mouth was drier than a summer wind. His insides tossed and turned as though in a
tumble dryer.

'Mitch, take it. Please.' A tear oozed from the corner of her eye.

He had always been able to turn a blind eye to women's tears. Until now. That solitary drop of water inching down her cheek arrowed straight to his heart. Jodi. Jamie.

His fingers weren't steady, probably never would be again. The phone slipped through her hand and his to the carpeted floor. Jodi didn't move to pick it up, sat there peering up at him with those stricken eyes. Finally he reached down, swooped it up, turned it the right way round and, with a suck of air, met his son.

He stared at his own reflection. At least, that's what it looked like. The eyes looking out at him were the same shade of blue he saw in the mirror every time he shaved. The only difference about the straight dark hair was the style. Slightly too long and wild. The generous grin with even, white teeth; the straight, pointed nose. Even the 'to hell with the world' attitude in the little lad's stance. This was himself thirty-three years ago.

But this photo. The modern background and clothes. This *was* different. Not even he could deny this boy was his.

Jamie was his son. He was a dad. *Oh, my God.*

'Mitchell?' His name hiccupped off Jodi's lips.

'Why now? Why not three years ago?' He swallowed the bitter comments hovering on his tongue. He mightn't want to be a father, or to even know he was one, but she should've told him, given him the choice of what to do about the situation. Except Jodi knew him all too well, had known he'd resist with every fibre in his body. What had changed her mind about telling him?

Jodi grimaced, went back to twisting her fingers round and round. The desolation in her face drilled him. 'I am very, very sorry.'

He waited quietly, while his heart thudded hard against his ribs. He couldn't have enunciated a word if he'd tried. *I've missed out on so much. Three years of growing up that I'll never know about.* Surprising how much that hurt. Even when it was partially his own fault. Especially because of that. Jodi had carried the weight of his blind need to protect himself, had paid the consequences. Until tonight. 'Tell me what brings you here now.'

When she finally answered it was with dignity. 'Jamie's very ill. He's going to die if I don't get the right care very soon. You might be able to help him.'

The strength went out of his knees. Gripping the edge of the table, he held himself upright. He'd asked and got the answers. Damn it. He stared at her. Her unwavering gaze spoke the truth. All of this nightmare was true. All of it. And more. His head whirled with angry questions. With denial. With acceptance. With—he didn't know the hell what with but it sure as blazes hurt. Pain needled him, squeezed him, shook him like a defenceless kitten in a dog's mouth.

Groping for his chair, he sank down into it and dropped his head into his hands. Could he rewind the clock an hour? Back to when the biggest problem he'd had was keeping his staff happy during the coming week? Back to when he'd been snoozing before going to a party?

'What do you want from me?' He didn't recognise his own voice it was so croaky. 'Money?' He lashed out, trying to step through this mire of problems he'd never expected to have, trying to come out on top of it all. His way. The way he felt safe. The way he had some control over everything.

'I'll forget you said that.' Ice chipped off Jodi's words. 'Jamie has renal failure. Cystinosis, to be exact. Our specialist in Dunedin believes he's got a better chance up here. In this hospital.'

'Bloody hell.' Mitch leapt up and strode across the room, turned at the wall, strode back. Turned and slapped his hands on his hips as he bent down towards her. 'Kick me in the guts, why don't you?'

'I know how you must be feeling.'

His eyebrows disappeared over the back of his head and his jaw clanged down on his chest. The situation got the better of him. 'You know how I'm feeling? That's rich.'

Her eyes were murky, like mud. Wet, brown and so, so sad. 'I've been dealing with Jamie's illness all his life. But I haven't forgotten the day I was told about his condition. The terror, the sense of failing my baby, wanting to believe the doctors had made a mistake and that someone's else's son was sick and not mine. And then guilt for thinking that. So, yes, I do know.'

Did she have to sound so bloody reasonable? And so disappointed with him? Couldn't she cut him some slack? It was all too much, too new, too raw. He tried to breath, struggled. Paced across the room and back, swallowed the lump blocking his throat, and strove for control. Back and forth across his office, which got smaller with every turn. He needed to get out of there, get some air. Stop thinking for a bit to give his mind time to settle down and absorb everything he'd learned over the last few minutes.

'I'm going for a walk.' He headed for the door.

Jodi was out of her chair and in his face so fast he hadn't even reached for the door handle. 'I'm coming with you.'

'No, Jodi. Give me a break here, okay? I need time to myself. It's not like you've given me a weather forecast or told me the cat's got fleas. This is huge. I need to absorb it all before I decide what I'm going to do.'

Her lips tightened. 'I understand. It's been a big shock. But I'm coming with you. You'll have plenty of questions once you start getting past the initial disbelief and I want to be there to answer them.' When he narrowed his eyes at her she added quickly, 'I won't say a thing unless you ask me to.'

Maybe this really was a lookalike Jodi.

His phone sang a tune. He groaned as he read the message. 'Samantha's wondering why I haven't turned up at the party yet.'

If looks could kill, he'd be a goner. Holding his hands up in a placating gesture, he added, 'I'm definitely not in the mood for a party now.' Probably never would be again. His finger pressed the 'off' button. Shocking how quickly life could change.

'Samantha is?'

'Not my girlfriend.' He hauled the door open and Jodi slipped out right alongside him. She stuck to him all the way through the hospital corridors, through the car park and onto the street, where he strode blindly along the footpath, trying to outrun this nightmare.

And, true to her word, she didn't utter a word.

Which was even more disturbing. He did not know this Jodi at all.

Jodi shivered in the chill night air. Wrapping her arms around her upper body, she tripped along beside Mitch.

Engrossed in thought, he didn't seem to realise she was still with him, which gave her a chance to study him uninterrupted. Every time they passed under a streetlight she saw the raw shock still in his face. And the serious bent of his gaze. The clenched jaw.

At least he wasn't shucking Jamie off like a used coat.

That had to be good. Mitch was the champion of avoidance when it came to getting close to someone. He knew all the moves to keep people at arm's length. Even in the best times they had together she'd known she had no future with him, that eventually he'd be gone.

That had made it a little easier to toss him out. Only a very little. The weeks and months following that disastrous day had been hard. Learning she was pregnant had added to her grief, but hadn't broken her resolve to stay away from him after the conversation she'd overheard between him and his twin.

'Here, put this on.' Mitch shrugged out of his jacket and handed it to her.

'Th-thanks. Wh-what about y-you?' Her teeth hurt as they chattered from the cold.

'I'll be fine.'

The jacket came down to her knees and she could've wrapped it around herself twice. 'A-anything y-you want to ask m-me?'

'What field did you finally qualify in? Paediatrics or general practice?'

Okay, not about Jamie, then. 'I opted for general practice when I learned I was pregnant.'

'Why?'

As warmth seeped into her chilled muscles she concentrated on telling him what he wanted to know. 'I didn't like the idea of the horrendous hours that working in a hospital entailed. I wanted to be home at the end of the day for my child. Turned out it was a good move. Since Jamie became ill I've only worked part time.' Very part time, some weeks.

'Do you like being a GP?'

Still avoiding the real issue. She sighed. Maybe this was the way to the heart of the matter, giving him time to assimilate everything. 'I love it. I see the same people regularly, get to know their families, watch the children growing.' Her words dwindled away as she thought of Jamie and how he didn't seem to grow at all these days. How a good day for him was one without pain or not being admitted to hospital.

'Yeah, I can see you fitting right in there. You always could empathise with people as easily as breathing.'

Whereas he'd never enjoy spending his days working with the same people, getting to know their strengths and weaknesses, having them believe they had a connection with him beyond a fifteen-minute consultation. But she took the compliment, held it in her heart; a small warmth in an otherwise frosty situation. 'You obviously still love the adrenalin rush of emergency medicine, though the hours seem to have taken their toll if that little snooze I witnessed is anything to go by.'

His elbows dug into his sides briefly. 'Caught. But in defence I've been working for ten days straight. And before you say it, I haven't changed in that respect. I do love the rush and drama of ED.'

Had he changed at all? In what ways? She hadn't noticed anything different yet. 'What about being HOD? More paperwork, less action, surely?' Definitely not his forte.

'Not in my department. Head of Department isn't a job to be turned on and off. The paper stuff gets done when it gets done, which lands me in hot water too often. Tough. The patients come first. The work's demanding and absorbing. How many people can say they get a buzz out of their job every single day? Do you?'

No, sometimes she was so tired after sitting up all night with Jamie it took everything she had to even turn up. 'I used to love the buzz when I was training in hospital too, but I never let it take over my whole life.' Ouch. Snippy.

Settle down. Antagonising the guy wouldn't win her any favours. 'Sorry.'

Mitch stopped and took her elbow to turn her. Looking down into her eyes, he smiled tiredly. 'I guess we've got a few bones to pick over. But maybe not tonight, eh?'

Staring through the half-light, she could see how confused, lost even, he looked. Yet his hand on her elbow was reassuring. Standing here with Mitch, something she'd never thought she'd do again, a sense of homecoming washed over her. The strength she'd loved in him, the gentleness, the caring. She'd missed all that and more.

They might never become real friends, might always bicker and try to avoid each other, but he knew about Jamie now. So nothing would ever be the same for her again, ever be as bad as the last lonely, heartbreaking three years had been. Mitch was back in her life, no matter how tentatively. As if he'd ever truly left. Reaching up, she palmed his bristly chin for an instant. 'You're right. Not tonight.'

In silence they continued along the footpath, dodging Saturday night revellers outside The Shed, a bar that appeared to be very popular. After half an hour they started back towards the hospital and her car. With growing exasperation Jodi waited for Mitch to ask her something, anything, about Jamie. Surely his head was full of questions? Didn't he want to know what Jamie's favourite food was? What toys he loved to play with? Did he take after his father or his mother in temperament?

Mitch would've seen from the photo how physically alike he and his son were. That had been hard at times. There had been days she'd looked at Jamie and cried for Mitch. Not only to be with her, supporting her, sharing the agony of watching her boy getting sicker and sicker, but because she'd missed him so much.

There'd been times when she'd seen Mitch in her son's face and had wanted to charge up to Auckland to tear him apart, to rant and yell at him for being so neglectful of her that she hadn't been able to tell him about his child.

But now the silence hung between them and she didn't know how to break it without upsetting him and she'd already done that in bucketloads tonight. But surely he wanted to know about Jamie's illness and what lay ahead?

They reached the car park and she thought Mitch was going to walk away from her without another word. Anger rolled through her. That wasn't going to happen. 'Mitchell, you can't avoid this one.'

His jaw jutted out, his eyes flashed as angrily as hers must be doing. 'Where is Jamie? Did you bring him to Auckland with you?'

What? 'Like I'd leave my seriously ill child behind while I came up here? Who do you think I am? I'm a very responsible mother, and you'd better believe that.' The words fired out at him and there were plenty more coming, except he put a finger to her lips.

'Hey, stop it. You wanted questions yet when I ask one you take my head off.' Those blue eyes were so reasonable it infuriated her.

She took a deep breath, stamped on her temper and tried for calmness. 'This hasn't been easy, coming to see you.'

'I'm sure it hasn't, but that's also kind of sad. I'd have thought we were better than that.' His gaze remained steady. 'So where is this lad?'

'With Mum in a motel down the road at Greenlane.' She named the motel and reluctantly smiled when he whistled.

'That's a bit trashy, isn't it?'

'Money's tight. And before you say anything, that's not a hint. I hope to find a small flat in the next few days.

The hospital did offer to put us up in one of those homes they provide for families with sick children but I don't think I can cope with living with other people, strangers, right now.'

Mitch studied his feet for so long she wondered if he'd fallen asleep standing upright.

'Mitch?'

He didn't look up. 'I'd like to see him.'

Yes. Her hands clenched. Yes, yes. Fantastic. 'Any time you like. We can go there now. The motel's only ten minutes away.'

Lifting his head he drilled her with his gaze. 'Whoa, slow down. Tomorrow will be fine. Let's leave Jamie to his sleep tonight.'

Mitch was right. But wait until tomorrow and he might change his mind. All those hours to come up with reasons not to see his son. 'Are you sure?'

'Yes.' Then, 'What's your plan for seeing specialists?'

'We've got an appointment with a renal specialist on Monday morning. Lucas Harrington. Know him?'

'Yes, a little. An American who moved here with his Kiwi wife a year ago. He's about the best you can get anywhere.'

'That's what I've been told. I also researched him on the internet and liked what I saw. He's written some interesting papers.' But could he save her boy?

'What time on Monday?'

'Huh?'

'Your appointment. I'll come with you. It might help if he knows I'm in the background.'

Her jaw dropped. She hadn't seen that coming. Mitch might not be owning up to fatherhood yet but he was supporting her in the one way he'd be utterly confident. 'Um, great. Yes, that's wonderful. Thank you. Ten o'clock.'

'Your enthusiasm's overwhelming. I thought this was why you knocked on my door,' he grumbled, then gave her a genuine smile for the first time since she'd walked into his office.

As far as smiles went it wasn't huge or exciting or welcoming, but it was warm and sincere. And her mouth dried. Her empty stomach sucked in. She'd once fallen in love with that smile.

I can't afford to do that again.

But it was going to be good seeing Mitch occasionally over the next few months while Jamie hopefully got the treatment he needed.

'There's something you should know.' Mitch's drawl broke into her thoughts. 'That party I'm supposed to be at? It's an early farewell party. My farewell. I leave for Sydney in less than two months' time, where I've accepted a job in the city's busiest hospital. It's a very prestigious position.'

She gasped, 'I don't believe it. You can't.' Shock rippled through her. Gripping her fists under her chin, she stared up at this man who seemed to slip out of tricky situations more easily than a greased eel slid from a man's hands. 'Of all the things you could've told me, I'd never have picked that one.'

'Bad timing, isn't it? Really bad.'

Her mouth fell open and she gaped at him.

He did sound apologetic. That didn't help one iota.

She almost cried. 'You have no idea.' *What have I done? Can I undo it? How totally unfair it would be to introduce Jamie to his dad only to have Mitchell disappear on him. No, that could not happen. No way.*

Mitch looked directly at her, fixing her with those intense blue eyes. 'It's not right for a child to lose parents at an early age. Better not to have known them at all.'

By the time she found her voice and could get a sound out around the rock in her throat Mitch was long gone.

From the corner of the car park Mitch watched Jodi drive away from the hospital, his heart knocking and his head spinning.

Jodi Hawke had come to town, bringing with her problems he'd never expected to have to face.

'I'm a father.'

Heading for his four-wheel drive in the underground park, he tried to think what this meant to him. Was he thrilled? Excited? Terrified? Angry?

Damn it. He'd go to Samantha's party, drink a tankful and sink into oblivion. Forget Jodi was here. Forget the bombshell she'd dropped.

And how's that going to look in front of your staff? Their HOD off his face at the party they'd put on to say farewell to him? A farewell he couldn't look forward to anymore. Staff who expected better of him.

'I'm a father.'

Yeah, he got that. Sort of. When would it really kick in? To the point where everything he did or thought had to take into consideration a small person? It might never happen with him. He wasn't exactly qualified to be a parent.

Turning, he headed back to the road. The Shed Bar would be crowded and heaving but he could get a drink and not be able to hear himself think. Perfect.

Or he could change into his gym gear, which was in the back of his vehicle, and go for a run up at Auckland Domain. Build up a sweat and tire his body so that it would go to sleep when he finally crawled into bed. Pound the paths that circled the museum.

Yeah, and probably break an ankle tripping over a kerb.

Anyway, he liked the bar idea better. Shoving his hands deep into his trouser pockets, he headed for bourbon. On the rocks.

CHAPTER FOUR

'MUMMY, WHY DO the sheep smell funny?' Jamie leaned through the fence wire peering at the animals grazing on the lush green grass.

Jodi forced a grin but couldn't keep the weariness out of it. 'That's their woolly coat. It keeps them warm and dry, like your jersey does for you. That's made out of sheep's wool too.'

Jamie's brow furrowed as he looked from his fire-engine-red top to the muddy sheep. 'Are there red sheep, Mummy?'

'No, the wool is coloured with red dye, like I did with the icing for your birthday cake. Remember?' Rubbing her eyes with the back of her hand, she stifled another yawn.

What with Mitch's bombshell about Sydney and all the questions buzzing around her head, she hadn't slept a wink last night. Worse, with her mother sleeping in the main room and Jamie in the small bedroom, she hadn't been able to get up and read to distract herself. So Mitch had dominated her mind all night long. Nothing new, really. He'd been dominating it ever since she'd made the decision to move north. Come on, he'd never really left. Mitch had always held a place in her heart. They might be over as far as a loving, sexual relationship went, but she'd never been able to completely let him go. She'd loved him deeply. Missed him more than she'd believed possible.

'Mummy, that man's looking at me.'

She knew. Just knew it was Mitchell. Despite everything that had gone down between them last night, she'd known he'd come. Despite him saying a child shouldn't have to lose a parent, she knew he wouldn't be able to ignore Jamie for long.

Turning slowly, warily, she studied the man standing twenty metres away, who looked as though he didn't know what to do next. 'Hello, Mitch.' He looked so…bewildered. Which was totally unlike him. What would it be like to hold him again? To feel that chest under her cheek? To have his arms around her? Darn, she'd missed him. Really, deep inside missed him.

'Hi, Jodi.' His eyes were glued on Jamie as he slowly closed the gap between them. 'I called in at the motel and Alison told me I'd find you here.'

Mum had probably told him a whole heap more than that. 'Cornwall Park's the perfect place for a small boy who's bored and feeling chained up in a motel unit the size of a gnat's house. All this acreage, the sheep, trees—it's wonderful. I'm going to take him up One Tree Hill shortly.'

Shut up, Jodi. Let Mitch speak. Let him tell you why he's here. Has he come to meet Jamie? Or to explain more about why he's soon heading to Sydney? As if she didn't know the answer to that one. A very prestigious position. One to rub his brother's face in, she'd bet. The guy couldn't stay still if there was an outside chance of getting one over Max.

They were both the same, had a gene that kept them moving on through anything life handed them that hinted at commitment to another person. They couldn't even front up to each other and admit their feelings. And who knew what those were? Mitch and Max probably didn't have a clue. Kind of sad when they were the only close family either of them had.

And now, when she'd turned up with his son, Mitch had got lucky. Or was that nearly lucky? He'd already made plans to go away. Mitch's heart must be doing leaps in the air. Timing was everything. What if she'd been a month earlier? Two months? He'd have immediately started searching for another position far away. Wouldn't he? Or was she justifying her actions again?

'Mummy?' Jamie's little hand crept into hers, his fingers twining tight around her thumb.

She dropped to her haunches, drew her baby into her arms. To protect him? Or herself? From what? 'It's okay, love. He's a...' Swallow. She looked over her son's head at the man who'd helped her create him. 'This is Mitchell, a friend of Mummy's.' Define friend. Define Mitchell Maitland. Impossible right now. Pulling her head away from Jamie, Jodi looked up into the bleak blue gaze of her boy's father. 'Mitch, I'd like you to meet my son, Jamie.' She slowly turned Jamie to face him, holding his frail body against her.

Mitch blanched. She'd hit a tender spot. Tough. This was a battle. If he was about to disappear she wasn't going to introduce him as Daddy. That might antagonise him, and her son's life depended on Mitchell coming onside. She'd do whatever it took to save Jamie. So, Mitch, you're toast. She pushed Jamie forward. 'Shake hands with Mitch like Mummy showed you.'

Her heart swelled with pride and pain as she watched Jamie trot across the space to this man he'd never met, holding out his right hand in greeting. So trusting, so totally unaware how important Mitch could be to him. Who he was. Until now Jamie had never asked about his father, but it wouldn't be much longer before he started noticing he didn't have one.

'Hello, I'm Jamie Hawke.'

Thankfully Mitch reciprocated. She'd have killed him if he hadn't.

'Hello, young man.' Mitch's hand swallowed his son's for a brief shake. Then it was as though he couldn't let go. Like his hand had frozen in place around Jamie's. 'I'm Mitchell Maitland, but you can call me…' He blinked, swallowed hard. 'Call me Mitch, like your mummy does.'

'Okay.' Jamie tugged his hand free. 'Want to see the sheep with me, Mitch?'

Mitch looked stunned at how easily he'd been accepted. 'Um, all right, I guess.'

But as Jamie ran towards the fence Mitch remained fixed to the spot, studying him. 'He's small for his age, isn't he? And so pale. All part of the renal failure, I know. Does he suffer a lot of pain? Headaches? What's his urine output like?'

Jodi took his arm and led him across to join Jamie. Again Mitch was dealing with this the only way he knew how. But that didn't explain the tremor running up his arm. 'He has intermittent bone pain, lots of headaches, urinary tract infections are a regular occurrence, and there's a score of other symptoms. He also has a sense of humour, loves chicken nuggets and fries, prefers orange juice to fizzy drinks, and wants to be a fireman when he grows up.'

'Not a doctor, then?' A wry smile tweaked Mitch's mouth.

'They're boring. Anyway, I think he's had his fill of medics for a while.'

'That makes sense. Poor little guy. Of all the crappy things to happen to him.'

Jodi pursed her mouth. 'I know. I've spent hours berating the fact *my* boy got sick, but as a doctor I know better than that.'

'I guess if there's anything to be grateful about it is that you are a doctor.' When her eyebrows lifted he grimaced. 'Doesn't make the slightest bit of difference?'

'Not a jot. Sometimes I think it's worse. I've always known what's ahead, and probably spend too much time looking for symptoms that aren't there. Yet.'

Mitch astonished her by dragging her into a hug. His chin rested on her head as he said, 'Jamie's very lucky to have you as his mum. I can't think of anyone else I'd want looking out for my child. To love him, cherish and care for him.'

Blimey. That was so unexpected. But then again, this was one of the charming Maitland twins. Of course he'd know exactly what to say to make her feel good.

Hang on. Was that a kiss on her head? Couldn't be. Not from Mr Enjoy 'em and Leave 'em. But they were in an odd situation. Maybe he was starting to see the whole picture, not just the *Oh, my God, I'm a dad* bit. She'd take it to be a kiss, a kiss given in friendship. And hope she was right.

'Mummy, I want a hug too.'

'Coming right up, my man.' Turning out of Mitch's arms, she leaned down to pick up her boy and hugged him tight. And got the shock of her life when Mitch's arms wrapped around both of them. A giant step forward?

Suddenly Mitch stepped back, his face inscrutable. 'I'll see you tomorrow at the appointment.' He spun on his highly polished shoes and almost ran to his four-wheel drive.

'That went well. Not,' Jodi muttered under her breath as she watched his rapid retreat. 'What next? Huh, Mitch? What am I supposed to do if you don't want to face this?'

Confusion boiled up in her head. If he was going to

Australia soon, why had he made an effort to meet Jamie this morning? Had he decided to take an active part in Jamie's life? Or was he just doing what he thought was the right thing? Putting in a cursory appearance? Maybe the reality of meeting Jamie had proved too hard to deal with. Now that he'd seen and met Jamie there was no denying he was a father. So why had he taken off as though a swarm of bees had been after him?

Could it be that—and the breath stuck painfully in her lungs—he'd thought the whole renal failure situation through and realised what she was hoping for?

Then again, last night when he'd told her about Sydney, she'd been unable to hide her anger and disappointment at him leaving—just when he'd found out about Jamie. He'd been ambivalent, saying he thought she'd done the right thing unless it was going to stress Jamie even more. At that point he had still been grasping the fact he was a father, nothing else. Of course Mitch leaving would cause Jamie grief. He mightn't ask why he didn't have a father yet, but to learn he had one only to lose him almost immediately would certainly create problems.

And right now she and Jamie didn't need any more of those. They already had more than their share.

Except there were more. Her unexpected need for Mitch, for one. It sprang up at her in full force, denying the difficulties lying between them, ignoring the fact that Mitch Maitland would never settle down in one place for longer than necessary, pushing aside the number of times he'd left her waiting. The fact was he was undeniably as gorgeous as ever. He'd be very easy to fall in love with all over again. Big problem, that.

Three attempts and the key still wouldn't fit into the ignition. Not surprising when Mitch's head was in turmoil.

He wanted to vent his frustration, to shout at the damned thing and bang the steering wheel with his clenched fist. Why did he feel such a strong yearning for that child out there in Jodi's arms?

No ordinary child. His son. Where had this sense of belonging come from when most of his life he'd been happy to believe he didn't want kids of his own? It had arrived, bam, the moment he'd seen Jamie standing by the fence, his little face puckered in wonder as he'd watched the sheep.

Was this how a father felt when the midwife handed him his baby for the very first time? Couldn't be. That would be more poignant, seeing the birth, holding the brand-new baby. Or would it?

When he'd decided to follow Jodi to Cornwall Park he'd believed he was prepared to see Jamie. He'd spent most of the night thinking about him. And about why Jodi hadn't told him earlier. And about Jodi herself. Part of him still didn't want to believe that the rumpled-looking woman now heading for her rental car was the vivacious, fashion-conscious lady he'd once lived with.

'Damn it.' His hand unclenched, clenched again. He'd thought he'd just meet the boy and be able to remain impervious to him—at least until he'd worked out what he was going to do. But that first glimpse had brought reality crashing down on him like a load of bricks. Shock and fear had fought with something like pride as he'd stood drinking in the unbelievable sight of the small boy who had his genes. The kid was beautiful, cute.

And so bloody sick. His heart squeezed tight. His fingers gripped the key. Inside his head a drum began beating a steady rhythm. Jamie. Bang. His son. Bang. Jodi. Bang. On and on it went.

Nothing Jodi had said had prepared him for what he'd seen when he'd studied Jamie. He knew sick kids, dealt with them daily. But this was his boy. Jodi had done the right thing, bringing him to see Lucas Harrington. The man was the best in his field in New Zealand, and close to it on the world stage. He had access to other top specialists too, including Max Maitland, transplant surgeon extraordinaire.

His teeth were grinding and he swore under his breath. Max was going to love this. He could see his brother's eyes lighting up now at the thought of Mitch needing something from him. Worse, somehow he had to tell Max about Jamie and his illness. How did he do that when they rarely talked? On the occasions they had to work together with a patient they were very professional. Thankfully, they didn't cross paths too often, though when they did there wasn't a civil word spoken between them. But all that was about to change. Jamie would be Max's patient.

Angrily shoving any thoughts of his brother aside, he concentrated on Jodi and her telling *him* he was a father. Had that been the right thing to do? Of course it was. He had two healthy kidneys. That had to be the biggest motivator for Jodi. His kidney—for Jamie. Anger should be enveloping him. She'd manipulated him. Perfectly. So was he going to follow the path she'd mapped out for him? He shrugged. Too soon to know yet. He still had to get his head around being a parent.

Across the road Jodi was buckling Jamie into a child's car seat. Her body was bent at the waist, her long legs seeming to go on for ever. His body tensed as memories of caressing those legs with the satin skin, of kissing his way from her knees to the apex where her womanhood waited, warm and moist, for him.

He shoved the key hard. Finally got it into the ignition. The engine roared as his heavy foot hit the accelerator. The wheels spun as he pulled away.

Jodi raised a startled face as he passed. A shocked, sad face with disappointment blinking out at him. That Jodi he remembered without any trouble at all.

Jodi Hawke, the woman who always sneaked into his skull in that still hour before the sun lightened night into day. Reminding him of what he'd lost.

Huh, you didn't lose Jodi. You handed her an excuse to leave you and then felt hard done by.

Forget those emotions. Forget why she'd suddenly turned up with Jamie. He wasn't ready to contemplate that can of worms. Not today.

Strange how already he felt some strange connection with the lad, as though there was a thread running between them. Which was frightening. Terrifying. But he was leaving for Sydney soon. That concerned him too. One thing he was an expert on was living without his father. He took a glance into the rental car as he drove past. 'My boy.'

That thread connecting them was tightening, pulling him inexorably closer to the kid, no matter how far away he drove. As though genes cut through all the words to the heart of the matter. If he hadn't felt so wired, confused and downright terrified, he'd laugh at himself because never once had he envisaged this moment. He'd sworn he'd leave children and parenting to the rest of the human race.

Driving through the park, he watched out for Sunday strollers and kids chasing each other, more aware than ever before of those children and the dangers they placed themselves in as they played.

What was it like to play ball with your son? To help him get dressed in the morning? To read him bedtime stories? His head swirled with images of him and Jamie together. Alien images, but kind of intriguing and warm and nice as well. Damn it.

And in every picture flicking across his brain was Jodi.

The real Jodi or the lookalike Jodi? The woman he'd once thought he might love? Or a complete stranger?

He needed to know. Now. Before he could digest anything more about that child and what to do for him. He had to find his Jodi amongst all those heart-wrenching emotions continually scudding across her beautiful face.

Lifting his foot, he slowed and turned back the way he'd come, pulled up behind her car. Climbing out, he went to meet her just as she hauled the driver's door open to get in.

'Mitch?' She tilted her head back, blinking as the autumn sunlight caught her eyes.

'I need to find you.' He tapped her sternum with a finger. 'Somewhere in there is the Jodi I once knew.' And then he took her shoulders and pulled her close. His lips covered hers as she gasped. Hot air spilled into his mouth. But he didn't pull away. Instead, he eased into her, hauling her up close against his chest, his stomach, his thighs. And tasted her, recognised her. This was his Jodi. Not that worried woman holding him to ransom. This warm, responsive woman not pushing him away but sliding her hands around his neck—that was the real Jodi.

He breathed her in. She still used lavender-scented shampoo. His hands splayed over her waist. His tongue danced across hers. Finally everything was beginning to make sense. This was the real deal.

Which meant so were all the problems she'd brought to town with her.

Jodi watched Mitch's vehicle until it was lost from sight behind the oak trees lining the park roads. Her finger traced her lips. 'What just happened?'

Worse. Why had she let it happen?

No. Worse was that she'd enjoyed the kiss. More than

enjoyed it, had felt it was right. It made her feel she'd finally come home, come in from the cold.

Which was so stupid because it didn't solve a thing. Their son was still ill. Mitch was still leaving for Sydney. She still didn't have a clue what came after Jamie's transplant.

Slumping against the car, she couldn't stop the warmth creeping through where her body had been chilled for weeks. Mitch had said he hadn't recognised her until he'd kissed her.

'Why? Have I changed that much?'

Must have. But she liked Mitch's technique for finding her. Except it would probably complicate things even more to have that kiss hanging over them.

No, the complication came from the fact that she'd enjoyed it, hadn't wanted Mitch to stop.

This was not what she'd come to Auckland for.

Or was it? Deep down in that dark corner had she been hoping for a reunion with Mitch? A kiss-and-make-up, fairy-tale ending to the years of anguish?

'If that's what you're wanting, you're in deep water. Mitch is still on the run from himself. You're going to get left behind and be angry at him for that when it will be your own fault for even thinking you could make it work again.'

Straightening up, Jodi turned and opened the car door again. Peeking in the back, she saw Jamie was dozing. At least he wouldn't have seen that kiss. Did it matter if he had?

Who knew? He might accept Mitch more readily if he thought Mummy liked this new man who had started hanging around a bit.

What Jamie wouldn't understand was that Mummy more than liked him, had always more than liked him.

Time to head back to the motel and put Jamie to bed for an hour. But as she drove slowly along the road the thought of that dark, cold unit did not excite her. At the intersection she looked left and right. To heck with it. She'd head for One Tree Hill. If Jamie stayed asleep then he was getting his nap anyway. If he woke up she'd show him the sights of Auckland.

And try to push that kiss down into the dark hole where all her other great Mitch memories were stored, gathering dust.

At the top of the hill she parked and went to sit on the stone wall where she could see Jamie and yet have the fresh air blowing around her cobweb-filled head. She tried not to think about anything.

But that kiss had startled her, not to mention it had quickly awoken a need inside that she doubted would be easily ignored.

Cars came and went, disgorging tourists who talked in many languages as they pointed out landmarks to each other. When Jamie grizzled she went and freed him from the seat belt and lifted him down to the pavement.

'Let me carry him.' Mitch stood in front of her, wariness in those unsettling eyes.

'That's the second time in less than an hour you've sneaked up on me.' There was a wobble in her voice that annoyed her.

'It wasn't intentional. Either time.' He reached down for Jamie. 'Hey, sport. Want to see Auckland?'

She followed slowly, wondering why he'd returned. She had no idea. It was as though he was on an elastic rope, pinging back and forth. Now she saw him. Now she didn't. Now she did.

At the wall, Jamie stood on the top so he could see the

city sprawled out below. Gripping her jacket, he asked, 'What's that over there, Mummy?'

'That's the harbour bridge,' she told him, hoping they were looking at the same thing. 'And that skinny tall building with a knob on top is the Sky Tower.'

'Can I go up there?' Jamie asked.

'When you're a bit bigger.' *When you can go alone and I don't have to suffer vertigo.*

'Why do I have to be big?'

'It's a Mummy rule.'

'That works?' Rare amusement laced Mitch's question.

'On a good day.' She tried to smile back and managed some sort of twist to her mouth.

His amusement faded, replaced by seriousness. 'Why did you come to Auckland? Was it only so Jamie could get the best medical care? Or did you come for my undivided attention and support? Hoping I'd drop everything to be by your side now that you've decided to tell me I'm a parent?'

Jodi flinched. And considered his questions. He had every right to ask. 'Both reasons.' She paused, thought it through some more. This was too important to muck up. There was a third reason, the most important one. But she was afraid to bring that out into the cold light of day yet. More than that, she'd prefer Mitch to broach it first. 'At least I think so.'

'Explain.'

I'm trying, without pushing you too hard. 'From the moment I heard about Lucas Harrington, nothing would've kept me from bringing Jamie to see him. At first I thought that's all it would be—a visit. Maybe a few visits, depending on the outcome of the consultation. Then back to Dunedin while we waited to see what could be done.' She rubbed Jamie's back absentmindedly. 'You've got to understand that Jamie comes first, second and third with me. Whatever's important for him is important for me. Nothing and no one will get in the way of that.' *Not even you. Despite that bone-melting kiss.*

'I'd never doubt it. You've always had the right instincts when it comes to other people so you'd be no different with your own child.'

So what did he doubt? That her altruistic claims regarding his role were false? 'I was wrong not to tell you I was pregnant. It was wrong not to let you know we had a son. But at the time it felt like the right thing to do for me. I can't change that.'

'I'm happy to let it drop, Jodi. As you say, we can't undo anything.'

Astonishment caught her. Blinking back sudden tears—darn, but there were a lot of those this weekend—she leaned over and kissed his cold cheek. 'Thank you.'

Together they stared out over the city, Jodi wrapping her arms around Jamie for added warmth. Then she gave Mitch a little more of herself. 'When Dad went to prison, Mum worked every hour of the day and night, trying to get ahead, trying to prove to the townspeople she could be a success and that Dad's criminal habits hadn't rubbed off on her. I really didn't factor into her plans in any way other than as a child to be fed, clothed and educated.' She paused, added quietly, 'I know Mum loved—loves me. But it was a lonely, cold way to grow up. She was never there for me. I didn't want sandwiches. I wanted hugs and mother-daughter talks.'

'Did you think I'd act in a similar way with my child?' There was no condemnation in his voice, only a need to know. Which was kind of sad.

Yet she couldn't keep the bitterness out of her voice. It had been collecting for a long time. 'And wouldn't you have? Isn't that why we broke up? You were always too busy for me. I was like your car: handy when needed otherwise best left parked up. Not the sort of man I wanted for Jamie's father.' But she could've dealt with that if only she'd given him a chance.

'That night of your birthday I was dealing with an emergency and couldn't get away.' He ground out the words.

'Mitch, you could never get away. There were always emergencies. There were other doctors available. You didn't try hard enough. You didn't even consider that a text to say you weren't going to make it would be preferable to leaving me sitting in the middle of the restaurant while I copped pitying looks from all the other diners.'

'I was pushing you.'

'I don't understand.'

'Like a test. Waiting, watching for your breaking point, which to me was inevitable. The closer we got, the harder I pushed.'

'So I passed the test with flying colours. And in doing so failed you.' And me. It was all beginning to make sense at last. If only she'd known more about Mitch's insecurities back then, how different the last three years might've been.

'Mummy, I'm cold.'

Oh, heck. 'Jamie, love, sorry. We'll go back to the motel now.' She had a lot to think about regarding Mitch and her role in this screwed-up situation.

'Don't want to go to bed. I want chicken nuggets.'

She picked Jamie up and headed for the car.

'Jodi.' Mitch spoke softly as he opened the door for her to place Jamie in his car seat. 'You're right. I should've let you know I wasn't going to make it that night. I let it get out of hand. I didn't text or phone and you kicked me out. Over and done. That's history. Since you've turned up again I'd like us to find a way to get along, at least for Jamie's sake, while his health is sorted.'

'And afterwards? Will you want to be around for him? It was you who said it would be better for him not to meet you than to have you walk away later. And yet here you are. Does that mean you want to be a part of his life?'

'Why wouldn't I be?' He had the audacity to look startled.

Something in her head exploded. 'Because I wasn't worth the effort of something as easy as a text so why would I expect more for my son?'

'Don't I deserve a second chance?'

'Aren't I giving you one?'

His hands slid into his pockets and he leaned against the front of the car. 'I'm trying to get my head around it all. Please be patient.'

'Sure.' Her hands fisted in the air between them, her teeth dug into her bottom lip. 'Sure.'

'There's something else that's bugging you, isn't there? Something from the past you're busting to get off your chest.'

How did he know that? How could he read her so well after all these years? He couldn't read her at all back then. 'Why did you ask me out that first time?'

'Because I wanted your company. I liked you.'

Narrowing her eyes at him, she forced the words out. 'Not because you wanted to show Max you could do better with his old girlfriend than he had?'

Mitch reared back, horror twisting his handsome face. 'Where did you get that crazy idea?'

'I heard you. You and Max, shouting at each other one day when I came around to your flat to tell you I was pregnant. Max yelling that brothers never, ever went out with each other's girlfriends, current or otherwise. You taunting him about how I preferred living with you than him.'

'Sh—'

'Don't swear in front of Jamie,' she snarled. 'There was more. Max taunted you by saying he was surprised you hadn't got me pregnant to prove how much better than him you were.'

'And I told him I didn't intend wrecking my great career because I had duties at home with a family.' Mitchell slammed his hands on his thighs and leaned back, staring up at the clouds scudding across town. His throat worked hard and he swallowed fast. His eyes blinked rapidly. 'That wasn't about you. It was about me. And Max.'

'Of course it was. How stupid of me to think any different. But I'll tell you this for nothing.' She paused for emphasis. 'I don't believe you. I hated being used as a scratching post between you two. I'd liked Max until then. I'd loved you. More than anyone, anything.'

His head snapped up. 'Jodi, no, you didn't.' His face lost its tanned look as all colour drained away. 'You couldn't have.' There was a tremor in his voice.

She shook her head, afraid to say anything more in case she really tore him apart to the point of no return. She'd said too much already. Her temper had got the better of her at the worst possible moment. She'd held that hurt in for so long now that a few more weeks wouldn't have mattered. But, no, she'd opened her mouth and slapped him over the head with her words.

'Maybe Max said that to me because he cared deeply for you, and when I picked up with you he saw red.'

Her chin dropped a little as she contemplated that. 'No, he didn't. It was Max who called our relationship off.' Not that she'd been broken-hearted. They had got on well but she hadn't been in love with the guy. And he certainly hadn't loved her.

'He's a Maitland, remember?'

'A commitment dodger?'

'Yeah, exactly.' Mitch's sigh hurt her.

'You're wrong. Max and I got on okay but there was no chemistry. None at all. We should never have dated for as long as we did. It became a comfortable habit, really.'

Mitch's eyes widened. 'Truly?' When she nodded he continued. 'Still, you should never have heard that particular argument. It was pure Max and Mitch vitriol, each trying to hurt the other. You know how good at that we are.' He drew a breath. 'And I swear the only reason I asked you out that night was because I liked you, was attracted to you and wanted to get to know you better.'

'Oh, okay. Thanks.' She nibbled her lip, trying to ignore the elephant between them. She'd loved Mitch. And now he knew. 'I had hoped we'd had more going for us than your antipathy towards your brother.'

'Jodi, we had much more. My problems with Max never had anything to do with why I was with you. For me it was all about you and me.'

She'd put it behind her. She had to. For Jamie. And maybe even for herself. 'Let's go feed our boy.'

Let's forget my tongue has a mind of its own sometimes. She slapped at her cheeks. When would this watery stuff dry up? She never did tears. Yeah, sure.

CHAPTER FIVE

MONDAY MORNING WAS grey and wet. The clouds oozed drizzle. It suited Jodi's mood.

'You sure you don't want any toast?' Mum asked for the fourth time.

Jodi shook her head, irritated by her mother's persistence. 'I wouldn't be able to keep it down.' Even the tea she'd drunk sat like a puddle in her stomach. She wanted to be at the hospital now, meeting Lucas Harrington, getting to the nitty-gritty of Jamie's medical issues. But it was barely gone seven-thirty.

'Want me to do anything with Jamie?'

'Thanks, Mum, but I'll leave him for as long as possible. He had a bad night.' Which meant so had she. There was grit in her eyes, a dull throb in the base of her skull, and her limbs were lead-lined.

'Then I'll take the dirty clothes down to a laundry I saw when I went for a walk yesterday. I can take my laptop with me and do some work while I wait.' Mum started stuffing Jamie's clothes into a plastic shopping bag.

'Thanks, Mum. I do appreciate it.' More than that, she really loved it that her mum had come up to Auckland with them, even if only for the first few days. It had made all the difference, being able to leave Jamie with her while she'd gone in search of Mitch. Mum's support was always practical, and she'd come to recognise it for what it was—love.

'Jamie's my concern, too.'

Mum seemed to make more time for him than she'd ever done for *her*. In fact, since they'd learned about Jamie's kidney disorder Mum had changed, putting more effort into helping her, being there to give her a break, and sometimes offering to pay the overdue bills. As she hated parting with her hard-earned money, that was huge. Despite being wealthy due to her own hard work, she hadn't learned to relax. Work had been her saviour, money her prize.

Jodi jumped. Someone was knocking on the door. Opening it, she gasped, 'Mitch. What are you doing here?'

'I thought that since I'm going to Jamie's appointment with you I may as well give you a lift to the hospital.'

'But we're not going for more than two hours.' He looked absolutely fabulous in his grey suit and light blue shirt. The darker blue tie matched his eyes perfectly.

A sheepish look crept over his face. 'Is it a problem? I can come back later.'

Was this about Mitch wanting to see Jamie again? Or to make himself useful? She stepped back, holding the door wide. Or did he have things to say to her? 'Come in.'

'I brought breakfast.' He held up a grocery bag. 'Bacon and eggs.'

Nausea swamped Jodi. No way would she be able to hold that down. 'We had toast a little while ago,' she fibbed to save his feelings.

Her mother stood up. 'Bacon and eggs might be good for you, my girl.' She switched her fierce look to Mitch. 'I'm glad you're going with Jodi and Jamie to the specialist. She needs you there. So does Jamie.'

Here we go. Mum had never had any time for the charming Maitland brothers, always warning her that she'd get into trouble if she hung around with either of them. How true, if having the most gorgeous little boy on the planet was trouble.

Mitch gave Mum one of his serious smiles, wisely withholding one of his charm-filled variety. 'Alison, you're right, which is why I'm here. I will do what I can for Jamie and Jodi over the next couple of months.'

'Okay.' Jodi went for the peace plan. 'Mum, I've got a few things from yesterday that need washing.'

'Where's Jamie?' Mitch asked, before her mother could say anything more to him.

'Dozing in bed. Not a good night. I'll get him up shortly.'

Thankfully, Mum decided to leave well alone and, picking up the laundry, she slung her laptop carry bag over her shoulder and disappeared outside.

Jodi switched the kettle on, more for something to do than the need for a hot drink. She still couldn't get her head around the fact that she was in the same city as Mitch, let alone the same motel room with only an arm's length between them. While she'd lain awake beside Jamie during the night she'd had plenty of time to think about this man who'd once made her heart sing. If only he hadn't been so commitment shy. But he had been, still was, so there was no point in rehashing her old feelings for him.

'Aren't you entertaining a TV crew this week?' she asked, vaguely remembering something that doctor had said in Mitch's office on Saturday night.

'I've been into work already and arranged for Aaron to cover for me this morning. For all his grizzling I think he's stoked to be fronting some of the documentary.'

She gave him a quick grin. 'And you wouldn't be?'

His answering grin was self-deprecating. 'Not at all.'

A cry sounded in the other room. 'Here we go. Jamie

doesn't wake up sweetly. Especially after a rough night.' This was sure to send Mitch charging out of the motel faster than an angry bull.

Pulling the curtains open, she sat on the edge of the bed and ran her hand over Jamie's damp hair. 'Hey, sweetheart. It's time to get up and have some breakfast.' She kept talking softly while rubbing his head, then his back, slowly coaxing the crying to a sniffle then to a few hiccups. 'That's my boy. Shall we put your tiger top on today?'

'Okay.'

Really? That easily? Jodi studied Jamie and realised he was looking beyond her to the doorway. A quick glance showed Mitch leaning against the doorframe. That's why she'd won the first round in the dressing stakes so easily. Mitch was a huge distraction.

'Let's get you some toast and honey.' That usually meant Jamie would automatically want cereal.

'Okay, Mummy.'

Blink. Was something wrong with her hearing this morning? Where had this little angel come from? She plopped a kiss on her boy's cheek. Noted the slight temperature from the warmth on his brow. Paracetamol coming up with that toast.

Mitch spoke up. 'Can I put the toast on?'

'Thanks, that would help. I'll give the tiger a face wash.' Swinging Jamie up into her arms, she winced as her back clicked.

'He's heavy for you.' Mitch reached out to Jamie. 'Hi, sport. Can I carry you to the bathroom?'

Jodi held her breath, certain that this gesture would lead to tears, if not tantrums.

Jamie jammed a thumb in his mouth, staring at Mitch warily. Then he nodded and held his free hand out to him.

Stunned, Jodi handed him over to his father. 'Guess I'm on toast duty, then.'

'Ahh, are you sure? What if Jamie doesn't like me washing him?'

'Then I'll be right with you. Coffee?'

When Jamie trotted out to join her a few minutes later Mitch was right behind him, a bewildered smile lighting up his face. 'That was easy.'

Jodi handed him a mug of black coffee. 'Beginner's luck.' But it warmed her heart that he'd done something for Jamie. The first hands-on thing and he'd come out of it with a smile. That had to be good. Didn't it?

'Now, about that breakfast.' Mitch leaned against an impossibly small bench and eyeballed Jodi. 'You could do with feeding up. I don't believe you've had anything. Facing today on an empty stomach is not a good idea.'

'I don't want to carry a rubbish bin around with me either,' she grumped as she elbowed him out of the way to make coffee.

'If I cook it, will you at least try to eat a little?' Mitch slid back against the bench. He wasn't giving up on her that easily. 'I'll carry the bin.'

She glared up at him from under lowered eyebrows. 'Persistent, aren't you?'

'That's a yes, then.' He ignored the flush spreading across her pale cheeks and delved through the two small cupboards to find a pan. 'I can feel your eyes boring holes in my back.' He unpacked the groceries, opened the packet of bacon.

'Which part of no didn't you understand?'

'Which part of persistent don't you?' He turned around and was fixed with a look that told him to back off. A look distinctly lacking in humour. 'Here's the deal. I'll cook some food and if you still don't feel like eating then that's okay with me.'

It wasn't true but he wasn't about to have a big argument over what she ate for breakfast. Somehow he doubted Jodi could take too much angst this morning, even if he was only doing it for her own good.

She dipped her head in acknowledgment. 'Deal.' Those brown orbs were filled with exhaustion, and behind that he saw her need for someone to take care of her, to stand at her side while she faced a new round of specialists today. A need she'd never in a month of birthdays admit to.

'I've told my staff I might not be available for most of the day. I intend spending it with you while we talk to Lucas and anyone else he might refer Jamie to.' Including Max. Damn it. He needed food in his stomach to manage that.

She didn't move, didn't say a word. But her gratitude was in the welling up of tears and the lightening of the brown of her eyes.

If only he could give her everything else she required as easily.

One step at a time, boyo. One step at a time.

Lucas Harrington turned out to be a genial man who immediately won Jodi over by simply spending time getting to know Jamie and putting him at ease. He acted as though he had all the time in the world for her little boy, and yet he had to be extremely busy. The examination he eventually gave Jamie was thorough and gentle.

Jodi nibbled her lip and watched Lucas's face the whole time, looking for clues of what he thought. Not that she expected any nasty surprises: she'd already had them all. But worry held a permanent place in her head when it came to Jamie's health.

Beside her, Mitch picked up her hand and held it in his. His thumb rubbed her wrist, softly, soothingly. When she dared to shift her vigil from Lucas to take a quick peek at Mitch she was surprised to find his eyes fixed on her, concern and care staring out at her. If only she'd had him beside her right from the beginning. It would've been so much better to have someone to share the burden, to talk about Jamie's health and future. But that couldn't be changed. She'd chosen not to tell him. And if he had known, it still wouldn't have changed Jamie's situation.

Mitch whispered, 'Hang in there, Jodi. Jamie's doing fine.'

'He's so brave.' Her teeth nibbled her already tender bottom lip. 'If only I could swap places with him. It's so not fair.'

'I think you're very brave too. I'm only beginning to understand what it's been like for you, and I'm probably so far off the mark but, hell, Jodi, you're a marvel.'

'I'm a mother. It comes with the territory. And I wouldn't have it any other way.'

Understanding filled his gaze. His thumb stilled on her wrist. Then he lifted her hand and kissed her palm. 'Thank you from me for Jamie.'

Shock rippled through her. What a difference thirty-six hours made. Mitch had gone from denial to acceptance that they had a child together. He'd made her breakfast—which seemed to be staying in place. Now he was sitting with her throughout their appointment, totally supportive. Blimey.

'Right.' Lucas's deep voice blasted through her wonder. 'Let's get Jamie back into his tiger suit and then we'll talk.'

With Jamie dressed and sitting on her knee, Jodi braced herself. She knew what was coming but hearing it from this man would take away her last, futile grain of hope.

Lucas cleared his throat and looked at her. 'I've read

all the notes sent up by your specialists in Dunedin and I don't see any reason to disagree with their prognosis.'

Her stomach churned. She tasted bacon at the back of her throat and not a rubbish bin in sight. In a strange, quivery voice she asked the specialist, 'Are you going to run more tests?'

Mitch gripped her hand tight. She gripped back, probably crushing every bone in his.

'I'm going to keep everything to a minimum. Jamie doesn't need any more distress than is absolutely necessary,' Lucas told them.

Jodi liked this gentle man even more.

Tapping his pen against the desk pad, he added, 'But I can't avoid all the tests, I'm afraid. We need to take some bloods.' Tap, tap, tap. 'We need to put him on stronger antibiotics too. I'm sure you're aware of his temperature.'

'That's happened overnight,' she told him. 'Please, just tell me.' Everything. Nothing. Make it all go away.

Lucas's voice was very matter-of-fact. 'Jamie does need a kidney transplant. Urgently.'

She knew that. Had heard it in Dunedin. That's why they were here. But it still caused her breathing to cease, her heart to stop. The truth hurt, like a knife turning in her tummy. Shredding her to bits. Her boy was dying. Slowly, painfully. Horribly. And now she had to depend on someone else volunteering a kidney. Or, worse, another mother losing her child so Jamie could live. She opened her mouth to answer Lucas, but nothing came out. Not one word, not even a sound.

Mitch's hand still held hers, but it was the specialist he spoke to. 'Lucas, do you do the transplant surgery?'

'No. As you are well aware, we have an excellent transplant team here, headed by none other than your brother. I'd prefer that Max does this.'

Beside her Mitch tensed, then shocked her with, 'He is the best.'

Max to do the operation? Jodi could not swallow the lump blocking her throat. Max? Too weird. Too family. But she'd always known it would come to this. 'What about Carleen Murphy? I hear she's very good.'

Lucas studied her so long Jodi knew he had to be seeing right into her head, seeing her confusion, her unwillingness to have Jamie's uncle operate on him. 'You'll be meeting with the whole transplant team. We'll leave deciding who does the operation until afterwards.'

She couldn't ask for better than that.

Mitch wanted to run from the room, to get as far as possible from the kind eyes and disastrous words of Lucas Harrington, to block out the horror. But he couldn't. He'd run out of time. This was when he stood up to be counted. Acted like the strong male he'd always pretended to be.

Unwittingly he looked at Jamie. Another look at the boy with the pale face and the small frame. Wished he hadn't because what he saw made his heart tighten painfully. Surprisingly it continued pumping.

Face the truth. Face what I've been hiding from since Jodi told me about Jamie's illness. This kid needs a new kidney. He'll die without it. And I've only just met him. My flesh and blood. I don't want to lose him before I've got to know him.

I don't want to lose him at all.

My flesh and blood. My kidneys might be compatible.

'Mitch?' Jodi nudged him. 'We're finished with Lucas for now. I need to take Jamie up to the lab.'

He saw the pain for Jamie in her eyes. Saw the way she held on to her son for dear life and knew she wouldn't let him carry Jamie for her. Not now, at this moment, when she'd faced the truth of the situation—again.

'Hell, Jodi, how have you held yourself together through all this?' He wasn't managing very well after one doctor's consultation. Jodi would've had plenty of those. She'd done it all alone. Her mother might've helped but Alison wasn't known for dealing with the emotional stuff when it came to her daughter's needs. Just like him. He could blame the fact he hadn't had long to get used to having a son who was seriously ill, but that was a cop-out.

Jodi might've been right not to want involve him in Jamie's life.

But it was too bloody late. He was involved. Like it or not. And he was coming to like it, horrendous problems or not.

In the corridor she peered at him over the top of Jamie's head, those beautiful, suck-him-in eyes filled with resignation. 'There's never been any choice. Jamie needs me to be strong, to fight his battles, to love him. If I fail he has nobody.'

Time to start thinking about these two, not himself. Mitch swallowed hard. 'He has me. For what it's worth, I accept I'm his father and therefore have a role to play in his life.'

As Jodi's eyes widened in relief he felt a surge of pride. And astonishment. It hadn't hurt a bit to say that. Would that come later when he thought through the consequences? No, actually, he didn't think it would.

You've just taken a giant step forward, boyo.

Then dismay shivered through him, knocking down the good feeling. What about Sydney and that fabulous job he'd been angling to get for over a year now? Was he prepared to give that away? He hadn't thought about that for a few hours. Relax. Jodi and Jamie could join him over there. After the transplant, of course. Yeah, that would work. Jodi could find work in a general practice if she wanted to, and he'd be able to spend time with Jamie in his downtime. They might even find adjoining apartments somewhere central.

Definitely a solution to everything. For the first time since he'd opened his eyes to find Jodi in his office, things were looking up.

If he ignored the axe hanging over them.

Jamie needed a new kidney. Fast.

And he had one to spare.

As Mitch took her elbow and eased her through the throng of people streaming in the opposite direction, Jodi tried to assimilate the full extent of what he'd just said. Did he understand how big the role of father could be? Why wouldn't he? He'd spent all his adult life avoiding getting into the situation where he'd have to be a dad.

'Mummy, can we go home?' Jamie sniffled against her neck. 'I don't like it here.'

'Oh, sweetheart, I know you don't.' She tried to avoid saying an outright no. 'We'll go back to the motel soon.'

Despite the phlebotomist being so careful and gentle, Jamie had still felt the needle that had drawn his blood. His little face had puckered up with resignation. She'd had a sudden urge to pick him up and run. Run from all the uncertainty, the kind medical staff, the big question of Mitch. Run and hide in a warm place where they could pretend none of this was happening. If Mitch hadn't been there, watching over them like a fierce male protector, she really might've taken off.

'I don't want to go there. I want to go home and see Bambi.'

'Who is Bambi?' Mitch asked.

'My cat.' Jamie's head twisted around as he sought out this man who didn't seem to understand anything.

'A cat named Bambi? That's novel.'

Jodi smiled despite everything. 'Better than Knickers, which is the name of the boy next door's puppy.'

Mitch chuckled. 'I didn't realise there was quite such a wide range of pet names out there. Whatever happened to Socks or Blackie?'

'My cat's not black. He's ginger,' Jamie informed him through a sniff.

'And he is really a she, proof being the litter we found in the bottom of the hall cupboard last month.' Jodi smiled her thanks at Mitch for the diversion. Hopefully they'd got past Jamie's need to go home for a little while longer, at least until they'd collected his prescription and dosed him up.

Mitch asked Jamie, 'Feel like going to the canteen and getting a juice, sport?'

'I think so.'

'What do you say?' Jodi nudged her boy.

'Thank you, Mitch. Are you going to get Mummy a coffee? She likes one when I have a juice.'

'Then, yes, that's what we'll do.' His hand tugged her left along another corridor. 'This way. The canteen shouldn't be too busy at this time of the morning.'

Thankfully Mitch was right. Only a few people sat at the scattered tables. About to give a sigh of relief, Jodi suddenly froze, her feet unable to propel her any further forward as she stared at the man seated in the far corner reading the newspaper as he drank from a mug.

Max Maitland.

She so wasn't ready for this man. She hadn't sorted everything out with Mitch yet, so how could she explain to his twin about Jamie? Because the way these two didn't get on, always tried to outdo the other in absolutely everything, Max was going to want to score points out of her sudden appearance with a child in tow. Mitch. Her head flipped back as she sought his face. But he was staring across the room with the same emotions racing through his eyes as she was feeling.

'Let's go.' She nudged him in the side. 'We can get a juice somewhere else.' Preferably on the other side of the moon.

Mitch turned to propel Jodi out of the canteen. He definitely wasn't ready to have Max learn about his son. Probably never would be, but there'd be no avoiding it. All he asked right at this moment was that they got out of here without being seen so they could go somewhere quiet and discuss how much Max should be told. One day. One whole day, that was all he wanted.

'Why can't I have it now, Mummy?' Jamie's voice rose to a loud squeal. 'You promised.'

Mitch bit down on his frustration. The little guy didn't understand what was going on. 'We'll find a better place, okay?'

'Mitch?' Max called across the room. 'Disappearing before you've even got here?'

Damn. Luck was definitely not on his side today. But maybe it would be better getting this out of the way. Huh. As if. Resigned, Mitch braced himself and tucked Jodi under his arm to turn around with her—and met the startled glower of his brother as he noticed who was with him.

'Jodi? Is that you?' Max unfolded himself from the chair to stand tall, a smile spreading across his handsome face. 'What brings you to town?' Then his eyes widened further still. 'And who's this?'

Mitch felt her tremble but she stepped forward, away

from his side. 'Hello, Max. It's good to see you. And this is Jamie, my son.'

Mitch would've laughed if the situation hadn't been so damned serious. Instead he groaned and held his hand tight at his side. Max's jaw had dropped, and for once he seemed lost for words.

Jodi crossed the remaining gap to his brother. 'It's been a long time but you're looking as good as ever.'

She hadn't said that about *him*. Mitch studied the expression in her bold eyes. Aha. She was pandering to Max's ego, softening him up, trying to prevent a tirade of questions. Especially when it was blatantly obvious who Jamie's father had to be. And what was *he* doing about the situation? Letting Jodi down.

'Max, Jamie is also my son.' There were a million things he wanted to add to that bald statement. He and Max had an unvarying pattern to their conversations and arguments, which always included getting one over the other, a power struggle to come out on top. But not today. He couldn't abide Max saying anything wrong about Jodi or Jamie.

Max blinked then drawled, 'Even a blind man could see that.'

Jodi murmured, 'Strong Maitland genes.'

Then Max got his second wind. 'Jodi, it's great to see you. Really. I've wondered what happened to you.' And the guy hauled her into his arms for a hug, Jamie and all.

Mitch glared at his brother's back. What was it about Jodi Hawke that attracted them both? Jodi had said Max had dropped her and that they didn't have a strong relationship, not a lot of chemistry between them, but they had gone out for a couple of months.

Then after she and Max had split he'd been feeling particularly low about his adoptive parents' bad financial situation and the bankruptcy suit that had been filed against them so he'd given Jodi a call to ask her out for a drink and a meal. One thing had led to another with Jodi that night. The chemistry between *them* had been hot, sparking and wild. He had to believe her when she said she hadn't felt anything strong for Max.

Jodi backed away from Max, the thumping of her heart unnaturally loud. She'd seen the utter disbelief in Max's eyes, quickly followed by shock when the realisation he had a nephew clanged into place. But he had hugged her as he always had, like a special friend.

Moistening her dry mouth, she filled him in a bit. 'I've been in Dunedin all the time, working for a general practice when time allows. Jamie keeps me fairly busy.'

'I imagine he does.' Max was studying Jamie carefully. Seeing the illness? Of course he was. Anyone with half a medical brain would know this wasn't a child brimming with good health.

'Jamie has cystinosis and he's been referred to Lucas Harrington. We've just come from seeing him.' Max's eyes widened, darkened as he absorbed this bit of news. She could see the thought processes going on in that bright intellect as he digested everything. Compassion clashed with surprise. Sadness nudged medical interest.

'The poor little guy,' was all he finally said, but there was a weight of concern behind each word. He really did care, really did understand what she might be going through.

'Guess you never expected to have a nephew,' she muttered.

A Maitland smile lifted the grim outline of his mouth. 'There's a good surprise in every day.'

Stunned, she could only gape at her son's uncle. No nasty words, no snips at Mitch for obviously not knowing he'd fathered a child. This Max was new to her. Swallowing the lump sliding up her throat, she managed, 'Thank you. Hopefully you'll get to see him on a day when he's got more energy and can chatter to you.'

'I look forward to it.' Max's gaze fixed on his nephew, and a flash of hunger zipped through his startled eyes. It was gone so fast she wondered if she was mistaken. Replaced by his usual professional, don't-think-you-can-touch-me demeanour. But, no, she had seen it, knew he'd be around to see Jamie some time soon. Her heart softened. Bring it on. *And sorry, Carleen Murphy, we don't need you after all. I've just touched base with the best surgeon in all respects available for Jamie.*

Jamie's eyes were closed as he sniffled against her neck. Her hands tightened around his thin body. 'I'm sorry, Max, but we have to go. Jamie's exhausted after seeing the specialist and having bloods taken.'

Mitch reached for Jamie, lifted him into his arms to relieve Jodi of her load, knowing she'd let him go now. She'd reached an understanding with Max that he hadn't been a part of but which he found he didn't mind. His brother was Jamie's best hope and so all animosity had to be set aside. He'd seen the instant Max had comprehended his role in Jamie's future.

Mitch also knew the exact moment Max fully understood the implications of Jamie's disease. There'd been a glint of compassion in the sharp glance Max had flicked him. A big question hovered behind the reality of what he'd just worked out. If Jamie needed a transplant, who was going to be the donor?

To dodge that bullet, Mitch told him, 'Jamie's to be seen in your department next week.'

Jodi murmured, 'We haven't got an appointment yet.'

Max stood absolutely still, concentrating on Jamie. Finally he shook his head and focused on Jodi. 'Bring him to see me tomorrow. Three o'clock. All right?'

And then he was gone, charging out of the canteen, a man on a mission.

'How can he know he's got a space in his schedule at that time?' Jodi stared after him.

'He'll make time. Guaranteed. But, Jodi, just because he's seeing Jamie tomorrow, it doesn't mean you can't have Carleen Murphy do the operation if that's what you want.'

She looked at him with those big imploring eyes. 'I haven't a clue what or who I want. Except…' She stopped, and shook her shoulders as though pushing aside something very difficult.

He fully understood. Especially when it came to having his brother on the case. But they had to put all grievances aside in the interest of getting the absolute best care and help for Jamie. And as much as it galled him to admit it, Max was the best transplant surgeon in the country.

Jodi leaned in against him for a brief moment. He had to bend his head to hear her say, 'No, I do know. Max has to do the transplant. If it's not asking too much of him, considering the family ties.'

That was something they'd have to wait to find out.

CHAPTER SIX

'YOU'RE NOT SAYING MUCH.' Jodi's understatement jolted him as he concentrated on the motorway traffic. 'You must be feeling annoyed that Max has found out about Jamie before you've had time to get used to the idea.'

'You could say that.' He pulled out to pass a truck and trailer unit.

'Working in the same hospital, the odds were always tipped that way.'

'We hardly ever bump into each other. Mostly keep to our own areas.' To avoid each other and the arguments that the hospital staff had come to expect as much as they did.

'What is behind all that antagonism between you two?'

He breathed deep. 'Did you know our parents died when we were six?'

'Yes, I think it was you who told me. What happened?'

He should've told her everything years ago. That's what couples did, shared their pasts as well as their futures. But they hadn't been planning on a long-term future together. At least, he hadn't. The closer Jodi had got to him the more he'd pushed her away until she'd left him and he could feel justified for his actions. Self-preservation? Or self-destruction?

'Mitch, talk to me. I need to know more about your past. Jamie will start asking questions as he gets older.'

She hiccupped and twisted her head to stare out the side window, sniffing back tears.

Mitch's heart lurched as he glanced across and saw her swallowing hard. He had to fight the urge to pull over to the side of the motorway and hug her in a vain attempt to take away her fears. She lived with Jamie's situation every minute of every day. It must hover on the periphery of her mind, suddenly blinking into full focus whenever she talked about anything but Jamie's immediate future.

But until he worked through what his role was then he had to keep his distance from her. At the moment all he could give her was some background stuff. 'Dad and Mum loved sailing, especially offshore. It was their passion.' More than their kids had been if they could go away and leave us for months at a time. 'They were on a trip to Fiji when a storm blew up. There were mayday calls for a few hours, then nothing. An air and sea search went on for days until eventually a few broken planks and a life jacket with the yacht's name stencilled on it were found a long way from their last known position. The court ruled death by drowning.'

Jodi turned to look at him through watery eyes. The hand she rested on his arm trembled. 'That's dreadful. What happened to you and Max?'

'We were separated and sent to live with different uncles, both brothers of our father. They got to choose one twin each.' A chill permeated his warm muscles, set bumps on his forearms. Like how did anyone pick between two kids?

'Twins shouldn't be separated.'

'Want to tell me something I don't know?' he snapped. 'I get that we were a handful, but we'd just lost our parents. Who wouldn't be?'

Jodi laid her hand on his arm again. 'Hey, that's shocking. Why did neither of them take both of you?'

'The uncles never got on, always competing against each other in everything.' He sighed. 'Yeah, like Max and I.' He concentrated on the car in front, keeping a perfect distance behind it. 'From what I learned over the years, Harry and Fred carried that competitive streak too far and couldn't agree about who took us so their wonderful solution was to take one each. And to hell with the consequences for us.'

It had been like losing an arm to lose his twin, only worse. And there had begun the slow build-up to the animosity that now lay between he and Max. The families had been completely different; the situations and attitudes of their adoptive parents poles apart.

'That is so cruel.'

'My adoptive family is loving and sharing. Ma and Pa were always putting their hands in their pockets for anyone to the detriment of themselves. They now live in a run-down bungalow in a bad part of town.' And refuse any offer of financial help. After all they'd done for him it saddened and maddened him. 'But despite everything they did for me, gave me, how much love I got, they weren't my parents. And my cousins were exactly that. Cousins. Not my twin brother.'

'Yes, that would suck, big time. What about Max's family?'

'He landed into a very wealthy home with people who made high demands on their adopted son. I'm not even sure they wanted children so why they adopted him is a mystery, except to get one over Harry. I lived in Ashburton; Max lived in Auckland. We never saw each other except for a couple of awkward visits.'

As a young boy, Mitch had spent years searching for

Mum and Dad, and Max, at every turn of the road, in every shop, on the bus. When he had been a teen he'd run away to Auckland in search of his brother, only to be rebuffed. He couldn't do any of that to Jamie, no matter how much he might want to be a part of the lad's life. He knew how desertion hurt deeply, irrevocably.

Mitch flicked a quick glance in the rear-view mirror at Jamie, sitting in his special seat. *My spitting image. How could I leave him?* How could he not get to know the boy?

How could he ignore the burning question he saw in Jodi's eyes every time he looked at her?

Focusing on driving so he could briefly abandon thoughts of Jodi and his son, he took the Greenlane turn-off. But the despair and worry over what to do did not back off. As if it was likely to. Somehow over the next few weeks he had to come to some decisions about Jamie.

But, wow, he was a dad to a cracker of a little guy. Despite thinking he wanted to hightail it as far away as possible, there was a spark of interest and yearning that, if he admitted to it, would never let go of its hold over him. He wasn't going to do a runner. He didn't know what he would do, how he'd make it all work, but he would do his damnedest for Jamie. And Jodi.

Could he commit to this child? If he gave Jamie his all, would it work out for them both? Doing so would keep Jodi in his life one way or another, too. Did he want that?

His gut clenched. Was that a no? Or a yes?

Why would he suddenly get a relationship right when he'd not managed one so far in thirty-six years?

Back at the motel, Jodi held the door open as Mitch carried a tired and grizzly Jamie inside to his bed and laid him down. 'Time you had a wee sleep, sport.'

'Don't want to,' said Jamie around a big yawn. 'Where's Mummy?'

'Right here, sweetheart.' Jamie had looked so right in his father's arms. Startling how similar they were, not only physically but also in their expressions. Right now Jamie wore that frustrated expression that twisted his face whenever things weren't going his way. She'd seen that expression on Mitch's face more often than she could count.

She was still getting her head round Mitch's shocking revelation about his parents' deaths and the upbringing he'd had afterwards. She couldn't begin to imagine what it must've been like to be separated from his twin. No wonder he had commitment issues. If only he'd listen if she told him she believed that having had an unusual upbringing didn't mean he wasn't capable of being a great dad. More than many men, he'd understand how important it was to be there for his child. Unfortunately she had no chance of getting that message across.

'Mummy, where's blankie?'

She hurried to fetch the old baby blanket Jamie refused to go to bed without. 'Here it is, and I've got some medicine, too.' When Jamie opened his mouth to protest she slid the full spoon into his mouth.

'Yuck.' He shook his head in disgust.

Her heart expanded. She loved her boy so much. Today's confirmation from Lucas about the transplant had been hard to swallow, despite knowing it was coming, and yet now that she'd had time to calm down she found she was ready. Bring it on. Then they could get on with their lives.

'Who's a good boy, then?' She kissed the top of his head. Felt the heat on his skin. A flare of worry almost blinded her. She'd need the thermometer. In a moment. First things first. 'Okay, let's take your clothes off and tuck you in all nice and snug.'

Mitch held a squirming Jamie while Jodi deftly whipped his top and trousers off. 'Want to take his temp when he's settled? I'll get your medical kit.'

'Thanks,' she muttered. So Mitch had noticed the heat on Jamie's skin too. Didn't he get the urgency of a transplant? Or was he avoiding the real issue here? He was a possible donor, a stronger candidate than anyone else. With a kidney from a compatible parent Jamie had far better odds of an excellent recovery and long-term good health. The first thing she'd done on learning Jamie had cystinosis had been to find out if she was compatible in preparation for this moment. Unfortunately, her own history of renal disease as a child had put her out of the running. And that had felt as thought she'd failed her child badly.

'Want anything else?' Mitch put her bag on the floor.

Your kidney. Closing her eyes to hide those words from him, she held her breath. Fought the impulse to grab Mitch and shake him into seeing things her way. Like that would really help. Even she knew Mitch had to make his own decisions on that score. Surely he got the urgency? Lucas did. Max did. She did.

'Jodi? You all right?'

Of course not. Who would be? Part of her knew that if she rushed him into a decision, she was less likely to get the result she wanted: help to save Jamie's life. The other part of her couldn't care less if he was hurried, she needed to know. It was too late to keep Mitch away so she'd just have to deal with the fallout of whatever he decided to do.

Sighing, she said, 'I'll be a little while here. A story always helps calm Jamie down so that he drops off to sleep. Hopefully that'll help bring his temperature down.' Otherwise they'd be back to the hospital before the end of the day.

'I'll phone into work and see how they're coping with the TV crew.' Mitch backed out of the tiny room.

'I like Mitch, Mummy.'

'Me too.' When she wasn't thinking about kidneys and transplants. But now that she wasn't stressing about tipping Mitch's world upside down she was starting to see the man she'd once fallen for. Behind the concerns and questions lurked the charming side of him. Plus the caring, tender man. The humour hadn't come to the fore but that was hardly surprising.

She could hear him talking on his phone, the words indistinguishable but that deep, velvety tone sent heat curling through her, reaching the tips of her toes, the muscles in her neck, and everywhere in between. She could almost feel his body under her palms, the smooth skin, the taut muscles, the latent strength.

For the first time since she'd taken her house key off him, memories of all the good times flooded in without any of the baggage getting in the way. It was as though, since arriving on Saturday, all that mess in her mind had washed away, finally leaving her free to get to know the father of her child all over again. Last time she'd known Mitch as a lover, a partner. How would she know him this time round?

How do you want to know him? Apart from as Jamie's father?

The book in her hand shook. Moving her head left then right, left, right, she quashed the flare of panic. No, she wasn't going down the Mitchell path again. He might be stepping up to the line about Jamie but she still couldn't trust him to be there for her. Not as a husband or even as a lover. Definitely not for ever. That would be asking too much of him. Way too much. He'd openly admitted he couldn't do it.

And since the only kind of relationship she'd ever agree to partake in involved total commitment and stability, she and Mitch were yesterday's news.

Her stomach sank. Her blood slowed. Really?

Really. There was no future for her with Mitch.

So why did her whole body feel so sluggish at that thought?

'Jodi,' Mitch whispered from the doorway. 'Jamie's sound asleep.'

'Oh. That was quick, but I guess he's exhausted after all the drama of meeting Dr Harrington.' At least Mitch didn't know where she'd been in her head. Tucking the cover under Jamie's chin, she tiptoed out and carefully closed the door.

Mitch stood in the middle of the main room. His size made the walls shrink in on her. His gentle, caring gaze made her heart trip and her breathing falter.

This was a Mitch she'd not met before.

This was a Mitch she had to be very wary of if she wanted to remain untouched by him. She needed to keep her head straight and not give in to any fantasies about falling in love with him again.

Her heart stuttered in defiance. Why not? He's the only man who'd ever made her pulse beat as though she'd run a marathon, made her body feel starved until he touched her.

She gasped. What's happening here? She'd tracked down Mitch for Jamie's sake, not because she needed him. Not because she'd never forgotten him. Or because she'd never stopped wishing he was still a part of her life. Within two days all those pent-up emotions and feelings that only Mitch could evoke were roaring around her head, through her body, centring at her core. Making her want to drag him off to bed and have her wicked way with what she knew that superb suit covered.

Heat swamped her face and she turned aside before Mitch could read the emotions that surely must be spreading through her eyes, over her cheeks and curving her lips into a sultry smile.

'Want a coffee? I have to warn you, I've only got instant.' Not that she wanted another hot drink but she did want to keep her hands busy and away from Mitch.

'No, thanks.' Mitch watched Jodi's lips press together with worry as she dropped onto the arm of one of the two chairs in the room.

He needed her, wanted her, had the urge to haul her into his arms and hug her until she finally relaxed and smiled that beautiful, gut-wrenching smile he always used to look for at the end of the shift when he finally walked through the front door of the flat he'd shared with her.

It might be a dumb move but he put all his reservations aside and moved to lift her up and wrap his arms around her thin frame. Damn, but she needed feeding up. 'Hey, let me hold you for a moment. You look shattered.' Pulling her against his chest, he tucked her head neatly under his chin and held her. Right where she belonged: in his arms.

Until this moment he hadn't realised he'd missed her so much. Hadn't understood that he was only half a man without Jodi in his life. Until now he'd believed he'd had everything he needed. That there was no room in his life, his heart to fit someone close. Someone special. Jodi. He'd known he'd screwed up. But now it was as though someone had taken a bat and banged him over the head until he got the message. Jodi was the only woman for him.

He'd neglected her back then. Big time. He'd let her kick him out, taking the easy option, thanking his lucky stars that he'd escaped unscathed. But he'd been lying to himself. Pleased that he'd proved she wasn't a stayer.

Unscathed? Yeah, right. As if. If that cold, lonely town house of his, the one-night stands that he never took back to his place, no one to share a birthday or Christmas with, was what he really wanted, then fine. Go for it. Enjoy it. Make the most of what he had. If that was his definition of unscathed and happy then he was a sad puppy.

He'd definitely been lying to himself. All along. Worse—he'd always known he had been.

So what now? Declare his feelings? Tell Jodi he actually cared for her, about her? That he wanted to be right at her side over the next months as Jamie battled for his life? That he wanted to be there for her beyond that? His stomach crunched, his heart dived for cover. Go ahead, tell her all that and then stand back while she laughs herself sick.

Jodi was not stupid. She would not believe a word of it. And who could blame her? Certainly not him.

So what now? Slowly, slowly, sort one problem out at a time. Over her head he stared at the crappy motel room, the marked walls, the grimy windows and shabby furniture. Unwinding his arms from around her body, he stepped back. 'Have you done anything about finding a flat to move in to?'

She tensed. 'I've hardly had time.'

'Good.' He reached into his back pocket. 'The key to my front door. It's only a small place, and we'll be a bit squeezed, but pack your bags and move in. Today.' When her mouth fell open, he couldn't help adding, 'For as long as you need somewhere to live in Auckland.'

It felt great to surprise her in a good way. He caught up one of her hands, wrapped her fingers around the key. 'You can't stay in this motel. It's awful. Not good for a sick child. Not exactly cheerful for you either. Oh, and here's another key. Get rid of that heap on wheels you've rented. From now on, my vehicle is yours.'

Those brown pools fixed on him, filled with amazement and gratitude. 'Are you sure? There are three of us. Mum's not going back down south until Friday.'

'No problem. I've got two spare bedrooms. Anyway, I'm not there very often.'

'To sleep and shower, according to your cleaning lady.' Jodi looked guilty. 'I met her on Saturday when I went looking for you.'

'I wondered why you turned up at the hospital in the evening. Get tired of waiting for me to come home?' Just like old times. He swallowed the bile rising in his throat. Hell, home wasn't his favourite place. Not a lot going on there.

'How will you get around if I've got your car?'

'I'll grab a taxi. Or give you a call.' It was less than two months until he left for Sydney. Oh, hell. Sydney and the job of a lifetime. So much to sort out. So much to consider. Too much to think about. Slowly, slowly, one small thing at a time. 'I'll go and talk to the motelier while you pack up.'

Jodi watched Mitch stride across to the motel office, his shoulders back and his chin forward. So full of confidence. His way was the right way. No doubts at all. 'You still don't ask what I'd like to do.' Her mouth curved upward. 'You just tell me.' Funny how today she couldn't care less when in the past she'd have refused just to spite him.

'I take it you're not talking to yourself.' Mum spoke from the doorway, laden down with full recycle grocery bags. 'And as I see Mitch disappearing into the poky space the owners of this dump call an office, you must be berating him.'

Jodi opened her hand to show the keys. 'We're moving into his house as soon as Jamie wakes up. And the other key is for that fancy four-wheel drive parked outside.'

Mum dumped her shopping on the bench and turned to study her daughter in a disconcerting, this-is-your-mother-talking kind of way. 'Good. He's come through for you both. Always thought he would if he was pushed hard enough. And there's nothing harder than being confronted with the son he didn't know he had. Good man.'

So much for wondering if Mum would move into Mitch's place with them. She'd probably have come up with the idea herself in a day or two if Mitch hadn't beaten her to it. 'Mum, you've never liked the guy. Remember all the things you used to warn me about? Newsflash—most of them came true.'

'Selective memory, my girl. I also used to say Mitch Maitland would make a fabulous husband if he ever got over his past. It can't have been easy, growing up without his parents there and never seeing his twin brother. He's done amazingly well considering the circumstances.'

Jodi gaped. 'You knew all that? How? He never even told me.'

'You didn't think I wouldn't check up on my grandson's parentage, did you? I always thought there was more to Mitch and Max than was obvious. They might be charmers who're used to getting what they want from everyone they cross paths with but essentially they're good men.' Mum winced. 'I should've told you what I learned but I figured you had enough on your plate with Jamie's illness. How did the hospital consultation go, by the way?'

Stunned at her mother's revelation, Jodi took a moment to answer the sudden question about something totally different, and then she didn't have to.

Mitch answered for her as he came inside. 'Lucas Harrington is excellent and I have every confidence in him. But even though I knew what was coming, he still managed to shock me to the core. I presume Jodi's heard what he had to say before, but hearing it again rattled her too.'

'It's so different when it's my...' Jodi swallowed. 'When he's talking about our child. It doesn't matter how many discussions I've had with Jamie's specialists, the details still scare me sick.'

Mitch's eyebrows rose endearingly. 'Yes, that must be it. Not any old patient but our son.'

Mum looked from Mitch to her and back again. 'So, is this Dr Harrington putting Jamie on the transplant waiting list?'

'Yes. We've got an appointment with the transplant team tomorrow afternoon.' Mitch moved closer to Jodi and casually dropped an arm over her shoulders.

His warmth and strength immediately filtered through to her, touching that chilly place where all things to do with Jamie's health hid. She snuggled even nearer. Drawing a breath, she told her mother, 'Max is arranging the appointment. We bumped into him at the canteen and the moment he heard about Jamie's problem he gave us a time to go and see him.'

Mum didn't even blink. 'I'm glad. We want the absolute best treatment for Jamie, and in Max's hands he'll get it.'

So she'd known Max worked at Auckland General too. Just how much had Mum found out about the Maitland twins in that research she'd done? And why hadn't she talked about this before now? Could've saved some worry about how to tell Mum that both brothers were here and that there was every possibility they'd both have something to do with Jamie's care.

Mitch shook his head. 'We're waiting to see how tomorrow's meeting goes before deciding that.'

We are? She wasn't so sure, though she was still struggling with Max being a part of this. In the meantime she'd back Mitch even if he was definitely against his brother doing the transplant if at all possible. Presumably they had time to think it all through, that a kidney wouldn't become available in the next day or two. 'Yes, that's right.'

Mum said nothing, just rolled her shoulders and looked away, lost in her own thoughts.

Mitch squeezed Jodi's shoulder. 'I've checked you out of here as from whenever you're ready to go. You've got all afternoon if you need it.'

'Jamie will sleep for a couple of hours, then there's nothing else to keep us here.' From under his arm she turned to look at him. 'Don't you need to go to work? That TV crew could be having a wonderful time without you there to restrain them.' It was one thing for him to accompany them to see Lucas but quite another to hang around all morning with her.

'Aaron will be more of a ball and chain with them than I'd ever be.' With one finger he lifted her hair out of her eyes. The steady blue gaze he fixed on her sent electricity zipping along her veins, reminding her of how well they'd played together. Unfortunately his voice was solemn, reminding her how out of kilter they were now. 'But I do have to put in an appearance. I can't ask Aaron to work my whole shift and then do his tonight.'

Plastering on a smile, Jodi gave him the answer he would want. 'Then go. We've only got three bags. I can get us packed and moved to your place easy as.' And she needed space to sort through these weird feelings ambushing her every time Mitch touched her.

Not to mention how, as much as she wanted Mitch in on everything to do with Jamie's treatment, she was so used to going it alone that it felt a little stifling having him just hanging around now that they were back at the motel.

'There's a GPS in my vehicle.'

'Handy.' If she knew how to use one. 'Can you warn Claire she's going to be overrun with Hawkes?'

'Done already. She's making beds as we speak.' Mitch didn't move, didn't shift that penetrating gaze.

What did he see? She'd changed in the time they'd been apart. Having a sick child did that. Blast it, she didn't even take care of her appearance anymore. Her smile deepened. She'd set a new fashion trend—grunge. Oh, but that had already been done; she was just running behind the times.

Mitch leaned forward and placed the lightest of light kisses on her cheek. So gentle that it brought tears to her eyes. That kiss spoke of affection, care and support. It told her she still held a place in his heart, even if only that of the mother of his son.

And then it hit her. Pine with a hint of spice. His aftershave. The one she used to buy him. He hadn't been wearing it over the weekend—she'd definitely have noticed. But now he was. So there was more to his kiss than affection. But just how much more? What was he telling her? She was afraid to find out. Didn't want to go there. To break her heart over him once had been bad enough; to do it again would be stupid. And she was a lot of things, but stupid wasn't one of them.

CHAPTER SEVEN

MITCH PAID THE taxi driver and shoved open the door. Home at last. The television crew had trailed after him all afternoon and right into the evening. Their endless questions had at times annoyed him but in the interests of getting a real and true picture of how an emergency department worked he'd sucked it up and done his best to be helpful.

All the while wanting to go home and check out Jamie. To make sure that temperature had gone down. Check Jodi was okay after their eventful morning.

His legs dragged with weariness as he headed up the path, but his heart lifted at the welcoming scene. Lights were on behind the drawn curtains, the light on over the front door. The first time that had happened since he'd moved in last year.

The large bag with the toyshop logo swung back and forth from his fingers. He'd snatched a quick break and gone out to the toyshop next to the hospital, strategically placed for softies like him.

Humming tunelessly, Mitch pushed the door open. Swallowed hard as the words, 'Hi, honey, I'm home' nearly spilled off his tongue. Repeating something that had amused her three years ago would only make her think he was deliberately trying to use the past to win her over. Which he was—kind of. Cramming his size-ten foot into his mouth to shut him up might be a better option. Jodi would probably brain him with a pan if those words reached her pretty ears.

Another memory assailed him. Where were the earrings? He hadn't seen Jodi wearing any since she'd appeared in his office on Saturday. She was queen of earrings and bracelets. Not a bracelet in sight either. The woman had jewellery boxes full of them. Surely she still did? Had they gone into storage along with all those swanky clothes she loved to wear? Maybe she'd given them to the op shop. But why? The woman he knew couldn't have changed that much. Had she? Nah, he kept seeing hints of the old Jodi. Surely beneath that worry and fear for her boy lay the happy, jokey Jodi who loved to dance and tease.

'Hey there, you obviously got busy.' Jodi didn't add *considering it's after nine*, but he heard the words anyway and bit down on a retort. They hadn't moved along that far in their relationship. Yet. If ever. That kiss at the park hadn't changed a thing.

Yeah, it had. He'd rediscovered his Jodi, remember? Yeah. That had something going for it.

Striding towards the kitchen where she stood in the doorway, he told her, 'It wasn't horrendously busy with patients but the TV crew made up for that. Then I told Aaron to stay away until nine to make up for filling in for me this morning.'

Her cheeks reddened deliciously. 'Oops. I spoke without thinking.'

'An old habit?' he snipped. Then, 'Sorry. Uncalled for. It's odd finding people in my house at the end of a day at work.' He looked around. 'I take it Jamie's asleep?' He put down the bag he held, ignoring a flare of disappointment. Of course the lad would be in bed at this hour.

'Out for the count despite his excitement about staying

in Mitch's house.' Her smile was shy. The lookalike Jodi
had returned. The old Jodi had never done shy.

Sniffing the air appreciatively, he said, 'Something
smells wonderful.' How easy it would be to get used to
this. Even if it meant coming home earlier? 'Never thought
to tell you I hardly ever eat here and that the cupboards
were bare.'

Jodi stepped backwards into the kitchen, a gorgeous
smile lightening up her face. 'All taken care of. Mum went
shopping, and I put together a lasagne and salad. Hope
that's okay?'

'Okay? You have no idea.' Anything edible would be
okay. Lasagne and salad made his mouth water. 'Have
you eaten?'

'Thought I'd wait for you. Mum had hers and has taken
herself off to her room to start reading her financial reports.'

Unless Alison was a ditz she must've made a fortune
over the years with all the financial shuffling she'd done,
and she was no ditz. Yet there was no sign of wealth. That
motel and the rental car he'd dropped off on the way to
work indicated a distinct lack of funds. Puzzling, but not
important. What was important was spending the rest of
the evening with Jodi. 'Do you want a glass of wine before
we eat? That is one thing I do have plenty of.'

'I opened a bottle of Cabernet Merlot to breathe. Hope
you don't mind?' Jodi handed him the bottle and held out
two glasses to be filled.

'You certainly knew which one to pick.' He grinned at
the top choice she'd made.

'That's quite a collection in your cellar. Since when did
you become a wine buff?'

'I've always enjoyed a good wine, but until I came to
Auckland I'd never really done much about it. Besides, med

students drink beer. These days, when I take a weekend off, I like to get out of town and away from the possibility of being called into work, so I've started visiting the North Island wine-growing regions. Funny how those bottles seem to find their way into my car with no trouble at all.'

'Right. You open the door and shoo them in. I can see it now.' Laughter tinkled in the kitchen air.

Mitch felt his eyes widening as he realised that was the first time he'd heard Jodi laugh these past days. 'You should do that more often.'

'Do what?'

'Laugh.' He took a gulp of wine. 'You used to always be laughing about something.' And when her face dropped he hastily added, 'I know you haven't had a lot to laugh about. Believe me, I get it. But hearing that just then brought back some wonderful memories.' Another swallow of wine. 'We weren't all bad together. There were plenty of fun times too.' Mostly in the sack. Because there hadn't been time for much else. What an idiot. He'd gone and made things worse, just when they'd started getting along a wee bit better.

Any minute now she'd throw her wine in his face, tell him he was a selfish pig and that she was moving back to that rank motel. He waited and watched.

Jodi blinked. Stared at him. Then her mouth lifted into a wide, beautiful smile. That gut-wrenching smile all his dreams and memories were made of. 'Thank you for re-minding me. Sometimes all I've been able to think about is the wrong memories.' The colour heightened delight-fully in her cheeks, over her throat. The tip of her tongue grazed her lips. 'I've been having some memories of my own since yesterday.'

Since he'd kissed her? 'Really?'

'Some of the good ones.' The heat in her eyes scorched him, told him exactly which good times she recollected.

Memories skittered across his skin bringing back exquisite sensations of his body sliding over hers, his hands recalled touching the dip of her waist and that soft place on her inner thighs, and cupping those curvy buttocks. His tongue knew the taste of her. Below his belt his maleness definitely remembered the very centre of her femininity. It sprang up, hard and hopeful. 'Down boy,' he growled under his breath. Wrong place. Wrong time. Bad, bad—good.

He lifted one foot to close the gap between them. Panic flared in those coffee-*au-lait* eyes. Her sweet mouth flattened. A slight jerk of her head negated his move. His shoe slapped on the tile floor. Bad, bad, bad.

Spinning around, Jodi was suddenly very busy serving up dinner. The dinner he no longer wanted. But what he wanted he couldn't have. Not now. Not ever.

Over lunch in his office the next day Mitch spent a lot of time answering the TV documentary director's questions methodically, keeping the medical content to a minimum without actually dumbing everything down too much. Now he needed to do some real work. He pushed his empty coffee cup aside. 'If that's all for the moment?'

Carl stood up, smiling good-naturedly. 'Sure. I know you're busy and I'm a pain in the butt.'

Mitch grinned back. 'We understand each other. So how do you think your documentary is working out? Are you getting some good footage of the patients and what we deal with?'

'Absolutely. Your staff have been extremely accommodating to my crews.'

'Right down to getting their hair done and wearing

more make-up in a couple of days than any of them normally use in a year.'

Carl chuckled. 'I'm used to that. The moment the word "camera" is uttered, out comes the lipstick and hairbrush.' His face grew more serious. 'We're getting good footage but what I want now is a human-interest story that can run through the whole doco, tie it all together.'

Mitch winced. They'd discussed this prior to the crews starting in the department and he wasn't so sure that he liked the idea. 'Have you given consideration to how patients might come to regret it if they say yes while they're dealing with pain and serious injuries?'

'They'd have the opportunity to change their minds later. Whether that person is the patient or the patient's parent or caregiver,' Carl reminded him.

'So you don't think any of the patients you've filmed so far suit your criteria?'

'Mitch.' Samantha flew in the door. 'Mitch, you've got to come now. The ambulance has brought in a little boy with acute renal failure.'

Mitch's heart stopped. 'Do we have a name for this child?' The question squeezed through his clenched teeth.

'Jamie Hawke.' Samantha's eyes were huge in her face, and there was a hint of something awfully like excitement as she added, 'Jamie Maitland Hawke.'

Mitch's chair flew backwards. Snatching up his phone, he scanned the messages as he raced for the cubicles. Nothing. Jodi hadn't phoned or texted. Why not? If he was picking up the reins of fatherhood then she had to include him in everything happening to Jamie. 'Where is he?' he demanded.

'Cubicle four.' Samantha ran alongside him. 'Is Jamie a relation of yours?'

'Yes.' More information than she needed to know.

'I'll tell the cameraman to head your way.' Carl was with him too.

'No. You. Won't.' He snarled. 'Stay away from this patient.'

'I didn't think Max had any kids.' Samantha had skin thicker than a rhinoceros's.

'He doesn't.' Oh, hell. Mitch cursed under his gasping breath. Now the whole department, no, the whole hospital would know he had a son by dinnertime. Not that he wanted to hide the fact, but he wasn't ready to share any of Jamie's story with *everybody*.

At cubicle four he jerked the curtain open and strode in. And stopped. Jamie was attached to more cables and tubes than a cat had lives. 'Jamie.' His gut clenched, threatened to throw his lunch back at him. Closing his eyes, he willed his belly to behave.

'Mitch?' Jodi's hand gripped his. 'We need Lucas here now. I told the nurse that but he insisted we wait until you arrived.'

Mitch blinked, stared down into the terrified face of his boy's mother. 'I'll call him. Don't you worry about that. Where is the PRF?' He snapped his fingers at Chas.

The head nurse on day shift pressed the patient report form from the ambulance into his hand. 'Severe vomiting and bloody stools. High temperature.' Chas continued talking, filling in all the details he'd gleaned from the ambulance crew.

Mitch was grateful to him. There was no way he could see the obs on the page in front of him for the tears blurring his eyes. As he listened he stepped up to the bed, ran a finger lightly down Jamie's arm, careful to avoid all the gear attached to him. 'Hey, sport,' he whispered around the lump cutting off the air to his lungs.

Chas finished the report and told Samantha, 'Get the phone and the phone number list for Mitch.'

Jodi muttered, 'Thanks, Chas.' Then her fingers squeezed Mitch's hand again. He could feel her fear through her grip. 'It happened so fast. He was a bit grizzly and his temperature had crept up some more so I put him down for a nap. When I went in to check up on him he was vomiting. I called the ambulance to save time. The way I was panicking I'd have got lost for sure.'

'We'll get Lucas down here ASAP.' He wrapped an arm around her shaking shoulders, drew her close. 'Where's that damned phone?' he yelled through the gap in the curtains. Carl stood to one side observing everything, his cameraman filming from an unobtrusive distance. Doing exactly what he'd been asked to do when any urgent cases presented. 'Not this patient, Carl.' And when Carl made to reply he held a hand up. 'Not open to negotiation.' His son was not going to make headlines on national television.

Then Samantha handed him the phone, her demeanour now serious and concerned. Had one of the nurses put her in her place? 'Extension 324 for Mr Harrington.'

Punching in the numbers, Mitch watched over his son, despair gnawing at him. The little lad hadn't moved in the minutes he'd been with him. At least he couldn't see the pain and fright behind those fragile eyelids. But he knew it was there. He'd give anything to make it all go away for Jamie.

Even your kidney?

Even my kidney.

Wouldn't Carl love that story for his show?

Mitch shuddered. He could see the show headlines already. 'Carl, go away.'

* * *

'How's Jamie doing?' Mitch's hand cupped Jodi's shoulder, his fingers firm yet calming, strong yet tender.

She hadn't heard him enter the room but, then, she hadn't heard all the hospital noises going on around her either. Jamie was her only concern, her only focus. Jodi leaned her head sideways so her cheek touched his fingers, gathering strength from him. 'Lucas just called by and gave him a top-up of antibiotics and a whole heap of other things.'

'I passed him on my way here. He's going to talk to Max, who's rescheduling our appointment with the transplant team.' Mitch squeezed her shoulder and dropped a kiss on her head.

That felt so right—as though they were on the same page. 'Everyone's being awesome.'

'We figured you've had enough drama for one day, and another twenty-four hours isn't going to bring the transplant surgery any closer.'

'I guess you're right, though I'd feel a little bit better knowing we had everything under way.' Her bottom lip trembled when she looked at him. 'But you're right. Tomorrow will do fine.'

'It's going to mean more tests, another round of poking and prodding for the little guy.' His voice was so sad, hurting even.

Jodi reached up, laid her hand over his. She didn't feel any better. In fact, she felt like crap. 'I'm glad you're here for him. Sorry to dump you in at the deep end, though. If it helps, I wish I could turn back the clock to when I learned I was pregnant. You'd be the first to know.' Her sigh was sad. 'But I guess that doesn't make you any less angry at me.'

Mitch lifted her chin with his finger. 'Anger hasn't come

into it. Disappointment, yes. And sadness. But there's also guilt. If I'd come knocking on your door and explained a few things, we might've worked something out so that you'd have trusted me to be a good dad. Even if we hadn't got back together.'

His tone was so sad she had to wonder if that's what he might've wanted after all. Them together, permanently. No way. Mitch was always too busy, too tied up in his own world to make that work. Or was she being unfair? Using that to justify her own actions? Ironic when now she'd change everything if she had the chance. 'Only one way to go now. Forward.'

He didn't say anything for a while. Nothing to say, she supposed. They were parents grappling with a huge problem and finding their way back to each other with all that was going on wouldn't exactly be easy.

Finally Mitch asked, 'How's the dialysis going?'

'Doing its job, thank goodness. With the cycler working overnight, hopefully Jamie will be feeling a lot better in the morning. But I never get used to this,' she murmured. 'No matter how many times we end up in hospital, every visit is as frightening as the first one.' With her other hand she stroked Jamie's arm. 'Even with all the swelling he looks so small in this enormous bed. So frail. So darned ill.' Tears pricked the backs of her eyelids and she squeezed tight to prevent them spilling down her face. She had to be strong for Jamie. It would never do for him to wake up and see her crying.

Mitch must have sensed her fragility because he wrapped his arms around her from behind, his hands meeting beneath her breasts and pulling her back against his waist. 'Shh, you're doing fine. Just fine. How the hell you've managed to stay sane this long I can't begin to understand. I'm new to this and I'm already feeling wrecked.'

Sniff, sniff. Winding her hands around his, she told him, 'Not a lot of choice. One of those situations that when faced with you get on and do what has to be done. And that's another thing. There's not much I can do for Jamie. As a doctor or as a mum. Some days I feel so utterly helpless.'

His chin dropped onto the top of her head. 'Being a mum, being with him all the time, is the most important role. I'd bet anything that if you could ask Jamie he'd agree with me. Nothing, nobody, is as important to have around as your mum. Especially when life is going horribly pear-shaped. Believe me, I know.'

Was this the little boy whose mother died speaking here? 'Thank you. I really needed to hear that.' How had Mitch survived that shock and hurt? Even if his adoptive family had been kind and loving he'd have always carried a deep sense of loss. Even more because his twin had been taken away as well. Without thinking, she lifted his hand and kissed his palm.

He asked, 'Want a break? Take a shower? Grab something to eat? I'll sit with Jamie. The staff will page me if anything urgent comes up in ED.'

Shaking her head, 'No, I don't want to leave him in case he wakes. He'll panic if I'm not here. I'm sorry, Mitch, but he's not used to you yet. Not enough to be happy I'm not in sight when he wakes in a strange place anyway. Not that hospital is strange to him, I suppose.'

'It's okay, I get it.'

Leaning over the bed, she tucked Jamie's blankie closer to his pillow so he could see it when he woke up. 'Mind you, when he sees that teddy bear you brought him he might be more than happy for you to be with him.' A tired chuckle escaped her. 'I don't suppose they had any small bears in that shop?'

'Define small.'

'Something not as tall as Jamie.'

'Nope, not a one. Not a good-looking one, anyway.' Mitch was studying her with a serious gleam in his eye.

'What?'

'You mightn't want to leave Jamie but you do need to eat. I'll go and get you something, plus some decent coffee.'

'Thanks, but I'm not hungry.'

'Jodi, you've got to eat. Look at you, fading away to nothing. I'm guessing that's because your appetite goes every time Jamie has another serious bout of his cystinosis.'

'I needed to lose weight.' As much as ten kilos? None of her gorgeous clothes fit anymore. Not that she ever went out anywhere to wear them. At work she tended to stick to simple trousers and blouses. No point tarting herself up to be coughed or puked on.

'I'm going to the café. Any preferences?' When she shook her head he leaned closer. 'I liked you exactly as you were. Your figure was fabulous. Not that it's as important as what's on the inside. And that's fabulous too.'

By the time she'd dredged up a fitting retort Mitch had gone, leaving her to wonder what the hell was going on here. He was being so helpful and caring, supportive and bossy. Needed fattening up indeed.

Oh, okay. Fabulous on the inside. Wow. She could take as many compliments as Mitch wanted to dish out, but where did they come from? Why now and not when they had been together? Hugging herself, she enjoyed the warmth seeping through her.

Then her stomach rumbled and she had to concede another point. 'I get the picture. I'm apparently hungry. I'll do my best to eat whatever Mitch brings me.'

* * *

Mitch stood in the doorway to Jamie's room with a pizza box in one hand and a soda can in the other. He was late back, having been called to the ED just as he'd stepped outside the hospital. A teenager who'd been huffing gas. God damn it, when were these kids going to learn they couldn't abuse their bodies and keep getting away with it? It had been touch and go but, fingers crossed and with a lot of intensive medical care, the girl would make it through the night.

He studied Jodi. Quiet, slumped and yet very busy. Watching over her boy. Watching every breath he took. Observing the tubes putting goodies into him. Keeping a wary eye on the cycler that was emptying Jamie's abdomen of wastes, chemicals and extra water. Hopefully reducing the fluid retention that made Jamie so bloated.

'Ah, Jodi, sweetheart, you're awesome.' The words were so quiet even he didn't really hear them. Which was just as well. He did not want to see the disbelief in her eyes if she'd overheard.

He'd swear that she'd breathe for Jamie if she could. She'd certainly stick the needles and tubes into her body if that would save Jamie any discomfort. A true mother. An extraordinary woman. But, then, he'd always known that. That's why he'd been attracted to her.

Her looks and figure had drawn him first, but it had been her sense of joy—now missing—in everything, her love of life, the kindnesses and selflessness, her inner strength that had had him going back to her again and again for just one more date. That was what had stopped him leaving her after only a few weeks, as he'd done with all the other women he'd known. Before and after Jodi.

Jodi had set a benchmark that he'd not found since in any woman he'd taken out. Not that he'd been actively looking. Too busy avoiding staying around too long. Whereas Jodi had come from behind and slapped him on the head while he hadn't been looking. Unfortunately he'd probably made the biggest mistake of his sorry life when he'd let her get away. He hadn't recognised the emotion he'd felt for her that had churned through him as love. Plain and simple. Love. Complex and distracting. He hadn't wanted to be distracted from his game plan of getting the top job in his chosen path. A little longer and he'd have had it all.

Talk about dumb. And now it was too late. He couldn't make up for not being there during Jamie's illnesses. Even if Jodi hadn't given him the opportunity, he had to take the blame. It had been his ho-hum attitude to their relationship that had had her packing his bags. His lack of commitment that had prevented her telling him he was a father. Because, to her, he was as irresponsible as her own father. How stupid could a bloke be?

'Is that real coffee I can smell?' the woman who had his hormones and emotions on a roller-coaster ride asked.

'Sure is. And a pepperoni and triple-cheese pizza.'

'Very tempting.' Her eyes gleamed with gratitude, making him feel pleased he'd done something right for her. And then her tongue licked the corner of her mouth and he tripped over his own feet as he crossed to the bed.

More than his feet were having difficulty ignoring that gesture. South of his belt his maleness sat up, so aware of her it frightened him. Definitely not the time or place to be thinking anything sexual. That tongue flick must've been a subconscious move on Jodi's part, surely? She didn't look at all interested in anything but her coffee.

Guess it was good one of them had their priorities right.

'Hey, hope I'm not intruding?' Carl hovered in the door. 'Came to see how the little guy was doing.'

'You didn't bring the film crew with you?'

'Everyone's taking a break.' Carl gave an easy smile. 'Even we're learning to grab five when it's quiet.'

Jodi was watching Carl, caution tightening her mouth. 'You're one of the TV crew members? Is that why you were in the ED?'

Mitch made the introduction. 'Carl is in charge of the crews and does all the planning required.'

Carl stretched a hand in Jodi's direction. 'You're Mitch's wife?' In the silence that followed only Carl looked totally comfortable. 'Partner?'

Jodi shrugged and sucked a breath through her teeth. 'We're Jamie's parents.'

Mitch gave the guy credit for not making any ridiculously obvious comments, instead shifting along the bed to look down at Jamie. 'How's he doing? Better than when you first brought him in, I hope.'

Jodi answered. 'Dialysis makes him more comfortable but the catheter irritates his tummy, which he hates. He's always weary. His day is filled with short naps.'

'What's the treatment for—what was it—cystinosis?'

'Yes, cystinosis. Jamie gets regular dialysis to remove all the poisons and waste that kidneys do in healthy people. Long term?' Jodi stared at Carl, drilling him with her dark eyes. 'We wait for a kidney to become available.'

'That's all we can do,' Mitch added, to forestall the questions that smart brain opposite him was coming up with. Give Carl time and he'd know all there was to know about Jamie's condition and the odds on a kidney becoming available. He'd research everything and learn that the head of the department he was filming in had to be the most likely donor. Then try keeping the guy and his cameras away. 'Impossible situation,' he muttered.

'I can see that it is.' Carl looked pensive, craftily hiding the questions that had to be popping up.

'So you can see why I'm not interested in you filming Jamie. This is too traumatic for him as it is.'

'What's this?' Jodi reared up. 'What are you talking about? Filming?'

Carl spoke quickly. 'Wait. Don't jump to conclusions. Mitch knows I'm looking for one case coming from his department that I can follow through on. You know, the patient moving from the emergency department to a ward and then the treatment they receive, whether it's surgery or cardiac intervention. Whatever.'

'And you think Jamie is the perfect choice?' Jodi whispered.

'Truthfully? Yes, I do. It is a great human-interest story. But...' he held his hand up as Jodi's mouth opened '...I have a daughter about Jamie's age and I doubt I'd want me poking a camera in her face to make a documentary. So, good television or not, I'm not going to ask you to allow my crews near your son. Unless you change your mind, of course.' He turned to Mitch.

'Not likely.'

'It could help with making people aware of donating their organs,' Jodi commented thoughtfully, chewing at her fingernail and watching Carl with a more cautious gaze now.

Shocked, Mitch could only stare at her.

'Exactly.' Carl studied her back, trying to fathom where she was going with this.

Jodi looked too damned thoughtful. 'A lot of people indicate they want to be a donor, go to the trouble of registering the fact on their motor-vehicle licence, only to have family members refuse to follow their loved one's wishes.'

Carl sat on the end of Jamie's bed, careful not to disturb the sleeping boy. 'Not many people realise that small children are the recipients of a lot of these organs. I believe if we can show that then the donor numbers will rise significantly.'

Forget this guy going to do his research. He'd already done it. 'Leave it, Carl. Jodi has a lot to deal with already, without having cameras in her face.'

'To a certain extent I agree. But I'll leave it with you.' Carl nodded at the box Mitch had forgotten was in his hands. 'That pizza's getting cold.'

What he hadn't forgotten was the result of the blood-group test he'd had done that afternoon on the spur of the moment. Just in case he did decide to look more seriously at donating a kidney. It would be silly to put himself through making that decision only to find his blood group was no use to Jamie.

The result had told him he was Type O. Perfectly compatible with Jamie's Type A.

But it was too soon to tell Jodi. No point in getting her hopes up until he knew for sure what he would do.

CHAPTER EIGHT

JODI COULD FEEL Mitch beside her, fuming at his brother as the whole transplant team crowded around Jamie's bed, talking and reading notes. Overkill, surely? She'd have been happy to talk to Carleen Murphy. Or Max. Just not the whole bang lot of them. Even Lucas had turned up. They had Jamie's interests at heart but didn't they understand how terrifying this was for the little guy?

And while Mitch was fuming, Jamie was fretting. The corner of his blankie was stuffed in his mouth, slobber soaking the thick fabric. Tears streaked his pale cheeks. The shock of his admittance and then being put on dialysis had taken its toll on her boy. Leaning closer, she ran her hand over his head, and gave him a wink. 'Hey, Jamie, love, Mummy's here.'

'Want to go home,' he hiccupped, his eyes wide as he tried to beguile her into taking him out of there, away to where it was quiet and nice, not noisy and scary, not hurting.

'Not yet, sweetheart. These people are going to make you better.'

When the bewilderment filtered into his eyes she felt bad. Lying to her son had become a habit. Even Jamie understood that these people might not make him better. No other doctor had fixed him. When kids were seriously ill they seemed to mature so much in some aspects of their lives. There was no fooling Jamie that his body was improving.

But she could do something for him. Straightening her spine, she took her despair out on those who might understand it. 'If you're all going to hang around discussing Jamie's problems then you can at least sit down. You're huge from his perspective. Intimidating and scary,' she snapped.

'There aren't enough chairs to go round,' someone, she didn't know who, muttered.

He could go. She didn't need anyone on the team who couldn't see this from Jamie's point of view. 'Find some or leave.'

One of Max's eyebrows rose disconcertingly but there was a hint of approval in his gaze before he turned to a hovering nurse and flashed his charming smile. 'Find some more chairs, please, Charmaine.'

The nurse smiled ever so sweetly before dashing off to do Max's biding.

Ignoring the byplay, Jodi sighed. Was she overreacting? Damn right she was. This was her baby. And as if that wasn't bad enough, Mitch had been fuming quietly from the moment Max had walked in and said something to him. What, she didn't have a clue. When would these two get over their differences and act like family? They didn't have anyone else. Surely they needed each other?

Her eyes returned to Jamie. He was their family too, damn it. Mitch's son. Max's nephew. Family. Like it or not. 'Max…' She curled her forefinger to beckon him close. Thankfully he joined her and Mitch, otherwise she didn't know what she'd have done. Probably shouted at them, turning the ward into a zoo.

Keeping her voice low, she said, 'This is not an ideal situation for you both, but I don't care. This is about Jamie and not whatever you two have going on.' She stabbed the air between them and growled, 'Bury it while we make Jamie better. Nothing else matters at all.' Her finger hit Mitch's chest. 'Your son.' Then Max's arm. 'Your nephew.'

Sinking back into her chair, she returned her focus to Jamie, feeling uncomfortable. Had that been wise? Had she gone too far? Probably. But she was allowed to. She was a mother.

Mitch studied Max, trying to really see him, to see past all their angst. This was the man Mitch always wanted to outdo, and yet now he was about to rely on him for the biggest dilemma of his life. Jodi was right. He knew that. But there was too much history between him and his brother just to bury it in an instant. He'd spent his life being told that if he wanted to get ahead he had to do better than Max. And because the relatives that had adopted him were dirt poor he'd felt justified in proving to them they were right to believe in him and that he didn't need the wealth Max had lucked into.

What if Max had been fed the same line of rubbish about him? It was something to consider. But not now. Today was about Jamie, not them. If he couldn't at least talk to Max for the duration of Jamie's treatment then he had to leave now, head to Sydney on the next flight and never look back.

Sucking in his gut, he met Max's eyes and stuck out his hand. 'Let's put aside everything other than Jamie for as long as this takes. I want to be able to talk to you or your team at any time about anything and know I'm not having to worry about other issues.'

Max stood ramrod straight, his mouth tight as he stared back. The silence was laden with all the arguments and rivalry of their past. All the current angst and dislike.

Then he shoved his hand into Mitch's and they shook. 'Fair enough.'

Mitch felt his twin's warmth through their grasp, and was staggered at the sense of need that assailed him. When had he last touched Max? What would it be like to be able to walk up to him and ask how his day was going? To pick up a phone and suggest a drink at the pub?

Then the surrounding silence trickled into his brain and he looked around to find everyone watching him and Max. Max must've noticed at the same moment because he tugged his hand free and stepped back. But that severe look Max reserved entirely for him had lightened a little.

Ignoring everyone, Max dropped his gaze to Jamie and his countenance softened further. His chin moved down and up in agreement. 'I still can't get my head around the fact I'm an uncle.' Turning a gaze filled with something like need to Mitch, he added, 'Ask me anything you want. I'll always tell you exactly what's going on and where we are at.'

'Fair enough.' More than he'd expected. And yet why? Max was the consummate professional and an exceptionally good surgeon. Even when it came to his own flesh and blood. Especially when it came to his own family. 'Thanks. A lot.'

Very few words and yet he felt as though he'd taken a giant step towards his brother and maybe a slightly brighter future. Could be that Jamie was going to turn out to be the best thing that had ever happened to him in more ways than one. But he'd take things slowly, carefully. There was a long way to go if he and Max were even going to be on easy speaking terms.

He watched as Max tapped the back of Jodi's hand. 'For a moment on Monday I thought you'd lost your toughness, but I was wrong. It's there in loads. Jamie's lucky to have you on his side.'

'You didn't think I'd let this turn me into something as soft as spaghetti, did you?' Jodi gave him one of her megawatt smiles.

'I guess not.' Max smiled his Maitland smile then turned away to face Mitch.

Mitch met his twin's steady gaze and shock slammed into him. Compassion blazed back out of those eyes that mirrored his.

Nah. Couldn't be. Never once in all the years since he'd screamed for Uncle Fred not to take Max away, for Max to turn round and come back to him, had he known anything from Max that might indicate they were on the same side.

Even at their eighteenth birthday dinner with supposedly loving family—the uncles who didn't like each other, the aunts who tolerated one another—the underlying competitiveness between him and his twin had risen to the fore, each being encouraged by their respective adoptive uncle. The evening had quickly been ruined. That had been the last time they'd even pretended to want to get together and be buddies.

And now Max goes and shows empathy for his situation. Mitch looked away, around the group of medical specialists gathered for Jamie, and saw their admiration for his brother. He had to agree with them. Max was very good at what he did for his patients.

Mitch's gaze dropped to his boy. Jamie. Seemed this kid was stirring up the Maitland family all by himself. Might as well get this next bit over before he changed his mind—which in the circumstances would be foolish and selfish. Breathing deeply, he opened his mouth and turned to his twin, told him, 'You're to do the operation when the time comes.'

Jodi gasped. 'Excuse me?'

Guilt assailed him. So much for discussing something as important as who the surgeon would be. Jodi's lips were tight, her eyes spitting at him. He hurriedly said in as placating a tone as he could manage without seeming to grovel, 'We'll talk later.'

She knew Max was the best transplant surgeon available. And they wanted the best.

Max's eyes had widened and he gave Mitch the full benefit of that infuriating twist of his mouth he'd perfected. But his eyes were devoid of anything other than acknowledgement of the statement. He nodded slowly, as though digesting a lot more than the fact he was to do the life-saving operation on his nephew. 'I hope that won't be too long away.' Spinning away, he gathered his team around him and began an in-depth discussion about Jamie's case before they all moved on to examine a teenager further down the ward.

A chill slid under Mitch's skin as he watched him go. Had his brother already reached the far point of this whole transplant equation? Come to the conclusion that Mitch was going to have to put his hand up and volunteer a kidney? Did Max understand him better than he realised? Why wouldn't he? They were twins, after all. Despite living most of their lives apart in very different circumstances, they knew each other—very well.

Which meant Max totally understood the arguments he was having with himself. Not that he was trying to get out of the situation. He'd already started down the track of finding out if he'd be a suitable donor by getting Lucas to arrange further tests now that he knew the blood types were compatible.

But it was the wider picture that frightened him. The whole thing of committing to helping his son and the ramifications afterwards—the ties to his lad that were building day by day, hour by hour. The fear he'd fail Jamie. Nothing to do with giving the kid a kidney and all to do with giving him his heart. And Max, blast him, could see that as plain as day.

'Can Bingo sleep with me?' Jamie's big blue eyes, filled with trust, stared at Jodi.

'Bingo? Is that teddy's name?' Where did he get these names?

'I like Bingo.'

'He's very cute.' A smile tugged at the corners of her mouth as she tucked the teddy bear in beside him. Two days after being rushed into hospital, Jamie was sounding more like himself. But he was still tired, which was why he'd snuggled down after his breakfast in preparation to having a nap. There'd be more dialysis treatment later in the day.

'Where's Mitch, Mummy? He hasn't seen me for ages.'

Mitch had been the favourite person in Jamie's life since he'd been handed the big bag and told to take a look at his new friend. Just to see Jamie's eyes popping out of his head had brought warmth curling through her where she'd been cold for the past night and day. Also making Mitch the most favourite person in her life at that moment.

Despite not talking to her about Max doing the surgery. That annoyed her, but it was so Mitch. Taking charge was as natural to him as charming everyone he wanted something from.

'Mitch is busy at work but he'll be up to see you soon.' Now she was defending the guy for being at work. Funny how things went round in circles. To think that a few days ago she'd intended to drag Mitch away from that department of his to be with her and their son until this was over, until he saw how ill Jamie was and how desperately his son needed his kidney.

Stretching her legs out to ease a light cramp in her calf muscles, she couldn't help smiling. Now she was happy that Mitch had his work to keep him balanced while he adjusted to being a father and all that involved.

Nothing that Max and his transplant team had discussed with them had made her feel any better. Except, maybe, that they were all agreed that the sooner Jamie had a new kidney the better. It couldn't come soon enough in Jodi's mind, while at the same time she battled the fear of knowing her little boy had to go under the knife.

Mitch had been acting a bit strangely since he'd told Max he had to do the transplant, going vacant on her at inopportune times. Was he finding it hard that he had to rely on his brother to help them? Maybe this could lead these two stubborn people towards some sort of reconciliation. Or was that like wishing every day to be sunny and warm?

While Mitch hadn't intimated so, she felt he was seriously considering the whole kidney donation thing. And while that's what she hoped for and thought she'd be able to ask him to do, being with Mitch these past few days she'd found she just couldn't do it. That it was Mitch's decision alone, and that she had no right to ask such a huge thing of him. Mitch being Mitch, he'd get there in his own way and time.

Max had talked to them about the odds of a kidney becoming available in the near future. Not good. No one had mentioned that it was in the lap of the gods unless Mitch put his hand up to find out if there was any reason why he couldn't donate a kidney. No sign of Mitch doing that, either. Not a dicky bird.

'Mitch,' shrieked Jamie. 'You came.'

'Why wouldn't I, little man? Hmm?' Mitch gave Jamie's hand a squeeze. Then did the same to Bingo. 'Hey, bear, how're you doing?'

Jamie giggled. 'Grandma, look what Mitch gave me.'

Jodi's head spun. Mitch and Mum coming in together? Seemed Mitch was knocking down a few fences at the moment.

Mitch slid a hand onto her shoulder, his fingers gently squeezing warmth into her. 'Hey, there. We've come to sit with Jamie while you go and have a shower, refresh yourself.'

When she looked up at him she noted Mitch was focused on Jamie, his eyes making a rapid medical scan, as all doctors were prone to do. What about fathers? Yep, they tended to do that too even if they weren't medically trained. It was an instinctive thing.

'I've brought you clean clothes, and your shampoo and conditioner.' Mum handed her a small bag before dropping a light kiss on Jamie's cheek. 'Hi, sweetheart. How's my boy? And who's that in bed with you?'

'Bingo.' Jamie tried to lift his new mate but he was too tired. That short burst of excitement had already drained what little energy he had.

'Here.' Jodi reached for the teddy and sat him on top of the bed for everyone to admire.

'Granny, can I have a story?'

'Sure can. I've brought all your books with me. We'll read while Mummy goes and spruces herself up, shall we?' Mum was really laying it on about her looking a mess. If she thought a quick shower and clean baggy jeans and top would impress Mitch, think again. He liked his women looking sensational. Not to mention stylish. For a fleeting moment she thought longingly of all those outfits hanging in the wardrobe of her spare bedroom back in Dunedin.

But, no, her bedraggled appearance was the real her,

the newer her. It came with the job of being mother to a sick child. Anyway, she didn't have the energy to care.

Mitch was pulling back her chair and taking her elbow, hauling her up. He handed her a key. 'Go on. This is for the on-call room. It's all yours for as long as you need it. You'll feel better after a relaxing time under those jets of hot water to ease out the cricks and tight spots in your muscles.'

'Sounds delicious.' And too darned exhausting to even walk the distance to wherever this on-call room was. She didn't have the strength to move, let alone argue with these bossy people. Every muscle in her body groaned and her backside aimed for the chair. The drums in her head were playing a heavy beat.

'No, you don't,' Mitch muttered.

She'd have to give it her best effort. 'See you soon, sweetheart.' As she leaned over Jamie to plaster his cute face with kisses the mug of disgusting instant coffee sloshed in her stomach. It was always like this whenever Jamie was in hospital.

'Come on, I'll show you where the on-call room is.' Mitch swung the bag off the floor and waved to Jamie. 'See you in a few minutes, sport.'

'Okay.' Jamie's mouth widened into a huge yawn.

Jodi yawned in sympathy. 'I hope this room isn't too far away.'

'I could find a wheelchair.' Mitch grinned.

The grin disappeared when she muttered, 'I could almost take you up on that.'

An arm came round her waist, holding her upright and close to Mitch's warm, strong body. 'I've put some chicken in the little oven to keep hot for you. Claire's been cooking all morning.' As she opened her mouth to protest he shook her gently. 'Don't even think of saying you don't need food. You do. You're shattered and you haven't eaten since I brought in that panini for breakfast.'

'The thought of food makes me feel ill.'

'You need to keep your strength up for Jamie.'

'Since when did you become such a nag?'

'Just looking out for you.' That grin had returned.

'I know.' She did, truly, but it was too hard.

'In here.' Mitch took the key from her fingers and opened the door for her. Then he followed her in.

'Hey, thanks, but I'll manage from here.' Jodi leaned against the wall. Liar. The moment Mitch walked out that door she'd slide into a heap on the floor. Probably fall asleep right there.

'It's all right. I'm not about to offer to wash your back for you.' Couldn't he look at least a teeny-weeny bit disappointed? 'But I'll pour you a glass of juice and dish up the chicken.'

She dredged up a smile. 'You're going to force-feed me now?' Having those fingers slipping food across her lips would be nearly as good as him washing her back.

'If you don't move soon I'll toss you over my shoulder, march you into that bathroom and put you under the shower.' His eyes widened and that grin slipped a little. 'Except there's less room in there than a mouse needs.'

Her head rolled from side to side as images of Mitch carrying her over his shoulder, his hands on her thighs, filtered through the murk that was her brain at the moment. If only she had the energy. Forcing herself upright, she took a step in the direction of the only other door in the room. 'On my way.'

Mitch looked down into her eyes. 'Just taking care of you. For Jamie.' His head lowered. 'And this is for me.' His lips brushed her forehead, strong and firm yet as light as a butterfly landing on her skin.

Then he stepped back and turned her to face the bathroom door. With a gentle shove he said, 'Go on. You'll feel a lot better afterwards.'

She stumbled into the bathroom and banged the door shut behind her. Leaning back against it, she brushed her forehead with her fingertips. He'd kissed her. Not a proper, lips-on-lips, tongue-circling-tongue kiss but something so sweet and caring that her heart felt as though it might burst with some strange emotion she couldn't identify.

Didn't want to identify.

Knock, knock. 'Jodi, you all right in there?'

No, I'm totally confused by you. About you. 'Couldn't be better,' she lied as she flicked the shower mixer on as hot as it would go.

Letting the water pour over her, through her hair, down her back, over her face, she tried to blank everything out of her mind. But images of a naked Mitch crammed in there with her, his hands massaging her back, took over, dominating her brain. They'd be so squashed into the shower that every movement they made would involve wet skin sliding over other wet skin. Desire unfurled deep inside her, sending heat coursing along her veins to all her extremities and every place in between.

She wanted Mitch. Now. And he was only a couple of steps away, on the other side of that door. She swallowed, trying to dampen down the flames roaring through her passion-starved body. 'Mitch?' she croaked.

She felt the memories of previous showers with him; her body knew exactly how those firm hands would touch her skin, pummel her muscles to replace the aches with hot desire, with a raw need for him.

'Mitch?' His name came out louder than she'd intended. Full of need and love and plain old horniness.

'Did you call me?' The door cracked open two inches.

Yes, no, I don't know. Her knees trembled. Confusion reigned. The gripping exhaustion had to be why she'd uttered his name. Not the best circumstances to be considering this. Better to wait until she'd slept a straight twenty-four hours. Which wasn't about to happen in the foreseeable future. 'Yes, Mitch, I did.'

The door opened slowly and then closed again, this time with Mitch on her side. Even as he twisted the lock shut he was unbuttoning his shirt enough to haul it over his head. 'Is this wise?'

'Probably not but I need you. Really need you.' Was she being selfish?

Not if Mitch's reaction was anything to go by. Gulp. God, he was stunning in his naked glory, his manhood erect. He needed this as much as she did.

Her eyes widened at the majestic sight filling her vision. Dreams had nothing on the real thing. Memories didn't do the man justice. Her stomach tightened to stop the ball of need from exploding through her. How could her throat be dry when she was immersed in all this water?

He squeezed in beside her, pulling the glass door closed behind him. The blue of his eyes smouldered with desire. Whether this was right or not, she'd make the most of the moment. 'I need you so much,' she whispered. 'I've missed you.' Too much information. But she didn't care. Whatever the result was of this, she would not regret it.

Mitch moved and his skin slid over hers just as she'd known it would, teasing, tantalising, unbelievable. The heat that spiralled over her, through her from that first naked touch tipped her into him. And as his hands spread across her backside to pull her even closer she closed her eyes and gave herself up to him. To Mitch, the man she'd never really stopped loving.

His mouth was hungry, devouring her lips, her throat,

tracking down between her breasts. When his lips closed over her nipple she shuddered with excitement. Then his teeth grazed her and she gasped.

She was so ready for him. Slipping her hand between them, her fingers found his erection, stroked the length of him, revelling in the silky feel, in his heat.

Rising onto her toes, she pressed hard against him.

'Jodi,' was all he said as his hands on her backside lifted her enough for him to gain access to her centre.

There was so much passion in the way he spoke her name she almost came. His passion twisted around her, branded her. She was his. Always had been.

And then he was slipping into her and her brain couldn't think at all. All she knew were the exquisite sensations dominating her body, overriding everything else, taking her higher and higher until she was floating. 'Mitch, come with me.'

He did, instantly. And she hung on for dear life, crying out his name over and over as her world shattered into lightness around her.

When he could breathe again, Mitch reached around Jodi and flicked the shower off. Keeping hold of her, he edged the door open and helped her out onto the bathmat. Her body was limp and she swayed on her feet. 'Hey, steady.' Knocked her socks off, did he?

'What happened? That was out of this world.' Her mouth curved into that smile he craved.

He had to kiss her. Taste her. Have more of her. And as soon as his mouth touched hers he could feel his body getting excited again. Whoa. Pull back. As much as Jodi had instigated this, he doubted she had the energy for a rerun. He was surprised she'd managed the first round, given that she'd barely been able to stand up when she'd first gone into the bathroom.

The lips under his moved. 'Don't stop.' She shivered.

Mitch reached for a towel. 'You're getting cold, Jodi. Let me dry you off.'

'Cold? I'm burning up.' Her smile widened as another shiver shook her.

'You're good for my ego, woman, but catching a chill isn't such a brilliant idea.' He rubbed the towel gently over her breasts, biting down on the flare of need slamming through him. Finish the job and get her dressed, hide all that flesh before you really lose your head and take her again. 'Turn around,' he growled softly. But the sight of those round buttocks stalled the air in his lungs.

Closing his eyes, he counted to ten, twenty, thirty. Finally his breath eased out and his muscles loosened up a little. 'Here, you're dry. Get some clothes on, will you?'

She didn't have to give him that wicked smirk as she opened her bag to find something clean to wear. Bloody woman, she'd be the death of him. She tugged on underwear and a T-shirt that only came down to mid-thigh—and ramped up his heart rate dangerously high.

Now that he'd made love with her he knew he wanted it again and again. Once was not enough. Jodi was back in his life in another way now. This was one way he knew her well, what he'd missed so much, and wanted for the future.

His head reared up. The future? With Jodi? *Yeah, well, weren't you getting to that? Hasn't the idea been flapping around in your brain for days now? As the shock of learning about Jamie has ebbed you've been more and more aware of Jodi as the woman you once loved.*

Food for thought.

'Time for that chicken,' he muttered, trying desperately to get back on track.

Jodi looked up at him from under her eyelashes and swayed some more. 'Think I'll have a snooze first.'

'Yes, you're asleep on your feet, sweetheart.'

Her eyes widened at that but for once she remained quiet. Not having second thoughts, he hoped. Tugging down the covers, he said, 'Come on. Climb in.'

'Mitch,' she murmured as she snuggled down.

'Ye-es.'

'We've still got what it takes, haven't we?' Her eyes closed and he'd swear she'd fallen asleep on her last word.

'Yes, sweetheart, we have.' He brushed a kiss on her forehead and tucked the sheet under her chin. Then crept out of the on-call room and went to sit with his son.

CHAPTER NINE

THE FOLLOWING AFTERNOON in the ED Mitch gently felt along Mark Williams's arm. 'Any pain where I'm touching?'

The fifteen-year-old nodded. 'Hurts like stink everywhere. That prop was a big guy.'

'You're no midget yourself.' Mitch gave the mud-covered lad a smile. 'Did his head crash into you or his shoulder?' Not that it mattered. The damage was done.

'Think it was his head, but then his whole body slammed on top of me as I went down. Pow. But I got the try.' Mark grinned despite his obvious pain.

'Good for you. Hope your team wins and makes the mess you've got yourself into worthwhile.' Mitch filled out a form requesting X-rays of Mark's humerus and ribs.

'Inter-school rugby matches tend to be physical,' Carl said from the corner.

'All rugby is physical,' Mitch muttered. 'Hang around here on the weekend and see how many bodies we get to patch up.'

'Am I going to be on TV?' Mark grinned at the camera being directed his way.

'You might,' answered Carl. 'Depends on the editing process and what other cases we get over the next couple of days.'

Mitch pulled in a lungful of air. *Yeah, focus on Mark and forget all about Jamie.*

'Cool,' Mark said. 'Wait till I tell my mates. They'll be green.' Then he jerked round to offer a better profile to the camera and groaned in pain.

'Take it easy. You have some broken bones that won't take kindly to sudden movement.' Mitch carefully pressed the boy back against his pillow and glanced across to Samantha. 'Can you arrange for an orderly to take Mark up to Radiology, please?'

Mitch headed to the station where he picked up the next patient file. Turning, he almost bumped into Carl. 'See, plenty of willing patients for you and your crews to make an excellent documentary about.'

'You're right. Mark's rugby accident will resonate with many teenage boys and their parents.' Carl's gaze was steady. 'But nothing like the human-interest story we could have about the head of this department and his very ill son.'

Mitch bit down on an expletive. He still couldn't get used to other people knowing he was a father when a week ago he'd been blissfully unaware himself. At least no one knew that. They might be wondering, since he'd never mentioned his son, and he could almost hear the debates going on about the situation, but he'd leave them to it. He wasn't about to make an announcement to all and sundry that he'd never been told he was a father.

In the meantime Carl was standing there, expecting an answer to his ridiculous suggestion. 'No.'

'So it's all right for us to interview your patients but not all right to interview you as a parent of one of your patients?'

'You've got it in one.' This guy wasn't going to pull the guilt flag on him. He would protect Jamie, and Jodi for that matter, from all the publicity this man's documentary would generate.

Carl shrugged. 'Believe me, I do understand. As I said,

if my daughter was going through what Jamie is I don't know how I'd react to a request like mine.'

'Good, then we understand each other.' Mitch pushed past him, on his way to examine Jocelyn Crooks, who'd apparently been found an hour ago lying on her bathroom floor in a dazed state. 'Anyway, Jamie is no longer a patient in this department.' Just so the guy really got it.

'You know my thinking about that.' Of course Carl was right behind him.

'Right from that very first conversation you and I had about your crews coming in here we established that any patient uncomfortable with your presence could request that they be left alone. As a parent I'm exercising that right for Jamie. Leave him be. He and his mother have got more than enough to deal with.' He snapped his mouth shut, his teeth banging together hard enough to vibrate in his ears.

'We'll talk some more later on.' Carl was so damned calm, so sure of himself.

Whereas he could feel his blood heating to boiling point. But he couldn't lay the blame on Carl. The man was doing his job while he himself was struggling to deal with absolutely everything at the moment. What had happened to his busy but orderly life? Jodi Hawke had happened, that's what. Instantly his temper eased. Jodi. Jodi had come to town. And turned his life around. And given meaning to his existence. And woken his heart up, as she had once before.

Surely this time he could manage to do things the right way and not lose her again. Because if Jodi walked out on him a second time he doubted he'd cope half as well as last time, and he'd barely managed then.

Chas poked his head around the cubicle curtain. 'Rescue Helicopter One on way in from Waiheke Island. Touchdown in ten minutes. Sixty-three-year-old male, chainsaw accident, partially severed leg.'

Mitch looked up from reading Jocelyn Crooks's obs. 'Get the on-call general surgeon on the phone. Call the blood bank and have someone on hand for an urgent cross-match. Let me know the moment the patient is here.'

He glanced across at Carl and saw the guy go grey. 'This one will be messy. If you or your crew can't deal with that, please stay well away.' His staff would have enough to deal with without having to pick up fainting sightseers.

'I'll talk to the cameraman now.' Carl pushed out of the cubicle.

Mitch called after him, 'This could be a good one to follow up on if the man's agreeable. You'd probably get the Department of Occupational Health and Safety to come on board too.'

Carl turned to shake his head at him. 'Nice try.'

I thought so. Mitch turned back to his middle-aged patient. 'Now, Jocelyn, has this happened to you before?' Pretty much everything was normal, including her blood pressure.

'Never.'

'Do you remember what you were doing before you ended up on the floor?'

Jocelyn looked away. 'No.'

Okay, what was going on here? 'Were you alone?'

'I think so.'

'Drinking alcohol?'

She muttered, 'I only had a couple.'

'I see you're on codeine. Alcohol and codeine don't mix.' Why didn't people adhere to the warnings that came with their drugs? Mitch wanted to lecture the woman but what was the point? If this incident hadn't taught her anything then nothing he could say would have any effect.

Sam arrived with an intern in tow. 'Patient's being brought down from the helipad. Rob will take over here for you.'

Mitch filled Rob in on the few details he had about Jocelyn then headed for the chainsaw patient, rolling his tight shoulders. He really needed to go for a run sometime soon. He'd been missing a few of those since Jodi had turned up.

A nurse called from the desk. 'Mitch, Radiology on the phone. You're late for your appointment.'

His chest X-ray. Damn it. 'Can you get me another time, Sheryl? I can't get away right now. But not tomorrow morning.' He was having an arteriogram done on his kidneys then. And he used to think he had a busy life before.

'Is it really Friday already?' Jodi stirred sugar into her coffee. Round and round and round.

Until Mitch reached for her hand, effectively stopping the movement. Removing the teaspoon from her grip and putting it on Jamie's bedside table, he said, 'All day.'

'One day looks exactly the same as the next, or the last one. Except Jamie sometimes looks a little bit better, then he looks terrible and so sick. And then...' Her voice faded away and her teeth nibbled her lip. The continuous rounds of dialysis were distressing for Jamie, even though they did make him feel less sluggish and took away that horrible bloating.

'Lucas said Jamie's got an infection around the catheter site.' Worry deepened Mitch's voice.

'A small one. At this stage.' Any infection was too much. Another problem to be dealt with, more drugs to be pumped into Jamie's body.

And suddenly the tears started. She tried to stop them but how did anyone stop a torrential flood? It was one that had been building up for days, beating at her eyelids to be freed, only held in place by all the willpower she could muster through her fading strength. She'd been determined not to show Mitch any weakness, and afraid that she would never get back up if she gave in to this gripping worry and fear.

Falling forward, she rested her head on the edge of Jamie's bed and gave in, no longer able to fight her grief, her anger, her sense of failure for not being able to do more for Jamie. Throw in the guilt for not telling Mitch about Jamie sooner. What a bloody mess.

Mitch lifted her into his arms, holding her as though she was made of spun sugar. Taking her place on the chair, he sat her on his lap. 'Let it go, Jodi,' he whispered. One hand stroked her back, the other cupped her head to tuck her under his chin. 'You've got to let it all out, sweetheart. It's eating you up.'

If only he knew the half of it. How bad she felt about the way she'd treated him. 'I—I'm sorry,' she tried around the lump clogging her throat. 'For everything.'

'Hey, come on. Two can play that game. I could've come home more regularly, been more attentive, come begging you for another chance. So I'm sorry, too. Okay?'

'But—'

'But nothing.' His chin rested on the top of her head. 'You're here now. We're in this together, no matter what. That's our boy lying there and we'll do all we can for him. And we'll talk over everything, any time.'

'That feels good, really good.' To have someone with a vested interest to share all the horrible medical facts with, to watch over Jamie with, would make a huge difference to her coping mechanism. 'A new beginning.'

Under her cheek Mitch's chest rose high, dropped back. Did Mitch realise his shirt and suit jacket were getting soaked?

'Something like that. New, but different.'

Pulling her head from under his chin, she twisted round to look him in the eye. 'I like that.' She especially liked what they'd done together in the on-call room yesterday. Maybe she could take a shower every couple of hours.

'I passed Max on the way to the canteen earlier. He asked how Jamie was doing. Said he's getting everything in place in case a kidney becomes available.'

They knew he would. The man wasn't going to play games with something this serious. The stream of tears slowed to a trickle as she shook her head. 'Can't do better than Max.'

'You're right.' Not even a hint of the old angst lined Mitch's words. Blimey.

She settled back against that wide expanse of chest. A great place to be—warm and comforting. And the hand still soothing her back brought other memories back. The day she'd had to have her very old cat put down, Mitch had come home early to be with her. He'd held her just like this until the tears had dried up and then taken her to bed and made exquisite love to her to blot out the sadness for a while. And afterwards he'd gone into town to get a miniature rose bush to plant on her cat's grave.

The rose bush she had pruned every year and remembered the cat, deliberately shoving aside all thoughts of Mitch. How could she have been so single-minded about him? Why hadn't she wanted to recall all the wonderful times they'd had together? Ashamed, she craned her neck and placed her mouth on Mitch's. 'Thank you for being you.'

He shifted his mouth to cover hers fully. His arms wound around her, like a safety net, only this time there was an exciting kind of danger in their hold as well. As though there might yet be something for her, for them, if they could only step cautiously and carefully through the minefield they found themselves in.

'A very salty kiss,' Mitch murmured against her mouth. When she made to pull back he added, 'I like salt. Don't you remember?'

'On your fish and chips, yes, but—'

'Shh, you talk too much.' And his lips covered hers again, shutting off anything she might say.

She'd missed this. Lots. Slipping her tongue cautiously into his mouth to find his, to taste him, she felt the mistake she'd made when she'd kicked him out of her life. How could she have given this up? Must have been on something toxic. Because no one in their right mind would deliberately banish from their life a man who could kiss so superbly.

Mitch's hands had somehow worked under her top onto her waist, holding her against his body. Each fingertip scorched her skin, sending out lines of hot desire, filling her body with a longing so strong she shook. Pressing her breasts hard against him, she revelled in the feel of his rapidly rising and falling chest. Her fingers slid through that thick, dark hair, walked over his scalp. And still she wanted more.

Under her backside Mitch's growing need was becoming more apparent. She wriggled and he gasped. Pulling his mouth away, he stared at her from lust-filled eyes. 'Wrong place, I think.'

Heat seared her cheeks as she abruptly returned to reality. Hurriedly standing up, she turned round and smoothed her top down over her bony hips. 'You're right. I don't know what came over me.'

'That's a shame.'

Snapping her head round, she was confronted with

Mitch's wide grin as he stood up. Sighing out a laugh, she told him, 'Thank goodness no one caught us.'

His grin disappeared. 'Would that bother you?'

How the heck did she know? It was too soon. There were too many problems facing them. 'If I think about it, it probably does.'

He leaned in and placed a soft kiss on her cheek. 'Then don't overthink it.' Then he was gone, striding out of the room as fast as those long legs could take him.

Picking up the coffee from where she'd put it earlier, she took a sip and shuddered. Cold. She'd get another one. Jamie was still asleep. He wouldn't notice her absence if she was quick.

But she stayed by the bed, staring down at her son, not seeing him. Instead seeing the older version of those blue eyes and dark hair, smelling the pine and spice aftershave that his dad wore, feeling the ripple of well-developed chest muscles under her cheek.

What had she started when she'd called Mitch into the shower yesterday? A rerun of an old, not-so-good relationship? Or a new version of that, with more honesty and understanding to help it along? They'd talked more in these few days about real things concerning both of them than they had in six months when they'd been together.

Did she want to get back with Mitch? There'd been as many good times as bad, she realised now that she'd let all the memories in and not just selective ones. But if they had any hope of making a success of being together again, they had a lot of things to clear up first.

And before any of that Jamie had to have his transplant and get well.

And she still didn't know how Mitch felt about donating a kidney. Did she have the right to even ask?

How would I have felt in the situation? Truthfully? I'd hate for someone to tell me that.

But Jamie's nephrologist in Dunedin had done exactly that and she hadn't taken offence. It had been a professional move, not an involved, emotional one. Unfortunately the nephrotic syndrome she'd suffered from as a youngster had precluded her being able to give a kidney to Jamie.

No, whatever was going on between her and Mitch did not give her permission to back him into a corner over a very personal decision. She had to wait. Best to hold off on any more of those kisses, then. No more sex in the shower, or anywhere else. Because of the way her body melted when his lips devoured hers, the chances of her brain remaining in good working order were next to none. And then she'd surely spill the words he and she wouldn't want hanging between them.

'Guess we'd better get back to the hospital and relieve Alison,' Mitch murmured against Jodi's throat. It would be so much better to curl his body around Jodi's and hold her throughout the night while she got some sleep. Okay, not only sleep. He wouldn't be able to refrain from making out with her again. His body was warm and languid right now after making love but it wouldn't be long before everything was up and about, wanting more action.

'Mum did say to take as long as we wanted.' Jodi laughed.

He loved it when she laughed. 'But even she knows dinner only involves a couple of hours. Coming back to the house has stretched those into half the night.'

'I doubt she'll be surprised. Mum doesn't miss much. She probably even guessed we'd grab takeaways and head back here.' Jodi winked at him. 'Though you needn't think you're getting out of taking me to dinner at one of those fabulous restaurants down on the Viaduct.' Jodi trailed her fingers through the light hairs on his chest. 'I was really looking forward to that, but somehow we got sidetracked.'

Yeah, the moment he'd thought about them having a deep and meaningful discussion over dinner he'd changed his mind about going to the amazing restaurant he'd chosen. That was for fun, for romance, not for dissecting their past relationship. 'I'll definitely take you there another night. Soon, I promise.' He crossed his fingers briefly.

Jodi chuckled. 'I'll keep you to that.'

'Anyway, you sidetracked me. Not the other way round.'

She blushed. 'I did, didn't I?' Her eyes widened, big brown pools that drew him in. 'I'd decided this wasn't going to happen again. At least not until everything else was out of the way.' The smile she bestowed on him was wicked and cheeky. 'But when you came out of your bedroom looking so mouth-wateringly gorgeous I lost the argument.'

'So why did we get into my four-wheel drive and start heading into town?' It was Jodi who was gorgeous, not him. Dressed in a knee-length dress that floated around her as she moved, the colour—not quite emerald, not quite turquoise—suited her perfectly. His heart had thumped wildly at the sight of her. Wild horses wouldn't have stopped him from kissing her then. And that stunning dress hadn't stayed on very long.

A while later they'd had to get ready all over again, only to get as far as the first Chinese takeout shop before buying some food and racing home again.

'I'd just bought the dress. I had to wear it out somewhere.' Had she thought this might happen when she'd packed it? Her finger circled his nipple. Her tongue replaced her finger, licking slowly, tantalisingly.

Hot need shot through him, waking up every muscle in his body. Again.

'You want more? So soon?' He pushed up on his elbow and leaned over her, kissing those fingers, taking them into his mouth.

'It's this, or having a quick shower and going back to the hospital.' Her hand reached down between his legs. 'Your call.'

It was no contest. Sliding his body over hers, he gave her his answer.

CHAPTER TEN

'JODI? CAN WE COME IN?'

Jodi dragged herself upright from Jamie's bed and ran her hands over her hair and down her face. 'Claire? Of course you can. I'm a bit of a mess but, hey, it's good to see you.' Exhaustion dragged at her muscles, numbed her mind.

Claire stepped closer, tugging a little girl with her. 'I've brought you something for your lunch.'

'You're an angel, you know that?'

'Don't talk daft. How's Jamie doing?' she whispered.

'It's okay, you won't disturb him. He wakes and sleeps as he needs to and no amount of noise will unsettle him.' She stretched her kinked back as she looked at the child hanging on to Claire. 'Hello, you must be Lilly.'

'Lilly Silly Billy.' The girl grinned and shook her head in all directions. 'That's what my friends call me cos I'm always dancing and singing and laughing. Want me to show you a dance?'

Claire quickly cut off that line of thought. 'No, Lilly, no. We're in hospital, remember? Sick people don't like lots of noise.'

'I'd do it quietly, Mum, promise.'

Claire rolled her eyes. 'You don't know the meaning of the word.'

Jodi smiled at Lilly. 'Maybe another time. I know, what about when we're at Mitch's house? Do you go there with your mum sometimes?'

'After play centre I do. Can I see Jamie? Why's he asleep in the morning?' Lilly began climbing up on the bed.

'It was a mistake, bringing you here.' Claire lifted Lilly back down to the floor.

Jodi pushed a chair towards Claire. 'No, I'm glad you dropped by. Lilly's not a problem. It's okay if Jamie wakes up. Truly. A little distraction would be good for him. But, Lilly...' Jodi lifted the girl onto her knees. 'See all those tubes?

'They're stuck to Jamie with plaster.'

'Yes, those ones. Now, you have to be very careful not to bump any of them because you could hurt Jamie if one gets pulled out by accident.' Her heart ached for her boy who, if he woke up, would be gutted that he couldn't play with Lilly. He'd missed out on so many opportunities to have fun with other kids over the years. It seemed so unfair. Sometimes having all the stories in the world read to him just didn't cut it.

'I'll be good,' Lilly assured her earnestly. Then her face split into another wide smile. 'I'm always good, aren't I, Mum?'

Again Claire rolled her eyes. 'Of course you are.' Then she turned to Jodi. 'I dropped your mum off at the airport.'

'You're kidding! Mrs Independence accepted a lift?' Mum held on to her money like it was a lifeline but she also never took offers of help from people she didn't know very well. Oh. 'I get it. She grilled you on Mitch.'

Claire looked uncomfortable. 'A little bit.'

'Mum doesn't do little. All or nothing is my mother.' She'd changed her flights by a day so that she could sit with Jamie last night. But now she was heading back to Dunedin to check on her shop, but she'd be back in a week.

'You're right. I got a barrage of questions thrown at me. I think she was disappointed when I explained Mitch was my boss and I wasn't prepared to talk about him behind his back. When I added how much I need my job and why, she backed off.' Claire grinned. 'A little. Actually, I like your mum. She cares about you all.'

'Yeah, she does.' Even Mitch.

Claire sat up straighter on her chair. 'Mitch, hi. I've got your groceries in my car. I'll drop them off after we leave here.'

Looking around, Jodi gaped, then smiled at the man standing a couple of metres away, studying Jamie thoroughly. 'Max, what brings you here?' But she knew already. He'd come to check out Jamie, to take another look at his nephew. He'd been doing that regularly since the team consultation.

Claire stared at Jodi. 'Max? Who's Max? This is Mitch.' Then her eyes widened further. 'Blimey, has the guy been using two different names? That could get him into all sorts of trouble.'

'Claire, meet Max Maitland, Mitch's twin. Max, Claire is Mitch's housekeeper.' She'd never had any trouble telling them apart. Max's eyes were set slightly wider, and his smile didn't have that lopsided thing going on that Mitch's did.

'I never knew Mitch had a twin. Or any family, for that matter.'

Max's mouth tightened but he sounded his usual charming self when he spoke. 'Nice to meet you, Claire.' Then he instantly turned those knowledgeable eyes on Jamie.

Actually, no. Try hungry eyes. Now, there was something to think about. Did Max want kids of his own? Why wouldn't he? She'd judged him on Mitch's standards, which was hardly fair. She stood and crossed to Max, gave him a hug. 'I'm glad you came.'

Max returned her hug before gently setting her aside. 'Just keeping an eye on my patient.'

Sure, buddy. 'Not a problem. He's doing fine, if you call having daily dialysis fine. Which I don't.'

'Okay, watching over my nephew. Feel happier?' He chucked her under the chin with his forefinger, a smile lightening his face.

'Absolutely.' More than happy, ecstatic.

Then the smile slipped. 'Jamie hasn't had a lot of fun in his short life, has he?'

'Very little.' She tried to read his eyes but Max had always been good at hiding his true feelings. It was a family trait. Came with the twin gene. Only one way to deal with either Max or Mitch when they did this. Speak bluntly. 'No fresh kidneys on their way from somewhere around the country, then?'

'You'd be the first to know.' He grunted, shoved his hands deep into his pockets. Another Maitland gesture. 'Ever felt you wanted to step outside and knock someone off so you can save your child? Because that's how I've been feeling all week.'

When Claire gasped, Max turned to her with a self-deprecating smile. 'It's all right. I have no intention of spending the rest of my life behind bars. But this is my nephew. It's a whole different ball game now.'

Claire was staring at Max again. 'You and Mitch must cause a lot of problems around here, being so alike and all.'

'We don't work in the same departments.' Then he shrugged. 'Yes, occasionally I get grumped at by a staff member for forgetting something when it wasn't me they talked to.'

'Bet you two have caused all sorts of trouble over the years.' Claire grinned as she took her daughter's hand and said, 'Okay, come on, Lilly. We'd better go and unpack those groceries before the ice cream melts. You can see Jamie another time.'

Jodi and Max watched them leave, neither saying a word. As Lilly, looking over her shoulder and waving hard, disappeared around the corner, Jodi turned back to her boy, who had slept through everything. Which brought tears to her eyes. Just another little thing he'd missed out on. A visit from a sweet little girl who wanted to be friends. When was this going to end? How was it going to end? Where was Mitch? Suddenly she wanted him there with her more than anything. His arms around her, sharing his strength, sharing her fears. Guarding their son together.

'How have you managed?' Max's shoulders rolled. 'You still look sane. And strong, which I guess answers my question. But to do this on your own? Obviously still stubborn too. You should've told Mitch. Hell, you should've told me,' he growled.

'Too late for this conversation.' Jodi shivered.

'How's Mitch taking it? It must've been a hell of a shock. Is he okay? I know he seems to be stepping up but what's going on inside that skull of his? Does he need to talk to someone?'

Jodi's jaw clenched as she tried not to gasp in surprise at Max's apparently genuine concern for his brother. Totally out of left field. Perhaps Jamie would be the catalyst that got them talking to each other. Really talking, not sniping. 'Maybe you should be talking to Mitch about those things.'

He huffed. 'I'm more concerned about you and Jamie. Mitch is a big boy. He can look after himself.'

'Who's been suggesting I can't?' Mitch snapped from behind them.

'Mitch, no one, not even me, was suggesting you can't,' Max snapped in an identical tone to his twin's.

Mitch studied his brother. 'Okay.'

'I dropped by to see how Jamie was holding up,' Max explained. 'I always feel frustrated waiting for an organ for my patients, but this time it's far worse.'

Mitch nodded. 'Sure is.'

'Mummy.' Right on cue.

'Hey, Jamie, love.' She wrapped his hot little body in her arms and stroked his back.

'Mitch?' Jamie squawked. 'There are two Mitches.'

'No, love. One's Mitch.' One day you'll call him Daddy. 'And the other's Max. You met him the other day.' One day you'll call *him* Uncle Max.

'No, I didn't.'

Okay, not going there. Too complicated. 'Want a juice? Or some water?'

'No.' Jamie yawned and snuggled in against her, his big, bewildered eyes peering out at the two men standing together at the end of his bed. Side by side.

'Thought I might find you here.' Carl strolled into the room, dressed comfortably in jeans and an open-necked shirt. 'Didn't expect to see both the Maitland doctors in the same room together.'

Mitch spun round. 'Carl. I've said no. You are not coming near Jamie or Jodi. Not now, not ever. Which bit of that don't you get?'

Carl held up a hand. 'Take it easy. I'm not here to badger you or Jodi. I wanted to see how the wee lad was getting on. Nothing more than taking an interest in your child.'

Max turned slowly and eyed the newcomer up and down appraisingly. 'I don't believe we've met.'

The man thrust his hand out. 'Carl Webster, TV Aotearoa. I'm filming a documentary in this hospital's emergency department.'

Jodi wrapped her arms tighter around Jamie. 'Are you still hoping I'll agree to you filming my son?' Her voice was rising. Frantically swallowing, she tried to lower the pitch of her voice. 'The answer is no. Absolutely not. Get it? I know I thought it could be good for the donor service but I just can't have anyone coming near Jamie with a camera. Not so you can give your viewers some excitement while they eat their dinner and argue over whose turn it is to clear the table.'

Mitch came to her, laid a hand on her shoulder. 'Jodi, he won't. Trust me.'

Carl stepped up to the bed. 'Jodi, I apologise for giving you the wrong idea. I genuinely wanted to see how Jamie was. I've overheard conflicting snippets of talk from the staff. I feel for you all. There is no ulterior motive in my visit.'

He had guts. She'd give him that. 'I see.'

Max looked at Jodi, something like sympathy in his eyes. He smiled kindly then read the charts at the end of Jamie's bed. 'He's holding his own. I'll drop in again later.' With that he strolled out of the room, as if he didn't have a worry in the world. But he had been concerned about Jamie. About Mitch, even.

'I'll be getting back to my crew.' Carl turned to follow Max then turned back. 'But if there is anything I can do for you, please don't hesitate to ask. I'd really like to help if I can.'

Jodi stared after him, even when he had turned the corner and disappeared from sight. 'I think he meant it.'

'I guess we'll never know. I'm not asking him for anything.' Mitch sat on the edge of the bed. 'How'd you like to go home for the night, Jamie?'

'Ah, excuse me?' Jodi glared at Mitch.

'Wouldn't you like to spend a night in a bed, not sprawled out beside Jamie?' When her eyes widened he smiled. 'On your own, getting some much-needed sleep.'

'Oh.' Disappointment flared. It hadn't taken long to get used to having sex again. But Mitch was right. She did need sleep—very badly.

He was still smiling. 'What about a quiet night without nurses shining torches as they check on Jamie? Not to mention a meal that hasn't been reheated in the microwave?'

'Low blows, Dr Maitland.' She weighed up the pros and cons. It wasn't as though Jamie wouldn't have medical care on hand. 'I guess Jamie's well enough for an overnight stay away from here.'

'We've got Lucas's approval.'

'Stop looking so smug.' Her sprits were suddenly lifting.

'Can I take Bingo home?' Jamie asked.

'Where you go, Bingo goes, sport.'

If only everything could be sorted out as easily.

Mitch put the last pot away and hung the tea towel on the oven door handle. Leaning back against the bench, he folded his arms across his chest and breathed deeply. 'Jodi, how would you feel about us telling Jamie who I really am?'

Her head snapped up so fast it must've hurt. The gaze that met his was filled with surprise. Then she studied him as though she was looking at every single cell of his body.

He waited for all the questions about his intentions. He was ready for her, knowing deep within he'd never back off from being a father to Jamie. Now Jamie was in his life there'd be no letting go, no changing his mind. There were a lot of things to decide still, like Sydney and whether Jodi moved over there with him, but he'd make it all work. He had to.

Jodi smiled. 'I'd like that. He should know.'

'Truly? Just like that?'

'I can see you mean it, that you didn't just decide this between washing the dishes and putting them away in the cupboards. You really care about Jamie, love him, and that's all that matters.'

The tension gripping him eased off. His mouth spread into a smile. Warmth sneaked through him.

'Let's tell him now before I put him to bed.' She pushed up from the table.

Mitch looked through to the lounge where the TV was tuned to a cartoon programme. Jamie lay curled up on the couch, his blankie in his fist, thick pyjamas keeping him snug. Bingo was perched on the arm of the couch. Mitch could feel his heart swelling with love for the little man who carried his genes. Reaching for Jodi's hand, he walked through to his son.

But Jodi took over before he could utter a word. 'Jamie, sweetheart, we've got something to tell you, something good.'

'Not now, Mummy. I'm watching the dogs chasing the rabbits.' Jamie's gaze didn't waver from the screen as he pointed. 'See?'

'I see,' his mother answered, without looking around. 'Jamie—'

Mitch shook his head at her. 'It's okay. Only a few minutes till the end,' he said. 'It's kind of funny, really. When I finally want to tell Jamie I'm his dad he makes me wait for the cartoons to finish.'

He sat down on the other end of the couch, stretching his legs half across the room. He watched the enjoyment flitting across his boy's face and the resulting giggles making his cheeks screw up. Saw the gap where Jamie had lost a tooth this week. Noted the dark too-long hair so like his own. The tiny scar on his chin where Jodi said he'd once banged into the corner of a table. The little-boy things that made Jamie who he was.

Sitting beside him on the arm of the couch, Jodi swung her legs and played the piano on her thighs with her fingers.

Suddenly Mitch's stomach squeezed. Was this the right time to be telling him? Why not wait until after the surgery? But almost immediately the panic abated and he relaxed again. He wanted this.

The credits began to roll on the screen. 'Finished, Mummy. Can I have a drink?'

Jodi leapt off the couch and went to kneel beside Jamie.

'In a minute. Do you know what a daddy is?'

Jamie nodded. 'He's a man-mummy.'

Mitch felt his mouth drop open. *I'm a man-mummy? Couldn't have put it better myself.* And he grinned.

Jodi blinked and swallowed a laugh, but the look she shot him was one of pure fun. 'Jamie, Mitch is your daddy.'

At least she didn't say I'm his man-mummy.

Jamie looked over at Mitch and shrugged. 'Okay.'

'You can call him Daddy now, not Mitch anymore.'

'Okay. Can I have my drink now?'

Mitch stared at this kid whom he'd fathered. Who'd taught him to be so offhand? If he hadn't known better he'd have thought he'd been around Jamie all his short life. Well, he, for one, was changing. 'Hey, Jamie, want a hug first?'

'Yes, please. I like hugs.'

And when small arms wound too tightly around Mitch's neck, he grinned. 'So do I, Jamie. So do I.'

'Phew. For a moment there I thought we were in for

an argument.' Shock receded from Jodi's eyes, replaced
by love for her boy. 'But he came through. As he always
does.' She scrubbed her eyes with the back of her hand.

Mitch was torn between holding the squirming bun-
dle in his arms and reaching for Jodi to haul her against
him. Somehow he managed to juggle Jamie and snag his
mother. They sat in a squashed heap on the couch holding on to each other until Jamie wriggled out. Which was
almost immediately.

Mitch didn't care. His heart was bursting. He'd done
something right for Jamie. And himself. Another step ticked
off. Except this one was so huge. Was this how mountaineers
felt? Exhilarating now the worry was over, huh?

'Man-mummy, want a coffee?' Jodi asked as she extri-
cated herself from his hug.

'Watch it,' he growled, trying to hold in a laugh and failing. As the laughter rolled out of him he felt the best he'd
done in a very long time. Since the day Jodi had dumped
him. Yeah, he could get used to all this commitment stuff
after all. So far it hadn't hurt a bit.

Still feeling the effects of a good night's sleep, Jodi wandered out into the kitchen in her thick pyjamas and warm
bathrobe, looking for a cup of tea.

'Hi, sleepyhead. Thought you'd never wake up.' Mitch
sat at the table with Jamie on his knee getting stuck into
a plate of toast and honey.

'Hi, Mummy. Mitch let me make my own toast.'

'That explains the honey on your forehead.' Jodi kissed
his cheek. And got a whiff of delicious aftershave. Hurriedly stepping away, she busied herself with filling the
kettle, finding a mug and the teabags. Too early in the
morning for thinking about sexy men. Gees, showed how
bad things were. There had been a time when it was never

too early. Or too late, come to think of it. 'So you're still Mitch, then?'

He shrugged, apparently totally unfazed. 'Better than man-mummy.'

'You should've woken me. You'll be late for work.' She yawned and stretched her arms high above her head.

Mitch's gaze seemed stuck on her chest. 'It's Saturday. I'm not going in.'

The mug banged down on the bench. 'What?' Was he all right? Never had Mitch not gone to work on the weekend. Saturdays and Sundays were just normal days in his book.

'I've got more important things to do than look after patients today.' He sounded so smug.

Grabbing the milk from the fridge, she poured some into the tea and dropped down on a chair before her legs gave out in shock. 'What's more important than your department?'

'My son. And my son's mother.' Definitely smug. And smiling. 'You never thought you'd hear me say that, did you?'

'Honestly? Not before aliens took over the planet.' The tea scalded her tongue. Damn. 'Okay, spill. What's going on?'

'Jamie's got dialysis at ten.'

'Ye-es?'

'You've got an appointment in Parnell at nine-thirty.'

'I have? Since when? You've got the wrong woman, surely?' Weirder and weirder. She held up her hand in a stop sign. 'Mitch, did you take something you shouldn't? Should I be taking you to get your stomach pumped out?'

Jamie wriggled off Mitch's knee and took his plate over to the bench, reaching high to get it over the edge. Jodi automatically reached too, and saved the dish. When she sat back and reconnected with Mitch she saw his gaze had focused on her chest again. Glancing down, she muttered under her breath and tugged her robe closed over her breasts.

Mitch stood and began clearing the table of crumbs. 'I thought I'd take Jamie for his appointment while you go to a spa. The Indulgence Spa, actually. I've booked you a half-day session, longer if you want it.'

It was hard to talk when her mouth was hanging halfway to her knees. 'A spa?' Her? When was the last time she'd pampered herself? How old was Jamie? Three years four months and some days. That's how long ago.

Mitch towered over her, tilting her head back with his finger under her chin. 'If you really don't want to go then I won't argue. But before you say flat out no, think about it. You're exhausted.'

She nodded. 'But that only means I'll fall asleep on the massage bed.'

Mitch ignored her. 'I doubt you've done anything for yourself in all the time since Jamie was born. I want you to feel better within yourself, to luxuriate with a massage, facial and any other woman thing you want.'

That was quite a speech. 'Thank you, but I always go with Jamie for his treatments.'

'Jodi.' Mitch lowered his head to brush her mouth with his lips. 'He'll be fine with me. I am a doctor. More than that, I'm his father and I'm trying to be one. You have to let me do things like this.'

'That includes looking out for me, too?' The moment she'd spoken her lips sought his again. Finding them, she pressed up against him. How had she survived all this time without these lips to kiss, lips that teased and tormented, caressed and heated her up?

'You're part of the deal. Jodi and Jamie.' He leaned into the kiss, opening under her mouth, his tongue slipping across hers. His hands gripped her shoulders holding her in place. He needn't have worried. She wasn't going anywhere.

'Mummy, what are you doing?' Jamie tugged at the belt on her robe and she jerked away from Mitch whose eyes were filled with laughter.

'I'm kissing him.' That's what mummies and daddies did in an ideal world. Not as good as the whole works—commitment, love, sharing. 'It's a start.'

'It sure is,' said a bemused Mitch from the other side of the kitchen, where he'd suddenly become frantically busy running water into the sink. Then he twisted the tap off and turned to face her, his face now completely serious. 'I don't know what you want from me other than to be a part of Jamie's life. I haven't thought that far ahead yet. But you can believe me when I say I accept my role in Jamie's life. I am his father and nothing is ever going to change that. Nothing will take that away from me.'

CHAPTER ELEVEN

JODI SCRAPED THE roast lamb and vegetables off her plate into the rubbish bin. The racket made by dropping the plate and cutlery into the sink jarred her teeth, and cranked up her temper even more.

'You haven't changed one bit, Mitchell Maitland. All this talk about wanting to help me, to be there for Jamie, and where are you now? Dinner was ready two hours ago.'

All that pampering at the spa last weekend did not make up for this. All the sweet words, the kind gestures, doing the involved-father acts did not make up for his lateness.

'You could've at least phoned or texted.' Yeah, right.

She'd gagged, trying to swallow a mouthful of the delicious-smelling dinner she'd prepared. After waiting an hour and a half, giving him the excuse that he really had got caught up in an emergency at work, she'd carved a slice of the succulent meat and spooned gravy over that and the vegetables. But the moment she sat at the carefully laid table her stomach had started churning. Not wanting to let Mitch win, she'd forced her teeth to chew, her throat to swallow. She hadn't got past that first taste.

Covering the rest of the meat, she left it to go cold. The vegetables looked soggy and flat in the cooled roasting pan sitting on the stovetop. She lifted them onto a plate to set aside. The pan went into the sink to soak.

'Note to self: don't ever think you can prepare a meal for Mitch that he's going to sit down and eat with you on time.'

She flicked the kettle on. Maybe tea would be okay in her delicate stomach.

'Second note to self: remember the lessons learned the first time you had anything to do with Mitchell Maitland.'

The teabag steeped in the boiling water. Jodi tried to swallow the disappointment that had engulfed her but that was as hard to do as swallowing her dinner. Had she expected too much of Mitch?

She nudged the teabag with a teaspoon, squished it before removing it. Stirring in milk, she stared at the murky liquid. Not very appetising but better than nothing. Unlike Mitch. Very appetising but definitely not better than nothing.

'Third note to self: don't fall in love with him all over again.'

She dropped the teaspoon on top of the dirty plate and taking her mug in a shaky hand she headed for Jamie's bedroom. Her heart was squeezing, fit to bust. Her lungs were struggling to do their job. Just before her brain closed down on this bleak discussion it added one more warning.

'Fourth note: it's too late. Too bloody late. You're already completely in love with him.'

Mitch leaned his elbows on the railing and peered down into the dark sea metres below, his hands clasped tightly in front of him, his fingers feeling as though they'd never straighten again. The wind tossed spume in the air and across his face. His tongue tasted salt on his lips. He was impervious to that and the rain running down his neck. The anorak wasn't doing its job. In the scheme of things, getting wet didn't even register.

On the road behind him cars whizzed through the puddles, horns blared as impatient drivers hogged the road. Thursday-night clubbing and drinking awaited them. All so darned unimportant.

He was compatible. With Jamie. In every essential aspect.

The tissue typing showed no problems with their white cells. The crossmatch had come up negative, telling him that Jamie wouldn't reject his kidney. The X-rays showed all was good inside, and the arteriogram showed his renal system was in superb working order.

Jamie could have one of his kidneys. Any day now.

Which was good. Great, even.

The relief was huge. His boy would be safe, could start to live a normal life for the first time. Whether that life was in Dunedin or Sydney had yet to be sorted, but he wasn't overly concerned. Somehow he and Jodi would make that work. Even if he had to give up the new job. That idea didn't gut him as much as it would've a few weeks back.

So what's your problem?

That was the problem. He didn't know. Couldn't say why he felt so drained, so unexcited. When Lucas had given him the good news he'd been thrilled. At last he was going to do something worthwhile for his family. Because, unmarried, not together, Jodi was his family as much as Jamie.

So if that's how you feel, shouldn't you be at home, telling her the good news? Celebrating with a glass of wine and watching her face light up with wonder? Seeing that worry and fear slip away from those sad brown eyes?

Too right. He'd even bought the champagne on the way home, before he'd turned round and headed out here to think. The good mood had evaporated, leaving him with more questions than ever.

Did people celebrate donating one of their kidneys to their son? Or was the situation too grim for that?

Jodi would be relieved at the news. More than relieved. This was what she wanted, what she'd come to Auckland and him for. He'd known it the moment he'd heard the word 'cystinosis'.

Not that he could find fault with her over that. Their son's life was at stake. Of course she'd do whatever was necessary. Even knock on his door.

But what if after the transplant Jodi didn't need him to be a part of her life? What if that was all she'd wanted from him and the kisses and lovemaking had been incidental? Or just a big mistake? She'd never stop him seeing Jamie. He knew that as well as he knew anything.

I definitely do not want to be a part-time dad, having Jamie to stay in the holidays, spending every second Christmas with him, flying to Dunedin for his birthday.

More than that, he wanted Jodi in his day-to-day life. Not as his child's mother but as his partner, his wife. His lover. His friend.

He loved her. *I love Jodi Hawke.*

That had been creeping up on him since she'd dropped back into his life. There hadn't been any fireworks blinding him. No clashing cymbals awakening his heart. No, the realisation that he loved, still loved, her had been a slow slide in under his skin to take over his mind.

Right now he didn't know what to do about his love.

He wanted to marry her, have the whole enchilada, not just the hot sex on the nights they were actually at the house and when Jodi wasn't so tired she fell asleep the moment they finished. He didn't want to have their relationship deteriorate into passing in the hallway of his totally impersonal house as they went their separate ways.

But to tell her this, at the moment, might backfire. He

was between a rock and a hard place. He could see Jodi misinterpreting his kidney donation as a way to win her back when the truth of it was he'd never wanted to lose her in the first place.

Stick to the plan, boyo. One step at a time. Everything will work out in the end.

Water trickled down his spine. He shivered and his skin rose in chilly bumps. The next step should be to go home and get into some dry clothes. He smiled as he popped the locks on the car Aaron had lent him for the night. Home to share his news over a glass of champagne and the meal Jodi had said she'd be cooking.

He could almost taste the roast as he turned into the driveway. That sense of homecoming that had gripped him on Jodi's first night in his house washed over him as he noted the lights shining through the gloom, beckoning him inside where it would be warm and cosy Where hopefully his son slept and Jodi waited, ready to serve up dinner.

Pushing the front door open, he inhaled the delicious aroma permeating the house. His mouth watered as he headed down the hall to the kitchen. 'Hey, Jodi, that's smells wonderful. You're spoiling me. I could get used to this.'

Silence greeted him. 'Jodi?'

The lounge was in darkness. The dining room lights were on and the table set for two. Candles in the middle, wine glasses gleaming. A quick glance around the kitchen told him all he needed to know. He was in trouble with Jodi. *Big time, boyo. You're late home, just like always.*

Except this was different. He hadn't been working, hadn't used patients as an excuse not to come home. He enjoyed coming home these days. She wasn't playing fair. Especially when he had the best news imaginable to share with her.

'Jodi,' he called as he strode towards his bedroom. 'Jodi, where are you?' Disappointment warred with anger as he strode through the door, snapping on the light as he went. 'We've got to talk. Now.'

His bed was empty. A deep chill, colder than that from his wet clothes, bit into him. She'd gone? No, she wouldn't take Jamie out in this weather if she didn't have to. Unless he'd taken a turn for the worse. And then she'd have called.

Mitch spun round, began to stride back to the kitchen. Stopped in the middle of the hall. Jamie's bedroom door was firmly closed. Something Jodi didn't do unless she was in there with him because she was afraid she wouldn't hear him if he became restless or cried out.

His hand shook as he cracked the door open.

Jodi shot up in bed, reaching for her thick robe to keep warm. Her boiling anger had died away to a slow, cold throb as she'd lain there unable to fall asleep. 'Be quiet. You'll wake Jamie,' she hissed. 'He's very restless tonight.' Like mother, like son.

'Then can you come out here so I can explain why I'm late?'

Did he have to sound so reasonable? Had she made a terrible mistake? 'You'd have to have a very good reason.' Now she sounded like a fishwife. But she was so damned angry with him.

'I do.'

'Cellphone not working?' she snapped, barely remembering to whisper. But she did climb out of bed, careful not to disturb Jamie. Keeping as far away from that heart-stopping body as she possibly could, she slipped past him and headed for the lounge. Why was she even giving him the time? She'd heard all this before. The old leopard-doesn't-change-its-spots thing.

In the centre of the room she spun round. 'I don't want to hear how busy it was at work. I know you're the best specialist they've got. I know you're addicted to working every hour there is. Hell, you'd work fifty hours a day if there were that many. But, Mitch, haven't you proved to yourself yet that you're good, that you can do whatever's required of you without foregoing a life? What drives you to be so single-minded about what you do?'

She stopped her tirade. Not because she'd run out of steam. There was plenty more where that had come from. But Mitch wasn't answering back, wasn't defending himself. He hadn't followed her into the lounge.

Instead he stood at the door. Just stood there, not leaning against the doorframe, not folding his arms across his chest as he often did. As though he was waiting for her to have her say and shut up. No emotion flickered over his still face. Nothing showed in those intense blue eyes. So still, so quiet.

So not like Mitch.

A ripple of fear caused her to shiver. 'Mitch?' His silence got to her, started her off again. 'What? No answers? Because I'm right? And here I was thinking you'd changed, that you wanted to be a part of something bigger than just you. A relationship, relationships.'

He sighed.

And she shut up. She'd spewed her guts and he'd sighed. Where was the Mitch who raced to give her all the excuses under the sun? This guy had sighed when she'd read him the Riot Act. Had she got it all wrong? If she had then she'd just blown any chance of them ever getting together again.

'Mitch,' she croaked.

His steady gaze fixed her to the spot. 'Thought you'd like to know that I've found out I can donate a kidney to Jamie.'

All the air in her lungs hissed out over her lips as she collapsed in on herself. Squeezing her eyes shut, she tried to exorcise that image of Mitch as he told her what she'd wanted to hear for weeks. But she couldn't get his face out of her head. His totally emotionless expression pressed at her.

A kidney for Jamie. From his father. And she hadn't even known he was getting the tests done. Because he'd wanted to find out first? Whichever way it went?

Jodi sank to the floor, her legs unable to hold her upright. She wanted the ground to open up and swallow her for ever. Mitch was doing the most generous thing possible for his son. And she'd been ranting and raving at him for coming home late. When had she become such a witch? Had Jamie's illness taken over every part of her so that *she* was the single-minded person she'd accused Mitch of being?

Dragging her head up, she met Mitch's steady gaze. 'I am so sorry, Mitch. I didn't think, didn't consider you might have another reason for not coming home as you'd promised. I'm so sorry,' she repeated.

'We have an appointment with Lucas at eleven tomorrow to discuss what we're doing next, when we might schedule the operations. I'll see you there. In the meantime, I have a job to get back to.'

As Mitch turned away, Jodi noticed a bottle of champagne in his hand. She gasped. Never, ever had she got something so wrong. And the consequences were huge.

She'd just lost the only man she'd ever loved, still loved. Again.

At five to eleven the next morning Jodi was pacing the general waiting room outside the surgical consultants' rooms. Every time the swing doors opened she looked up expectantly. When a stranger walked though her stomach dropped, and she went back to pacing.

Jamie sat sprawled sideways in the wheelchair Mitch had arranged for him, half-asleep, his blankie tucked around him. Since learning he had to go to see the doctor today he'd been grizzly but his lethargy had finally quietened him.

Eleven o'clock clicked over to one minute past on the wall clock. Where was Mitch? And Lucas? According to Lucas's nurse, he hadn't arrived on the floor yet.

She wouldn't even begin to think anything other than that Mitch would be here as soon as he could get away from his department. And that he'd put Jamie first unless it was absolutely imperative for a patient that he stay in the ED.

The doors swung wide and Lucas marched in, Mitch at his side looking quite cool and calm in his perfect suit with matching shirt and tie.

'Hey, sport.' Mitch crouched down by Jamie. 'How's my boy?'

'I want to go home.'

'As soon as we've talked with Dr Lucas, okay?'

Jodi's heart twisted at the love for Jamie emanating from Mitch's face. He had taken this whole situation from a place of shock and horror to something vibrant and caring. How had Mitch done it? It must've taken a massive amount of courage.

'Morning, Mitch,' she said quietly.

'Morning, Jodi.' He dipped his head abruptly in her direction before pushing Jamie's chair after Lucas. 'Let's get this under way.'

'Daddy, I don't want to see that man.'

What? Now? Shock slammed Jodi and she stumbled.

Mitch gaped at Jamie, then leaned down and brushed the hair out of Jamie's eyes with the gentlest of movements.

A quick glance at her showed shock and delight mingled in his beautiful blue eyes. Then he straightened up and continued pushing Jamie towards Lucas's office.

Jodi followed in a daze. Jamie had called Mitch Daddy for the first time. Why today, of all days? He'd had days to start saying Daddy and until now she'd not heard the slightest acknowledgement from Jamie that he understood Mitch's special place in his life.

Lucas let Mitch push the wheelchair through to his office before turning to Jodi. 'Are you all right, Jodi?'

'Of course. Jamie's got a very real chance now.'

Lucas caught her elbow to stop her moving forward. 'I don't know anything about the situation between you and Mitch other than you haven't had a relationship for a few years.'

'That's true.' If you didn't count the recent mind-blowing sex. Or that they were sharing his house. Make that had been until last night. Mitch must've slept over here because he hadn't come home at all during the night.

Lucas jiggled her arm. 'I'm probably speaking out of turn—no, I am definitely interfering—but it's important. Please give Mitch some space while he works through this. It's a huge undertaking to donate an organ and while he's willing to do it there are going to be moments when he'll wonder if he's going to be all right afterwards.'

'I understand.' It was great that Mitch had Lucas batting for him. And a shame that he thought she'd be impatient with Mitch while they got everything under way.

'And, Jodi…' Lucas paused and locked eyes with her. 'I'm thrilled for you and Jamie. There's sunshine coming for you. Now, let's get this show on the road.'

It was the first ever medical discussion about Jamie that Jodi sat through without saying a word unless asked a direct question.

She listened carefully as Lucas explained that Mitch would have some sessions with a counsellor before he signed the paperwork required. They discussed how long all this would take, but Lucas hoped to fast-track the last few ends that needed tying up.

'Then,' Lucas added, 'before you get totally excited, there's one final round of blood tests to be done before we go to Theatre. More often than not we don't find any problems at that stage. We'll have covered all the bases in the previous tests.'

Jamie grizzled as Lucas checked him over once more but with Mitch making faces at him and Lucas talking softly Jamie was soon smiling.

Jodi felt estranged from them all. Like she was in a vacuum. She'd got what she'd come to Auckland for: help to save Jamie's life. More specifically she'd got Mitch to offer his kidney. And yet it was as though she'd made a terrible mistake. Not for getting Jamie what he needed— hell, she'd even got him a father. But she'd lost Mitch. Really lost him for good this time. And there was only one person to blame. Herself.

The appointment seemed interminable but at last she was standing and pushing Jamie's wheelchair out of the small room. Mitch held the swing door open for her. He walked beside her down the long corridor to the lift. He pressed the buttons for the floors they both required. At level one he stepped out the moment the doors slid open.

Jodi watched his stiff gait, saw his hands clenching at his sides, and reached out to him with her hand. 'Mitch.'

He stopped, turned to face her. 'Yes?'

Whatever she'd been about to say froze in the chill pouring off him. Her mouth dried, her tongue stuck to the roof of her mouth. Her arm dropped to her side, effectively letting the doors close and the lift continue its downward journey. Down to the underground car park where she'd left Mitch's vehicle in his reserved slot.

Strapping Jamie in to his seat, she proceeded to take them back to Mitch's house, where Mitch's cleaning lady had country music blaring and the laundry flapping in the winter wind.

Inside the house she tucked Jamie into bed in Mitch's spare room and went to make a strong coffee with beans she'd bought the other day—one of the few things she'd contributed, and that had been more about her than Mitch.

Claire filled another mug and joined her in the dining room, where weak sunlight cut through the windows to create a semblance of warmth. Not that it reached the cold rock that was Jodi's heart.

'Hey.' Claire dropped heavily into a deep armchair, miraculously not spilling a drop of her coffee. 'You look pooped.'

That was putting it mildly. 'Try blind with lack of sleep.' The lethally strong coffee hit her stomach, sent her caffeine-craving senses into raptures. And set the drums in her head beating again.

'Mitch's starting to look a bit like you these days. Like you're both space trekking.' Claire sipped her well-milked coffee and winced. Her focus appeared to be on the small spider's web in the corner of the room. 'I used to think he ran on empty all the time and still managed to come up looking fabulous. But not anymore. When I saw him yesterday he looked like crap.'

Rub it in, why don't you? 'I'd say it's the worry about Jamie that's doing that.'

'You're probably right. He's used to working all those hours and dealing with everyone else's emergencies, not his own.'

Jodi stared at the woman. Had she been talking to Lucas

by any chance? Of course she hadn't. But two similar messages in one morning? Didn't they get it? She knew she'd messed up big time. What she didn't know was how to fix it. None of them had any answers there. 'It's not the same looking after someone who's a patient as it is looking after your own child.'

Claire changed the subject. Slightly. 'Fancy Mitch having a twin brother. It freaked me when you called him Max. I thought you were having me on.'

'That happened a lot at med school.'

'Did you ever make a mistake?' Claire grinned. 'Ever think you were with Mitch when it was actually Max?'

'Not once. I know the difference between Mitch and Max.' Max, who only the other day had told her she was strong. Because she fought for her son. So why wasn't she fighting for Mitch?

The phone in the kitchen rang. 'For you,' Claire said moments later. 'It's Mitch.'

Mitch was phoning her? Her heart rate lifted. 'Hi, Mitch. That was a positive meeting with Lucas.'

'I'm calling to inform you I'm flying to Sydney on Friday for two days. I'll email you my contact details so that you can reach me if something happens with Jamie.'

Sydney and his prestigious job. Of course. How silly of her to forget that.

Mitch dropped his phone on his desk and ran his hands over his stubbly chin. 'Going to the pack, boyo.'

'Talking to yourself now.' Aaron stood in the doorway.

'Come in and take a pew.' Mitch waved at him. 'You sure this is all right? Me disappearing for a couple of days?'

'No worries.' Aaron turned the chair around and straddled it. 'How'd the meeting go with the boss?'

The big boss. 'It's going to work out just fine.' For who? Him? Jamie? Or Jodi?

'Good. I like what you're doing. For purely selfish reasons, of course.' Aaron talked shop for a bit then stood up. 'Coming to the farewell bash the TV crew are putting on? It looks impressive. Probably because they overstayed their welcome by a week.'

'I guess I'm expected to. At least that's one thing done and dusted.' Thankfully Carl had seen reason and stopped harassing him about doing a clip on Jamie.

'Then shift your butt. Kick-off is in thirty minutes. You could do with some spit and polish before then. Can't have the HOD turning up looking like something the dog chewed. They'd probably film you just for the hell of it.'

Mitch rolled his eyes. 'Bloody chirpy, aren't you?'

'Got what I want, didn't I?'

Mitch flapped a hand at his colleague, and the guy who'd become a good friend. 'Get out of here. I'll see you shortly.'

'I'll come looking for you if you're late.'

'Getting far too clever for your own good, Dr Simmonds,' he called at Aaron's rapidly disappearing back.

Aaron flipped him the bird and continued down the corridor.

Mitch unfolded himself from his chair and stretched his back, easing the kinks in his spine. Jamming his hands into his trouser pockets, he crossed to the window to stare out at the busy street below. End-of-day rush hour traffic queued for lights, going nowhere in a hurry.

Last thing Friday he'd fly to Sydney. A quick trip. If everything went to plan he might even make a flight back late the next day. The thought of being out of the country when Jamie could take a turn for the worse worried him more than anything. But he had to go. No way around it. Not and keep his reputation from being ripped to shreds.

'What does your rep matter if you don't have the two most important people back in your life?'

He'd worked too hard to let it go easily, even if it wasn't the most important aspect of his life anymore.

He muttered to himself, 'You're working at keeping Jodi and Jamie around for long? Or just until the operation is over and done with?'

No, that was only the beginning of everything. Jamie would be well, able to do all the things little boys did. The kid would have a future, a long future. He'd be able to grow up and decide what he wanted to be as an adult.

'There'll always be the side effects of anti-rejection drugs.' He continued his monologue.

A small price to pay for Jamie's life. As long as someone explained it all to him thoroughly and often. Mitch pinched his lips together.

'That's my role. Among others.' From now on, Jamie had a dad. A father who was never going to leave him to grow up with another male figure. A father who'd put his child first, over everything else.

'And Jodi?'

Yeah, well. Lots of work to do there. Did he even want to try? Risk not being believed, not being listened to and actually heard?

Jodi had cut him right through to his heart with her accusations about not coming home when he'd said he would. It wasn't that she'd made a mistake that got to him. It was that she hadn't given him the opportunity to explain first. Neither had she believed he might've changed.

Hell, when it came to Jamie he'd got up to speed in a very short time. Accepting that Jamie was his. No questions asked. Okay, not many. After the initial shock he'd had no doubt that the boy was his.

And he'd put his kidney on notice for Jamie. Which was what Jodi had wanted all along. What was a guy supposed to do? Beg forgiveness for an argument that was three years old?

Whether Jodi noticed or not, he had changed. Was still changing. He was making plans for the future that involved all of them. Those plans would continue.

CHAPTER TWELVE

JODI'S CELLPHONE VIBRATED on her hip, waking her from a doze. Tugging it free, she read 'Mitch calling' and flicked the phone open.

Exhaling a deep breath, she said, 'Hello. You got my text?' In her worried frame of mind she'd feared it mightn't have reached Mitch in Sydney.

'How bad is he?' Blunt and to the point. No change there.

Jodi glanced at Jamie lying with tubes seemingly coming out of every aperture he had, and then some. The white hospital sheets made him look paler than he already was. 'He's got a fever, higher temperature than last time we were here. He's been on dialysis all day and it doesn't look like Lucas will stop that for a while yet. Basically he's getting worse and there's no stopping it.' She knew the despair in her voice would reach him and that made her feel guilty. But she couldn't help it.

'Hang in there, Jodi. Everything will work out. I promise.'

How can he promise that? 'Sure.'

'I'll get home as soon as possible.'

'Mitch, wait. Do what you have to do. Getting back a day earlier isn't going to change anything here.' Except give me the strength and courage to carry on watching over my boy.

'I want to be with Jamie. And you. I'm missing you both.'

Really? Missing me? Mitch had said that? 'Um, great. Looking forward to your arrival.' *I'll be counting the hours, except I haven't a clue what flight you're booked on.* 'What time tomorrow do you get in?'

The dial tone answered her. He'd hung up. Right. Okay. Now what? Mitch was heading home to Jamie—and her. Did that mean he'd give her a chance to apologise properly? Would he give her a second chance?

She hoped so because she had news for Mitch. Once Jamie had his transplant and had recovered, they were moving to Sydney, too. If possible she'd find a flat near Mitch so he could spend lots of time with Jamie. She'd get work at a local medical centre. And they could both take active parts in raising their son.

'Go to the on-call room and get some decent sleep.'

For a moment Jodi thought Mitch had got back early. She lifted her head and blinked in the half-light of a ward full of sleeping patients. 'Max?' In her dazed state his deep voice had sounded so like his brother's. 'What are you doing here?'

'I heard Jamie had been readmitted.'

'So you wanted to check up on him?' Cool. Max couldn't deny he was an uncle. All the right instincts seemed to have kicked in.

'Seriously, go and grab something for dinner, then put your head down for a while. I'll sit with Jamie until Lucas finishes surgery, which should be by eight o'clock.'

'What has Lucas and surgery got to do with Jamie?' Had she missed something here?

'Lucas says you need a break and there's no one else to sit with Jamie so he's coming as soon as he can.'

Huh? Mr Lucas Harrington was going to sit with her boy for a few hours? 'Heck. He doesn't have to do that.' She studied Max. 'Neither do you.'

'Can't have people thinking Maitlands are no good at looking out for their own. Jamie's my family, too.' He gave her an eloquent shrug. 'I know that much.'

Cool. But—

'You look whacked. Don't want Mitch seeing you like this.' Max sat on the end of the bed and reached to brush her hair out of her eyes. 'Do you trust me with Jamie?'

'Why wouldn't I?'

'Then why are you still here?'

The pillow was soft and tucked around her neck to keep the cool air out. The sheets were heavy and crisp. Luxury after sleeping huddled in a chair by Jamie's bed last night. She rolled on her side and tucked her knees up, wrapped her arms across her breasts.

Half an hour more and then she'd relieve Lucas. Or was it Max? Her eyelids dropped shut.

Mitch immediately wandered into her mind. Laughing Mitch with Jamie, holding his boy ever so carefully. Angry Mitch walking away with a bottle in his hand. Mitch with his feet up on his desk snoring as though there was nothing in the world that could disturb him, only to wake up to hell.

She yawned and stretched her legs, pulled the covers tighter and snuggled further down into the bed. If only Mitch was here now to hold her while she slept, or to make love to her. Those strong yet gentle hands on her skin would stroke her alight, would take her places where all the worries couldn't follow for a short while. That muscular body would slide over her as he entered her and she could feel his heat, her heat mingling.

Oh, Mitch.

A hand rocked her gently. 'Hey, Jodi, wake up.' A persistent voice from her dream spoke too loudly.

She blinked, snuggled back into the pillow.

'Jodi.'

What? Mitch? For real? Not a dream? She sat straight up, and Mitch had to jerk back to avoid their heads clashing. 'You're not due back till later.'

'I swapped flights. I was already at the airport when I called you.' He handed her a mug. 'Instant only. I'm sorry.'

'No problem.' She placed the mug on the floor and got out of the bed to pull on her jeans and jersey.

Mitch didn't even look at her. Which only went to show how bad things were. She asked, 'Is Jamie sleeping?'

'Yes. Max is sitting with him for a few minutes while I came to see you.'

She blinked. 'He sent me in here hours ago.'

'Sent Lucas home, too. Seems Max quite likes babysitting his nephew.' Mitch looked bewildered.

She changed the subject. 'How did Sydney go? Did you do everything you wanted?'

'Yes, I did.'

The coffee wasn't flash but she drank it down before her shaking hands dumped most of it over her jeans. Then, 'Mitch, I'd like to move to Sydney when all this is over so that Jamie can be near you. He needs both of us in his life—all the time.'

'Yes, he does.' Mitch stood up, paced the three steps to the door and turned, his face relaxed and open. 'I'm not going to be taking up that position. I went across to talk to the general manager of the hospital and explained the situation. I also had to cancel the lease on an apartment

I'd arranged and tidy up a few things so I didn't leave a bad taste in anyone's mouth.'

'What? You're staying in New Zealand?' When he nodded, she asked, 'Where? Haven't you been replaced here?' Why was he doing this?

'The board hasn't decided on a candidate for my job; they're still doing interviews. I've been told I can stay on. So would you consider moving to Auckland rather than Sydney?'

'Of course.'

'You haven't even thought about it,' he pointed out.

'Nothing to think about. You're giving up your prestigious job. That's huge.' She would be giving up a job she enjoyed but hadn't been able to give her full attention to anyway. And then there was Mum. Who knew what Mum would do? But one thing was certain—she'd approve of this.

'It wasn't that hard. It feels right, good even. I want to get everything right with Jamie. I want to be a great dad.'

'Thank you.' Tears blurred her vision. A part of her was happy, happy for Jamie.

He returned to sit opposite her, took the mug out of her hands. Then he folded his hands around hers. Warmth seeped into her, giving her strength and courage.

'Mitch, I got it all wrong. I didn't give you a chance. I guess I hadn't learned how much you've changed, didn't want to admit you're not the man I knew three years ago. I seem to have fallen into my old habits when I'm around you and so I expect that you're doing the same. I blew it. I'm sorry.'

His fingers squeezed her tight. 'It's okay. I get that. And it doesn't matter anymore.'

Her heart dropped. So there'd be nothing developing between them. Their up-close-and-personal encounters weren't going to be repeated. Unless she was honest. About everything.

She tugged her hands free and stood up, stepping around him while her brain worked overtime. Finally she said, 'I loved you last time. I never said so because I felt vulnerable. I understood enough about you to know you wouldn't stay for the long haul. But I loved you and when I packed your bags it nearly killed me.

'I thought I'd got over you. But I hadn't. I haven't. Coming here, seeing you again, being with you, talking, making love, even arguing, I feel complete. I still love you. I've never stopped. I—I wondered if we could try again.'

A smile broke across his mouth, his whole face, into his eyes. He reached for her and sat her on his lap. His hands cupped her face. 'Try keeping me away.' His lips brushed hers. 'You're the only woman who makes my knees knock or my heart skip. I've always loved you right from that first date when you spilled your red wine over my grey suit. You were so embarrassed because it was the only suit I owned and I had an interview the next morning.'

'Do you have to remind me?' He loved her. That had to be good, didn't it?

'You still owe me.' His smile widened into a grin. Then he grew serious. 'Jodi Hawke, I love you with all my heart. Do you think we deserve a second shot at our relationship? Will you marry me?'

Her eyes widened while inside her heart swelled with love. 'Yes,' she breathed. Leaning in, she covered his mouth with hers and repeated, 'Yes.'

He kissed her back long and hard, before pulling away. 'We've got a tough time ahead with Jamie and the transplant, but I was hoping we could get married as soon as possible. A very quiet, private service. Just you, me and Jamie. Your mum, even Max.' He stopped, sucked a breath.

'I'd feel more comfortable knowing we were legally together before I have the surgery.'

'Yes, definitely, if that's what you want.' Tears spurted from the corners of her eyes. So the surgery worried him. Yet he'd do it for his child. A true father.

There was a knock and the door flew open. 'Mitch, sorry to barge in but you're needed in the ED. Now.' The man in blue scrubs nodded at Jodi. 'Hi, I'm Aaron, Mitch's second in charge. There's been an accident on the Harbour Bridge involving three cars. We've got three priorities due within the next five minutes.'

Jodi leapt up so Mitch could stand. 'Go, Mitch. I'll be with Jamie.' She reached up and kissed him quickly. 'Yes. Absolutely yes.'

Aaron said over his shoulder as they tore along the corridor to the stairwell, 'Bad timing, huh?'

'For me, yes; for the patients, no. An extra specialist might make a difference for one of them.' Jodi loved him. Holy Toledo. They were getting married. Next week if he could get everything organised.

'So no more plans to leave us?' Aaron shoved the fire door open, shot through.

Mitch was right on his heels. 'Not in the foreseeable future.' His future involved family now. He grinned despite the urgency driving him down the stairs to his department.

The first ambulance was unloading as they reached the department. 'Yours,' Aaron told him.

'Right.' He followed the stretcher being wheeled straight into Resus.

The paramedic handed over the PRF. 'Janet Lees, twenty-four years old. Driver of one of the cars. Hit the side window with her head when the car spun. High blood loss from femoral artery.'

Nurses and interns stepped up, suctioning the patient's mouth, swapping the oxygen supply from the ambulance tank to theirs, putting in lines for fluids, applying pressure to that artery. Organised chaos reigned. Mitch oversaw everything, making decisions, ordering X-rays, working to stem the blood loss from the torn artery.

Phoning a neurologist, he said, 'Tom, I think we've got a severe brain injury due to trauma. Can you come down?'

A couple of minutes later Tom Grady blew in like a winter wind, immediately reaching for the report form and the latest obs. And Mitch continued doing everything possible to save Janet Grady's life.

But an hour later he had to step back and listen to Tom. The news was grim.

He said, 'We'll put her on life support and send her up to IC. The family will need time with her.'

Mitch sucked a breath. And swore long and hard under his breath. Tragic deaths happened. But he hated them.

The family would be asked if they wanted Janet to be an organ donor. Donation was a gift. More than one gift to more than one desperate person. But how did families make this decision at the worst possible time of their lives? He'd dealt with other cases where the patient had gone on life support until the organ retrieval team had done their thing, and he'd accepted it for what it was. Death giving life. Someone's loss giving another person a better chance at a future. Nothing wrong with that. Hell, he was signed up as a donor if something happened to him. He'd gone as far as making sure his adoptive family knew and understood his wishes. But now he suddenly found it entirely different, that the right thing to do wasn't that easy.

More than that, he finally really understood why parents might say no. Mitch took one last look at the young woman as she was wheeled out of his department and wondered which way her parents would react. Sometimes life sucked.

Handing over, he headed for the shower. He threw his filthy scrubs at the basket. Missed. Shoved the tap hard to the right. Leapt under the water. Leapt out again. 'Bloody cold.'

Thank goodness Jodi had brought Jamie to him. Thank goodness he could save his boy without anyone having paid the ultimate price.

The water was warming. He stepped into the shower again and tipped his face under the water, let it stream down his body. He needed to cleanse away the smells of the ED, then he needed Jodi's arms around him.

Jodi was curled up in a chair beside Jamie's bed when she saw Lucas walk in. 'It's two in the morning. Why aren't you at home?'

Mitch appeared behind him, looking dreadful. Not just exhausted but hollowed out. Despair oozed out of him as he met Jodi's gaze.

A trembling started deep inside her. 'No.' Her head swung from side to side. 'No.' She wasn't ready. Hadn't prepared for this enough. 'No.'

'Jodi?' Mitch lifted her into his arms and held her tight. 'It's all right, sweetheart. Everything's going to be fine.'

She'd never be ready. Jamie needed a new kidney to survive. She'd signed the papers, understood the consequences and risks, wanted it for him. But she wasn't ready for her boy to go under the knife. To have such major surgery. 'He's too little. Too frail.'

'He's tough. He's a Hawke. He's a Maitland.' Mitch spoke with conviction. With tenderness and understanding.

She shifted in his arms, looked for Lucas. 'Tell me.'

Lucas was sitting on the end of Jamie's bed, watching her. 'There's been an accident in Nelson. Two people died and one is an organ donor. The retrieval crew are on their way down there. We'll know more in a couple of hours. But, Jodi, you have to prepare yourself. It could be a match.'

Under her hands she felt Mitch's chest rising and falling far too rapidly. 'Mitch?'

His chest rose high and stuck there. Then as his lungs slowly let the air out he said, loudly and clearly, 'Lucas, phone Max and get him and his team in here. He'd be coming to do the op anyway. But he'll be taking one of my kidneys for Jamie. It's time to do it. We were only waiting for one more counselling session. I don't see the point. I'm ready.'

Lucas nodded. 'Fair enough. Your kidney is a far better option for our lad here anyway. It's a go, then. I'll go and make some calls.' He stood up and looked from Jamie to Mitch to her. 'Jodi, you're going to have the hardest job of all of us. You have to sit around waiting.'

For both my men. She wanted to shout at the world for letting this happen in the first place. She wanted to cry and fold into Mitch for his strength. She wanted to pick Jamie up out of his bed and run.

Instead she straightened her spine and looked first at Mitch and then Lucas. 'Think what I've got. Mitch and Jamie. How can I not be okay? I'll be like a soccer mum, cheering and encouraging from the sidelines.' Gulp. At least she'd got that out without a quaver in her voice to give her away. Her stomach turned over, wanting to reject the meal she'd eaten hours ago. No way. Not now. She sucked her belly in against her backbone. She was strong. And today she'd just have to be even stronger.

'I'll be back when I know more.' Lucas headed for the door, turned back. 'Mitch, nil by mouth from now on, eh?'

Mitch nodded slowly and sank down on a chair, pulling Jodi with him. The reality was hitting home. This time tomorrow he'd have one kidney and Jamie would be on the road to a full recovery. 'It's happening.'

'Faster than you'd thought.' Jodi brushed a lock of hair behind his ear. Love radiated from her eyes. Love for him.

'Better that way. The decision's been made, nothing to wait for. It's not as though I need to listen to that counsellor spouting on about what my emotions are going to be doing. I get it. Time to get on with the whole damned process.' So stop raving and give Jodi your undivided attention. Support her.

Under his hands he could feel the occasional tremor rock through her body. But she sat straight, not melding into him. There was confidence in her face, that earlier fear long gone. Amazingly brave. Because she really would go through hell when he and Jamie were wheeled away to Theatre.

Mitch wrapped his arms around her and dropped his chin on the top of her head, smelt the lavender of her shampoo, remembered the night he'd woken up to find her in his office. She'd brought him so much. She'd given him a life worth living. How did he thank her for that? A lifetime together, cherishing her, would not be enough.

'One step at a time, boyo.'

'What are you talking about?' Jodi mumbled against his neck.

'Thinking that our wedding will have to wait a few days.'

She sat so she could meet his gaze full on. 'We could try to get a special licence, if that's what you want.'

He shook his head. 'I think we've got enough to deal with.'

'Mitch, we're a family now. A piece of paper isn't going

to change that.' She kissed her finger tip, placed it on his lips. 'I love you. More than you can imagine.'

He kissed her finger and tapped it on her lips. 'And I love you. We've got each other, and our son. We're as married as anyone who has said their vows.'

His mouth covered hers to give her a kiss full of love. A kiss that would get them through what lay ahead. A kiss that sealed them together. For ever.

Max stood in the doorway, watching Mitch holding Jodi, understanding, in his role of transplant surgeon, what they were all about to go through. The time had come.

His heart swelled—for Jamie, Jodi and Mitch.

And for himself.

How he'd manage it he didn't know, but he swore that once Jamie was out of danger, he would talk to Mitch.

Really talk to him. About the lives they'd both lived after they'd been separated. And hopefully one day in the not-too-distant future, he might be able to meet Mitch at The Shed for a friendly drink.

* * * * *

HOW TO RESIST
A HEARTBREAKER

BY

LOUISA GEORGE

To Christine
With best wishes!
Louisa George ♥

MILLS & BOON

First published in Great Britain 2013
by Mills & Boon, an imprint of Harlequin (UK) Limited.
Harlequin (UK) Limited, Eton House, 18-24 Paradise Road,
Richmond, Surrey TW9 1SR

© Louisa George 2013

ISBN: 978 0 263 89902 3

Harlequin (UK) policy is to use papers that are natural, renewable and recyclable products and made from wood grown in sustainable forests. The logging and manufacturing process conform to the legal environmental regulations of the country of origin.

Printed and bound in Spain
by Blackprint CPI, Barcelona

A lifelong reader of most genres, **Louisa George** discovered romance novels later than most, but immediately fell in love with the intensity of emotion, the high drama and the family focus of Mills & Boon® Medical Romance™.

With a Bachelors Degree in Communication and a nursing qualification under her belt, writing medical romance seemed a natural progression, and the perfect combination of her two interests. And making things up is a great way to spend the day!

An English ex-pat, Louisa now lives north of Auckland, New Zealand, with her husband, two teenage sons and two male cats. Writing romance is her opportunity to covertly inject a hefty dose of pink into her heavily testosterone-dominated household. When she's not writing or researching Louisa loves to spend time with her family and friends, enjoys travelling, and adores great food. She's also hopelessly addicted to Zumba®.

PROLOGUE

'WE HAVE A DONOR.' Max Maitland put his hand on his brother's shoulder. A first step to making things right between them all. God knew, they needed it. That, plus a hefty dose of courage and his surgical skills.

Little Jamie's life depended on this being a success. Failure wasn't an option. Not now. Not when so much was at stake.

'Yes, we do have a donor.' Mitchell's eyes lit up with hope as they walked towards the nurses' station. 'Me.'

'What? No. There was an accident—the kidney's being flown in. We have to run some tests, but first thoughts are that everything's compatible.' Max couldn't risk his brother on the operating table too. 'I'll be the principal transplant surgeon, obviously. We're just waiting for the rest of the team.'

'No. I want to do this. I want to donate my kidney to my son. I have to do this, goddamit.' Mitch's Adam's apple bobbed up and down as he swallowed. He gripped the edge of the desk, knuckles blanching.

Max knew how hard coming to terms with being a father had been for his brother. Harder still to learn the child he'd only just met would die without urgent help.

Dragging him away from the screaming telephones, the bleeping monitor and babies' wails, Max looked Mitch squarely in the eye. The steel gaze he knew was mirrored in his own eyes bored into him. Eyes so eerily identical to his. Maitland eyes. The same ones Jamie had. His nephew. *His brother's son.*

Max's chest tightened. How long had he wished for this kind of connection with his own flesh and blood? How many nights had passed in a fit of fantasy—about a family with people who cared, who believed in him?

Now Max could do something to make a difference, bridge that gap between himself and his estranged twin—make a real family. 'Are you sure? You know the risks? It's major surgery.'

'I know that I'm a positive match. I know that adult-to-child transplants work best. That living donors work better. I know I'd do anything. Anything. For my child.'

Max nodded. In the Maitland gene pool determination beat anything else hands down. Stubbornness came a close second, which meant he hadn't a hope of changing his brother's mind. But he had to try. 'Let's see what the tests show on this donor kidney. Then we'll take it from there.'

'No. Give it to someone else.'

'This is a good chance for Jamie. Donors are few and far between. At least wait and see…'

Mitch shook his head, sucked in air. 'Would you do that for your child? Would you wait to see if things panned out okay? To see if the higher chances of tissue rejection from an unrelated donor made him sick again? Watch him suffer when you could easily make things better for him? Or would you give him the best chance? Would you do it?' *For your nephew? For me?*

Mitch didn't have to say the words. Years of frustration and jealousy, anger and grief hovered round them tainted with the thick disinfectant smell that coated everything in the hospital ward. *Would you put yourself on the line for your family?* Even if that family was something you hadn't spent a whole lot of time with.

Without hesitation Max answered. 'Of course I would. I'll make it work.'

CHAPTER ONE

THE SHED PUMPED with the throb of techno beat. A deep bass rhythm resonated off Max's ribcage, as if the music came from within him. Hard. Loud. Raw. Through a glass door leading out back he saw silhouetted people dancing, arms punching the air, the way he wanted to right now. The way he felt whenever surgery had been a success. But today—hell, nothing came close to that kind of buzz.

Mission accomplished.

Bill, the barman, nodded towards the bottles in the fridge. 'Hey, Max. Usual?'

'Sure. Line them up.'

'Celebrating?'

'I think so.' It paid to be cautious. The first twenty-four hours were often the decider, although with transplants the decider could be years down the track. He'd laid it all out to Mitch and Jodi, plain and simple; Jamie's operation had resulted in a functioning kidney, but a lot could still go wrong. Too much.

He didn't want to go there. Emotions had no place in a surgeon's work and in his career he'd always managed that—but saving his nephew's life? That was all kinds of different.

Bill slid the beer bottle across the bar, his eyebrows raised in understanding. The great boutique beer, plus the fact the staff never asked questions or gave advice, was the reason The Shed was Max's home away from home. After a heavy day of intense surgery he relished the chance to de-stress the best way he could in familiar surroundings, followed by some kind of hot physical workout—a bed was optional.

Here in the public bar there was no one save a couple from the phlebotomy unit and a single woman a few seats down with her back to him. A mass of thick dark curls covered her shoulders.

His gaze drifted down her straight back, stopping short at the taut line of the black long-sleeved blouse stretched across her spine. Her dress was more funereal than fun, so much so he wondered why she'd be in party central. Most girls here showed far more skin. Intrigued, his gaze travelled over the narrow dip of her waist. The flair of her skirt over a decent amount of hip. The right amount.

He imagined running his palm over those curves.

Running a cool hand over the back of his neck instead, he eased the tension in his shoulders. Man. After eight hours of surgery his hyped muscles needed a release. And he knew the perfect way.

A quick drink first. Then hit the back bar. Then... maybe...who knew? The night was still young.

'Barman? Excuse me? Hey.' The curls shivered as the woman raised her hand. 'Excuse me. Another mojito, please.'

Bill's pupils widened as he leaned across the bar to Max, his voice low. 'Been here an hour. Had three already.'

Following Bill's line of vision, Max caught a view of her face. In an urgent and acute response something twisted in his gut, tightened with an awareness that was full and powerful. Hell. It had been a long time since he'd had that kind of immediate reaction to a woman.

Her hair framed a soft face, kissable lips with a smattering of red lipstick. Almost perfect features—cute nose, a dusting of freckles. She was the kind of woman any man would give a second glance to. And most would chance a third. But the clip in her voice screamed that she was a woman not to be messed with.

So of course his interest ratcheted up the scale. Fiery women always presented a challenge. And, boy, did Max love a challenge. He hadn't become Auckland's most successful transplant surgeon without pushing a few boundaries.

Okay—a lot of boundaries.

She caught him looking at her but he refused to look away.

Her eyes. Wow. Large, dark, almond-shaped, glittering with something. Hurt? Anger?

Which in itself was a warning sign. But, hell, a conversation didn't mean a whole lot of anything. And if it went further—he'd lay out his intentions from the get-go. Starting with nothing deep and meaningful. Ending with don't ask for forever.

Max leaned across the bar to Bill. 'Is she waiting for someone? Been stood up?'

The barman shook his head. 'Nah. Don't think so. She hasn't checked her phone or looked at her watch.'

Good. Not stepping on anyone's toes. He didn't break that brotherhood code as easily as others. As easily as Mitchell had. Max raised his beer to her. 'Tough day?'

'And getting tougher by the minute.' She took her refreshed drink and turned her back to him.

'Okay, I get it. You don't want to talk, right?'

Swivelling round, she gave him a full-tilt death stare. Definitely anger in her eyes. Hurt was a distant cousin. 'Gee, whatever gave you that idea? Very sorry, but my back's not feeling very chatty tonight.' She turned away again, but not quite as far as she'd gone before.

'Watch you don't get whiplash with all the swivelling around.' He caught her profile. The uplift of her chin. Tight lips.

And very possibly the hint of smile.

He'd been on the verge of leaving, but the fading smile reeled him in.

Never one to admit defeat, he slid into the seat next to her, determined to make that smile last a little longer. 'It's okay. We don't have to talk.'

'Get out of here. Really?' Her ribcage rose and fell quickly as she turned to face him, slim fingers running a diamond locket along a thin silver chain at her throat.

Her dark gaze slid from his face down his body and back again. 'People actually say that? Is it from *Cheesy Pick-ups for Dummies*?' She held up her hand. 'Wait. No. It's a phone app, right? *Lame Lines for Getting Laid.*'

'Ouch. Cruel. I'm mortally wounded.' He touched his heart for effect. 'Actually, it's from *Just trying to be friendly dot com.* But forget it. I'll leave you in peace.'

She blinked. 'No. I'm sorry. Come on, hit me with another line.'

'That was my best shot. I'm all out.' He winked, took his phone out and whispered, 'Quick. Help me out here. What was that app called again?'

'Yeah, right. Like you'd need it.' She laughed. The glitter in her eyes turned to one of humour. Her mouth kicked up at the corners—she was fighting it, but he'd made her laugh. And that gave him a sharp punch of pride to his gut. She clearly got a kick out of the sparring and, hell, judging by the effect of that smile on his libido, so did he.

Her eyebrows lifted. 'You must have some more lines? Surely? Tell you what—you try them on me and I'll rate them out of ten. Then no other poor unsuspecting woman has to put up with the bad ones.'

'Okay.' He took a slug of beer and rose to the bait. If it meant a few more minutes laughing with her, then game on. Then he'd go out back. 'My friend's all-time favourite was "Hey, darling, do your legs hurt from running through my dreams all night?"'

'No. No. No. Stop. Running away from a nightmare, more like.' She grimaced and put her fingers in her ears. 'That's terrible. A very poor three. Please don't tell me people actually use that?' Her head tipped back a little as she laughed.

He was mesmerised by the delicate curve of her throat. Imagined placing a kiss in the dip lined with the silver chain. When she leaned forward again he got a delicate scent of flowers. Made him want to inhale way more deeply than he should.

Boy, he definitely needed to get out more.

She shook her head. 'Was that your best shot? You are so bad at this.'

'Thank God, I've never needed them. Obviously.'

'The worst one I ever heard was "Is your dad a baker? Because you've got a nice set of buns."' She snorted into her drink, then pointed to her face. 'Hey. Eyes up here.'

'Clearly he was a good judge of…character.' Max reluctantly dragged his gaze from the swell of her blouse-covered breasts back to her smiling mouth. Whatever shadows had been haunting her when he'd arrived had gone. Her eyes shone clear and bright. Job done. 'Seriously, you just looked like you could do with cheering up.'

'And you voted yourself cheerleader? How sweet.' Her eyes narrowed and she pointed at him. 'But I was managing just fine without the benefit of your help. Now you should go. Thank you.'

Huh? This was new. He hadn't been knocked back for a very long time.

Adrenalin pumped round his veins. Instinct told him they could have fun together—and his instinct was rarely wrong. That and the fact he always liked to win meant he'd have to up his game. The chase usually lasted all of two seconds once they knew who he was, what he did. 'And yet here you are, *smiling*...er?' He held out his hand. 'I'm Max.'

'Max...' She paused, clicked her fingers together. 'Max...Max Maitland. You're that guy. Thought I'd seen you before.'

'Seen me where?' Because he sure as hell hadn't seen her. He'd have remembered.

'I had my first-day orientation on the paediatric high dependency unit today. While you were doing your rounds I looked after little Jamie for a few hours. He's gorgeous.'

'Yes. Yes, he is.' A weird tightness squeezed his chest. He breathed it out, chalked it up to the long day. He'd just left Jamie sleeping soundly in his mother's arms, tubes and drains permitting. He'd looked so small, still a baby really. Renal failure sucked at any age—but at three? The world wasn't fair. He quickly checked his phone. No messages. No news was good news. 'He's my nephew.'

'I get that. Same name. Same eyes. Cute kid. That must have been hard, watching your nephew fighting for his life then having to operate on him. Takes guts.'

The guardedness she'd had in her eyes relaxed a little as she watched him. She held his gaze as if weighing him up—no, more, as if she could see right through to his core. A hazy connection snapped between them—he sensed she understood some of what he'd been through.

Weird. The women he usually met only wanted a good time, a turn on his boat, expensive dinners, the high life

of a successful surgeon. None of them ever saw past the
label and the cash. Certainly none of them had X-rayed
his soul before.

Her lips formed a small pout. 'You did good today.
Very good.'

He leaned in. 'That's because I am good.'

'Now, that's better. Rising up the scale, Mr Maitland—
maybe an eight.' Raw need flared behind her gaze. Her
lips parted a little as she ran the tip of her tongue along
her bottom lip.

This was dodgy territory.

Mixing business with pleasure was a definite no. Too
much gossip, too much to live up to. Hell, he'd had enough
of that.

And yet…there was something simmering between
them. A tension building, an awareness they both acknowl-
edged, if not with words then with those fleeting looks.
Like a gathering storm, intense, alive with static.

Then the connection fractured as she frowned. 'But I
know all about men like you. Big-shot surgeon. Work too
hard. No time for friends or relationships.' She glanced at
his hand. 'No wedding band. No one to go home to—or
you'd be there already. You just want something quick and
hot and uncomplicated.'

And now she was stamping on a raw nerve. No woman
had ever challenged him so blatantly. Pure lust fired inside him. He whispered in her ear. 'You reckon you fit
the picture?'

'Not today. So if you don't mind, I need a little privacy.'
She held her glass out to Bill. 'Another one, please.'

Max didn't want to ask why she was so intent on getting tanked. The woman was free to do what she liked. She
certainly looked as if she could handle herself. In truth, the

less he knew about her the better—that way things could stay strictly professional.

But his interest was way off the scale.

He wrapped his hand over her wrist, gently pulling the glass onto the bar. His fingers were drawn to her hand. He turned it over and rubbed her palm with his thumb. Checked for wedding rings. None. Good. The static jumped and buzzed around them at his touch. 'Don't you think you should be slowing down?' And why did he care?

Her fingers shook free and the frown deepened. 'Seriously? I've had four drinks. I can still walk, talk and count. No big deal. Don't bust a gut over me. This is a once-a-year indulgence I allow myself. I'm having a ball, so don't go spoiling my party.'

He wanted to ask why. Why once a year—what had happened? Why here? Why the hell had things aligned for him to bump into her today, when he needed something, as she'd so rightly said, hot and quick. With her it felt complicated already, not least because they were going to be colleagues. And there was that thing...that invisible tug between them. 'Hey, I'm a transplant surgeon. Livers fail. I worry.'

'Oh, sweetie. Don't.' Her mouth twitched. 'Once a year. The rest of the time I'm a saint.'

'Well, lucky I found you tonight, then. Your liver will be eternally grateful.'

'Sure it will. But my brain will never forgive you.' Gabby shook her head. The man was beyond irritating. Okay, she conceded, and not a little gorgeous with his dark messy hair, tight black jeans and startling blue eyes that drew her gaze every time she looked in his direction. They were a deep-set, mesmerising, intense blue framed by eyelashes bordering on illegally long.

Not to mention the way his white shirt clung to thick biceps and broad shoulders dragging her eyes to his body.

She tried to ignore the fire smouldering in her belly as he touched her hand.

But really? The man was rude and way too self-assured. Six feet plus of trouble.

His reputation went before him—first time she'd had an orientation that had come with a health warning—Max Maitland, legendary surgeon, serial heartbreaker.

If she hadn't seen the softening in him at the mention of Jamie she'd have believed the hype—chalked him up as a self-centred charmer.

She had to admire him, though. He could spar as well as she could. But his ego was spilling out of that crisp cotton shirt. From previous ugly experience she'd erased over-confident and über-charming from the list of qualities she liked in a man. Nonna had been right about one thing, men just couldn't be trusted.

She rolled her eyes. 'Next time I need some advice from the fun police I'll know who to call.'

'And I'll make sure I'm right there in my superhero outfit.'

'I so did not need an image of you with your undies over your trousers.' She shrugged, stifling a laugh, trying hard not to look at the way those jeans hugged his long legs. His perfect backside. Fascinating.

'It's the twenty-first century. We don't do outfits like that anymore. I'll let you into a secret…' He finished his beer. 'We *transform*.'

She mustered indifference, holding her laugh back. 'I'm only interested if you transform me another mojito.'

'A virgin mojito for sure.' He motioned to Bill to bring an alcohol-free drink despite her protests. 'Er… I still don't know your name.'

'You are very annoying.' And damned gorgeous, and way off-limits. And all the things she'd been warned about. And funny and sexy, too, and there was that strange pull to him that she was trying to ignore. But they were going to be working together so he'd find out her name soon enough. 'Charge Nurse Radley. Gabby, to my friends.'

'Well, Gabby, pleased to meet you.' He stuck out a hand. 'Do you have any interesting secrets you'd like to share?'

Not even if hell froze over. She'd moved to Auckland to restart her life, not relive it. Freedom. At last. Space of her own. No one to tell her what to do.

She regarded his hand with as much disdain as she could muster. God, she'd met her match here. Most men had run a mile by now.

In another life this could be fun. He could be fun.

Dodging his question, she bristled. 'Like I said, you don't get to call me Gabby. I'm Charge Nurse Radley.'

'*Gabby*. So that is Gabrielle? Gabriell*a*?' His grin widened as she stuck her tongue out. It was as if he knew exactly which buttons to press, and definitely how to tease. 'Ah, Gabriella, your eyes give so much away. Nice name, and I'll stick with Gabby, thanks.'

'Are you this forward with everyone or is it just me?'

'Considering it's your first day in a new job, I'd have thought you'd want to make a good impression.' He laughed, his chin jutting up. 'Here's a hint— you could make it easier for people to get to know you.'

'I do, usually. Just not people like you.' And not today, when she just wanted to be left alone. 'Don't worry, I can do professional and competent. Tomorrow.'

'I can't wait. Any more frostiness and we'll need to increase the central heating. I'll make sure I pack a scarf.' He checked her half-empty glass and then his watch. His smile turned from friendly to insanely wicked. '*Gabby*, you've got the wrong impression of me. Or you're delu-sional. Or drunk. Whichever, clearly you're a danger to yourself. So, if you're done, I'm taking you home.'

'Whoa, buster. You are not.' She'd had enough of peo-ple telling her what to do. 'I'm not ready to go home…' She paused.

Home? Where the heck was that? Certainly not the new shared flat she'd dumped all her boxes into yesterday.

Or Wellington, with its bittersweet memories and dark, dark corners.

But she'd determined not to think about any of that. Apart from tonight. The whole day had been exhausting—a new job, new people. A sweet baby fighting for his life. Piling a tumult of more emotions to the anniversary she kept, like a vigil, every year.

And now Mr I'm-sexy-and-I-know-it was piggy-back-ing on it. Adding a hint of danger to the heady cocktail of anger and hurt.

'Thank you, but I'm fine on my own.' She dragged on her jacket, lost her balance and slid off her chair, slam-ming into his hard wall of stomach. 'Oops.'

'Are you sure about that?' His voice sent a breeze against her neck followed by ripples of something hot pat-tering through her stomach. 'Because if there's anything I can help you with…'

Well, she had been sure. Sure she wasn't tipsy, sure she was going to walk away.

But now? Not so much. Maybe the mojitos had made her a bit woozy after all. She wasn't used to drinking, to meeting men in bars. To the dizzy lights of a strange new city, or the safe embrace of a man like Max Maitland.

Strong arms circled her waist as he hauled her upright and led her outside into the dark street. Heat fizzed through her body. His smell, woody and heady, washed over her.

She put her hands out to his chest to create space, but something held her there—her body flat refused to move. A wave of awareness jolted through her.

As her gaze travelled up his chest, over his too-damned-sexy mouth and up to his bright blue eyes, she realised it was no good fighting it. What he hadn't offered in words she could see from the spark, feel from his increased respiratory rate. God, she was still thinking like a goddamned nurse. How long had it been?

Too long.

She'd managed to keep that bridge between her and intimacy for so long, fortified by Nonna's rules and ugly experience.

But what he was offering her? What she thought he was offering her, hot and quick, would take her off that bridge with a wide leap. She'd spent ten years clinging on by her fingertips, frightened of what might happen. Of how much she'd have to give and lose all over again.

But this was different. He was different. Max wasn't asking for anything but a good time—he wasn't the type to make promises or offer her any more. She'd been warned about that already. Which was fine with her.

So, she could go back to the people she didn't know in her cold unfamiliar house and spend the night alone with her memories. Like she'd done for a decade. Or she could take him up on his offer. One night of heat and fun and danger.

She could scramble back onto the bridge tomorrow.

The mojitos made her bolder. Instead of pushing away from him, as she knew she should, she held on to his arm and looked straight into his eyes. Made sure he got the message. What she wanted. Where they were headed.

Never had she felt so brazen, so alive. 'Actually, I can think of a few things I need help with.'

'Then I'm your guy.' For a second he seemed to still, confused no doubt by her see-sawing signals. Then heat ignited in his pupils. He tipped his head, his mouth a fraction away from hers.

An ache spread from her abdomen to her groin, rushing through her blood to every nerve ending. When his hands reached for her waist and pulled her closer she stepped into his arms, pushing away any negative thoughts.

When his thumb rubbed against her hip bone her heart rate spiked. Then his mouth was covering hers with a force she'd never experienced before.

She wrapped her arms around his neck, deepened the kiss, opening her mouth to his tongue. His hardness pressed between them and she rocked against it. The desire he'd unleashed in her only seemed to grow more intense as she curled into his heat.

She didn't know where this temptress act was coming from. Something about Max Maitland made her feel so sexy—and knowing it was for one night only, she played along. God, if her nonna could see her... No. *No. No.* She hauled Max closer and lost herself in his heat, erased any thoughts of home from her brain.

Shivers tingled down her spine as he cupped her face and crushed his mouth to hers.

Eventually he pulled away, his breathing ragged. 'Okay, *Gabby*.' Still keen to play games with her. Good. She wanted to play. 'You want to rate me now?'

She pretended to think for a moment, pressed her lips together— relishing the unfamiliar stinging sensation from his kiss. 'Nine.'

'Nine?'

She bit her bottom lip and leaned closer to his ear.

Breathed in the scent that had started to drive her wild.
'Okay, nine point five.'

'Really? And I lost half a point for what, exactly?'
'It didn't last anywhere near long enough.'

CHAPTER TWO

'I CAN REMEDY THAT.' Max's forehead rested against hers, his breathing finally steadying. He'd met his match here. Hallelujah. Things could get very interesting between now and tomorrow morning. 'I'm not back on duty for a few hours. You?'

Gabby frowned. 'Early shift. And as it's my first day in charge, I have to make an impression—so watch out, Mr Maitland. I can be ruthless.'

'Woo—scary nurse lady.' But, yes, they would be colleagues from tomorrow. Damn. This was getting too complicated. He hesitated, his judgement getting the better of him. And his conscience too.

He didn't know her—but what he'd seen so far was that no matter how much of a front she put up, she had shadows, and a past—or else why would she be in the pub on her own, hell-bent on getting wasted?

And he didn't want to veer into that kind of territory.

But she was intriguing. Strong and strident one minute, sexy siren the next, and all the time with an undercurrent of vulnerability that tugged at his protective instinct.

And right now he wanted to bury himself inside her. Not just anyone. Not someone. Her.

'Hey.' She kissed him on the cheek. 'Earth to Max.'

'You want to talk about why you were in the pub?'

'No. I don't want to talk at all. Don't ask me anything, and I won't ask you.' She placed her finger to his lips. 'You don't want more. And neither do I. So forget the sensitive-guy thing.'

'But…?'

'But nothing. Tonight we are…friends. Tomorrow we are co-workers. I can cope with that if you can. Seriously. Cross my heart.'

Her fingers tiptoed down his shirt buttons and she drew a cross over his heart. When she peered up at him through thick black eyelashes he caught the flash of desire in her eyes. 'Now you are severely dropping in my ratings. If you want to get back up to at least a seven, you've got a bit of work to do.'

'Seven? How did that happen?'

She wiggled her hips against his thigh. 'You, Mr Maitland, are all talk and no action.'

'You want action? Right.' Max walked her across the deserted street and into his apartment block. Crazy stuff. He never offered his place. One of his rules, and he had a few—no staying the night. No promises of anything. Anything. No sharing his private cave. That was way too personal—and he didn't do intimacy on any level, not if he could help it. But his apartment was close by. And what they needed right now was hot and quick. He punched 'P' and the lift jolted.

'You live in the penthouse? Wow.'

'Sure. You have a problem with heights?'

He couldn't resist the smile. It had taken a lot of damned hard work to earn enough to get this place—but it had been worth every hour and every cent just to see the look on his uncle's face. 'We could go back to the ground floor. I own an apartment there too—but it's rented out at the moment—could be a bit crowded.'

'Now you're just showing off.'

'Oh, believe me, I haven't even started.' He nibbled her ear and watched her squirm with delight further into his arms. Her scent coated everything—her hair, her skin— his skin. And it fired a zillion nerve endings in his groin.

He swiped his card and opened the apartment door, activating the lights.

He couldn't help the smile when Gabby gasped. Whether it was at the one-eighty-degree view of Auckland's glittering night skyline or his kisses on the back of her neck he didn't know. Either way, with her sharp intake of breath he was all turned on as hell. He took her hand and led her into his space.

'Wow! Look! The lights. You didn't even touch a switch.'

He laughed. 'There was me thinking my kisses made you gasp.'

'You really do have a high opinion of yourself, don't you?' But she traced a finger down his cheek and over his lips. 'Do it again.'

He waved a hand and the room plunged into darkness again. 'Like that?'

'Oh, yes.' Palms worked their way down to his chest.

Then the lights came on again.

Then off.

Then on.

She grinned as he caught her, her arm in mid-air. 'Oops. In the real world we have flicky switch things. This is so cool.'

As the room plunged into darkness again he found her mouth, the pressure of her fingers on his back stoking the fire in his belly. He guided her to the couch, raking his hands through those thick curls he'd been aching to touch all evening.

With every stroke of his tongue she moaned with pleasure, sending him dangerously closer to the edge. He undid the buttons on her blouse, slid his hand under her bra, felt the delicious contraction of her nipples against his palm.

He struggled with an intense need to take her. Here. Now. But he sensed he needed to take it more slowly with her. *Wanted* to take it more slowly. They only had a few hours before morning and he felt as if time was running out. If he hurried, the magic would be lost too soon.

When he pulled away slightly he watched her face transform from beguiling to bewitched as she gazed across the room to the city view.

'This place is freakin' huge! Incredible! Look at all those lights, the harbour. I can see a cruise ship down there in dock. It's magical.' Then she glanced around the moonlit room, her delight evident, like a kid in a sweet shop. 'The glass…so much glass…must cost a fortune in window cleaning.' She laughed, ran her hand along the top of the couch. 'And all these white fixtures, the blonde wood…but no knick-knacks? Pictures? Photos?'

'No.' He wouldn't explain.

'What about Jamie? Your family? You must have photos of them.'

'I don't like clutter.' He'd managed to live like that for a long time. No mess—physical or emotional. 'I keep things simple.'

'I see. Noted.' She paused and seemed to take that in. Then she nodded, understanding his hint not to probe further. 'It's stark, but breathtaking. I've never seen such a space. It's like something out of a magazine.'

'*Metro House Monthly*—February edition.' At her frown he explained. 'The interior designer was pretty happy with it so she booked an editorial. There's a spa, too, out there in the garden.'

'You have a spa and a garden all the way up here? Oh. My. God.' She ran to the Ranchslider doors but he flicked the remote and they opened before she got there.

'Oh.' Disappointment laced her voice as she stepped out. 'That's not a garden, it's a desert. There's nothing here.'

'I don't have time to look after plants. I hardly have time to sleep these days.' He tutted, took her hand and walked her across the empty decking space towards the spa.

Looking at it all through her eyes, yes, it was kind of sparse. Just how he'd planned it. Uncomplicated, stress-free.

Just like Gabby seemed to be. Instead of all the pretence that he usually went through with women—the faux affection, the predictable seduction, the craning of their necks to see the colour of his credit card before they said yes—Gabby seemed undeniably, ruthlessly real.

Her bright-eyed reaction to his apartment was genuine, not greedy. She'd been honest about her expectations. And flirty and unexpectedly fun.

A pinky-orange glow shimmered across the balcony, illuminating the red and gold highlights in her hair, her dewy skin, warm eyes. She fitted perfectly into his arms, soft curves filled with promises.

No, it wasn't his flat that was breathtaking—Gabby was. How amazing to make love with her out here in the moonlight...in the spa.

Anywhere.

She leaned back against the railings, her forehead crinkled with frown lines. For a moment he felt like he'd disappointed her, but then she smiled. 'If I lived here I'd have an oasis—somewhere I could come sit and read, relax. A sky garden with lots of plants. A home isn't a home without flowers and plants.'

Where's home? The question almost tripped off his

tongue, but he remembered their agreement—no questions. His hands ran over her shoulders, down her triceps, and he realised she was shivering in the early-winter breeze. He locked her into his arms. 'I'm not into flowers and plants. That's girl stuff.'

'No. Real men get their hands dirty.' Taking his hand in hers, she examined it. 'You've got surgeon's hands. Wow. Just think of all the lives these hands have saved.' She pressed her lips into his palm, kept her eyes locked with his, then slowly placed his hand over her breast. Went up on tiptoe and filled his mouth with her tongue.

Maybe this was a dream. A post-surgery dead-on-his-feet hallucination. A beautiful woman. A still night. Promises... Anytime soon and his cellphone was bound to go off. He was going to wake up.

On paper she was his perfect woman: she didn't want a relationship, didn't want more than one night. Was happy to forget it all tomorrow. Just like him. Sure, on paper she was perfect, but there must be a catch. There was always a catch. 'Are you for real?'

'No, I'm a figment of your imagination. Open your eyes and I'll disappear in a puff of smoke...gone...' she whispered, and giggled.

'Then I'll keep them shut. I don't want you disappearing on me. Not just yet.' He kissed her again hard and fast, cupping her breast. Her excited moans of pleasure spurred him on. Just the simple act of kissing her was a sensual feast that he didn't want to end. Her hips ground against his and suddenly a fire blazed in his groin, hot and hard. Tearing at her straps, he removed her top, lifted her bra and took one nipple into his mouth.

Watching the reaction on her face—concentrated joy—spurred him to give the other nipple the same treatment.

She clutched at his hair. 'Oh, God, this is so good. I don't suppose this place has a bedroom?'

'I have three.'

'Goody. Which one do we start in?'

Her skin against his mouth fired spasms of need through him. He dragged his lips from her shoulder. 'Master. Now.'

'Don't stop, though. Don't stop.' Ignoring her groans of protest, he took her hand and led her into his bedroom. 'Wow. Just when I thought things couldn't get any more impressive.'

As she pointed to his bed he was hit with a surge of pride. Okay, so it was a handcrafted masterpiece, imported mahogany, Egyptian cotton. Yeah, it was impressive.

But when she said, 'It looks so perfect I daren't mess it up,' he swooped her into his arms and lifted her onto his bed—her dark hair instantly flaming against the white linens. Her skirt ruched up to her hips, revealing long shapely legs.

Palming her thigh, he joined her on the bed. She edged closer, fitted into his space. Kissed him again, soft and sweet. Then in an electric moment the tension ratcheted, the kissing became more frenetic, the need more explicit.

He slipped her skirt off, kissing across her bellybutton down to the edge of her panties. 'How am I doing on the rating front?'

'Oh…nearing eight…' she breathed out on a sigh.

'Only an eight? I show you this…I do this…and this…' He moved back up to her neck, nibbled her ear, slicked a slow trail from her lobe. Tweaked her nipple again with his hot mouth. 'And I only get an eight?'

'Hey, a guy's always got room for improvement.'

'We'll see about that.' Grabbing his condoms from the bedside-table drawer, he paused and looked at her. Realised he didn't want hot and quick. Wanted long and slow. And maybe again tomorrow.

He shook those kinds of thoughts from his head—useless and pointless. People walked through his life, no one ever stayed for long. That was how it worked for him. And for Gabby, too, it seemed. 'Are you sure?'

Placing her hands on his chest, she frowned. 'I want you to know this is not something I've done in a very long time. I don't usually...you know...do this... I am on the Pill but, yes, definitely use a condom.'

She seemed hesitant. Maybe the alcohol was wearing off. Good call—he wanted her head to be in full working order if they were going to do this. No regrets for either of them. He brought her fingertips to his mouth. 'It's okay, you know. I could take you home. We don't have to do this.'

'Oh, yes, we do. You promised me hot and quick.' Gabby's courage had begun to waver, but her need to have him hadn't diminished. No, siree.

Running her hands over his back towards his waist, she pulled him to her and crushed her lips against his. A surge of heat spiralled through her from the small of her back to the top of her head. Mr I'm Sexy was so different from any other man she'd kissed. Not that there'd been many— she'd made sure of that.

Dumb, really, that on today of all days she was doing this. When she should be staying away from any kind of risk. But the headier the risk, the more her body wanted to take it. Take him. Now. And nothing was going to stop her finally taking something for herself.

Because, for the first time in forever, she felt absolutely, totally free.

Scragging his shirt over his head, she slicked kisses down his hard chest, over a smattering of hair, across hard muscle. He pressed against her as he shucked off his jeans. His hands grasped her hips, slipping off her pants, fingers reaching her inner thigh.

For a moment she stiffened, worried about what could happen. If she even knew what to do now. If she would be enough for him. What would happen afterwards. Tried to put out of her mind what had happened last time she'd done this.

But unlike last time she wasn't an innocent grasping at a fairytale, looking for an escape and dreaming about happy ever after—this time she knew exactly where she was headed. Sex. Need. No promises. No illusions. She was a woman, powerful and in control.

His hands stroked her skin and it felt as if he was stroking her insides too. And she wanted more. His kisses heated her. Banished the cold she'd felt for so long. Stoked the fire that raged from her belly to her breasts and that didn't stop…couldn't stop…wouldn't stop until he was inside her.

Then there he was, edging into her, telling her to relax, calling her beautiful over and over. Until she truly believed she could be. His breathing quickened and his words stopped, and all she could hear was their sighs and the thud of her heart and the blood pounding round her veins. Until he took her over the edge, and all sounds splintered into one explosion of shuddering joy.

A perfect ten.

A harsh, tinny tune jolted Max awake. His first instinctive reaction was to feel across the duvet for the uncompromising Gabby.

His second was to reach for his phone.

God, he was doomed.

And she was gone. He'd opened his eyes and she'd disappeared, just like she'd promised. Which irritated him more than it should have. Most women wanted him to stay, had always been put out when he'd made up his excuses and left.

He'd never had the time or the inclination to invest in anything longer than a fling. And he'd certainly never given any woman time to do the walking—he'd had enough of people he loved disappearing from his life already.

But the room still smelt of her scent. The sheets did. And so did he.

His phone blared again.

Focusing on the lurid green message, his heart began to race. Jamie.

A rising temperature less than twenty-four hours post-op. Dipped urine output. Distressed kid.

Within minutes he was on the HDU, trying to keep his voice in check so as not to spook Jamie's mum, Jodi. He scratched his head as he approached the bed, still unused to her being round again after so long.

It was weird enough when Mitch had dated Max's ex. But even more awkward to have her back in his life, at his work after so long. Not that anything lingered between them anymore, except his wish they could all move on. But Jodi's hurt was still there, along with his brother's betrayal. Unmentioned. Unresolved. Like everything with Mitch.

His attempts not to growl at the surgical on-call house officer disappeared along with any trace of post-damned-fine-sex good humour.

'I need full blood and urine screens, swab drain and catheter sites, keep an eye on central venous pressure and his blood pressure. How long has his temp been this high?'

'An hour, maybe two.'

'And you waited to tell me. Why? I said I was to be contacted immediately if there was a change in his condition.'

'I thought we could control it. I was hoping the paracetamol would hold it in check.'

'Since when does paracetamol hold an infection in check? You wanted to mask the symptoms and not investigate them. Pretend he hasn't got a problem, right? Great.' God, he was surrounded by...

He took a breath. It was the middle of the night. They were tired. He was tired. And poor Jamie. Thick, dark shadows edged the little boy's eyes as he stared up at them.

Max's heart squeezed. He never allowed himself to feel anything but professional concern for his patients. But Jamie? Jamie was special. He was the sticking plaster they needed to stick them all back together. They hadn't come this far for the kid to get sick again. Not on his watch, anyway.

He should never have left them this evening. Even though he'd been exhausted by the surgeries and countless demands on his time.

He shouldn't have gone to the bar. Even though he'd left clear and strict instructions with his staff.

He shouldn't have taken Gabby to his apartment. Just in case something like this happened.

So that was a mistake he wasn't going to repeat. He didn't need a hefty dose of guilt to add to his conscience.

Although Jodi was a doctor, he tried to explain the turn of events in everyday language. Knowing that in the middle of a long night, with spiralling concern, technical terms wouldn't be much use.

'Jamie's got a spiking temperature. Which could mean one of a few things. Pneumonia, urine infection or just something sticky at the drain sites.'

'Or it could be rejection, right?' Her palm covered her mouth as she held in the tears Max knew she wanted to shed.

Accelerated acute rejection—death of the kidney soon after operation. He didn't want to imagine it.

He put a reassuring hand on her shoulder as he would with any other patient's relative, but did she think that was strange coming from him? So far he'd played out the ex card pretty well, but everything normally clear-cut had become muddied. He focused instead on upholding his professional manner. Hiding behind that was preferable to dealing with emotions.

'It's a very real possibility, but he has a reasonable urine output. We're doing a blood scan and antibody check. Honestly, it could be anything. It's quite common to have some sort of low-grade infection post-op. So we'll increase the antibiotics and titrate his fluid input. That should keep him comfortable.'

'Okay.' Jodi's lip wobbled as she looked equally uncomfortable. 'Er...thanks. For everything.'

'Hey, it's my pleasure. Anytime.' Although heading up the team operating on his twin brother and his nephew in a double-whammy of transplant surgeries was a one-off he hoped never to repeat.

As he injected more antibiotics into Jamie's Luer, Max dredged up a smile for Jodi. 'How's Mitch doing?'

'He's fine. He was wheeled in for a few minutes to say good-night to Jamie, but he was wiped out after his operation so he went to sleep. He says to say thanks, mate.'

Mate? Since when was he his brother's mate? Maybe they were finally getting somewhere. Such a shame it had taken something so drastic to get them talking again. Max huffed out a breath.

Jodi managed a tired smile in return and he felt a strange pang of regret. Not of losing her—because she had been so wrong for him and so right for Mitch—but because he'd never seen anyone have that love-filled, misty-eyed look over him.

Must be getting soft.

'You look bushed. Why don't you have a lie-down?' He dragged over a foldaway bed, grabbed some pillows and covers, and made her sit down. 'Get some sleep. I'll stay right here with him.'

'But what about his temperature? Or if he cries?' She was terrified and exhausted and what she needed was a rest, away from the eternal twilight of the hospital ward. A foldaway bed was the closest he could come to providing that.

Not for the first time he wished he could do something, anything, to prevent his estranged family from suffering through this.

'Then I'll wake you up. Trust me. We'll be fine.' Resisting an urge to drop a kiss on his cute cheek, he scruffed the boy's hair instead. Keeping a lid on his emotions at work was his mojo—and he intended to keep it that way.

The boy murmured a little but finally went back to sleep, leaving Max in the cold silence with too many thoughts.

Too many worries about the fate of this little chap.

Too many guilty stabs about where he'd been and what he'd been doing instead of keeping watch over his family.

Too many memories of a pool of thick black curls, a sarcastic mouth.

And a very sexy smile.

CHAPTER THREE

'HE'S HAD A LONG and difficult few hours, so don't wake him.' The night charge nurse finished her handover by parading the whole of the day staff in front of cubicle four.

Gabby's chest did a funny little hitch at the sight of a sleeping Max. Slumped half on a chair and half on Jamie's bed, he was completely and utterly comatose. And with stubble on his proud jaw he was completely and devastatingly gorgeous.

God. She glanced round at the rest of the crew. Could they all tell? Did she have 'Guilty' written all over her face? Did her smile scream *I've just had fabulous sex with Mr I'm Sexy here*?

She tried to make the smile more interested in the handover than the subject, as the unfamiliar ache of bedtime gymnastics thrummed through her body.

Bad, bad girl. Maybe her nonna had been right all along. She waited for the thunderbolt her grandmother had promised. The dark satanic music as she was dragged away to the bowels of hell.

Nothing happened. Gee—what a surprise.

If sex was so bad, why had it felt so good?

Her palm found its way to her throat. She tugged on the necklace she refused to take off. She knew exactly why.

Concentrate.

How would she ever concentrate with Max there?

'Where's Jamie's mum?' she whispered to the night nurse, dragging her eyes away from Max. God, he'd been amazing. She'd been amazing—and that threw her even more. She didn't know she could be like that.

'Mr Maitland sent Jodi home at five-thirty, once he'd got Jamie's fever under control. Said she needed a good rest and a hot shower. He's been here ever since. Wouldn't leave him. Wouldn't even let go of his hand.'

Gabby's heart constricted as she noticed the tiny hand wrapped in Max's fist. No. *Harden up, Gabby.* Don't get involved. Don't let a little boy tug at your heart. Or a grown man snag a piece of it.

Hurriedly closing the curtain and shushing the staff away, she took a moment to compose herself. Tried to think through the thud of her alcohol-induced headache and the wave of lust fizzing all the way down to her knees. She'd allocate Jamie to someone else. That way she wouldn't have to spend any more time with Max or his family. No looking into too-blue eyes that made her feel weak. Then she'd avoid him, for the rest of her life.

The sluice was looking pretty attractive right now. The treatment room. Cleaner's cupboard. Africa...

Coward.

Sure, sleeping with him had been epic. Fan-bloody-tastic. The best and most wild thing she'd done in a decade. Liberating. Affirming. Crazy. But now?

Not so much.

She didn't regret it, though. It had been one amazing night that she'd always treasure. But focusing on him took her brain power away from the things that mattered—her new job, her future. Putting the cloistered past behind her. And that included Max and his far-side-of-minimal apart-

ment. She refused to let everything go to hell again because
of a man. Especially a man like Max Maitland.

She found one of the house officers loitering too near
the biscuit tin at the nurses' station. 'Hey! Hands out. Are
they clean?'

The HO snatched his hand away from the chocolate di-
gestives and looked down at his fingers. 'Er…yes.'

'Makes a nice change.' She refused to smile. She would
start as she meant to go on. Her reputation as efficient and
no-nonsense had preceded her. Give them a smile and before she knew it there'd be chaos…and no biscuits left.
Every hospital ward was the same—the doctors always
devoured the biscuits. 'And you're waiting here for…?'

'Mr Maitland's ward round. It started five minutes ago
but he's not arrived. That's not like him. Should I call him?'

Cripes, and it was her job to accompany the ward round
too.

So much for her well-constructed avoidance plan. 'I'm
sure he's very busy and has just been held up. He'll be
along in a few minutes. Why don't you chase up those
blood results for Peter Brooks in the meantime?'

It was no sin to fall asleep when off duty but no doctor would want to be found sleeping on duty, even if he'd
been up most of the night.

Scanning round for someone to go wake him up, she
saw a very organised ward—her new staff all working under her strict instructions, getting patients up and
washed, doing pre-op checks, dressing changes, no idle
chit-chat. A hive of activity that left no one, *no one* else she
could ask to stop their work and go and wake Mr Maitland.

That was the first time her efficiency had been back to
bite her in the backside.

One steaming mug of coffee and a round of toast and

jam later she dragged open the cubicle curtain. 'Max? Mr Maitland?'

Placing the tray on the over-bed table, she bent to his ear. Resolutely did not breathe in that delicious smell that had driven her wild and that she'd been reluctant to shower off only hours ago.

Did not look at the stubbled cheek she'd dropped a kiss on as she'd left.

Did not allow herself any spare emotions other than that she was very busy and he was taking up her time. 'Oi! Maitland, wake the hell up.'

'Lovely to see you again, too.' He lifted his head from the sheets, creases streaking down his cheek. The sweet curl of his lips made her heart hiccup in a peculiarly uncomfortable way. She'd kissed that mouth. It had roamed over her body into places no one else's mouth had ever been. That mouth had given her so much pleasure she felt the heat seep into her cheeks at the memory.

But there was a line between kissing and fun and a bit of *harmless* sex, and the cold harsh reality of relationships. Harmless sex? Boy, she'd been dreaming that day ten years ago. And after her heart had been shattered into too many pieces she'd made sure she kept on the right side of that line.

Even though last night she'd tested it, seen how much the line could bend, nothing Mr I'm Sexy could do would drag her to the dark side.

He sat up and stretched, glanced over at Jamie—satisfied himself with his observation—and then turned back to her. 'So you didn't disappear into thin air after all, Gabby. Here you are. Lovely…and fresh…and…so loud?'

'Busy ward, Mr Maitland. Busy day.'

'After what you did to me last night you can definitely

call me Max.' His smile morphed into that wicked look he'd had in the bar. 'How's the head? How are you?'

She so did not want to have this conversation. 'Fine. Now eat this. Quickly. Your ward round was due to start fifteen minutes ago. We need to get a wriggle on.'

And they'd done a lot of that last night, too. Her cheeks blazed.

His mouth twitched. He rested his chin on his hand and held her gaze, his eyes misty with sleep. His hair was dishevelled and annoyingly perfectly ruffled. Sex hair.

It would be so easy to just lean in and kiss him again. But she pushed the plate towards him instead. 'Hurry up. I haven't got all day.'

His hand covered hers. 'Not before we clear the air.'

'Nothing to clear.' She twisted her hand out of his grip.

'You sure, Charge Nurse Radley? You were an animal. I particularly liked that thing you did with your finger—'

'Do not…' His proximity was jangling the one nerve she had left. First proper day in charge and she did not need this distraction.

She glanced over to make sure Jamie was still asleep. Peered out through the curtains to see if anyone could hear.

The patient in the next bed grinned at her and waggled his finger. Gabby silently wished the poor sick teenager a swift dose of short-term memory loss and dodged back behind the curtain.

She jabbed her filed-to-a-sharp-point fingernail into Max's chest. 'Okay. You. Me. Sluice. Now.'

'But I've got a ward round.'

'Coward.'

'Never, ever challenge me like that. Because I have no fear, Gabby.' His words breathed down her neck as he followed her into the sluice and closed the door.

Trapped. In a small, hot room. Alone. No, not alone—

with six feet three of glorious out-of-bounds hunk. 'You want to taunt me some more? Just to see?'

'I am a professional person trying hard to get a little respect around here. You do not talk to me like that when there are patients close by.'

'So I can talk like that now?'

'Absolutely not.' Her mouth tipped into a smile. She tried to stop it. Bit her lips together, tensed the muscles, but the smile kept coming. 'And I was not an animal.'

'I meant it in a good way. Uncaged, wild.'

He leaned against the steriliser, folded his arms, his legs crossed at the ankles. So relaxed that clearly the one-night thing was a common occurrence for him. She'd probably been just a notch in his magnificently handcrafted bed. She'd bet anything his heart didn't pound and skip and jitter like hers did.

His eyes pinpointed her, fixed her to the floor. He started to lift his shirt up, inching very slowly over that fine line of hair that pointed straight down towards his zipper. She swallowed through a dry mouth. Watched as centimetre by centimetre his abs then pecs were revealed.

His voice was hoarse and inviting. 'I'm sure I've got scratches on my back. You want to check?'

'No, I do not. Put yourself away.' *Before I jump your bones.* 'We're not going to talk about this again. Okay? That person you met last night? That's not me. That was a different Gabby.'

'Not the real you? You seemed very real. You felt very real… Oh. No…the animal thing…' He hit his head against the steriliser. 'Please, God, don't tell me I've woken up in some sort of paranormal universe? You're not going to go all weird or hairy and shapeshift on me?'

Laughter burst from her throat. 'No. I was just drunk, which is a rarity. Thank God.' She'd been bewitched by

Max, or the mojitos. Either way, she wouldn't be giving a repeat performance. And she would never ever drink again. No matter how much she wanted to forget. She pointed to her scrubs. 'This is the real me. This is the only Gabby you're going to know. At work. Charge Nurse Radley.'

'Which is a damned shame all round.'

Yes, it was. 'And now we go out there and pretend we don't know each other at all. At least, not in the biblical sense.'

'Right.' His teasing grin told her he could pretend all she liked. But he knew her. *Knew* her.

'Right.'

'Excuse me…' The door swung open and Max Maitland walked through it. She did a double-take. Talk about a paranormal universe.

Max leaning against the steriliser, all cocksure and oversexed.

Max standing at the door in pyjamas, wheeling a drip that was attached to his arm, pale and tired-looking.

The in-patient one was minutely shorter, had longer hair and an air of worry around him. Unlike the doppelgänger in the corner. He was just downright smug. Or had been. His jaw tightened.

'Whoa.' She'd heard they were brothers, but no one had mentioned identical twins. How could there be two such beautiful men in the world? It made her head spin.

And did Max Two have the same freckle just above his…? Could he make her gasp and moan?

Stop.

She banished such thoughts as she held up her palms. 'This is weird. Can—?'

Her Max was by Max Two's side in a second. *Her Max?* What the…?

His cocky demeanour evaporated into concern, his

voice lowered. 'Are you okay? Who said you could leave your bed, Mitchell?'

'I did.' Max Two glowered.

'I was going to come and check on you. You should have waited until the ward round.'

'I was told you hadn't even started it. I came to see Jamie...' He gripped the drip pole as his jaw tightened to exactly the same tension as Max's. 'In case he needed anything.'

So alpha clearly ran in the family. She wanted to tell him that Max had spent a good part of the night looking after that scrap of life out there. And was running late because of it.

But she held her counsel. 'Would anyone like to introduce me?'

Max turned and smiled. 'Yes. Sorry. This is my brother, Mitchell. He was the transplant donor for Jamie. He's also consultant ED specialist here when he's not on the dark side. Mitch, this is the new paediatric HDU charge nurse, Gabby.'

'Gabby. Hello.' Mitch's eyebrows rose as he looked from Max to Gabby then back again.

There was a distinct edge between the brothers. So close in appearance, but a gulf stretched between them.

Oh, she knew enough about families that things didn't always run smoothly, that there were crises and ups and downs. Hell, she knew you could be angry and disappointed with someone for years and years, but you still had to treat them with respect.

Because they were family.

And family, she'd had drummed into her, was everything. Which was why things had turned out so perversely in the end. Why she wasn't going to have one of her own.

Because now she'd wrested some control into her life, she'd never give it up.

But this Maitland thing seemed different. The brothers stood aloof, distant. There was a strange cold charge between them. And yet a child's life hung in the balance out there. More than anything that should count. Surely they should be united in that?

Mitch nodded towards her. 'I came to find out who's looking after Jamie today.'

'I allocated him to Rachel. She's very competent. Last thing I heard she was just about to give him his breakfast. Why don't you come and see him? He's probably ready for some daddy hugs. Then perhaps we could alert your nurses to your whereabouts.'

She ushered them out of her sluice room. As things had been progressing with Max in a way-too-dangerous direction, Gabby was thankful for the interruption. But perturbed by the existence of not one but two very distracting Maitlands.

Surely to God one was enough.

Six hours later Gabby finally found a moment to breathe. Slumping into the soggy orange sofa in the ward staff lunch-room, she broke out her sandwiches and yoghurt and started to eat.

Luckily the ward round had run smoothly. Jamie appeared to be making it through his first day post-op with just a niggling temperature. And there had been no major events.

Apart from her near heart attack every time Max brushed past her on the drug round, at the nurses' station, along the corridor. Was it normal for a doctor to spend so much time on one ward?

Of course it was—he was dedicated, hard-working. And always, it seemed, there.

'Gabby? We meet again.'

There. See? Always there, his deep voice making her stomach do cartwheels. She swallowed her mouthful of tuna mayonnaise. 'I'm just leaving, actually.'

'No, you're not. Your feet are tucked up, your shoes discarded across the floor, you're only halfway through a magazine and if I know women well…' He let the *'and I do'* hang in the silence. Well, hell, he certainly knew how to please a woman, as she'd learnt last night. 'You won't go until you finish the article on best celebrity diets.'

He squished down onto the cushion next to her, mug in hand. The fabric of his scrubs stretched tautly against the muscle of his thigh. The thigh she'd caressed, gripped and, by all accounts, scratched. She dragged her gaze back to his mouth, his words. 'Which means, Gabriella, that we have time for a quick chat.'

'I don't think so.' She made a big deal of slipping her feet into her shoes, checking her watch, weighing up her options. Still ten minutes of her break left. She could leave now and attend to the piles of paperwork or she could last out her break. With him. In here.

She felt the heat in her cheeks and knew her stupid body was betraying her. What to do? 'I told you, Max. I'm not open to that.'

'To what?'

'More of last night. The whole sex thing…'

'Yes. No. Me too. Although…I could be persuaded. You have to admit it was good. We were good. Anytime you want a replay, I'm your man.' His eyes glinted and he appeared to be holding back a laugh.

Annoyingly, she liked it when he laughed. His whole body lit up and his attention focused totally on her. Made her feel he'd laughed just because of her. This was why she didn't date. Didn't want to get caught up in the lure and charm of someone like Max.

He leaned forward a little. 'Don't look so worried. I was only going to let you know I'm off to my outpatient clinic. Jamie's temp is still wobbly, so I'm going to arrange for some more scans to double-check everything. Should be later today. In the meantime, if you need anything, call the house officer.'

'Oh. Okay. Of course, that's fine. And I'll personally check Jamie's obs.' She managed to bluff her way through her embarrassment.

Of course he'd put their night behind him. He was a player. And at work. She'd already given him the brush-off and he'd moved on. A guy like Max wouldn't ask twice. Didn't need to—there would be plenty of other offers. The gossip machine whirred with his and his brother's sexual exploits. 'How's Mitchell doing?'

His eyes darkened and his back stiffened at the mention of his brother. She got the impression that, like her, he didn't talk about personal stuff. Even if personal stuff included a patient and a member of hospital staff.

'Mitchell is fine.' He stood to leave, but paused. 'I think I might need to apologise for him.'

'For what?'

'Let's just say that tact isn't his forte.'

'Believe me, I don't think anything you Maitland brothers do could shock me. Your reputations go before you.'

Because once she'd discovered they were identical she'd made it her business to discover as much about them as possible. Didn't want to find herself propositioning the wrong brother!

She knew about Max's history as a heartbreaker, sure, and there were lots of women queuing up to try to cure him of that. What she hadn't expected to hear was that he and Mitchell had barely spoken a word to each other for the last few years they'd both been working at the hospital. That some kind of feud boiled between them, making communication on any scale largely impossible. That no one really knew why.

No matter—she didn't need to know much past who to call in an emergency. She tore off the top of her yoghurt and licked the lid.

Max grinned, reached across the back of the sofa and stuck a spoon into her yoghurt pot. Ignoring her whack on the back of his hand, he licked, eyebrows peaked. 'So I have a reputation?'

'Oh, yes. Big and bad.'

'Tough job, but someone had to do it.' He perched on the edge of the sofa arm and finished the rest of the yoghurt she held out to him.

'It depends if good-time guy and commitment-phobe float your boat.'

'What can I say? Having fun isn't a crime.'

'Not just you—your brother too.' She didn't even try to lose the laugh. 'So who's the oldest? You or Mitchell?'

'Me. By twenty minutes.'

A blink of an eye really, and yet the responsibility clearly sat heavily on him. Operating on his younger brother's son must have played a part in the wisps of grey at his temples. Made him look sophisticated, self-assured. Belied the playful spirit she knew lurked underneath his professional mask.

'You must have had a lot of fun growing up with a twin. I always wanted a sister, someone to talk to. I've heard all sorts of stories about twins. Swapping clothes. Swapping girlfriends. Conning teachers. Secret languages…'

The grin slipped. 'We weren't close.'

'How so? That's unusual for twins. Were you always vying for position? Too much competition?'

'Geography.'

And with that he shook his head and left the room. It was as if a switch had been flicked. All his good humour and good manners had instantly evaporated, leaving her feeling uncomfortable and strangely bereft.

What did he mean? Geography? The academic subject? Or geography as in distance?

It didn't matter and it certainly wouldn't have any bearing on her professional relationship with him. And she really shouldn't care.

And if she did, it was only her innate reaction that a human being could look so hopelessly, horribly lost—if only for a second.

Before he'd managed to pull up the barriers again.

CHAPTER FOUR

So, HE'D SAID more than he should have. That was the trouble with sleep deprivation—it did funny things to a man's brain.

As did beautiful women. He usually handled it, no problem. But Max couldn't put a finger on what bothered him so much about Gabby Radley. Sure, she was distractingly beautiful. But he'd taken gorgeous women to bed before and had never sought them out the next day.

And she was funny. But he'd met plenty of amusing women.

It all came back to the way one look of hers could pierce his soul.

In the staff room she'd only been making polite conversation. She hadn't attached him to a lie detector and demanded answers. And yet for the first time ever he'd felt like talking about his past. About the way things had careered out of control, about everything he'd lost. And had never got back.

No matter. He'd survived so far—excelled, in fact. Spilling his guts to a woman wouldn't change a thing.

He exited the lift and huffed out a long breath. The day had melted into forty-eight hours of constant demands, an unexpected death, dealing with a grieving family. The gut-wrenching reminder that life was so fragile.

All he needed was a shower and bed. Where he could put everything out of his mind. Focus on rest and getting ready for more surgery tomorrow. Ensuring Jamie got better. Putting things back together with Mitch. Forgetting Gabriella.

Gee, there'd been a time when he'd had no one to think about but himself. *Be careful what you wish for.*

Turning the corner towards his apartment, a flash of colour grabbed his attention. Scarlet in the midst of the carefully designed neutral palette. A splash, vivid. Bright.

Weird. He got closer. A plant? A red plant. In a black ceramic pot.

Not a pretty plant either—this was gnarled wood, browny-green leaves, a bunch of itsy red petals. He picked it up and examined it. It had a strange smell.

Why the hell would anyone leave him a plant?

Shrugging, he let himself into his apartment where the fading remnants of Gabby's fragrance hit him square in the solar plexus. Between her and the plant they were going to fumigate him out of the penthouse.

He held his breath as he placed the plant on the kitchen bench. Stepped back. It didn't look right—too much red.

Moved it to the dining table. No.

The coffee table. No.

It was too eye-catchingly bright, a misfit, chaotic in the sea of…in Gabby's eyes, bland. God, now he was looking at everything from her perspective too. He really needed to stop that.

He didn't notice the note until he'd put the plant outside on the deck. Hoping for out of sight, out of mind.

Max,
I'd rate your so-called 'garden' a woeful one.
    And that's only because it's so cool to even have

a garden at twenty thousand feet. Here's something
to help it rise up the scale.
Charge Nurse Radley

He smirked and began jabbing numbers into his phone.
Made a few calls. On the last one she picked up. 'Hello?'

'What the hell am I supposed to do with this…mon-
strosity?'

'Good evening to you too, Mr Maitland. It's a geranium. They're very popular in France. People put them
in window boxes.'

He heard the laughter in her voice and immediately
relaxed. 'If I did that and it fell off the railing, it'd kill
someone. It's a long way down.' He peered down to the
city street hundreds of feet below. 'Why are you giving
me lethal weapons?'

'It's a flower, but you're a guy so everything has to be a
weapon, right? It was more about encouraging you to take
time out to smell the…er, geraniums. Besides, it's a sin to
live anywhere where there aren't flowers.'

'Looks like I veered deep into the dark side, then. I'm
good at that.'

'I know.' There was a catch at the back of her throat.
Sounded a lot like the sighing noise she'd made the other
night when he'd kissed her. Then her voice crackled back
down the wire, softer now. 'Hey, I heard about your day.'

'Yeah? It happens sometimes. We lose the ones we don't
expect and sometimes the sickest ones pull through.' Exhaustion washed over him. It was never good to let his
guard down, to share the toll a day like this took on him.
Much easier to push it all deep inside into a hard, tight knot
and hope it didn't get so big it strangled him.

All the time he'd been working on the kid he'd been silently thanking anyone who'd listen that it wasn't Jamie who was dying. What kind of a doctor did that make him?

Hell, it made him real. An uncle, with people to care about. But for the first time in decades he'd had a taste of what families must feel like, waiting, praying, hoping. So losing a child so soon after working on Jamie had hit him hard. 'I'm a last-resort surgeon. I get them when the only alternative is nothing at all.'

'I heard you wouldn't give up, though. I heard you did what you could and more.'

'Sometimes it just isn't enough.' But if he thought like that he'd never get up in the morning. Years of wishing he'd fought harder against his uncles and more for his brother had only given him a steely determination never to give up. And never to get close enough to anyone to care about losing them. Because, damn it, that hurt.

Her voice brightened a little. 'Okay, so here's the deal. Stick your nose close to the flower and take a big breath right now.'

'Why?'

'Do it.' Now she had that take-no-crap charge-nurse voice again. 'Now.'

'Okay. Okay.' He inhaled. Coughed. Stepped away from the plant. 'Ugh.'

'Now breathe out slowly. Geranium oil is supposed to help with stress and anxiety.'

'I'm tired, not stressed or anxious. At least I wasn't until I found a plant on my doorstep. I suppose you'll want me to look after it. Water it? It's like having another mouth to feed. Suddenly I'm responsible for another life. God, the pressure.'

That she'd even thought about the impact of today's loss struck a chord. Never mind that she'd left him a present. He heard her laughing, imagined the way her head tipped back, the light in her eyes. Remembered how she'd been out here, hot and hungry, on his balcony. How soft she'd been in his arms. How good a rerun would be. 'I do know a really great way to ease tension. Works every time.'

'Back to that again? No, Max. We agreed.'

'You agreed. So you get to have your wicked way with me, and then...that's it? I'm dumped?' He laughed. He was never the dumpee. It didn't fit right and he didn't much like the prospect. In far too many ways. 'You're as bad as me.'

'We both took what we needed, no questions asked. So, yes, I'm the same as you, Max. If that's bad then so be it.'

'Hmm. I like bad. Bad is good. And if we're so similar you'll know exactly what I'm thinking. Right. Now.'

'No. Hush.' It was part warning, part dare.

'Yes, Gabby. I'm thinking about how good we were. How it's even better that neither of us wants anything more than sex.' At the word 'sex' he heard her swallow, her breathing becoming rapid and heavy. Imagining her reaction fired his testosterone surge into hyperdrive. 'How good it would feel to do it again. Now.'

'We can't. I—'

'Where are you?'

'At...home. In my room. Trying to unpack. Finally.'

'I can be there in ten minutes.' He couldn't have her here again. Bad enough he'd broken that rule already. Bad enough he'd have the damned plant around, invading his space. 'I'm very good at unpacking.'

He was?

'No! You can't come here. Just stop. Please, this is ridiculous.' This time panic coated her voice. She clearly didn't want him invading her space either.

Why not? Did she have the same personal code he did? Or was it something else?

And that was none of his business.

He heard a shrill landline phone ring in the background. Voices.

'Mum. No. Of course I'm not avoiding you. I've just been busy. Just wait…I'm on the other line. What? For goodness' sake, I told you I don't want to talk about that ever again. You promised me. No. No. *Wait*. Don't cry. Please. I'm sorry, I know. Yes. I'm sorry too.' Then Gabby came back to him. Harassed didn't describe it. 'Max, I have to go. It's my mum.'

'Call her back.'

'No.'

Hell, if he had a mother to talk to he'd put her way up the priority list, too. And if she was crying he'd be there like a shot. 'Then call me back when you're done. Because I'm not done.'

'No.'

Then there was silence. Apart from the hazy noises of the city street. And nothing, but a bright flash of red in a pretty dull landscape.

And a whole lot of questions he wasn't allowed to ask.

The key to one-night stands was to walk away and not give a damn.

So Gabby had heard.

So she'd failed miserably from the start. Despite the bravado and the very frequent use of the word 'no', her body wanted to scream *yes, please* at every Max Maitland encounter. Which was becoming tiresome in the extreme.

Ten days later and she was bordering on lust exhaustion. But not for much longer.

'There we go, no more spaghetti to get tangled in. All ready for your transfer.' Gabby removed the last of Jamie's tubes and checked the dressing on his supra-pubic incision, just below his belly button. His little hands clutched his dad's and, as instructed, he hadn't moved. Hadn't whimpered or cried. Just stared up at her with wide, trusting eyes.

She allowed a ripple of tenderness to flutter round her heart. Wondered how things might have been different... then locked that thought away. No point in dwelling on things past. She'd made her decision and lived with it knowing it had been the best thing she could do. No matter how much it hurt.

But it was always so good to help the littlies get better. Just so very hard to let them go. 'You're pretty much all fixed up, little man. Just wait for Mummy to come back and then we can all go over to the paediatric ward together.'

And that would mean no more Maitland eyes staring at her from every corner of the room. Not Jamie's, his dad's or his uncle's—all too blue, too bright and too alluring.

'Urine output still okay?' Having let go of his boy, Mitchell stood at the end of Jamie's bed, his eyes fixed on the four-hourly observation charts. Gabby took a chance to have a closer look at the twin brother that Max had no pictures of. That he refused to have a dialogue about.

They were breathtakingly similar. She couldn't imagine having someone else just like her in the world. It would be disconcerting. Could they read each other's thoughts?

Perhaps that's why they'd had such a rift.

She considered asking Mitchell about their history—but, heck, it was absolutely none of her business. She'd be mortified if anyone pried into her past. 'It's so great he's off the critical list now, and his urine is absolutely fine. Liquid gold.'

His eyebrows peaked. 'Never thought about it like that before. Pee has really just been pee until now. Having a kid is a real wake-up call.'

'I can imagine. But don't worry, everything's fine.

Blood pressure's normal. Blood tests are within normal limits, that wobbly temp was just a blip. But they'll keep monitoring everything on the ward and slowly bring you all up to speed with the anti-rejection drugs, so you know what to do when you get home.' As she spoke she felt a blush start from her cheeks and spread. Fast. The guy was an ED specialist. He'd know the routine better than her. 'Oh. Gosh. I'm sorry. I'm just trying to… You're a doctor…'

'Hey, I'm a dad first. Which took a bit of getting used to.' He peered at her and chuckled. The first time she'd seen him smile since she'd started working there. Parental responsibility hung heavily on him.

Her heart ached to think how much that burden could be shared if he and Max were on better terms. 'You're looking much better, too. It'll be nice for you to get back to a normal family life at home. Try to keep him quiet for a while, though, he's still got a lot of healing to do.'

'Keep him quiet? Clearly you've never tried to parent a three-year-old.' Mitchell laughed, meaning well. But she felt her shoulders stiffen and the familiar emotions roll over her, slamming her heart against her ribcage.

Determined not to dwell on the past, she feigned busyness. After the last phone call with her mother she resolutely would not talk about it. Ever. Again. And that meant here. With her new friends. 'Well, if you don't mind, I'd better get on. There's always a pile of paperwork for transfers.'

'Hey, Charge Nurse Radley, all organised for going to the ward?'

She hadn't seen Max arrive but now he was there his voice soothed her nerves. Deeper and warmer than Mitchell's, it never failed to send shivers of something shooting through her. This time it was like balm to a burn.

She inhaled deeply and kept things professional. 'Sure. And now I have phone calls to make.' She gave them both a stern, matronly smile. Avoidance plan reactivated. The less time she spent with Max the better. Maybe then she'd get over the lust exhaustion more quickly.

Max nodded towards his brother. 'Mitch. You look much better.'

'Thanks.' Mitchell opened his mouth to say more then closed it, obviously changing his mind.

Communication between the two of them was robotic, only saying what was absolutely necessary. Brothers didn't act like that. Strangers did. People who had nothing to say to each other. Surely, after a lifetime they could show a little more warmth? And yet she could see in their eyes that they were both aching to reach out.

Almost two weeks of caring for Jamie and she'd barely heard a word between them. Interfering wasn't her style, but they needed a damned push. 'You two are priceless, you know that?' She stared at them both in turn.

And kept the simmering desire for Max in check. Yes, she'd kissed that stroppy, grumpy mouth. Yes, okay, if called to account she'd admit she wanted to do it again. And again. Either that or slap it.

And she really should not be checking out his backside in those scrubs. So, yes, she was all kinds of confused.

But one thing was very clear: after all the reports of how Mitchell and Max had been before the transplant she would not have her ward turned into a Maitland battlefield. 'It's great that Jamie's fixed up and on the mend. But for his sake you two could try being a bit friendlier to each other, especially when you're in front of the little guy. What kind of message do you want him to grow up with?'

'Sure. Sorry.' Mitchell scowled, picked up his son and

squeezed him close. 'Look. Here comes Mummy. Time to get going. Wave goodbye to Gabby.'

The kid waved his chubby hand and beamed. 'Bye, Gabby.'

'Okay, I'll catch you up once I've got the forms.' As always she held tears in check. Something about a cute toddler hit her full-on hard in the chest every time. They had that earthy, homey smell that drew her to sniff their heads. Huge eyes that showed every emotion. That little-man swagger—half baby, half toughy. All cute, and feisty, and enough to make her heart ache.

As she prepared to leave, her attention was briefly captured by Max's reactions to Jodi. He nodded towards her then turned away, unable, or unwilling, to hold her gaze. Gabby wondered whether it was her imagination or did he seem tense around his brother's girlfriend too?

Something was very wrong with this family set-up and gossip or no gossip she needed to find out what. If only to produce harmony in the hospital corridor.

'You be good now, Jamie. I'll be down to check on you very soon.' As Max pressed a knuckle to the boy's cheek, uncharacteristic tenderness flitted across his face. And swiftly on its heels came a blanket of indifference. Emotional shutdown.

She recognised it because she'd seen it in her mirrored reflection all too often.

Then he turned and walked back to the desk at the far end of the ward.

After she'd completed the transfer, Gabby offered Max a seat in her office and sat opposite him, keeping the large mahogany desk between them as a buffer. 'I know I'm way out of line here, but do you want to talk about what's going on with Mitchell?'

'What?' He shrugged.

'The monosyllabic communication. It's like working with automatons.'

'It's just brother stuff, you know how it is.'

'No, actually, I don't. I'm an only child.'

He laughed, pushing a hand through his hair, his mouth kicked up into a half-smile. 'Praise the Lord for that. I couldn't handle two of you.'

'Well, welcome to my world, Maitland One.' This was way off professional limits and she knew it. But she couldn't bear to see families fall apart. She'd been there. Was the poster child for how to stuff things up.

And ever since she'd hated seeing people tear each other apart when they should be loving, supporting, talking. Hell, it might be too late for her, but it didn't have to be that way for the Maitland men.

Infusing her voice with as much understanding as she could, she leaned across the desk. 'You want to tell me what's going on?'

'Some things just aren't worth explaining.' There was a warning in his eyes. *Don't go there.* His jaw tilted up. 'And it's your business because…?'

Apart from the fact her staff had apparently been dodging verbal bullets—oh, and the teensy-weensy fact that she'd shared his bed—she couldn't think of a single reason. Clearly he didn't attach any emotions to the other night and she needed to learn from that. Business as usual at the office. No time or space for emotions.

This one-night-stand thing was hard to get her head around. But if she was going to take charge of her life she had to get used to a lot of new things.

So she worked to keep it less personal. A pen lay on the top of a pile of files. She picked it up, twiddled it in her fingers, hoping it gave her more gravitas. 'Okay, well, here's an idea. You and Maitland Two could kiss and make up, at least at work. It would certainly stop us all having to duck for cover every time you meet.'

His eyebrows lifted, the message finally sinking into that messed-up brain of his. 'That bad, huh? No one's mentioned it before.'

'That's because you rule their world. Who would dare tell the marvellous Maitland twins off?'

'You?' For some reason that seemed to amuse him. 'Why doesn't that surprise me? You are quite surprising, you know. But you're probably right. It's been going on so long it's just the way we communicate. I guess it's just habit now.'

'Then go cold turkey, take a hypnosis course. Acupuncture? If you need help with the needles, I'm a pretty good shot.' She jabbed the pen in his direction, sat back in her chair and fixed him with her best evil stare. 'I know exactly where to stick them for maximum pain…er, effect.'

He leaned across the desk until his mouth was inches from hers. Kissing distance. Inhaling distance. Goddamn, the desk would never be big enough. 'You certainly had maximum effect on me the other night, Nurse Radley.'

Heat shimmered between them. She caught her breath. It had all been going so well. She'd actually got him to see things from her point of view.

But now she just wanted to kiss him again. She looked at his mouth. The way his lips parted ever so slightly. They seemed to be infused with some kind of magnetic force that attracted her. Pulled her. Coaxed her forward. Inch by inch. Until the only thing she was aware of was the lightest whisper of his breath.

Oh, no.

She shifted her gaze. Over his perfect nose. Past some freckles she hadn't noticed before, dark, thick eyelashes.

Up to his bright blue eyes. Saw the sparkle, the promise.
The heat.

Bad move.

She swallowed and edged backwards out of immediate
kissing range. 'Your nephew needs a solid loving family
behind him.'

'And he has that. We all adore him. Surely you can see
that everything we do, we do for Jamie?' His hand cupped
her chin. 'You really care about him, don't you? What's
that all about? What's it to you?'

How the hell had this shifted to being about her?

At his touch her breath hitched. She couldn't handle
him touching her again, not here. Not ever. Didn't want
the flash of need that he instilled in her, which she'd just
about kept under control for ten days. The way he made
her forget everything. Made her feel alive and hopeful.

But, God, he felt good. Smelt good. And she knew how
great he tasted.

Smacking her lips together, she moved his hand from
her chin and tried to focus on the conversation. 'I care
about them all. That's why I took up paediatric nursing.
They don't choose to get sick. They don't choose to grow
up in a world that's fighting. Or have a say in how they're
parented. Or by who.'

She sucked in air, trying to clear the tight knot that
had lodged in her stomach. It wouldn't budge. And then it
fused with the mish-mash of emotions Max stirred up in
her until she didn't know what she was doing. What she
was saying. She tried to refocus. 'I want them all to have
a nice life. Adults have too much to answer for.'

Before she realised it, he was on her side of the desk,
standing over her, his hand in her hair. Fingertips stole
their way up the back of her neck, into her ponytail. He
tugged it loose. And she let him get away with it.

His mouth dipped to her ear. 'Your kids are going to have a great mum. A bit scary…but you'll be fighting their corner. That's good.'

He didn't mean anything by it. It was just a statement, but he'd hit a nerve. He made a habit of doing that one way and another. The man had a lot of annoying habits. 'What's that got to do with anything? I don't want kids. A family. I don't want any of that.'

'Oh, yes, I forgot. You don't want more. That right? You don't want commitment. You don't want more sex. And now you don't want kids. Life's just peachy as it is.' His eyes darkened for a second, his breathing coming fast and erratic. She could feel how turned on he was as he pushed against her. 'But you're wrong, Gabby. All women want more.'

'Well, I don't.' And she didn't. She really didn't.

But there was his mouth again. So close. A breath away.

Okay, the guy was a mind-reader. He was right, she did want more. More of him. More kissing. More lovemaking.

But that would get her damned to hell. 'No. I don't. Want. More.'

'Sure you do. Every part of you tells me so.' His hands fisted in her hair and he pulled her to him. For a second he stared at her with questions running through his eyes. He looked as confused as she felt. Weirded out by the wild rush of pure feral need.

But then his focus cleared and his mouth was pressing hard against hers. His tongue stroked her lips apart then dipped into her mouth, filling her with an ache, a heat that she'd never imagined was possible, and now never wanted to lose.

As he ground her against the desk she grasped his shoulders, rocked against him. Knowing that at any instant someone could barge into the office and find them.

Knowing this was every kind of wrong. And dumb. And too risky.

But knowing that made her want him even more. It was like an illicit secret addiction that she had to feed. Each glance, each touch, stoked a need for the next fix. She moaned against him as he dragged her top up and palmed her breast through her bra.

She sighed with delight as he parted her legs and fitted his body between them. Through the thin fabric of her scrubs she felt the length of him, hot and hard. Scraping her nails down his back, she sat on the edge of the desk and wriggled against him.

His hot, wet mouth made her clamour for more kisses, his touch fired every nerve ending, every cell in her body into a frenzy of intensity. Putting all doubts aside, she writhed against him, and he ground back harder and faster. She heard gasps and moans, realising, with a shock, they came from her throat as he licked it.

And then, when she thought he just had to be inside her, somehow, condom or no condom, a release she wasn't expecting shuddered through her. He gripped her more tightly as she rubbed and rocked against his erection. Stilled as she let go. Finally let go. All the emotion and frustration and confusion, all the avoiding what was so totally obvious—that she wanted him with a passion that almost scared her—knotted into a tight, sharp fierce ball and exploded into a million pieces.

He held her gently and kissed her with tenderness as she came down from her high, smiled into her hair as she found her senses again. Stroked her head against his chest as she steadied her breathing.

Who the hell was this man who could satisfy her with just a touch?

Too soon he pulled away. Left her in her office, her

mind a blur, her scrubs dishevelled and creased, the smell of him everywhere.

As he reached the door he turned and pierced her with a steely look. 'You do want more, Gabby. You just have to decide how much.'

CHAPTER FIVE

'How are the first few weeks going? Settled in okay?' Rachel, the senior staff nurse, put her glass of wine onto the pub table and squeezed into the empty seat between Gabby and Andrea, the ward clerk. Somehow they'd all convinced Gabby that the weekly ward night out at The Shed would help break the ice with the team.

And, secretly, she surmised, they'd try to find out what made her tick, where her soft centre was.

Which was why she was sticking to lemonade. She was all out of showing people her soft centre, especially people like Max. She'd shown him way more than she'd planned. Those mojitos had been the beginning of the ruin of her.

But having people to laugh and joke with without endlessly feeling she was being judged was like a breath of well-needed fresh Auckland air.

'If you mean have I managed to unpack yet, then no. There never seems to be enough time between shifts. Roll on my next day off.' When she'd probably still not be able to manage the gargantuan task of putting those heart-twisting boxes away. 'But I love the new place. The flat-mates are great. And as for the job, it's everything I hoped it would be.'

'Great, yeah? There's a good vibe on that ward. Even better now you're there.'

'Thanks.' Heat rushed to Gabby's cheeks. Since that mind-blowing orgasm she'd barely been able to look at her desk without sinful thoughts. Which had had a seriously detrimental effect on her organisational management.

What had started as efficiency had puddled into just about satisfactory. She really did need to put Max out of her head. She was not kissing him again. Ever. 'I hope I've made things easier, but tell me if I get too bossy. It's my first charge nurse job and I don't want to blow it.'

'It was manic before, but you've organised us. We certainly needed it.' The woman's eyes lit up. 'I know, you should come on the ward trip to do the twilight kayak over to Rangitoto Island. It's in a few weeks. Put your name down. There's a list behind the nurses' station.'

'Ooh, I don't know. A kayak? Me?'

'Ah, you'll be fine. And if it's too much for you, there's always a double kayak. I'm sure we could find a burly volunteer to paddle you across.' Rachel winked. 'Randy Roger the porter's always looking for opportunities.'

Gabby was well aware of Roger the porter's heat-seeking palms. Her backside had come into contact with them way too many times already. By accident, of course—so he'd assured her. 'I'm sure I'll manage.'

'It's great fun. We paddle over, have a picnic, then kayak back with lanterns as the sun sets. It's gorgeous. Think about it. We'd love you to come.'

Gabby got the impression Rachel was being genuinely friendly rather than trying to suck up to her. The heat from her cheeks settled into a general warm glow all round. It had been a great idea to move here. She wished she'd done it sooner. She was surrounded by warm-hearted, fun people who accepted her, seemed to like her. Regardless of her mother's taunts that had turned into the usual begging and manipulation, now down the telephone instead of in Gabby's face, this had been a very positive move.

Across the bar the door swung open and in strolled Max. The happy vibe Gabby had been relishing wobbled, spiked, dropped, then swirled around in her stomach for a few excruciating seconds.

She felt a sharp nudge in her ribs as Rachel did a mock swoon. 'He's got his name down for the kayak trip... Would that entice you?'

'Me? Max? No!' The words came out too sharply, too quickly. If Rachel muttered anything about 'protesting too much' she'd just about die.

It had been a one-off thing. That had morphed into a two-off thing. But it was still no big deal. Not anything to get worked up about, despite her heart doing a silly jig.

Her friend's eyebrows dipped. 'Come on. What's not to like? Those Maitland brothers make great eye candy. Double trouble and twice the fun. Especially Dr Make-You-Weep over there.'

Her colleague had been more than happy to share her inside information on Max in the past so Gabby tried to pump her for more. Doing a silent three Hail Marys for being so sneaky, she asked, 'So what's the deal between the twins?'

'Well, no one knows for sure because it all happened in Dunedin.' Rachel cupped her hand over her mouth and leaned into Gabby's ear. 'But apparently Max had a thing with Mitchell's girlfriend. Word is, they haven't spoken a civil sentence to each other since.'

An affair? Max? With Jodi?

Now, that was interesting. Shocking. And would also explain the rift and the edge between Max and Jodi. But it didn't seem right. He might be a player and a charmer but Max wasn't the kind of man to do that. 'Are you sure?'

'Sure as eggs is eggs. Their lives are, oh, so compli-cated. None of us even knew Mitchell had a child until a few weeks ago. Strange, don't you think? There's a lot more to their story.'

'I don't believe it.'

'Don't believe what?' Max was leaning over her, the hint of a teasing grin fluttering over his lips.

Earth, swallow me up now. He had quintessentially bad timing. 'Oh…er…nothing. I mean…'

'Speechless isn't a word I'd usually associate with you, Nurse Radley.' Placing a glass on the table—a large glass, with a paper umbrella and lime squeezed onto the rim—he grinned. 'Your usual. Just the one. Wouldn't want you to get drunk, now. Don't know where that could lead.'

'Er…but…no…thanks. I don't…' And he damned well knew it. Knew she was here with her work colleagues. That she had no desire to be reminded about what had happened the last time she had been in here. With him. Drink-ing mo-bloody-jitos. And now to top off her mortification her words had got lost somewhere en route from her brain to her mouth. Judging by the wicked smile he gave her, he thought it was due to his hyped-up animal magnetism.

He was probably right.

His eyes locked with hers, glinting with mischief. 'Oh, go on. Have a sip. Taste it. Then you could give me a score…out of ten? For the drink…obviously.'

Before she could answer he'd taken everyone else's order and disappeared to the bar.

Rachel grabbed the glass. 'Well, if you don't want it, I'll do the honours.' She took a long gulp. 'Delish. And tell me, Gabby, how does Max Maitland know what your usual is?'

From the heady heights of fun and relaxation things were rapidly going downhill. Gabby played the indiffer-ence card and shrugged. 'He probably asked the barman.

I was in here a few weeks ago and tried the cocktails.' It wasn't technically a lie.

'Probably 'cos you're the charge nurse,' Rachel whispered, 'trying to get into your good books. Always good to have the boss on side.'

Trying to get into my... No. Do not go there. 'Yes, probably.'

'Or maybe you're in already...' Rach nudged her. 'You know what I mean? But be warned; he's broken a few hearts already, that guy. Won't commit. Maybe he's still in love with Mitchell's girlfriend.'

Gabby choked on her lemonade. 'I doubt it. On all accounts.'

Did he? Was he?

A small knot of anxiety tightened in her gut. She just couldn't imagine a scenario where Max would sleep with his brother's girlfriend.

If he knew the gossip machine wheels were greased by lies about his love life the man would be mortified. And worse... If they were true? Did she want to get involved with a man who'd do that to his brother?

Involved? Yeah, right. She was definitely getting ahead of herself.

Too soon he was back, edging into the gap Andrea had left. He slipped into the space, slipped into the conversation. Slipped far too easily back into the forefront of Gabby's focus.

She watched him laughing and joking with the others, the attention he gave the women. The jokey camaraderie with the guys. He dominated the conversation. The life and soul of the party. The centre of the group. All ideas bounced off him. All his comments were noted with due respect.

She watched the way he chatted with Rachel, her new

knowledge in him tainting the way she read his behaviour. Charming, funny, attentive, but definitely not stepping over the line. Not like the other night when something had connected between him and her.

And hopefully he didn't kiss other charge nurses the way he'd kissed her the other day. Maybe he did. Maybe kissing charge nurses was his hobby. Others did moto-cross or tennis. He did kissing. Hell, he'd perfected the art.

Perhaps Mitchell had read too much into a flirty con-versation between Max and Jodi. Perhaps... Oh, the whole scenario was making her brain hurt.

But asking him?

As if. How could she insist he didn't ask her questions and then break that very rule herself?

How she managed to get through the next two hours was beyond her. The more she focused on him, the more aware she became of the tiniest touch, the merest glance in her direction. The way he ran his hand through his hair when he talked about serious stuff. Or when his smile hit his eyes and she felt like the sun was shining.

Somehow she agreed to join the ward touch-rugby team. Stumbled through a conversation about the latest boy band to hit New Zealand. The best ski lodges for parties. The merits of beer versus spirits.

All the time trying not to inhale his scent. Trying not to react to the brush of his skin against hers. Ignoring the fire raging in her belly when he leaned back against her or when he glanced in her direction for her opinion on the dangers of snowboarding. When he caught her eye and gave her a cheeky wink or the heat of his palm on her thigh when he shifted to allow someone out of the group.

And the way that simmering tension between them seemed to grow exponentially until she felt she'd go mad if she didn't touch him. Run her finger down his cheek, through his hair. Press her lips against his.

Suddenly Rachel looked at the emptying table and checked her watch. 'Oh, goodness. Look at that, it's getting late. Got to dash. I'm on an early tomorrow. But it's been great. We should do this again.'

Gabby gathered her rapidly diminishing senses as she watched Rachel leave, realising that if she didn't go she'd be left alone with Max. 'Oh. Yes. I need to go home too.'

'You live in Boston Road, don't you?' Rach paused. 'I live round the corner from there—do you want to walk back with me?'

Did she? No. She wanted to lie in bed with Max Maitland. To stare out of his penthouse window at the sparkling harbour lights. Listen to his regular breathing as he slept with her in his arms.

But most of all she wanted him to make love to her. 'Yeah, okay, I'll come with you, Rach. Hang on a second, I'll just put my coat on.'

Max's hand on her wrist gave her pause. He turned her away from Rachel and hissed into her ear, his breath warm against her neck. 'Oh, no, you don't. Not so quick.'

'What? Why?' *Please don't touch me.* Her body remembered how he'd felt inside her. Every nerve ending screamed for his touch. Her nipples hardened as she brushed against him, her legs already weakened with desire. How could a man make her feel this alive? She had no idea how to deal with the stirred-up hormones racing through her system.

There was only one release, could only be one release. With him. But she couldn't go there again.

Vivid blue eyes fixed on hers, offering promises and chances, and a night of wicked pleasure. Hers for the taking.

'There's only one place you're going tonight, Charge Nurse Radley. And that's with me.'

'Don't think you can spend the whole evening flirting and teasing without some kind of comeback.' His hands were in her hair now as the lift sped them towards his apartment.

He brushed her curls back from her face and peered into those large, dark eyes that had such a strange hold over him. Running a thumb along her cheek, he watched her pupils dilate. They told him how much she wanted him, too. Again she wore a buttoned-up blouse that covered her skin. Again it was the sexiest thing he'd ever ached to remove from a woman's body.

All evening the only thing on his mind had been this moment. It had been inevitable from the first second he'd seen her in the bar.

He'd gone from determination not to act on his impulses to trying to work out how the hell to get her alone again. And now, after all his promises to the contrary, they were headed back to the penthouse.

Pressing his lips against hers, he drank her in. This time he wanted to treasure the taste, learn everything about her, hear her moan, feel her shiver under his touch. He backed her up against the lift wall, his hands zoning in on those curves that kept him awake at night.

She pulled away, smiling. 'I wasn't flirting with you. I was chatting with friends. Rachel's going to think I'm a loony, sending her home in a cab while we… What was it you said? Talk about ward policies?'

'I was thinking on the hoof. You were driving me mad.'

'You think you're mad? Because I was trying not to think about you…us…this… I've signed up to kayak across an ocean, run myself ragged on a touch-rugby field and do a three-day cross-country skiing event. And I hate sport.'

She laughed into his chest and he hauled her closer, feeling the press of her breasts against his diaphragm, inhaling the sweet scent of her shampoo. He'd never been so aware of a woman in his whole damned life.

'Really? I reckon you'd be good at anything you put your hand to.' He pulled her hand to his waist, ran his fingers over her bottom towards her thigh. 'With these gorgeous legs you'd excel at sport.'

'Oh, I used to. I was a pretty good athlete once, but it all…' Those pupils contracted. Heck, her whole body contracted. There was more to this but she'd clammed up. Turned away. 'Never mind.'

He grasped her wrist and turned her to face him, wishing there wasn't such a veil of secrecy over everything. Wishing trust wasn't something he'd heard about but never experienced. 'So what happened?'

The lift pinged and they were in his apartment before she answered. The vulnerability in her face tugged at his heart, raising more questions about her past. 'Life got in the way. You know how it is.'

'Do I?'

She wrapped her arms around his neck. Nibbled along his lip. 'Shut up and kiss me.'

He smacked a kiss on her mouth. Short. Hot. Hard. Pulled away before she got too comfortable. 'Stop avoiding my questions. You are allowed to talk just a bit.'

'Talking never achieved anything.'

'But it might help. This doesn't just have to be about sex.'

What? Since when had he encouraged a woman to talk? Since when had he wanted anything other than sex?

But Gabby—she was too many shades, too complex to get his head round. She wanted him to talk but refused to illuminate him on her past. She held back so far it was bordering on retrograde—but when she did let loose it was like setting off fireworks. He was caught firmly in her glare.

'Says the guy with commitment issues.' Frowning, she jabbed him in the ribs before walking through to the lounge.

He shrugged as he followed her. 'Commitment's over-rated.'

'So I heard.'

'From whom?'

Her eyebrows rose. 'The hospital grapevine.'

'Again? We've been over this. You'll probably hear a whole lot of stuff. Doesn't make it true.'

'It was about Jodi and Mitch.' She paused, dark eyes scrutinising him.

God, it had to happen at some point. Now he felt like he was being put on trial. The truth serum was no doubt burning a hole in her pocket. Why the hell had he been encouraging her to talk? Kissing. Kissing's what mattered. Losing himself in her. Not relating a sad, sorry tale that benefited no one. He sucked in air. 'So what about Jodi and Mitch?'

'Well, actually, Jodi and you. Apparently you had a thing with her.'

'I did.' He didn't need the damned truth serum. Just one look from those eyes had him spilling the facts. Or at least as much as she needed to know. He had to wipe that dark look from her. Stat. 'But it was before Mitch ever got involved with her. Me and Jodi had a thing. Not a big thing but a thing.'

'A relationship thing? Serious?'

He winced. So that's where she was going, digging to see whether he was capable of caring. The bad news was he didn't believe he was. 'It's complicated. My whole damned life is complicated. Which boils down to the fact that I'm not good at relationships. I can't do it. Apparently I don't give enough, I'm too driven and I work too hard. Women don't like that.' He didn't even want to acknowledge why he did that, why he had to be the best at the cost of everything else.

But his uncle's endless stream of insults came back to haunt him, along with the relentless competition to excel that marked both Maitlands as the top students through med school. The endless comparison that had been instilled into both of them from a young age. *Mitchell's got his driver's licence, you'd better pass yours. Make sure you get an A in maths—show Mitch how much better you are. Mitch doesn't want to see you at Christmas. He's too busy.*

The wedge that had been driven between them grew larger every year, until… 'After Jodi and I finished, Mitch asked her out.'

'Tacky.'

'Broke just about every rule as far as I was concerned. You don't date your brother's ex. Period. We were barely communicating as it was. But this just about finished us off.'

Similar to this conversation right now. Ignoring the barrier she'd thrown up between them, he stepped back into her space, wrapped a finger in one of her luscious curls and rested his forehead against hers. 'And that was a real passion-killer, right? I vote we forget about that stuff and rewind. Or fast forward or something.'

He also didn't want to admit how lately he'd ached to talk to Mitch. Just talk. Bridge that gap. Making Jamie better had been a good step, but he didn't know how to take the next one.

Gabby stared up at him. 'Not yet. I'm not done.' Hell,

she sure knew how to drive a hard bargain. 'So that's why you two are at each other's throats?'

'Yeah. Yes, it is.' She didn't need to know the rest of his ancient history. It was easier to finish it there.

She cupped his cheek and smiled, although there was still a slice of distrust simmering there in her eyes. But somehow she just knew when he was holding back. And somehow she knew when to stop needling him. 'Just so you know, I'm glad the rumours weren't true. I never thought you'd do something like that.'

'Good.' Finally. 'So where were we?'

Placing a finger to her lip, she thought. 'Commitment's bad, but talking is...?'

Clearly not a good idea. 'Oh, but there's all kinds of talking...' He kept his arms round her as he guided her to the kitchen in a kind of klutzy waltz, hoping to lighten the mood. Tightened his grip on her waist and swirled her round, then took the opportunity to kiss her again. 'There's sweet-talking.'

'Obviously you're good at that, otherwise I wouldn't be here.' Her palms touched his chest as she giggled. A jolt of awareness surged through him.

If he didn't get her into bed soon he'd go mad, but if she needed convincing he could do that. He could do slow. He could wait. God knew, she was worth it.

He reached for the top button of her blouse and carefully undid it, then whispered into her neck, 'And there's shop talk... We really could discuss updating the policies.'

'Woo. Infection control has suddenly got very attractive.' She stepped back. 'But now you've just reminded me of another good reason why we shouldn't be doing this. Work.'

'I can think of lots of reasons why all of this could be really dumb, but can't say I'm focusing on those right now.

Good God, woman. Let me kiss you.' Okay, so slow was killing him.

His lips brushed just behind her ear and he inhaled her sweet fragrance. Managed three more buttons. Just enough to reveal the lace of her bra and the creamy skin of her breasts. 'Extra-curricular bonding. That can only help team relations.'

'I don't know. It seems so wrong. Ooh.' Curling deeper into his arms, she gasped as he ran fingers over the lace cup of her bra. Her words and actions were out of sync. 'What if people find out? I don't want to be the subject of gossip, I've only just started there. I don't want my clean slate sullied.'

'Sullied? By me? I do not sully.' Reaching behind her, he unfastened the bra, skimmed his fingers over her skin and tweaked a nipple, enjoying the tight puckering at his touch. 'So we keep it to ourselves. Our secret. Seriously, no one needs to know.'

'I mean it. No one, not Mitchell or anyone.'

At the mention of his brother the familiar irritation rushed through him. He dropped his hand to his side. 'Like I'd tell him anything.'

'Don't you have some kind of spooky twin telepathy? Doesn't he know already?'

'Nah. But we do understand each other well enough to keep our distance.' His hand slid to her hip. 'Let's not talk about him. This…this is much more fun.'

She didn't look convinced. 'And we're both woefully bad at sharing things about ourselves.'

'But we're very good at making each other feel better about it. Neither of us wants to get involved. When it's over, it's over. We walk away.' He ran his thumb over her swollen lips. 'No harm done.'

'No harm done. Really? You think that's likely?' She

licked round the thumb tip, sending wild jolts of electricity through him. Then she sucked his thumb deep into her mouth. And out. And he felt powerless against this raging need zipping through him. 'We're consenting adults. We both know the score.'

She smiled hesitantly. 'So we do this? Bed buddies? Friends with benefits?'

'Can you stop it?'

She shook her head and stared at his chest, thought a while. 'I don't think so.'

'So we do it when we want to. Because we want to. As soon as we stop wanting to we call it quits. We may not want to spill our guts over our past lives, but we can at least be totally upfront about this. As soon as the spark dies, we're out.'

Tilting her chin up to him, he finally, *finally* held her gaze. Caught the need and the fire and knew it mirrored exactly what was in his eyes, too. But there was a glimmer of fear, too. Something that begged him not to hurt her. She was protecting herself. Had she been hurt before?

When her mouth opened he covered it again before she could add to her damned list. Add to his own list.

And he promised her, with his kiss, that he wouldn't hurt her. Not if he could help it.

They didn't need a conversation, didn't need a mating dance. Didn't need anything to convince them they were headed straight to bed. They both knew it was as inevitable as night following day.

When he pulled away her breathing was ragged. Her eyes filled with that mist he'd seen the other day. The one that told him she needed him. Now.

'Which leads me nicely on to the best kind of talking… pillow talk.' He nuzzled against her throat as his fingertips ripped her blouse off and dropped her bra to the floor.

Eyes feasting on her two perfect breasts, he felt the smile spread through his body. 'Would you look at that?'

'Oh.' She smiled and pretended to be surprised. 'Naked. How did that happen?'

'Not naked enough.' He gripped her hips and dragged her back to him, struggling with the need to have her now. On the kitchen floor. Against the bench.

Knowing that if he took her into his bed he wouldn't want her to leave. Would want to wake up with her tomorrow. And maybe the next day. But not knowing how the hell to control this ache inside him. 'I know, let's have some champagne to seal our deal.'

'Are you trying to get me drunk? Just one small one.' Standing behind him, she peered over his shoulder. The fridge light lit up her face. No—her laughter lit up her face. 'Max Maitland, you have four bottles of champagne but no milk. No food...at all. What do you eat?'

'I eat at work.'

'That's it? Don't you cook?'

'No. I can cook—I just don't. We could phone out for takeaway. But in my book eating is cheating.' He popped open a bottle and poured bubbles into two long-stemmed glasses. Offering her one, he pointed towards the bedroom. 'Now, Nurse Radley, we have a lot of policies to work through... Shall we...?'

Her mouth formed a playful pout as she pretended to weigh up her options. Then she smiled, long and slow, and led the way. 'Hell, yes.'

CHAPTER SIX

'How could you?' Gabby tied Max's shirt-tails into a knot at her hip as her post-the-best-sex-of-her-life-times-three glow withered, just like the poor scrap of life she was looking at. Wilting and thirsty, the geranium's head hung limply in the weak early-morning sunlight. 'What the heck have you done to my plant?'

A bare-chested Max stepped onto the deck and handed her a cup of coffee. 'Yours, is it? I thought it was a present.'

'It's a present that now needs life support. You clearly can't look after it, so I claim part custody until you learn. It's *ours* then.'

'Okay. But you have to take charge of feeding time.' His arms snaked round her waist as he hugged her from behind. His heat wrapped around her like a cocoon. She leaned against him, unable to be angry after such an amazing night. He'd made sure she'd got exactly what she wanted, and when. And now she was hungry for more.

But still she was confused by the new turn of events. She had a bed buddy. It was the kind of thing other women did. People she read about, women she heard chatting in bars, sophisticated women, women who knew what they wanted and where they were going. Not grown women who, in their families' eyes, could never make up for a mistake committed over a decade ago.

And yet here she was. In a penthouse apartment with six feet three of sinful sex. Making up for a long time of celibacy.

Her nonna would be screaming a tirade of insults down from heaven. *Brazen. Sinful. Devil's child.*

She fought the instinct to put her fingers in her ears and block out the imaginary noise. Old Gabriella would have hung her head, like the plant, and withered and conformed to what was expected. New Gabriella laughed. 'We have something. That's a hoot.'

But as she peered more closely at the droopy leaves the laughter melted away. Nonna would be grinning along now. *Serves you right, wicked girl.* Again.

'Well, we did have something. Maybe it's a sign.' Celestial retribution. She touched a leaf. It came off in her hand.

Max grinned and stooped to pour his coffee into the plant pot. 'I'm not good at these kinds of things. I did warn you.'

'Wait! What are you doing? It needs water, not a caffeine hit. What are you trying to do? Kill it off completely?' She dashed inside to get a glass of water and poured it over the wilting plant. 'And it looks so lonely out here.'

'It's just a plant, for goodness' sake.'

'It's the beginnings of a garden, Max. And it needs care and attention.'

'So do I.' He wrapped her in his arms and leaned in for a kiss. 'Starting right now.'

Her back arched as she leaned away from him, hands flat on his chest. The towel from after their shower hung loosely at his hips. One false move...one very good move... and he'd be naked. She could already feel how hot she was making him. How hard. 'Promise me you'll take more care of it. Or no more kisses.'

'Na-ah. No promises.'

She shook her head. Wove her leg around his and pressed her nipples against him. Gyrated her hips in a dance of wanton desire. 'Promise, or no more of this.'

'Uh…huh.' At her insistence he nodded. 'Okay. Okay, I'll take more care of it. You are one crazy woman.'

'That's me. The crazy plant lady.'

'Maybe I like crazy plant ladies. Maybe you're my ideal woman.'

What happened to just friends with benefits? Her heart hammered in her chest. Ideal woman wasn't what she'd expected to hear. She'd been led astray before with that kind of comment and it had been the beginning of her downfall. So she'd learnt that lesson all too quickly. Never be charmed by a charmer.

But coming out of Max's mouth on such a beautiful morning, it felt like being caught in a ray of sunshine. 'How so?'

'Apart from that amazing thing you do with your finger…' He tapped her on the nose and guided her back towards the bedroom, his hand cupping her backside. 'You don't expect anything. You don't ask for anything. And you're pretty damned hot… God, I have so many things I want to do to you.'

'Ooh…' She turned into his arms, laughed at the glint in his eyes. 'That sounds very, very promising. But I should be going.'

His warm breath stroked the nape of her neck. He unbuttoned the shirt, let her breasts fall free. Closed his eyes for a second and sighed. When he opened them again he gazed at her. First her face, then a long slow gaze down her body. 'My shirt has never looked so goddamned sexy. What do you say to taking it off and staying a bit longer? I have nothing planned all weekend except packing for a conference that suddenly seems deeply dull.'

'Oh? Where are you going?' Her teeth grazed the side of his neck as she arched against him. He hadn't mentioned anything about going away. It would happen, she supposed, as he was an eminent, internationally in-demand surgeon. She just hadn't expected the prospect of him not being around to feel so bleak.

'Singapore. Then a lecture tour in Malaysia.' His head dipped as he took a nipple into his mouth. Heat fizzed through her at every lick of his tongue. 'But what I really want is to stay here with you.'

'Gosh, the life of a surgeon is so glamorous.' She tugged playfully on the fold of towel at his waist, hoping to make the most of the time they had left. 'How long will you be away?'

'Too long. But you're not back at work until Monday, so how about we spend the next twenty-four hours in bed?'

'God, yes.' She couldn't help the moan escaping from her lips. He had a way of driving her mad with one touch. One look. But her stomach growled, reminding her she hadn't eaten for a long time. 'But at some point we really do need breakfast. I need to replace some of that well-spent energy.'

'Later… I'll phone out later. I have other plans for my mouth right now.' His lips were on her breast, sending arcs of need spiralling through her. He edged her back onto the bed, kissed a trail down her ribs.

Suddenly, uninvited and unwanted, a shrill, silly pop tune stalled them.

Max's phone.

Already anticipating much more of what they'd spent the best part of the night doing, Gabby placed her hand on his arm. 'Don't answer it.'

'I have to.'

She groaned. 'It's your day off.'

'I don't get those.' He slid out of her grip, snatched the phone and frowned. 'Maitland.'

For a second he said nothing. Nodded. His breathing sped up, his jaw tightened. But his voice was soft and warm. 'Oh, hi. No, it's fine. Fire away…' He covered the phone speaker with his hand and turned to Gabby. 'It's Jodi.'

Then he tightened the towel round his waist, turned his back on her and left the room, resuming the conversation with his ex-girlfriend-turned-girlfriend-in-law. 'Yes, that's right. Thirty milligrams, three times a day. But if you hang on I'll come in now to check. I'll be there in five. No…you're not interrupting anything…nothing important.'

'Oh.' *Nothing important.* Again? Had she not learnt her lesson? Shivering in the now-cold room, Gabby sat up and wrapped the duvet round her. A tight fist of disappointment lodged in her chest 'Oh. Okay. That's how it is. Well, I was going anyway.'

Although she knew he hadn't meant it quite the way it had sounded, she suddenly felt like a spare part. A tiny piece in Max's busy life. Insignificant. He'd told her it was over between Jodi and him, and she was just the mother of one of his patients. His brother's girlfriend.

But it all seemed so intensely complicated. The brothers. Their rift that set the whole hospital on edge at times. This. Here.

Keeping everything on a need-to-know, ask-no-questions basis was all well and good, but it meant there was little connection. Nothing real. And the realisation that she wanted either something real or nothing at all hit Gabby hard.

And she definitely wanted to be something important. Clearly bed buddies wasn't her thing after all. Who was she trying to kid? Fun, sure. But the flip side to fun was expendable. Superfluous. Not needed.

She didn't want to be picked up and dropped when it suited. Didn't want to be the one doing that either. Because they'd agreed on equal terms, so she could do the dropping too.

For goodness' sake. He'd just spent the last few hours caressing her, whispering to her, sleeping with his arms round her, refusing to let her go. They'd even dispensed with condoms, using her pill as contraception—so as to get the deeper connection, skin on skin.

But however connected they were physically, they'd never be connected emotionally. Not when either of them refused to give.

Putting her feet firmly on the floor, she gathered her wits. These weird displacement feelings were a shock.

She needed to get out. She needed to be sure of what she wanted. And that certainly wasn't to be a spare part.

As soon as the spark dies...

That didn't look like it would happen anytime soon. If anything it was getting more intense—at least for her. She was learning fast that Max was the kind of guy she didn't want to pick up and drop at will. The kind that she wanted to stay with way longer than was good for her, after the sex and the sleeping.

She needed to get out before the spark ignited and she got too caught up in the flashback.

As she got dressed to the sound of his laughter bubbling through from the lounge, a hot sting burned at the backs of her eyes. A love life was something she hadn't allowed herself to think of for ten years. *Ten years.* Doing penance for a mistake she would never repeat. And never truly recover from. So this was so not the time to discover she wanted the whole damned package and more. And with

Mr I'm Sexy, who wouldn't know commitment if it wal- loped him in that too-damned-pretty face. Not a chance.

He was still talking as she disappeared once again from his apartment when he wasn't looking. Hitting the city street, she hauled fresh air into her lungs.

And renewed her determination to never again lose con- trol of her life and her heart.

'I'm so grateful you've come.' Jodi's smile wavered as Max neared the cubicle. Even though her eyes were ringed with shadows and her hair wasn't as tidy as she liked to keep it, she was still breathtakingly beautiful.

Just an objective observation.

He checked his heart. No—no feelings there, except genuine concern for her and his nephew. And a little sad- ness, perhaps, that things had ended the way they had with Jodi. She'd been one in a string of women who'd berated him for his dedication to work and unwillingness to com- mit. They'd had fun, though, before they'd broken up. At least, he had.

Apart from being his brother's girlfriend, she was noth- ing to him now.

And yet when Mitchell had announced—no, bragged— that he was seeing her, their animosity had thickened. Years of frustration, hurt and lack of contact melded into a fierce rivalry.

Then, after she'd turned up with a child who was un- mistakably a Maitland, he'd had a mixture of feelings. Jealousy had been centre stage, although he hadn't been able to see it at the time. Anger, he'd thought, at a broth- er's bond being broken.

But now he had to wonder—jealous about what? The fact Mitchell had Jodi again? Or that he had a ready-made family? That, despite how sick Jamie was, Mitchell had found love and happiness?

And he himself had found what? A fulfilling career, sure. But there was little fulfilling about the rest of his life. Did he want kids? That thought whacked him square in the gut. Hell, he didn't know. Hadn't contemplated it until Jamie had come on the scene.

But today all he felt was just eagerness to help them get sorted out. Then he could get back home.

Amazing what hot sex with a prim, buttoned-up charge nurse could cure. He kept his smile in check. Finally he'd found someone just like him—wanting nothing more than a good time, even if she'd done her disappearing act again. One of these days, maybe, he'd actually wave her off or even accompany her out of his apartment, instead of turning round and finding she'd done a bunk. Again.

And it was no end of irritating to realise he missed her again, too. Somehow she'd grown on him in unexpected ways. She'd probably just popped out to get breakfast.

But, goddamn the woman, couldn't she have left a note?

He closed the cubicle curtain around the bed to create a little privacy, trying to focus on the matter in hand. 'So what's the problem, Jodi? The meds dosage is being titrated so it's going to be different on different days until he stabilises…but you sounded panicked on the phone. Something else bothering you?'

'I overheard one of the nurses say that a couple of the kids here had gone down with some sort of vomiting bug. I need to get Jamie off this ward now.'

Great. That's all they needed: a compromised child and a virulent gastro bug. 'Yeah, the anti-rejection drugs do silly things with Jamie's immune system. He'll be vulnerable.'

'You're the only one with authority to discharge him.

Mitchell said he'd sign a self-discharge form if you…disagreed.'

'I won't. Why would I?'

She paused. 'Oh, I don't know…'

'In case I was difficult? Right?' Max pulled at his shirt collar. Something was irritating him, but he couldn't tell whether it was outside his body or more than skin deep. He shrugged. Checked the charts. 'Jamie's doing fine. I'm still a little concerned about getting all the dosages right, but I agree he'd be better off at home than at risk here. You can bring him in to Outpatients and we'll take it from there.'

'You hear that, baby? We're going home,' she whispered to Jamie, her voice thick with tears. 'I didn't think this day would ever come.'

The little guy jumped up and down on the bed—thrusting an old fire engine into Max's hand, those brilliant blue eyes blazing with mischief.

Suddenly an image popped into Max's head of him and Mitchell—not much older than Jamie—in some sort of den they'd constructed with a clothes airer and a sheet in their old house. The one they'd been dragged away from in such a hurry that fateful night.

Under the sheet they'd been laughing about a shared joke, chatting in twin-speak, the strange gobbledegook language they'd made up. He'd forgotten. Forgotten they'd once had such a strong bond that no one else had even understood them. Just the two of them, inseparable. Emotion clogged his throat and he sucked in air.

So many things he'd blocked out in order to cope. Easier to push everything—everyone—away than risk emotional overload. Easier to forget than to drag everyone down with him.

Their mother's face had been a mix of emotions as she'd popped her head under the sheet and laughed in confusion.

'You two, what a pair! You're always up to something. Would you one day let someone else into your private jokes?'

The memory was infused with the pungent smell of flowers. Was that her perfume? No... He tugged at the memory to try make it more real, but the more he tugged the harder it was to grasp. It disappeared into a mist, leaving him heavy-hearted and face to face with a red fire engine and a toothy smile. 'Max...play.'

Taking the fire engine out of her son's hands, Jodi ran it along the bed frame. 'I don't think Uncle Max has time to play, right?'

It was an invitation to leave. He was torn. He wanted to sit here and play with his brother's son for a few more minutes. Be a part of their lives. But he didn't know if Mitchell would take kindly to that. Instead, he had to let them all go. The irritation seemed to thicken the back of his throat now, his words struggling to come out. 'No, 'fraid not, buddy. Uncle Max has to go. But I'll see you...'

Jodi nodded. 'At Outpatients.'

'Yes.' He turned to go, but realised he needed to say something more. 'I'm really sorry for how everything has turned out.'

She gave him a shy smile. 'You mean you and me? Or you and Mitch?'

'I should have treated you better. But I'm glad you're with Mitch now. You both seem happy.'

'We are. He's not that bad, you know.' She winked.

'That's what they said about Attila the Hun.' When she laughed again he joined in and it felt great. Strange, but great, to have made some inroads.

Gabby was right. Maybe he and Mitch should call a truce—he just didn't know how to take that step. Maybe have that beer in The Shed, and a chat. Would his brother be open to that? A chat? That was something they hadn't managed for a long time. Seemed Gabby was right about way too much for her own good.

Jodi patted his arm and smiled. 'I can't thank you enough for what you've done. Perhaps you could come round to the house sometime? See how things go? Jamie would like that.'

'And Mitchell?'

'Give him time. I'll work on it.'

'Okay. Yes. I'd like that. If it's not too much trouble.' He slipped a kiss on the boy's head and huffed out a breath. Things were starting to look up, a chance at making something better with Mitchell, being part of Jamie's life. And a damned fine night spent with a gorgeous woman—with promises of a whole lot more. Her plans for a truce were finally taking form. He couldn't wait to tell her he'd actually been invited to his brother's house.

Now all he had to do was find her again.

Hours later he sloped back to his apartment block, tired, hungry and distinctly annoyed. Not knowing the correct address of the woman he was sleeping with was an error he wouldn't make again. He'd hammered on half the doors in Boston Road. Hadn't clicked at first that it was a damned main road that stretched for miles. And why the hell did she have her phone switched off? She had hours before she was back on duty, and that meant hours to play.

Turning the corner towards his front door, he was semi-blinded by a riot of colour. And now irritation almost burst out of him. Damn. He didn't want her silly gifts, he wanted her. Now. In bed.

But she'd sneaked back when he'd been out and had brought him a trio of ghastly plants identical to the last one. Okay, not identical. These at least looked alive.

Three—the same number of times they'd made love. Ah, the reality started to sink in.

Plus, she'd left a basket of oranges, pineapple, bread and milk. A tub of plant food. This time there was no note. He checked. And checked again, his good mood rapidly degenerating.

Shoving the door open and backing into his flat with his arms overflowing, he finally nailed what was bugging him. This wasn't a thank-you gift. Or a friendly gesture. It wasn't an *I'll be back soon to share.*

It was a kiss-off. A goodbye.

CHAPTER SEVEN

Six weeks later...

'AND THAT, MY FRIENDS, is a wrap,' Max raised his voice above the upbeat rock music that accompanied every closure he did. As he finished securing the final clip on his patient's swollen belly, the usual wave of relief hit him in the gut. It was only the beginning of a long journey, but at least the old guy had a chance now. 'I'll check on him when he's out of Recovery. Any problems, call me. I'll be up in the paediatric HDU.'

'HDU? Why? We don't have a patient there at the moment, do we?'

Deflecting the strange looks from his registrar, Max lobbed his gloves into the pedal bin, flicked off his surgical gown and washed his hands. 'I think I left my keys up there. Just going to check.'

'I could phone up if you like. Save you the trouble.'

Goddamn, could the man not leave him alone? 'No worries. I could do with the exercise.'

Surgery couldn't go fast enough these days. Not when his body had a homing instinct straight to the HDU.

Turning the corner, he saw Gabby leaving the staff cafeteria, coffee in hand. He jogged to catch her up and fell into step. 'I was just on my way to find you. In your usual hurry again, Nurse Radley?'

She offered him a wobbly smile, hesitant and unsure. Despite the confident outward appearance she liked to show the world, he could read every emotion flitting across her eyes. Today it was embarrassment, uncertainty and a dash of heat.

It wasn't that she didn't want him, then. Even after all this time her cheeks still heated at the sight of him. It was that she'd decided she couldn't, for some reason. 'I'm trying to get back to the ward. Since that gastro bug hit the hospital we've been rushed off our feet and painfully short-staffed. It took everyone out in waves.'

'But we haven't spoken properly for weeks.' And since the moment he'd walked back into his bedroom and found her gone, again, he'd had a keen sense of loss. Something missing from his life. Something missing from his bed. Now he finally had her attention he was going to keep it. 'I liked the way we were before. When we had a laugh.'

'You're very busy and important, Max. You went away to a conference for a fortnight—can't blame me for that—and I couldn't help getting sick. You've seen me most other days.'

'And every time I hit your radar you disappear behind a curtain with a patient or into a meeting. The toilet. Lunch. Timbuktu. It's close on six weeks since…' Okay, so, yes, he'd been counting. No big deal. He just, well, he missed her.

Dating other women had been dropped from his agenda, as had mindless sex. Nothing seemed quite as vibrant and bright without her in it—particularly his apartment, although his deck was all kinds of Technicolor with those darned flowers.

Putting his hand on her arm, he managed to get her to

focus on him. Stopped himself from planting a kiss on those chocolate-stained lips. 'Look, we need to talk.'

Uncertainty flickered behind her eyes. 'We do? Why?'

'I have news.' His chest swelled. He'd been trying to tell her this for days. It was ridiculous to be so damned excited about something so inane.

Her lips tightened. 'What do you mean? News?'

'We're going to be parents.'

'What? What on earth are you talking about?' Her cheeks pinkened, her eyes narrowed. For a second she looked spooked—no, abjectly terrified. She shook her head. 'No…no, we're not. We can't—'

'Yes. One of the plants has a new sprout. I think it's having a baby.'

'Really? The plant?' To his relief her mouth relaxed and she laughed, running her fingers over that silver heart at her throat. 'I thought you meant… How could you…? Oh, never mind. Wow. You've done good.'

He nodded. 'I know. And thank you, by the way, for the three extra mouths to feed. Now that I have a jungle family to care for, I don't have time to sleep.'

'The geranium needed company. And seeing that champagne isn't classed as an essential food group, I thought you needed some decent nutrition in your fridge, too. It was the least I could do.' And she truly did look a little shame-faced that she'd sneaked out on him again.

'Especially after you vanished, leaving me hard and half-naked and wanting you so much I thought I was going to die.' Ignoring her frown, he steered her to the laundry loading bay. Luckily it was deserted, save for a very large truck. He pulled her behind it, out of sight from the main corridor. 'Thing is, I had a lot more in mind that day.'

Holding her coffee cup up as a barrier, she tugged away from him. 'Well, I considered what you had to do—whatever that was—a lot more *important* than what we had planned.'

Was he missing something here? She was making a point but it was beyond him. 'I had to go and sort out Jamie's discharge meds. Then there was that conference. I did come and look for you.'

'I know. I understand.' But she wasn't giving him much hope for any sort of reconciliation.

'We miss you.' At her frown he explained. 'Our family.'

'You are so ridiculous.' She started to walk away, chucked her coffee cup into the trash, along with his hope. The conversation ended.

He reached out for her, but she was too quick. 'Wait, Gabby.'

His phone rang. 'Wait…'

Her back stiff, she retreated into the main corridor. 'Busy day, Mr Maitland.'

Now they were back to 'Mr' again. 'Wait.'

In three strides he caught her up, grabbed her hand. His phone blared again.

She tugged.

His phone screeched louder. 'Oh…crap.' He lifted the phone to his ear. 'Maitland.'

She stopped. Waited for him to finish his conversation. The whole time she stared at him, unable to wriggle out of his grip. Her face darkened, reddened, lips tightening into the thinnest line he'd ever seen. Her eyes blazed raw and black. And all he could think of was how she'd looked sprawled on her desk, panting and spent. Vulnerable, but so vibrant. How he wanted to make her wriggle like that again.

He flicked his phone back into his pocket. 'Your desk is only two floors away. We could make it in five minutes. Two if we run. What do you say?'

'I say let go of me, Maitland, or I call Security.' Her voice was loud and unwavering.

Smiling as sweetly as he could, he leaned into that soft, sweet-smelling spot at the nape of her neck. 'Okay, we're at work, and it doesn't feel right, that's fine. But listen, I have a kidney on its way from Dargaville. And a recipient driving up from Cambridge. I have to operate. Today. Or both the kidney and the patient will die. But I will be free after that.'

'So?'

'So you are six hours away from the best sex of your life. Do not walk away from me now.'

'You have no respect.' Pinching his hand with her free fingernails, she sent jarring spiky pains through his skin.

'Ouch. What the...?'

Grabbing his moment of weakness as an opportunity, she wrenched her fingers out of his. Shoved her fists on her hips and looked at him the way his uncle used to. A long time ago, but he still felt that familiar sting of shame, usually two seconds before he'd felt the sting of the belt. He was expecting the *must try harder* retort. He'd clearly disappointed her and he didn't know why.

She scowled at him. 'You don't want a relationship, Max. That I can understand. You don't want to commit. I get that too, I really do.'

'So what's your problem?'

'*Your* problem is I will not be left waiting naked in bed...only to hear you describe me as "nothing important".'

He would have reached out to her again but valued his intact skin too much. 'You thought I meant you?'

'You *did* mean me. Us. Spending the day in bed.'

'I didn't mean it like that. It was a slip of the tongue.'

'It came out all too easily, Max. And as I lay there naked

and waiting, I got to thinking. I thought I was happy with our arrangement. It was fun, it sounded like a good idea. All grown up and sassy.' Her shoulders slumped forward a little and her voice got smaller. 'But I've never done anything like that before. I'm just not cut out to have sex and walk away.'

'You managed it quite well before.'

Her eyes blazed. 'But don't you see? I didn't manage it at all. It was a mistake. I thought it was the kind of sophisticated Auckland thing to do. I thought I could walk away unscathed, but I can't. I can't treat you like that and I definitely deserve more respect. I'm not a toy and I'm not going to be treated as *nothing*.'

'Whoa. I didn't realize. I messed up pretty big, didn't I?' He'd blown it. Acted like a jerk, trying too hard to please Jodi, look after Jamie, rise in his brother's unforgiving eyes. And had hurt her in the process. Not realised that, despite her bravado, in reality Gabby needed more from him. Trouble was, he didn't know if he was capable of giving it. 'I'm sorry, Gabby.'

'Yes, me too. But it wasn't working.'

He'd heard those words before. Too many times. And each time he'd thought it was someone else's problem. Not his.

But maybe she had a point. A small one. And worse, this time he didn't want to lose this thing they had. Sure, he was going soppy in his old age, but he liked having her around. Hell, he ached to have her around. He wanted to fall asleep with her, wake up with her again. He liked the way she added colour to his apartment. She just needed to be convinced. 'We can fix this.'

'I don't think so, Max. Not by taking me to bed again or having a quickie over my office desk. That won't work.'

'Then what would?'

She stalked away, her words trailing back to him on a hiss. 'Hell, if you can't work it out with all those fancy medical qualifications, you are six hours away from *missing* the best sex of your life.'

Atta girl. He smiled as he watched her retreat. He was not going to miss out on that sex for anything. Challenge was his middle name. And that was the kind of gauntlet he could run.

Six hours, three minutes and fourteen seconds later, Gabby carefully placed the last of her blue boxes into the bottom of her wardrobe with a heavy heart and dashed to answer the door.

'You're late,' she said, to the thick green spiky bush bristling outside on her porch. She wouldn't admit to the ridiculous rabble of butterflies flexing their wings in her stomach.

But… What. The. Hell? He'd actually thought about what she'd said. That he'd even turned up was an amazing step forward. That he'd come with a plant rocketed him to idol level.

It was scary, but it was a start. Her emotions hovered between *let's get back between the sheets* and *run for the hills*. For well over a month she'd kept a lid on her emotions, thought she'd conquered her weakness for irritating transplant surgeons. When she'd lobbed those words at him earlier she'd believed there wasn't a chance in hell he'd actually rise to the bait.

She should have known better. He was a Maitland, after all—they always played to win. 'And you have to go one better, don't you? A small plant would have sufficed. A bunch of flowers? Chocolates?'

The bush wobbled as branches edged their way through

the door. 'Give me a break, will you? Walking a tree down the road is harder than you think. And it's got teeth.'

'It's a cordyline *bush*, not a tree, and, no, it hasn't.'

He laughed. 'You know way too much about plants and all that.'

How could she take a talking cordyline seriously? 'I was brought up on a lifestyle block. We did outdoorsy things.' Too many. Then stuff had happened. Isaac had happened. And now she had to live with the fallout. They all did.

Sucking in a big breath, she closed that door in her mind. Some decisions she'd have to live with, but she was determined to move on. She'd been destined for great things, her nonna had said—so Gabby was going to make sure they happened. 'Come on, let's take it through to the garden.'

Max stopped short as he squeezed out the back door. 'Garden? Garden? This is worse than mine.'

'I'm working on it. The landlord has the audacity to describe it as an oasis. But, look, I have herbs and a flower bed.' Kicking the dry earth, she sighed. 'It's very different from the soil in Wellington.'

'Okay, so you're from Wellington.' His words were muffled slightly by foliage.

'Yes. Well, we live in a small township just north.' They truly knew little about each other yet had been so intimate. Talking to him now, without the pressure of work or sex, was easy. Her words just tumbled out, unguarded. She'd have to be careful of that. 'It's a farming community with people trying to scratch out a living. We have a few hectares.'

Land that had depended on her being there to help tend it in what little spare time she'd had. God knew what state it was in now. Her mother would have to cope without her. That would be a first. 'There were only three of us—

Mum, my grandmother and me—so I had to help out a lot around my studies and work. We sold our produce at the local farmers' markets.'

'Sounds fun.'

'Sounds stifling.' With her dominating grandmother and manipulating mother, it sounded very much like the prison it had become.

A dull ache squeezed in her abdomen and she ran her hand over her belly as a wave of nausea rippled through her. Memories affected her in too many ways these days.

'Not a lot of fun, then?'

She breathed away the pain. 'Hardly living life on the edge, no.'

Late-afternoon sun filled the dusty courtyard, giving the place a feeling of summer, although they were far from that. But the sunshine warmed her, gave her a sense of optimism. She was here in Auckland with a fabulous job and a gorgeous man.

Gabby leaned against the doorframe, watching Max bend to put the plant on the ground. Maybe she could get over her anxieties about spending time with him, maybe they could work on the friends thing. That would be nice. She'd been working so hard she'd barely had time to make friends. Maybe...just maybe the benefits could come later. Once she'd got her head around her emotions.

But watching him straighten up and turn to face her, his eyes squinting in the sun, hair mussed up from plant-carrying, her breath was stripped from her lungs. God, he was gorgeous. Getting her head around her emotions might take a little time. 'So, you came here for...? A reason? Surely not just to bring gifts?'

He stepped forward, his mouth curling into a smile. 'I came to apologise. Seems to me we've gone about this all the wrong way: sex first then trying to learn about each other afterwards.'

'Isn't that your mojo? You should be used to it, surely?'

'Kind of. But I really do think we should clear the air. Let's go out.'

Her heart began to hammer against her ribcage. She was scared that the more she learnt about him, the more she'd like. And then the harder it would be to let go. And she didn't want this to be a sympathy invitation either. Or just another of his games. Because she knew he liked to win and she wasn't sure she was up to fighting him. 'Are you asking me out on a date? Because I don't think so.'

'No. Not a date. It's a getting-to-know-you…meeting.' He grinned. 'And as you're newish to Auckland I thought I'd take you sightseeing.'

'And what about our commitment issues?'

His eyes widened in surprise. 'Whoa. Straight talking as always, Nurse Radley. It's a dinner invitation, not a marriage proposal. The issues still stand. But I thought you might consider overlooking them, at least for tonight.' He stuck out his hand; it was warm and firm as she fitted hers into it. 'Gabby, please do me the honour of accompanying me for the evening. If we have fun, we may consider repeating it again tomorrow. Much more than that, I don't know.'

'Well, I've never been asked out on a non-date with a guy who can't plan past tomorrow before. This could be interesting.' Everything about his words and what she knew about him should have sounded alarm bells. But how could she turn down a plant-bearing sex god who just wanted to clear the air? 'I'll get my shoes.'

She dropped his hand and dashed inside the house, aware of his eyes on her the whole time. Question was, could she get in and out of her bedroom without him actually glimpsing her space?

'Or we could just skip the dinner thing.' He leaned lazily on the doorjamb, the heat in his eyes stoking the charge in her stomach. 'After all, one thing I can do is give you a good time. But you know that already. This your room?'

'No! Don't come in here.' *No. No.* Her heart thumped loudly as she shook her head. She couldn't have him in her room. Not until she was certain everything had been unpacked into its correct place. Until there was no way he'd see her things and think she was more crazy than she actually was.

He kicked the door open gently with his toe. Then frowned at the neat and tidy space. 'What's wrong, are you hiding a dead body or something?'

'No. It's just personal.' *Ask no questions, I'll tell you no lies.*

'Hey, it was a joke.'

'Oh. Sorry.' Seemed she'd overreacted. But how could she explain the things she kept in there without breaking her heart all over again? She had to get him out and do some air-clearing herself. 'So, let's go. Where are we headed?'

The questions in his eyes faded a little as his smile found its place again. 'First stop, the Sky Tower... You did say you were okay with heights?'

'This was not what I thought you meant.' Gabby's heart jumped and skittered as she stood dressed in a deeply unflattering blue and yellow jumpsuit and clutching a large metal clip attached to a harness. The windchill at one hundred and ninety-two metres was surprising, and it whipped her voice away a little. Either that or she truly was scared out of her wits.

Okay, yes. She was truly scared out of her wits.

She had to shout to make herself heard, but knew Max wasn't listening anyway. He had that determined look on his face that told her the man wasn't for moving. 'I thought we were having dinner here in that fancy revolving restaurant I've heard so much about. I prefer being inside. I prefer eating. Can we go back in? Please?'

Smiling, he adjusted her harness. 'Come on, fearless Gabby isn't scared? Surely not. Time to live life on the edge. Didn't you say you hadn't had a lot of that?'

'Is being up the top of this thing not enough? Now you want me to jump off it, too?'

'It's not dangerous. You're held on by a wire. Not like real base jumping. This is tame.' He brushed back a wayward curl that had blown into her face by the sky-scraping hurricane. 'I will if you will.'

'It's still a long way down at eighty-five kilometres an hour.' Yes, she'd listened to the instructions, read the notices, memorised the safety routine. If she was going to jump to her death then she would be well informed doing it. She curled into the heat of his palm, hoping he'd cup her cheek and kiss her. Then she'd find the strength to do this. 'I'll only do it if I can push you off first. You deserve nothing less.'

Damn right she had enough strength to do that.

'Deal.' He gave Jason, the jump master, the thumbs up. 'Ready when you are, boss.'

But Gabby held on tight to the rail. She peered over the edge to the streets below, where antlike people went about their normal lives rather than self inducing heart attacks at the top of the tallest tower in the southern hemisphere. Oh, and the building was swaying too. Great.

Then she slowly lifted her head and gazed out across the panorama of the city buildings and further still to the ocean. Another cruise ship was docking—it seemed tiny from this height. 'But why? Why this?'

'Two reasons. Firstly, it's a rite of passage. You can't come to Auckland and not do this.'

'You want to bet? I'm sure there's plenty of people who have never done this. I want to be one of them. I like never having done this.' The wind whipped up harder now, making the platform shake. The noise of the rattling metal echoed her erratic heartbeat.

'Then they haven't lived.' His hand covered hers and squeezed. 'And, secondly, it's about trust.'

'Now I'm really confused.' She'd started to shiver.

Putting his arms around her, he drew her close. She hesitated slightly, but he nodded and she went willingly into his embrace—as far as the wires and the harness and the clips allowed.

There was something so protective about him—his regular breathing, the heat of his body, the way he held on to her as if he'd never let her go. Ironic, then, that he wanted her to jump into nothing, supported by a flimsy wire. He whispered into her hair, 'Would I do anything to hurt you?'

He'd already hurt her once with careless words. 'I don't know.'

'Okay, not quite the answer I was hoping for.' He blinked. 'Do you trust me?'

'No.' That she did know, categorically. How could she trust a man who said she was nothing? But, then, at least he was trying to make up for it. In a spectacularly lofty way.

'Do you want to start trying?'

'It's too hard.' She wanted to believe he wouldn't hurt her. But she'd been there before—trusted a man—and it had ended in way more than tears.

He tipped her chin up and gazed at her. 'Trust me on this, Gabby. This is the best fun you'll have in years. You won't believe you found the courage to do it, but I know you'll ace it.'

Jason tapped his watch. The sun had started to dip below the horizon and if they were going to get the most out of this they'd have to do it now.

She watched Max edge to the front of the deck. There was little now between him and the ground, many, many metres below. The closer he got to the edge the more her stomach felt like it was dropping.

As he stood with his toes hanging over the edge of the thin platform, her heart rate went into overdrive, her legs barely held her up. He craned his neck round and winked. 'You can do this, Nurse Radley.'

This was exciting. Life-affirming. She shuffled forward, caught an intake of breath as she pressed her palms on his back. Caught her own scream as she forced all her frustration, her fear, her anger, her excitement…her growing need for him into her hands.

And pushed. 'See you at the bottom, Maitland.'

Then he disappeared into the air and for a second she thought of all the bad things that might happen. But that wouldn't. That this was indeed about trust. He wanted her to let go.

He'd brought her here to do this because it wasn't just an epic adventure, it was something fun they could share. A platform on which to base a friendship. *Do you remember that time you pushed me off the Sky Tower? I remember your screams as you flew.*

A platform for trust. A beginning.

Slowly, slowly.

Then it was her turn.

God. It was such a long way down. Such a leap of faith; in the wires and technology, in Max. In herself. Her courage almost failed her. She couldn't do this, didn't have the guts. She didn't.

So, she could remove the harness and go back inside to safety, or she could embrace this danger. She could turn it into a line, a line drawn between what had gone before and whatever happened next.

Old Gabby would never have done this. Old Gabby would never have been allowed to step out on here and risk her life, risk anything. But new Gabby—well, she could do anything she liked.

You do want more, Gabby, Max had said. And he was right. She did. She wanted fun and excitement, friendship, a rewarding job. The things everyone hoped for, that she'd been denied too long. Most of all, she wanted him.

Looking at the tiny shapes below, she wished she'd gone first, wished that the last thing she'd seen had been Max's face, felt his mouth against hers. She could just about make him out down there, standing away from the big red X, his arms outstretched as if to catch her. Would he? Was she putting her faith in too much? How messy would it be when it ended? Because surely nothing this amazing would last.

Gripping the rail with both hands, she hesitated.

She did have a choice. She just had to make it.

Could she take a chance? Dare she?

She imagined him calling her name.

Then she let go and jumped.

CHAPTER EIGHT

'OH. MY. GOD. Oh. My. God. I don't believe I did that.'

'Good, eh? I told you it was fun.' Max laughed at Gabby's wide eyes and pink cheeks. She hadn't stopped cursing and squealing since they'd unhooked her. And the fact he'd put that smile there fed his satisfaction no end. 'Rate it for me?'

Her grin spread. 'Five hundred and fifty thousand out of ten. Can we do it again?'

'Oh, no, I've unleashed an adrenalin junkie.' He shook his head. Another upside of it was that she hadn't let go of him since then. She'd slipped her arm into his and leaned against him as if she was meant to be there. Amazing what throwing yourself off a building can do for a friendship. Never mind the libido. 'They've closed the jump shop for today, sweetie. Stop pouting. Maybe we can go another day. If you're good.'

'I can be.'

'I know.' He saw the flicker of need there, heard it in her voice. But he'd promised himself he'd take it slowly with her. She'd had a point earlier—they needed to learn how to communicate. Good sex could only get better when two people knew each other well, right? After that, he didn't know. Distance hadn't worked for him. Maybe getting to know her, discovering all the faults that he could find in her, maybe that would dampen down this incessant craving to be with her.

Yeah, she must have faults. Trouble was, he hadn't found any yet.

He walked her down past the city-centre shops, along the waterfront, stopping to point out the old harbour buildings nestled between new glass-fronted architecture. Tourists spilled from the cruise ship, smiling and laughing, some dancing to the buskers beating out an old popular song. There was a carnival atmosphere.

He squeezed her to him as they strolled, ignoring the guilt that he should be doing paperwork or preparing for a lecture he was giving to the undergrads tomorrow morning. And the fact he really didn't know what he was offering her here. 'There are a few cool bars over there where we can grab something to eat. This area's changed heaps over the years. It used to be just a working dock.'

'You know a lot about the place. Is this where you grew up?'

Although he usually felt uncomfortable talking about his past, he let it go. He could hardly encourage her to embrace new things without trying a few himself. Besides, she had this way of asking in such a way that he couldn't help wanting to give her answers. 'I'm a Jaffa, yeah—Just Another Fella From Auckland. I went to Marquis School in the city.'

'Marquis, eh? Very posh. You rich, then?'

He laughed at her forthrightness. 'Not really. Just circumstances. Then I had a few years at Otago University. A couple in Aussie, learning the trade. Then back here.' He chose not to dwell on the early part of his life.

'Did you both go to Otago?'

'Both?'

'You and Mitch. Duh.'

She often spoke about him and his twin as if they were joined at the hip. How to explain that from the age of six he'd been brought up as an only child? Any time he told anyone the truth it was greeted with too much pity. He didn't need that. 'Yes. We did the same course. It's the best med school in the country.'

'Must have been hard on everyone else there, all that Maitland alpha ego and rivalry. A real force to be reckoned with. Now look at you, both top docs in your field, at such a young age.'

'Yeah, right.' He didn't mean to put an awkward silence in there. But somehow it had happened. His tone had been too sharp, too quick.

He didn't know what to say next and he definitely didn't want to delve too deeply into the dark side and deflate her high, so he gripped her hand and steered her into an Asian fusion restaurant overlooking the millionaires' yachts in the Viaduct harbour.

The lights from the buildings reflected in the dark water, giving the place an eerie glow. Bittersweet memories dallied with his heartstrings. This was the last place he'd seen his parents, so it was kind of spooky and special in equal measure. 'Wine? Mojito?'

'For a non-date, you're trying pretty hard to woo me.' She cast him a sarcastic smile. 'Lemonade, please.'

He ignored the jibe. Some called it wooing, he called it trying to be friendly. 'You sure you don't want a mojito?'

'No. I've got a bit of residual stomach griping from that vomiting bug.' Swiping her hand across her abdomen, she smiled. 'No biggie.'

'Yeah, it hit everyone hard. Took some of my interns weeks to get over it, or so they said. I thought they were just pulling my string.' Underneath those rosy cheeks he saw shadows. 'You okay, though?'

'Fine.' And now she looked embarrassed to be talking about herself like that.

He took her to a table, ordered the drinks and let the subject drop. 'So what about you, Gabby? You trained in Wellington?'

'Yes. It was a bit of a hike, travelling in every day, but I didn't want to leave Mum and Nonna to do all the work at home.'

'And yet here you are.'

'I know. The black sheep.' She blushed. He got the feeling she was picking her words carefully. This was obviously difficult territory for her. 'I still feel bad, but I just had to leave. I couldn't bear it anymore.'

'Why?'

'Oh…' Again she seemed cagey and unsure but also like it was a relief to let it out. 'My mum and I haven't got on for years, but I stayed for Nonna. Because of Nonna. When she died a few months ago I decided it was time to start fresh somewhere else. So I chose here.' Her words tumbled out in a stream and he was grateful she'd chosen him to confide in. More than grateful, especially when he knew he'd struggle to do the same with her—with anyone.

When he looked deeper into her eyes he saw a flicker of trust there—tiny and wavering, but there. And for a moment he didn't know if he could bear that responsibility when he couldn't give it back. Something in his chest constricted but he directed his focus on her. This was about Gabby. Not him. 'Was your mum happy about that?'

'My mum is generally not happy about anything I do.' She laughed, but it wasn't forced, more like she accepted her lot. 'She's not a coper, and relied on me and Nonna for way too much. But I decided she needed to learn how to stand on her own two feet. Actually, I decided to be the adult, so I enlisted some cheap labour to help her out and then I came here. So let's just say I left under a cloud. But it's nothing new. I had a lot of those growing up.'

'Why?'

'Lots of reasons—I was a surprise, not a happy one. Then I was the great hope. Mum was a single parent. We had little cash. I was…' she raised her eyebrows '…*destined for great things*. Mum and Nonna pegged me to be a doctor and buy them out of their financial mess. It's safe to say I let them down.'

'But being a nurse isn't a let-down.' Although the pain behind her eyes told him there was something she wasn't telling him. Something deep that still hurt now. Had she failed her exams? Had she not been cut out for it? Had she plain not wanted to be a doctor? 'Believe me, I know it's hard to carry the hopes of those around with you. Never quite meeting expectations, always feeling that you'd failed.' He knew all about not being good enough. No wonder they shared a connection.

'Not being a doctor is more than a let-down in their eyes. My having an independent mind and spirit never sat easily with them. I was raised to do what I was told and be a good girl. Or else…' She toyed with her silver necklace, ran her fingers over the diamond locket. 'Okay, spotlight back on Max.'

'Ugh.' He took a drink. 'You are far more interesting. Do we have to?'

'Yes. Parents?'

'Obviously. It's difficult to be alive without them.'

'Thank you for that, Mr Maitland. I can see why you became a doctor. I bet you aced biology.' The death stare returned, albeit laced with a laugh. 'Your parents are where?'

Before he could sugar-coat it the word tripped off his tongue. Flat. Cold. 'Dead.'

'Oh.' Fiddling with the napkin, she dipped her head, bit along the bottom of her lip. 'Gosh. I'm sorry.'

'Don't be. It was a very long time ago.' He'd gotten over it. Gotten over the fact they'd waved goodbye and that had been the last he'd seen of them. That a few days later he'd said goodbye to his brother, too. His whole damned world had fallen apart and he'd been unable to understand any of it. 'It was a yachting accident. They were planning to sail from here to Fiji but got caught up in a storm and didn't survive.'

'How old were you?'

'Six.'

She looked like she was about to throw up. Tears threatened as she leaned forward and stroked his hair. 'That's terrible. You poor things. I can't imagine—'

'You ready to order?' Worse than the thick weight pressing on his chest was seeing the pity in her eyes. Hurt was bad enough. 'I heard the wagyu is delicious.'

'Whatever you think.' Her hand dropped as she stared at the menu. Obviously his clumsy shift in conversation topic had upset her.

Damn, he'd done it again. Driven a wedge through a perfectly innocent conversation. They were supposed to be getting to know each other, but he didn't know how to bare his soul. He'd held it all in for so long it was part of him. And he didn't feel ready to give her that part just yet.

With impeccable timing his phone hit top decibels.

Mitchell. The name flashed on the display and he knew Gabby saw it too. Mitchell never rang. Ever. So this was important.

But Gabby stared up at him with those huge wide eyes that showed a flash of irritation. Max knew he was walking a tightrope here, and he wanted to get it right. 'I'll leave it.'

'No. Take it. It might be important.'

'No way. I'm not falling for that one.' Smiling, he pushed the phone into the middle of the table. 'I know this test—it's double-woman-speak for "answer that and I spear you with this steak knife".'

She pushed the phone back, her eyes warmer now. 'Seriously, take it. You've more than learnt your lesson. But next time, any trouble and you're off that Sky Tower without the harness, right?'

Truthfully, Gabby didn't mind at all. Not if it was Mitchell ringing. The intense adrenalin of the jump, then the opposite slump of devastation at hearing Max's story had jumbled her up, and she was glad for a few moments' respite.

The more she learnt about him, the more he seemed to entrance her. Fabulous yet arrogant surgeon he may be, but he came from such tragedy. That could be the reason for his dedication and need to succeed. Motivation came from so many different sources—maybe he was looking for validation through his work. Through sex—he certainly made a success of that. But that didn't account for all the problems between him and his brother.

Oh, stop the amateur psychology and stop trying to read into things. What she did know was that the poor twins must have gone through hell. Her dad had never been in her life so she'd never missed him, but to lose both parents at the same time was devastating. And they'd been so young.

Who'd looked after them from the age of six? How had two little boys coped with the deaths of their parents? And had any of that had anything to do with their rift?

Staring out over the water, she pretended she was fascinated by the view, tapped her foot to the jazzy music in the background. All the time straining to hear what Max could possibly be saying to his brother.

His voice had become calm after an initial hardness.
'Not tonight. No. Another time. Soon, though.' He paused,
seemed to look for words. 'Thanks, anyway.'

Not wanting to pry, she smiled—okay, she did want to
pry, itched to pry, really truly desperately ached to pry,
she had so many questions she didn't know where to start,
so couldn't—and waited for Max to speak. When he just
stared at the phone in some kind of daze, she coughed.

He blinked and gave her a funny half-hearted smile
back. Suddenly he seemed so boyish her heart snagged.
For all his sophisticated suaveness the guy had issues that
ran deep, and he was obviously still working through them.
'That was weird. Mitchell has a night off tonight and wondered if I wanted to go round for a drink.'

'Oh? You should go, then.'

'Here we go again with the test. No.' He picked up the
menu and scanned it. 'I'm not having you run out on me
again.'

'Seriously, this is good news, isn't it? You should go
before you both lose your nerve or find something else
to argue about. Like who has the most bubbles in your
damn lemonade.'

'But I'm here with you. You're *important*.'

'I can wait.' Laughing, she rubbed her shoulder. Since
the jump she'd had a niggling pain there—probably pulled
a muscle or something. In fact, generally she felt pretty
wiped out with the adrenalin high leaching out of her system. She just wanted to crash. 'Seriously, I'm not really
hungry. You go and see Mitchell and I'll head off to bed.'

She stood to go. The room swam around and she
grabbed the table edge. 'Whoa.'

'You okay?'

'Low blood pressure, I guess.' The nausea swirled.
When she could focus again she let go. It was definitely

a good idea to go home, although it would be a shame to let the evening come to an end. But there would be more of him tomorrow. More tiny steps forward. 'I'm fine. But I really think I need an early night.'

'Alone?'

'Yes. Alone, Max.' She tutted, then looped her arm into his as they walked to the main road. He was such a muddle of contradictions. One minute he was intense and sad. The next he was cracking jokes about sex. He'd moved on swiftly from his dark mood. If only he'd give her the whole story. Then she'd truly feel like she understood him. But there was a way to go before that happened. 'This has been the best night, but we're still learning.'

'We could learn a lot faster...naked.'

Yes, please. She batted his arm, shoving away thoughts of how good he looked wearing absolutely nothing. Nonna had always taught her that you had to wait for your rewards because they tasted all the more sweet. Gabby hoped like hell Nonna was right. 'So, how did we do? You think you might want to do this again another night?'

'Well, we have the team kayaking trip tomorrow evening.' His eyebrows rose cheekily. 'Some watersport is always interesting to add to the sexy mix.'

'Do you really think about sex every five minutes?'

'Sex with you? Every three.'

'Honestly! You're incorrigible.' But she smiled. The fact he still wanted her and cared enough to let her know made her feel hot inside. She'd never had that—had thought she'd had it once with Isaac but that had been a fallacy.

Truth was, she didn't really want to go home alone. She didn't want him to go off and see his brother. She wanted to lie in his arms and go to sleep. But she knew if they spent another night together she would be committing herself to him. And that would mean opening her heart, her old wounds, her memories. And she wasn't ready for that. She didn't know if she ever could be.

'Let me take you home first.' His arms circled her waist and he pecked a nonchalant kiss on the tip of her nose. 'I'm worried about you. You don't look well.'

'I'm fine. Please, get to your brother's before it's too late.'

A taxi pulled up and he opened the door for her, paid the fare in advance and blew her a kiss. But as he disappeared into the darkness, her heart constricted.

It was already too late. Somewhere along the line she'd committed her heart to him and she couldn't do a darned thing about it.

She fiddled with her necklace, clenched the diamond in her fist. But then what? If she was going to let him like her, and have a decent chance at a relationship, she'd have to be honest, tell him what she'd done all those years ago.

And she couldn't do that. She just couldn't.

CHAPTER NINE

BAD IDEA.

Max squeezed the beer can in his hand while his brother left the room to tend to Jamie. Getting together with Mitch was always difficult. Growing up, they hadn't played board games, they'd played barbed games. Who could hurt who the most. Who could be the bolder, bigger, braver. Who was the best.

Distance had put paid to any kind of relationship. Hundreds of kilometres and lack of desire on their uncles' behalf to allow them time together had forced them apart. Until that distance had become insurmountable, geographically and emotionally.

On the few occasions they'd spent time together Max had been eaten away with envy at the cosy family set-up Mitchell had compared to his own stark, harsh one—and how little his brother had needed him. He'd believed Mitchell had had no space in his life for his twin. And that hurt had dissolved into anger. At Mitch. At the world.

He knew Mitch had been jealous of him too—jealous of the money, luxuries Mitchell's family couldn't afford. Gradually that mutual jealousy, fuelled by their uncles' own dislike of each other, had poisoned them against each other.

So he should have listened to his gut and stayed with

Gabby. But, for Jamie's sake, he had to try. And he knew if Gabby got wind of any kind of worsening of relations between him and his twin there'd be hell to pay.

Hell, since when had he answered to a woman?

Since he'd fallen, literally, for a stubborn, newly signed-up member of the adrenalin-junkie club.

The door swung open and Mitch reappeared. Like looking into a mirror, Max could read his brother's moods, his emotions. Today they connected somewhere round about clueless. Mitch sat down in a big leather chair that had seen better decades, his hands curled round a can. 'Max, I think it's time we sorted a few things out.'

'Jodi put you up to this?'

'Yes. And no.' Mitch at least looked like he was trying to find the right words. 'You saved our boy's life and I can't thank you enough for that. I really can't. I owe you. We all do.'

'It's my job,' Max countered. But they both knew it was more than that.

'Thing is, now Jodi has this fantasy that we'll all live happily ever after.'

'Is there such a thing?'

'I hope so. For my son's sake.' The guy looked exhausted. He'd had a hell of a few months, getting acquainted with a child he hadn't known existed and reconnecting with a woman he'd separated from some years ago. In reality both brothers had had a hell of a time— their whole lives. They were the only ones who understood what the other was going through, and yet were unable to make things right.

Mitchell's family had always been plagued by money worries. Max had hoped he could help ease the way a little. He took a deep breath, unsure how Mitchell would take this. 'I wanted to tell you, I've set up a trust fund for Jamie.'

'You've done what?' It was hard to read his reaction. 'I don't need your money.'

'Hear me out. I wanted to give him something and I didn't know what. I thought it might help.'

Mitch's fist closed around his can and the metal twisted and bulged. 'Because you don't think I can provide?'

'No. I just thought—'

'That you could do better?' Mitchell's eyes blackened. Ease the way? Laughable. Seemed he'd erected a road-block. 'That'd be right. You haven't got a son, so you thought you'd buy mine?'

But then Mitchell looked as shocked as Max felt. What to say now? There was nothing to reply to that.

A wavering silence descended. Max studied his shoes. Mitch stared at the wall.

Eventually Mitch leaned forward and shook his head. 'I shouldn't have said that. I was out of order.'

It was Mitch-speak for *I'm sorry*. Max took it gladly. 'Look, I know things weren't great for you financially growing up, that you're still sorting out things for your... for Uncle Harry.'

Mitch laughed. 'Yeah, I got the bum run there. Should have been picked by Fred.'

'No, we should never have been in that situation at all. Two uncles given a choice—*a choice*—as to which boy they'd have. Like picking out a new car or a house. *Dip dip dip. My blue ship.*'

So they'd been boisterous and grief-stricken and a hand-ful. So they'd fought and screamed and missed their mum and dad. So they'd run away, lashed out and cried. But no one should ever have split twins up so soon after their parents' death.

What the hell had been going on in the grown-ups' heads he had no idea—but it had been obvious to Max then, as a child, that their decisions were so wrong. So horribly wrong. And in true Maitland style the uncles had been fighting their own battles. Who was better than who? Who was most successful? Who had the better son? One-upmanship ran deep in the genes. They'd all been living with the consequences ever since.

Max spoke up, 'Harry tried hard, though, didn't he? I was always envious of you—you seemed to have a connection with them and their kids. All I had was a fancy education from Fred's Midas touch.'

'Lucky you.' Mitch sat back in his chair. 'You did well out of his cash.'

'Lucky?' Max remembered the frequent emotional blackmail and taunts. *We never asked for you. We didn't want kids.* How Max would never ever be good enough in Fred's eyes. Compared to Mitchell's poor but loving up-bringing it certainly had never felt like he'd won the jack-pot. Rich, yes. But desperately alone.

'No, Mitch, there's a lot more to life than money. I didn't feel lucky at all. All our lives you've compared what you had to what I had. You have no idea what it was like.'

'To struggle? To have to work hard? To try to be as good as your brother? Get real, Max. You had a charmed life.'

Although this was getting out of control, it was getting real too. Finally opening up about what they'd both endured. Was it his imagination or did his back still sting from his uncle's belt wound twenty-odd years ago? Hiding the reality from everyone was preferable to reliving it. 'It wasn't easy for me. Stuff happened.'

'What kind of stuff?'

'You don't want to know.' But Max didn't want to sound like a victim either. 'Forget it. Let's move on.'

Because that's what happened in their lives. People moved on, leaving emptiness, chaos and hurt. Which was why Max never invested in his emotions. He never again wanted to feel the way he had when he'd lost his parents and then his brother. His enduring memory was of being dragged away, his brother's screams stinging in his ears.

From somewhere in the small townhouse Jamie cried out, the noise echoing off the walls.

Following his brother out to the hall, Max decided it was time to leave. He'd tried. They'd both tried. Who knew if it was enough?

Just before he left, Max paused, his hand on the doorhandle. 'Just one thing, Mitch. Do you remember making a den out of sheets and the clothes airer?'

Mitchell shook his head and frowned. 'No. Why?'

'In the lounge. In our old house?'

'No.'

'Really? A den that we slept in one night. And we had a secret language that used to drive Mum mad, you must remember that?'

'Nah.' Mitch's shoulders lifted then dropped as he turned to mount the stairs. 'It was too long ago. I've got a new life now, I'm trying to make a go of it. Like you, I'm trying to forget all that stuff.'

Max let himself out, a heavy ache thickening across his chest. Maybe it was pointless to even try to reach out to his twin, to try to create a family. Not when they didn't even have the same memories.

When the phone rang Gabby was sitting on the floor of her closet, sorting through her memory boxes again. Even though he wasn't in the room she instinctively closed the closet door to hide them from view. 'Max?'

'Hey.' Although it was wonderful to hear his voice, it

filled her with concern. He sounded flat. Tired. In the restaurant he'd been so closed down she hadn't known how to handle it. All she could do was wait until he was ready to talk. 'Thought I'd ring and see how you are.'

'I'm okay,' she lied, infusing brightness into her voice to counteract his. That damned SkyJump had snagged something in her stomach as well as her shoulder. An ache she couldn't shake with regular painkillers, which only zapped her strength and humour. Maybe she wasn't cut out to be an extreme adventurist just yet, or it needed a level of fitness more than that of a flea. 'How did it go with Maitland Two?'

'In his eyes he's Maitland One—so don't be surprised if that nickname isn't a hit.' His laugh was hollow and it made her heart hitch. She imagined him in that huge empty apartment with nothing for company but the plants and his worsening mood. 'To be honest, it went exactly as I expected.'

Not good, then. 'You need a distraction. Why don't you step outside and busy yourself with watering the babies?'

'Thanks. But I don't think that will help.' His voice thawed a little.

'So, what would?'

'You.' So inevitable. So obvious. So honest. His breathing stilled as he waited for her answer.

She glanced at the clock, torn between looking after herself and giving him what he needed. Maybe he needed to talk. Maybe they'd end up back at nothing—where neither felt able to give any more. But she'd spent a lifetime doing things for other people, rightly or wrongly—now she felt a tug of responsibility for him too.

It wasn't a bad thing, though, far from it. She liked it. She wanted to wipe that sadness from his voice, knew they'd have a fun time. That if anyone could make him feel better tonight, it was her. There was no point denying it: she'd lost a piece of her heart to him. And maybe, just maybe, he'd done the same with her.

But if she went over now, there'd be no going back. The commitment would be there, blatant in her actions. He'd know it. And so would she. 'I'd love to, Max. But I have an early shift tomorrow then the kayak trip straight after. I need to get some good sleep. I'm bushed.'

There was another long pause while he weighed up her answer. He breathed out a sigh, 'Okay, sure. I understand. No worries. See you tomorrow, then.' Then he hung up.

Just like that. Max Maitland had hung up with no sexual innuendo. No cheeky repartee.

The man had hung up without a fight.

Damn.

Ten minutes later she leaned against his apartment doorbell, letting it ring until he answered it. 'Surprised?'

He didn't speak. He was wearing the faded T-shirt from before and tight washed-out jeans. He looked like something from an advert, surly and sullen. But relieved.

His blue, blue eyes stared at her with a kind of need and tenderness that she'd never experienced before. Like she'd saved his world. Like there was nothing else he wanted more in his life.

Pressing her into his arms, his lips hit hers with a force that snatched her breath away. He hauled her against the door as his mouth traced rough, greedy kisses over her cheeks, her neck, her throat. His passion ignited a desire in her that overrode her intentions, overrode her sensibilities. All the holding back and the frustrations and the fear of letting herself go entirely with him were shot. He needed her and she needed him right back.

'I want you. My God, Gabby, I want you so much.' His

hands clawed at her blouse, ripped it from her, dragged her skirt to the floor. 'I want to be inside you. Now.'

'Yes. Yes.' She couldn't, wouldn't deny him this. She reached for his T-shirt, threw it to the floor. Tugged at his belt, her fingers brushing against his hardness. She needed him now as much as he needed her. Once she'd freed his erection from the constraints of his jeans she took him in her hand, felt the heat, the strength of him.

'God. Don't...' He groaned into her ear. 'Wait. Please.'

His fingers parted her legs, slipped into her, sending jolts of pleasure spiralling through her body. His mouth met hers again and he kissed her long and hard, stoking the want. If she didn't have him, if she didn't...she'd die. Pure and simple.

A huge pressure built inside her and all she could see, feel, hear was him. Max. His smell. His touch. And her whole body craved him.

'Now. I want you now.' Her voice was cracked and desperate, her words coming between each tight thrust of his fingers.

All too soon he withdrew them, cupped her bottom with both hands and picked her up. She wrapped her legs around his thighs and positioned herself over him. Then he was sliding into her. Pounding her against the wall, hard and fast.

He gazed at her as he entered her, a different Max now from any she'd ever seen before—emboldened and savage. Glorious and powerful. And he wanted *her*. Wanted to bury himself inside *her*. Wanted to lose himself and his crazy mixed-up feelings in *her*.

She squeezed tightly around him, gripped his back. Felt ripped apart with emotion—the intensity of his need meshing with her own. The ache in her stomach waned, then intensified with every stroke.

Those cool Maitland eyes bored into her, making a million promises. That connection she never believed she'd have. That fusion of souls.

Harder. Faster. He pounded.

Just when she thought she couldn't handle any more he tensed then moaned into her hair. Long and loud. She bucked against him, reaching the same high. Higher. Higher. Until the world splintered and burst into tiny stars.

He held her against the wall, rocking with her, slowly, slowly, his forehead against hers as their erratic breathing steadied. His kisses were more gentle now, infused with tenderness.

A huge knot of emotion lodged in her chest. She wanted him. Wanted Max Maitland more than anything else in the world.

She wanted him fiercely. Desperately. She wanted him to hold her heart and treasure it, not trash it like Isaac and Nonna and her mother had done. And she would hold and treasure his, if he offered it to her. If he could make that step. If she could.

After a few minutes she was able to speak. 'That was the most amazing thing.'

'Yeah. And so are you.' He withdrew and wrapped her in his arms. 'Come to bed. And this time you are not allowed to leave without me. No sneaking off. Promise?'

'Promise. I'll stay as long as you want.' *Forever?*

He carried her through to the bedroom as if she were as light as candyfloss and fitted himself around her, pulling cool sheets over their spent bodies. She watched as his eyelids fluttered closed.

'Don't go to sleep just yet, Max,' she whispered into the darkness. 'Tell me about it.'

'What?' His eyes remained closed but he snuggled in closer and rested his chin on her head.

'Mitchell.'

'Oh, you know. Same old, same old.'

She sighed. Was he hedging? Or did he truly not understand what she meant? The way she saw it, the only thing holding Max back from committing to anything was Mitch. And their tragic past. And she understood his reluctance to share his story. After all, history held her back, too. But she needed that connection with him. 'I mean from the beginning. Tell me about the geography. What happened after your parents...went?'

Against her chest his heartbeat sped up. 'It's too long and too late.'

'I won't go to sleep until you talk. And you know I have that kind of willpower.' She nudged him gently and wiggled round to face him. 'You want to try me?'

'No, I know what you're capable of, scary nurse lady.' He inhaled deeply, the hollows and slants of his face darker and more defined in the moonlit room. He was clearly filtering the information before he spoke.

He swallowed slowly, then began. 'Okay, so after our parents died we were put in care. Just for a short while. We were distraught and a handful. And I mean a handful.' He laughed sadly. 'But we just didn't understand what had happened. They weren't coming back, the people kept telling us. What did that mean?'

She imagined the two boys, not much older than Jamie, vulnerable and scared, living in a stranger's house. Tears pricked the backs of her eyes. 'It must have been terrifying.'

'Not as bad as then finding out we were going to live in separate homes.'

'What? Why?'

His hand stroked her thigh, back and forth. Back and forth. The rhythm seemed to steady him. 'My father had two brothers. Seems they were put in a difficult situation by the authorities—someone had to take us. And pretty damned soon before we got too difficult and they couldn't place us anywhere.

'Our uncles had always argued, played the Maitland competitive games. Neither of them really wanted us and they couldn't agree who'd take us both. So, as they couldn't reach a happy compromise to keep us together, they agreed to take one each.'

'That's ridiculous.'

'It is what it is.'

'So you were grieving and then separated. Twins? It's ludicrous.'

'It was almost thirty years ago; things are different now. Back then it was about keeping the adults happy. No one thought about how we'd cope.' He shuddered. It was obviously traumatic for him to talk about this—but it explained so much about him. How he kept parts of himself hidden from public view and wouldn't even allow a private glimpse. Why he chose to flit from woman to woman instead of putting down roots. He didn't know how. Probably too damned scared that every single person he formed an attachment to would leave him.

'The worst thing I remember was being led away by Fred. I could hear Mitch calling for me. I wanted to run to him, to tell him that whatever happened I'd find him and we'd be together again. But I was too scared, they were adults and they were in charge. Fred wasn't the type of man you messed with. And I was the older brother, I was supposed to look after Mitch. But I couldn't. I couldn't stop what they were doing. And I couldn't bear to see the look on his face as I lost him, too.'

Her heart was breaking. She gripped his hand and encouraged him to speak again, hoping that some good would come out of letting out all that pent-up hurt. 'You must have seen him again, though? Surely? They wouldn't keep you separated for long? That would be criminal.'

'Over the years Mitch and I got to see each other less and less. One year Harry and Fred had an almighty blow-up and access was pretty much stopped altogether. When we did ever meet up it was like being with a stranger, a distant cousin. His life was so different. So full, with brothers and sisters. He didn't need me. And I was completely alone. It wasn't until university, when we met up again, that it totally came to a head. Over Jodi.'

Hence the reality in which they lived now. It all slotted into place. 'What about your aunties?'

'My Aunty Beryl—*Mum*—they adopted me so they made me call her that—was nice enough.'

At the word 'adopted' Gabby froze.

She grappled to find words to fill his pause, but couldn't find anything to say. Her throat had closed. She nodded against his chin, encouraged him to go on.

'She was meek and subservient to Fred and did whatever he told her to. And he was a bully—I grew to hate him. Nothing was good enough. He once told me he wished he'd never agreed to take me on. Kids were too much trouble.' He huffed out a breath, his body shaking with anger. 'I was supposed to call them Mum and Dad—they were supposed to be my parents. Can you imagine? Can anyone replace your real parents? The ones who love you unconditionally?'

God, she hoped so. She really, truly did. His story had so many echoes of her own it broke her heart.

For the last ten years she'd desperately hoped that parental love could come naturally to those who wanted it enough. But what if it didn't? What if they changed their minds? What if they decided their child wasn't what they'd dreamt it could be? What if they made life intolerable?

The pain she'd carried around for so long almost overwhelmed her. This was Max's story, not hers, but she grieved for him with every bit of her heart. He'd lost. She'd lost, too. But while he'd had all choice whipped away, she'd made the choice on her own. And with good cause.

He hauled her close, kissed the top of her head, his heat and strength cocooning her.

She was utterly torn between holding him close and fighting free from his grip. To stay in his heat, and get away from him so she could stop more hurt. She wanted to be alone with her memories and her thoughts. She wanted to scream. To run. To stay. To weep.

Her throat closed, her belly hurt. God, how her belly hurt—a tight knot of emotion that squeezed and twisted.

His voice was hard now. 'My parents sailed off on some second honeymoon trip. They were supposed to be gone a few months, but they never came back. How could they do that? How could they happily leave us with a nanny for so long? How could they go off and die and give us up to strangers?' He nuzzled closer, took three deep breaths as he calmed down. It seemed like an age before he moved or spoke.

She wondered if he'd fallen asleep, but no way could anyone rest with such rage surging through him.

Eventually, he whispered, 'I'm sorry—you didn't need to hear all this stuff. You must think I'm crazy. But you could say I got pretty messed up back then. Every child has a right to be loved, right? To be brought up by parents who love them more than anything in the world? Who won't harm them? Who treasure them? There is no end of hurt, knowing you aren't wanted.'

That was when she knew she had to leave.

She had to walk away and not look back.

Judging by his intense emotions and his cruel experience, Max would never understand how she'd been able to do what she had. How she'd believed the choices she'd made had been for the best.

She needed to put space between herself and Max. Had to get out of his life once and for all, and never, ever let him know her story.

CHAPTER TEN

'HEY, WOULD YOU LOOK at that? I just realised we left my apartment together. At the same time,' Max whispered, when he approached Gabby at the nurses' station. All day he'd thought of nothing but having a rerun of last night. As he remembered her legs wrapped round his waist, his grin spread inwards and through him like a light.

Having opened his heart to her, he felt pretty damned good—like they'd made headway into something important. But he felt disoriented, too, on shaky ground. Like any minute now he'd get the need to run. Far away.

Trouble was, she seemed a bit subdued. Had been very quiet over breakfast. Uttered hardly a word as he'd dropped her off on the way to his ward round. Had barely managed a kiss. She was probably tired, so he needed to pep her up. 'Must be a sign.'

'Of what?' She looked up at him as she wrote patient details on a large whiteboard. Dark circles edged her eyes.

'Good things. I don't know. You didn't sneak out. That has to be good, right?' Watching her buckle slightly as she reached up, he leapt forward. 'Hey, are you okay?'

'Watch it, Prince Charming.' She nodded and backed out of his arms. 'It's busy and I don't want anyone to see us like this. I'm fine, it's just women's stuff, you know.'

Ah. He knew not to say a word. Just nodded. Took a step

or two out of range. He hadn't known her long enough or well enough to know how she coped with periods, whether she got PMS, whether she growled like a bad-tempered lioness once a month. Heck, he didn't know her favourite colour, what she ate for breakfast. Sweet or savoury. Coffee or tea.

But he looked forward to learning more about her. What he did know was that he couldn't keep away from her. That she was the first woman ever to hold his attention for more than a few days. Weeks.

And he sure as hell needed to rein his enthusiasm in. Tiny steps, like she said. 'Okay, got you. Enough said. I've got stuff to do, anyway. I'll pick you up in thirty minutes or so for the kayak trip. There's a bunch of us going down to the bay in my car.'

'I don't think I'm up to it. I'm still feeling grotty.'

Having been in hibernation way too long, his possessive instinct pushed to centre stage, as it always did whenever Nurse Radley came onto his radar. 'Do you think you should get it checked out?'

'Being over-protective?' She threw him a small smile. 'I'm twenty-five. I've been dealing with this stuff a long time. I get heavy periods, that's why I'm on the Pill—not so I can pick up strange men in bars and have random sex. Right? And now you know way too much about me. I just need a cup of tea, my bed and a hottie.'

'At your service.' He gave her a low bow, raised his head in time to see the frown. 'Okay, I get it, not that kind of hottie.'

'You are so up yourself. Now go away and let me work. And I'll definitely give the kayaking a miss. Can you tell Rach?'

'Tell me about what?' Rachel wandered over, the expression on her face telling him that their attempts at keeping their liaisons secret were failing. She winked. 'We have news?'

'Gabby's not feeling great so she's going to cry off the trip this arvo.'

Rachel's face fell. It was clearly not the kind of news she was anticipating. 'Not you, too? We're getting very short on numbers. If we're not careful we'll have to cancel altogether.' Then she seemed to realise how callous that must have sounded. 'Gosh. Sorry. I mean, if you're not up to it then we can postpone until next month or something.'

He watched a flurry of emotions flutter over Gabby's face. She looked first at Rachel then at Max, then back to Rachel. Absently rubbing her hand across her stomach, she shrugged. 'Oh, okay, okay. I don't want to let you all down. I'll come. But be gentle with me, and bags I get that two-man canoe.'

Standing at the water's edge at Okahu Bay, Gabby looked over at the majestic humped-top island. Rangitoto, an extinct volcano now covered in bush, appeared almost close enough to touch. But she knew it would take more than an hour to get over there by kayak. That was on a good day.

Today was not a good day. She felt strangely lightheaded at the thought of expending energy on anything. Her legs didn't feel strong enough to hold her up, never mind keep her stable on a long paddle across an ocean, and the dragging sensation in her belly had worsened.

Maybe a workout would help soothe the pain, or at least take her mind off it.

As long as she kept a reasonable distance from Max. Confused didn't describe how she felt—more like she'd lost something precious and knew she'd never be able to find it again. Her heart ached for him, but her head knew it was better if she kept him at arm's length.

Her attempts at avoiding him were in vain, as usual. Maybe it was time to move on, get a new job somewhere else, a different unit, hospital. A different country. At least then she wouldn't have to face him every day knowing that things could have been so good.

Dragging on the lifejacket, she had a weird feeling of dropping. The island blurred, then came back into focus. Then blurred again. Her head pounded and the pain in her stomach stabbed and dragged.

'Looks like it's you and me in this one.' Max hauled a double kayak towards the water. 'Hop in.'

'I was thinking I'd go with Rach or something—you know, sisters doing it for themselves and all that.' She raised a weak fist.

'I think your *sister* has other things on her mind.' He nodded over to where Rachel was climbing into a kayak with Rob from the night shift. She looked very cosy and not the least sisterly. Giggling even. *Traitor.* Max grinned and handed Gabby a paddle. 'We'd better be quick or we'll be the last to set off.'

'And that would be bad, why?'

'Because we'd lose.'

'Is everything a competition to you?'

'You say it like it's a bad thing.' Dropping the kayak into the shallows he turned, strode over to her and zipped up her lifejacket. Made sure it was fastened and she would be safe. Damn him. Did he have to be so considerate? Could he not be difficult? Did she have to be turned on by everything he did?

His fingers ran along the lifejacket, skimming the sides of her breasts. Instinctively they pebbled, anticipating his touch.

She edged out of reach. 'Don't…'

'What's all this about? Are you okay?'

'Yes. But I'm uncomfortable with people seeing us like this. And this kind of makes it obvious.' And too darned hard for her to cope with. Next thing she knew she'd be kissing him in full view of everyone.

'Sure, because they all look totally bound up in our lives, don't they? We could be naked and they wouldn't notice.'

'I would.' *Hell, yes.* For all the wrong reasons. She loved to see his long sun-kissed lithe legs, his perfect bum, his broad chest. And now she was torturing herself with such delicious images.

She glanced over at the team. They were jabbering about the trip, pushing off into the sparkling water. Planning their picnic and volcano walk. He was right. No one even seemed to notice that she and Max were in the same hemisphere, let alone same kayak.

'Okay.' Time to pull on the big girl's pants again. She would do this one trip. To keep everyone happy and bolster the team. Then she would be honest and open with him. Explain how things could not work—especially in light of what he'd told her of his past and his fervent beliefs. Then they would both be able to move on.

The trip across the harbour was smooth, the water calm, and the dappled late-afternoon sunlight provided a gentle warmth that was nurturing rather than overwhelming.

Unlike Maitland One. 'How easy is it to have sex in one of these things, do you think?'

She almost dropped the paddle. 'Impossible. Especially with all the rocking. Don't go there, Max.'

'That would make it more fun, don't you think? Living on the brink.' His voice deepened to that irresistible groan that stoked her inside. 'You want to try?'

Yes, please. 'Max, I'm wedged into a two-foot-wide hole and I'm soaking wet. There's about fifty metres of water between me and the ground. And…' She gestured to the flotilla of sailing boats with their white sails fluttering in the wind. 'There are more sailing boats and kayaks around than America's Cup week. I do not have sex with an audience.'

'So I take it from that you're possibly not keen? Wavering maybe?' His laughter fanned the flames his voice ignited. Damn him. One day she'd look at him and find nothing attractive about him at all. She would. She prayed that day would come soon. Tomorrow? And in that tight navy T-shirt and bright blue boardies, did he have to define sexy, too? The man would look sexy in a paper bag. He kept right on laughing. And stoking. 'Look, I want to talk to you about something. I do need your help.'

'Oh, yes?' She tried for nonchalant, wasn't sure she could ever be nonchalant around him.

But any call for help and she was there.

'I've been nominated for an award at the hospital annual ball and I need a plus-one. How about you come with me?' he yelled now, as he pulled back effortlessly on the paddles, propelling them fast and furious into the path of another kayaker. He really did want to win. In everything. Thing was, she had trouble denying him, too. But she had to.

'No, thanks.' She offered him a smile. Firm and fair. And as honest as she could be right now. 'I can't. I've nothing to wear.'

'You look fine like that.'

Whacking the paddle onto the surface of the ocean, she sent an arc of water behind her. Hopefully hitting her target. 'In cut-off denim shorts and an old T-shirt? Yeah, right. Perfect evening wear.'

'You'd look amazing in anything. Hell, you look amazing in nothing.'

He was making this very hard for her. How was she

supposed to tell him it was finished when he said things like that? When he made her feel the things she did? Sexy. Desirable.

Want flickered around her nerve endings, tripped up her spine, spread to her breasts, her groin. She tried to ignore it, even though it was getting way past troublesome. 'New charge nurse attends ball in birthday suit—that would get tongues wagging.' She tutted. 'I'm sorry, no. But you could advertise in the hospital classifieds. *Mr Sexy needs a date.* I'm sure you'd get plenty of offers.'

'I don't want plenty. I want you.' Even though he was behind her she could feel the swell of his chest. 'Mr Sexy, eh? Come on, say yes.'

'No.'

'Are you sure? Really sure?' With a jolt he started to rock the kayak from side to side. Faster and faster. Water seeped over the edges. His laughter turned pretend evil. 'You want to live dangerously?'

'Stop that!' She laughed as she hit the surface of the sea with the paddle again, hopefully soaking some sense into him. Nausea curled in her stomach. 'Stop.'

'Not until you say yes.' He rocked harder. Now water gushed in on one side.

'Stop, or you'll capsize us.' *And I'll lose my lunch.*

'Then I can save your life too and you'll be forever in my debt. Dashing hero opportunities abound. Say yes or you're getting an early bath.'

Laughing, she gripped the kayak as a mini-tsunami soaked her legs. 'No.'

'Yes!'

'Ohmygod, yes! If it shuts you up, yes!' The thought of spending an evening with him in a fancy dress appealed. At the plush Heritage Hotel too. God, how she'd love to walk in somewhere like that on his arm. But she wouldn't.

She'd cry off later, once she'd explained. Right now land was in sight and she didn't want to have to swim the distance. 'Now, get me to that shore before I feed you to the plankton.'

The walk to the summit was planned to take an hour, but judging by the way she stumbled upwards over loose black volcanic rock, Gabby thought it could take a lot longer. Getting purchase on the slippery path proved difficult and took more effort than she thought she had. The route took them deeper into thick bush, where they stopped only briefly to read signs telling the six-hundred-year history of the volcano.

Gabby hurried forward with the front group. Since coming ashore she'd managed to get herself nestled into the hustle and bustle of the climb and was grateful not to be on the edge with Max. She didn't trust herself to be alone with him. Before she knew it she'd be agreeing to much more than the awards dinner.

At a fork in the path an orange arrow signalled an alternate route taking them to the top via lava caves. She hesitated, wanting to see what these amazing-sounding formations must look like. But the rest of the group ploughed ahead, oblivious, the race foremost on their minds.

She watched their disappearing backs. 'Hang on! Does anyone want…?'

'I do.' Max's voice was like chocolate sauce over ice cream. Melting and thick. And hot.

'But you won't win the race.'

'Like I care.'

'You mean you would willingly lose?' Her hands found her hips. 'You're really letting the Maitland side down, there.'

He smiled. 'I think I already have my prize.'

Then he was reaching for her hand. Dragging her into the seclusion of one of the larger caves. It was cool and dark and smelt elemental—earthy, sensual. He pulled her in further, his hands circling her waist. Those all-blue Maitland eyes gazed down at her. God, he was divine. And hers for the taking if she wanted. All she had to do was breach that two-inch gap between them.

She struggled to get away. At least her head did. Her body glued itself to him.

He ran his tongue over her top lip, slowly. Achingly slowly. 'Kiss me.'

'What?' She pressed her hands against his chest, ready to push away. But her fingers curled into the fabric of his T-shirt as if making a stand. *We shall not be removed.* Excellent, just what she needed—renegade hands. 'Kiss you, here? You think that's wise?'

'It's the wisest thing I've ever done. Look…' He pointed to the thick shrubbery covering the view of the inside of the cave from outside. 'No one knows, no one cares. Hell, I'm sick of hiding out. I don't care who knows. And I'm going mad looking at the sway of your backside as you walk up that hill. I've got to kiss you. Now.'

'One kiss?' She could do that. One kiss. One final kiss. What harm would it do? 'Just one.'

'Or two, if you insist.'

'One is fine.'

'Yes, Charge Nurse Radley. And then I'll claim another later. And another. And another. When we're on our own. In bed.'

A tight fist clenched in the pit of her stomach. She wasn't being honest with him. She shouldn't be here doing this. But, God, she wanted to. Too much.

'No…listen, Max. We need to talk. We can't—'

Before she could find the right words his mouth lowered

onto hers. Such a gentle pressure, sweet and soft, suckling her lip. The simple, perfect pleasure of tasting him. He could be so tender yet so strong. So brilliant and yet so endearingly silly, it made her heart ache.

His tongue danced a slow dance against hers, teasing, enticing. Making her yearn for more. His body told her how much he wanted her. His mouth told her how much he cared. And she hoped she answered him with her response—at least her body was honest.

She clung to him in the damp darkness, not wanting to let go. He was so powerfully addictive, took her to places that she'd never been to before. Made her heart sing a soft and hopeful song where before it had played a fractured lament.

For a few beautiful seconds she allowed herself to take what she craved. Before the dumb bass notes in her head told her this was all kinds of foolish.

Then she managed to find the strength she needed to take a step back, even though the space between them filled with a rush of air that made her feel cold and she wanted to nuzzle back into his heat.

This had to stop. Insane. Senseless.

She turned her back, ignoring his hurt and confused look. And shouted back to him in the lightest voice possible, 'Race you to the top!'

The roughly hewn path gave way to countless wooden steps, getting steeper and steeper. She began to think it'd never end, and he'd catch her up and ask her a zillion difficult questions. But suddenly a bright blue gap in the bushline announced her arrival at the summit.

'Wow. That was worth the effort,' she spluttered to one of the guides as she managed the final few metres. Her heart hammered hard in her chest and sweat ran in rivulets down her back.

There were three-sixty-degree views as far as she could see—across the ocean to the east, and to the west where the melting sun cast a warm orange glow over the city and harbour. And right in the middle the Sky Tower rose magnificently, dwarfing the other buildings, like a needle jabbing the darkening sky.

'Here, eat something, keep that energy up. You're going to need it later.' Winking at her, Max handed her a plastic plate of cheese and crackers from the backpack he'd lugged up the hill. 'For the kayak home, obviously.'

He seemed a little frayed perhaps but kept up the smile as he set out the rest of the picnic on one of the wooden seats that made up the hexagonal lookout. Hummus, chicken, potted salads. Delicious, if she'd had an appetite. And very cute that he'd brought enough for her, too. Food certainly wasn't top of her list today.

All around, happy faces munched and chatted, congratulated themselves on such a fun way to spend the afternoon, challenged each other to a race back down and across to the city. Someone proposed a toast, and champagne flowed into plastic flutes. 'To the Paediatric HDU, and friends.'

When she saluted them Gabby realised they were all raising their glasses to her. A buzz ripped through her. Knowing they'd accepted her had tears stinging her eyes. She was fast developing a group of friends she'd begun to care about.

Since coming to Auckland she'd done things she'd never imagined possible with her restricted upbringing. Breaking those shackles had been such a relief, she'd invented a new persona for herself. One she liked. Finally.

It was sad, then, that she had to let the best part of her experiences go. But she'd always known forever wasn't something she could do—and not with a man like Max.

She toasted them back, unable to drag her eyes away from his. So blue, fervent and vibrant. So trusting—that was there too. A first. So she really would have to be honest, as soon as they hit the mainland again.

The thought of that made her head pound more. Her stomach knots tightened. She tore her gaze away and focused on his apartment high-rise, where she'd finally come to life again. Then the Sky Tower, where she'd confirmed that life, with his guidance. Auckland was Max's city and she'd never think of it again without memories infused with him.

'Time to move off, everyone. Watch your step as you go back down,' the guide warned, as they all began to pack up. 'It's slippery underfoot and the head torches only allow a limited view. Keep close.'

Gabby hung back to walk with Rachel.

Big mistake.

'So, you and Dr Make-You-Weep over there. What's the story? He's getting very cosy.' Rachel's tone was friendly and sincere. But it sent a rattle of nerves down Gabby's spine. She didn't want to become the subject of office gossip.

'Oh? You think so? I can't say I've noticed.'

'Come on. He can't keep his eyes off you. And you go gooey every time you look at him—like you're melting right there on the spot. It's pretty damned obvious there's a thing happening.'

'There's no thing.' Gabby's voice crackled. She tried to keep it steady as she whipped up the pace. With Rachel's probing questions and having lost sight of the others, she suddenly felt uncomfortable. They were falling behind. It was dark. And cold. And eerily quiet. 'Let's catch the others up. I don't want to get lost.'

'Wait. Hang on. Tell me about— Wait,' Rachel called. Then, 'Oomph…oww.'

There was a slight shiver in the air, the crackle of breaking branches. A loud scream. A thump of bone versus wood.

'Rachel? Where've you gone? Are you okay?' Heart thumping against her ribcage, Gabby retraced her steps and shone the beam of her head torch onto the ground. Her friend had disappeared.

No.

'Rachel? Rachel? Where the hell are you?'

This wasn't funny. The darkness covered everything like a thick black shroud. Gabby squinted and tried to scan the area but it was too dark, too hard to see anything beyond muted shapes and shadows. She managed to make out a steep bush-covered ravine dropping off the side of the path. Through broken foliage, way down, she made out a shape. Her heart beat a panicked tattoo in her chest. 'Rachel? Is that you? Are you okay?'

The shape groaned. 'I'm here,' Rach whimpered. 'My leg…hurts… I'm bleeding. A lot. Please. Help me.' Her voice wobbled and Gabby heard the beginnings of a sob.

Rachel was a competent nurse who wouldn't freak easily. Which meant things were serious. On a tiny uninhabited island. In the dark. And now left behind by the others.

Okay. Breathe. 'Hold on. I'll come and get you.'

'No.' Panic filled Rachel's voice. Panic, and pain. 'You won't manage, it's steep and dangerous. Get Rob. Max.'

'I'll come down first and check you out.' With her first step into thin air Gabby lost her balance, grabbed on to roots and earth and then nothing with her flailing arms. Tumbled over and over down the ravine, scratching her skin on sharp twigs. 'Whoa! This is lethal.'

Her arm hit against a spindly trunk and she grabbed it,

held on with everything ounce of strength she had, tearing the skin of her palm to shreds. Bringing her catapulting body to a hard stop.

After a couple of seconds to catch her breath she pulled herself to standing and reassessed the situation.

Safety first—assess the environment. Should have done that before. 'Okay, Rach. Wait here. Don't move. I'm going to scramble up to the path and get the others. I'll be back as soon as I can.'

'Please hurry. Please.'

The pain in Rachel's voice spurred her up the slippery incline.

It was too dark and dangerous to run. The loose scoria slid under her weight and she had to concentrate on keeping upright. Stepping gingerly over the rubble, she called out to the others, trying not to sound like she felt. Lost and lonely, scared and hurting. 'Max. Max. Quick!'

In the distance she heard the low rumble of laughter.

'Max!' She called louder, unable to erase the panic from her voice. Kilometres of ocean stood between them and any proper medical help. And she still hadn't been able to assess her friend in any kind of way. A lot of blood, she'd said. Gabby didn't want to imagine the dark possibilities. But they were real. 'Max. Please. Please. Help me.'

The voices stopped. Then she heard a thunder of footsteps.

Never had she felt so relieved as when she saw his large shape hurtle towards her out of the gloom. He was a doctor. He'd be able to sort out her friend.

No. It was way more than that. Her heart lifted every damned time she set eyes on him.

When he reached her his hands gripped her shoulders as he scanned her up and down. 'What the hell...? Are you okay, Gabby? My God. You scared the living— You're okay?' Now he was holding her tight in his arms. His lips were pressing on her forehead. In front of the whole crowd.

Before she shoved away she committed the feeling to memory. His smell. The shape of him. The feel of him as his body fitted so perfectly to hers. One last time. Her throat closed over and she forced words out as she directed them to the damaged foliage and the drop. 'It's Rachel. She's down there. She's hurt her leg.'

And it's my fault. She shouldn't have hurried like that in the dark, shouldn't have made Rachel run to catch up just because she was avoiding a difficult topic of conversation. 'But be careful, Max. It's dangerous.' She wouldn't forgive herself if something happened to him, too.

Within seconds he was scrambling down the ravine, assessing the situation. After a few minutes his calm voice rose through the darkness. 'Hey, listen, I think Rach has an open fibula fracture. We're going to have to call the coastguard—there's no way she can kayak back. But I need a hand to get her out.'

Between them they scrambled together a wound dressing and fashioned a splint out of a walking pole. Then they carried Rachel down to the jetty and waited for help to arrive. Night clung to them, darker and colder, as they waited anxious minutes.

After what seemed an age, lights loomed out of the darkness and two paramedics jumped off a boat onto the jetty.

As they waved her off, Max grinned. 'She seems a lot better with Rob holding her hand. Job done.'

'Yeah. There's definitely something brewing there. I just wish it hadn't all ended like that.' Then she admitted the truth. 'It was my fault.'

'No, it wasn't.'

'I should have made us stay with the group.'

*Instead of trying to avoid you. I should have been hon-
est from the start, instead of trying to take what I wanted.*

*Greedy. Impetuous. Selfish. Nonna was right all along.
One day you'll pay, my girl.*

She'd been paying every day since.

With all the excitement, Gabby had forgotten her own
unease. But now it came back with force. Her legs turned
jellylike as her stomach stabbed and swirled. 'Please, can
we go now? I'm so tired.'

'Hey, you're shaking. Here.' Taking off his fleece jacket,
Max wrapped it round her shoulders. Despite his heat coat-
ing her limbs, she didn't think she'd ever be warm again.
'Too much excitement for one day, eh?'

Max held the kayak steady as she wobbled into it. Sitting down was the sweetest feeling she'd had for days. As
she turned round to nod to him her vision didn't keep up
with her head. Whoa. She needed to lie down. Now.

And she needed to find the right words to say to Max.

But her head was filled with cotton wool. And she was
so cold she longed for strong arms to warm her. His arms.
Please.

She began to shiver and had to focus hard on keeping
the swaying paddling rhythm.

She barely noticed the lanterns the guide had attached
to poles on the kayaks bobbing gently in the breeze, creating a magical soft glow across the jetty.

Barely felt the water spray her skin as Max powered
the kayak towards the city.

Barely realised she had no strength of her own to even
hold the paddle now that every ounce of energy had deserted her. Exhaustion finally oozed into her bones and
made her feel cold. So very cold.

As she pulled the paddle towards her the pain in her

belly intensified like a bright, sharp knife, twisting and turning. Sharper. Hotter. Harder.

And suddenly she was falling into a black space… She tried to grab something, grasped for the paddle, at the water, at Max. Grabbed at nothing…

CHAPTER ELEVEN

'GABBY! GABBY!' MAX's heart pumped into overdrive. She'd slumped to the side, her face skimming dangerously close to the water.

He couldn't get purchase on her, though he grasped at her. Tried to pull her upright. 'Gabby. Wake the hell up.'

After hauling in her fast-disappearing paddle, he took a huge breath and leaned towards her, cursing the damned lack of space.

If he leaned too far he'd capsize the kayak and have them both in the water.

A scenario he didn't want to contemplate.

'Gabby. Come on, girl.' He dragged her back by the shoulders and patted her cheeks, hoping his wet, cold fingers would jolt her awake. 'Couldn't you have done this when we had the coastguard out? Two rescues for the price of one? Hey, sweetheart. Wake up.'

Her face was white, her lips dry. Crap. Pushing her hair back, he found a pulse. Weak and fast. She'd just fainted. But she wasn't regaining consciousness. This wasn't a regular thing. This was bad news.

'Hey! Hey!' Trying to get the attention of the other kayakers, he shouted. But the wind dragged his voice back out to sea.

The shore was tantalisingly close. A few hundred metres, maybe. He could get there in a matter of minutes. Raise the alarm.

Hauling in a breath, he infused every ounce of energy he had into getting her to that beach. His arms pumped until they burned. His lungs craved more and more oxygen but he was too focused on that shoreline to breathe.

After moments that seemed like forever he was kneeling next to her on the damp sand. Using his lifejacket as a pillow, he laid her down and bent her legs against his chest. 'Gabby. Come on, girl. Gabby.'

God. Think. Focus. What could it be? Just a vasovagal? But why?

'Max?' Her eyes fluttered open and she cradled her stomach protectively. 'It hurts so much…'

Then she was gone again.

He couldn't even get her focused enough to answer simple questions.

A few stragglers from the trip hovered around but he swatted them away. There was nothing for it. 'I'm taking her in.'

'Ambulance?' someone shouted above the concerned huddle. 'I'll call one now.'

Wait? For how long? Until she became critical? No way. He dampened down his tachycardia and worked out a plan. 'I'm not prepared to wait. I'll drive.'

Picking her up, he stalked over the sand and across the road to his parked car. Edged her gently onto the back seat and made sure to keep her legs raised to stimulate oxygen flow back to her brain.

That was when he noticed the blood.

God. No. What the hell…?

In all his years as a surgeon he'd never felt panic. Even when working on his nephew he'd had faith in his own capabilities. But right now, as adrenalin surged through him, his heart rate rocketed and he wanted her fixed. Immediately.

Thrusting the car into heavy traffic, he cursed loudly. Then he put his foot down.

Running the length of the hospital car park barefoot, fuelled by a need to save her, he finally got her to the emergency department. Faster than an ambulance could have made it. And he'd managed to keep some kind of observation going in the rear-view mirror. Resps: too fast. Pain: severe. She'd flicked in and out of consciousness.

He tried to keep his heart out of it. But, man, he couldn't. Couldn't reconcile the vivacious woman he knew with the damaged body in his arms. He would never leave her side again. Never.

When he ran in and saw Mitchell his heart beat faster. The best ER medic in town.

Thank God. And like Max himself, he would put everything aside to help his brother.

Now he knew what Mitch had felt like when he had agreed to do Jamie's surgery. Someone who had a vested interest—someone who'd care. He hoped. At least, if not for him then for Gabby. Mitch would repay the debt.

He managed to haul in air and relay her symptoms as they found a trolley and laid her on it. 'Weak, rapid pulse. Bleeding, I guess vaginally. She has severe pain in her abdomen.'

'Where?'

'Lower right side.' He tugged hard at his tumultuous memory. What had she said...? 'She mentioned something about her shoulder, too. Now I assume it could have been referred pain.' They'd put it down to the jolt of the SkyJump.

His hands fisted. Stupid. Damned stupid. They should have acted faster. He was a doctor. He should have known.

His eyes were drawn to the blood on her shorts. Thick. Dark. Too much. His stomach twisted and he beat back nausea.

Mitchell examined Gabby, talking gently, but she was too lost in pain to answer much. 'Her blood pressure's very low. I'll fix some fluids to bring it up. And I'll page the obstetrics reg.' He attached an oxygen mask, heart and blood saturation monitors. 'Any chance she could be pregnant?'

Holy hell. It had flitted through Max's head as a possible cause. But they'd used contraception the whole time. Condoms, and then the Pill. She'd been definitive about that, and said he'd been the first in a long time. Unless she'd been lying. 'I don't think so. But I guess technically she could be.'

'We'll run some tests. And do an ultrasound scan.'

'I'll come with her.'

'You'll get in the way, Max.'

'You take her anywhere without me and there'll be trouble.' It was the first time he'd ever lost control. The first time he'd ever wanted to lay down his own life for someone else.

Gabby's eyes flicked open, searching around the room, and her frightened gaze fell on Max. She reached for his hand and held on as if her life depended on it. God, it just might if they didn't find the cause.

Hurry the hell up. 'Give her some pain relief first.'

His brother's palm fitted onto Max's shoulder. 'Max, it's okay. I know what I'm doing. I'll sort it.'

'Then do it.' He twisted out of his brother's grip and held Gabby's hand, brushed her thick curls from her face.

Damn her for not listening to him. Damn himself for not making sure she got checked out. It was his job to notice symptoms. But she'd been too caught up in making people happy, in putting herself at the bottom of the pecking order. And he'd been too caught up in letting her have her own way.

He ran his hands through his hair. 'Sort it now, Mitch.'

He wasn't prepared to lose her, not when he'd only just found her.

Five hours later, five damned hours, numbness ran through Max as he waited on a hard plastic chair outside Theatre Two. Okay, so he wasn't supposed to be here. But, what the hell, he had to be somewhere since they'd all but banned him from the OR.

Being a surgeon at least had some perks. They understood his panic. Cut him some slack. He drew the line at squinting through the blacked-out window, though. Couldn't bear to see her like that, lifeless and fragile. Because he knew he'd be in there otherwise, throwing his weight around and interfering in stuff he'd be better to leave alone.

A cup of weak hospital coffee was thrust under his nose. He took it, and when he looked up he was face to face with his mirror image. Only he knew he looked a damn sight worse right now. 'Thanks.'

'You okay?' Mitch sat down next to him.

It was comforting to have him here. Despite everything, there was a definite connection. Something that undercut the pain, something that went beyond the present and deep into a past that they both shared. Six years of the past where they'd been inseparable. So it was okay to be honest. 'Nah. Truth is, Mitch, I'm scared for her.'

'Truth is, you love her.'

Wow. That had come from nowhere. Did he? After such a short time? And how the hell did Mitch know?

Because Mitch had known everything, once. Whatever he himself wasn't, Mitch had made up for. A right and a left. Two halves that made way more than a whole. They didn't have that telepathy thing going but they did have some weird mutual understanding. 'I don't know if that's possible, Mitch.'

'I think you do.' Mitch bumped against him in a kind of friendly nudge. 'That's okay, you know. You can love someone.'

Max didn't want to. Had never wanted to, not if his emotions paid such a price. He'd been running on empty for so long. 'Can I? Can we? After everything that happened to us?'

'Well, I do. I love Jodi and Jamie more than anything. And it involves risk. You have to put yourself on the line. And God knows whether they're going to be here tomorrow—you and I both know the realities there. But it's worth every second you spend with them anyway.'

And that was about the most honest thing Mitch had said to him in nearly thirty years. Decades of pain welled up in Max's chest until he could barely breathe. 'But what happens if it falls apart? What if they…you know…?'

'What if they leave?' Mitch dragged his chair across the linoleum to face Max. 'Well, you'll survive. You will. You're strong. You're a Maitland, for God's sake.'

A Maitland. Brothers. Tied together by blood, the same DNA. Identical. But so many differences for so long.

Silence stretched across the gap between them, wound through the corridor, filled the spaces. And along with it came an immense need to talk to Mitch. Really talk. The way he'd wanted to since…since forever. 'I missed you like hell, you know. After they took me away.'

If he was surprised at this admission, Mitchell didn't let it show on his face. His gaze dropped to the paper cup in his hand. 'You didn't even look back. I thought you were glad to be leaving me behind.'

What? 'Glad?' It was so far from the truth it was laughable. Thick emotion filled Max's throat. Sucking in oxygen, he forced words out. 'Dumbass. I was your big brother. I was supposed to stop it happening, and I couldn't. It was bad enough that I failed you. I couldn't look back and let you see me cry, too. What would you think of me then?'

'That you cared.'

Holy hell. 'You thought I didn't care, Mitch?'

'I was six. I didn't exactly rationalise it. Everyone was leaving, and you didn't seem to kick up a fuss. Then there was all that competitive stuff. If it hadn't been for the spectre of your success, I'd have been happy. Especially since you didn't seem to care about me. I hated it, and in a screwed-up kind of logic ended up hating you too.' He paused. Breathed. 'And then there was Jodi...' Mitch's gaze hit him. Honest. Sincere. And filled with the same kind of feeling Max had churning round his gut. Something like an apology. A need to make things right. Mitch smiled. 'I love her. Honestly. I wasn't trying to play her. Or you. It wasn't a game to me.'

Max shrugged as he heard what he'd always known but had chosen not to believe. 'Yeah. I know that now. Didn't seem like that at the time, though.'

'Guess we need to grow up, right?'

'Yeah.' Taking a chance, Max stuck out his hand and Mitchell grabbed it. They hung on, way too long. Like two idiots.

Pretty momentous. This would be where girls hugged or something. They weren't there yet, but it was groundbreaking Maitland history.

Max's heart squeezed with relief. A stupid stinging sensation hit his eyes as he looked into his brother's.

They dropped their hands. Looked away. At the floor. At their feet.

But Max noticed the smile on his brother's face was as broad as his own.

Another silence followed, this time a more friendly one.

Eventually Mitch leaned across. 'The other day, when you were talking about Fred, you mentioned something about *stuff* happening. You want…?' Turning his palms up, Mitch offered Max his chance to explain.

But Max had shared enough today. 'Nah.'

'You sure?'

'Yeah. Long time ago. Best forgotten.'

'Maybe one day, right?'

'Maybe.' Goddamn, would that lump in his throat go?

One day he'd tell his brother the truth about the regular beatings, the pressure he'd had to excel, how much he'd wanted to be part of Mitchell's family, how jealousy had eaten away at him and turned into hate.

But for now it was enough his brother had asked.

Suddenly Max had to walk. Find some space. Breathe. For so long he'd wanted to end that rift between them. To tell the truth, finally.

Yeah, the truth was he'd missed and loved his brother. And he wanted him back.

He wanted a family. More than anything.

And more than that, he wanted to share it with Gabby. *Gabby.*

Max stood and shook out his tight muscles. Needed some air to unclog his throat. To think about his next step. 'Thanks, Mitch. Really. Thanks. I've got to go.'

'Anytime, mate. You know where I am.'

'Sure thing.'

Max walked out of the hospital, through the car park,

over to the patients' garden, where he found a bench lit by a slither of moon.

Some joker had planted a peace sign made out of squat purple bushes, and a border of bright scarlet flowers. They reminded him of his sky garden. Of her. Of what she'd brought into his life. Hell, everything reminded him of her. The Auckland skyline, sunshine. The hospital. His apartment. He looked at everything touched with her image or smell, or some memory.

He cared for her. That was the truth.

Love? He didn't know about that. Couldn't define it in such simple yet complex terms. But she was special. And he wanted her. Maybe they could agree to some sort of commitment. Make a first big step.

Even thinking about that word sent shivers running through him. This was so far out of his comfort zone he didn't know what to do. Say. Think. But he had a gut feeling they should try and take this to another level. He just had to wait out the hours it would take to fix her.

And while he sat it occurred to him that Mitch was way more evolved than he was. He had a girlfriend and a child. People he could share things with. To help him relearn the truth about love. And he wanted that so badly. With Mitch. With Gabby. Trouble was, he was scared. Because he knew that sometimes the truth hurt, too.

Finally the obs and gynae reg sauntered along the corridor as if he'd simply been to the park and not just saved a life. 'Hey, Max, she's out of surgery now. It was a bit of a mess really. Her right fallopian tube was just about to blow, so we removed it. But her left one is scarred too. She has grade-four endo.' The doc smiled gently and put his hand on Max's arm. 'I'm very sorry, but the chances of her getting pregnant naturally again are virtually impossible and very risky.'

Whoa. Hold on. This was too much to take in. Pregnancy? 'How far along was she?'

'Five, six weeks. We could talk about assisted fertility anytime you want. There are options.'

Endometriosis. Infertility. All added up to a bleak future. But she was safe and alive. And that's all he damned well cared about. 'No. Thanks. I don't need to talk about this right now. I need to see her.'

The doctor shrugged. 'Of course. When she's out of Recovery we'll take you up to the ward.'

'I'll walk her up from Recovery.'

'You and I both know that's not a good idea.'

Yeah, well, he hadn't had many of them recently.

She'd been pregnant. With his child. And had nearly died.

God. Clearly due to their recklessness. The Pill had failed, probably due to the vomiting bug they'd all had. He was surmising. Trying to make sense of it.

Had she known? He didn't think so. And now he had to tell her not only had she lost her baby but she couldn't have any more. Not without intervention. And there were never any promises there.

She didn't want kids—she'd told him that. And neither did he. He hadn't ever given it much thought on top of not settling down. Not having kids had completed that picture for him.

But this—this was a game-changer. Emotions he hadn't known he had seeped through his skin.

A baby. His baby. *A father.*

Wow.

No one had warned him about the intense possessiveness a man could feel just hearing a word. One simple word. And the crushing hopelessness. The heavy weight that pressed on your chest and stole your breath. The pumping of adrenalin. The way for a second the joy unfurled enough to create hope, before it was whipped away on a senseless, cruel wind of reality. A father no more.

Truth dawned, crystallised in front of him. He did want a family, to be a father, to give a child the kind of things he'd never had. It was a shock. It was too cruel to realise that now, when it was too late, that he wanted what Mitchell had.

Without giving a second glance to the doctor, Max stalked away.

His pacing outside the ward probably gave the nurses a scare but he didn't care. The second he saw them walking towards him he darted past and in to her bedside. She was all wrapped up in blankets and tubes. The regular beep of the monitors assured him that she was mending.

He took a seat next to the bed and held her hand until her eyelids fluttered open.

She blinked up at him with groggy eyes. 'Hey.'

A hot, unfamiliar feeling washed over him. Gratitude and relief mixed with that tight ache in his chest. She was safe but their baby wasn't. 'Hey. You gave us all a bit of a fright. We had to operate, but you're okay. And everything's going to be just fine.' He promised her that much. He'd make it right. Somehow.

'What was wrong? Appendix or something?'

He didn't answer directly, didn't want to upset her so soon after the surgery. 'Rest now, I'll explain it all later. You're doing great. How do you feel?'

She coughed and ran a palm over her dry lips. Her voice was crackly and hoarse from the intubation tube. 'On a scale of one to ten? Minus three. How do I look?'

'On a scale of one to ten? Eleven.'

'You are so full of—'

He squeezed her hand. 'Quiet now. The nurses said you weren't to get excited.' So how the hell he was going to tell her about the pregnancy and the scarring he didn't know.

Coward. She needed to know.

All in good time.

'Don't kid yourself, Maitland.' She managed a weak smile. 'You don't excite me. Irritate, obviously. Annoy, intensely.'

He couldn't help grinning. At least she hadn't lost her spirit. The one thing that kept her so beautiful, so different from everyone else. One of the many things he admired in her. 'They clearly didn't insert a "nice gene" while they were rummaging around in there.'

'Nice is so overrated.' As her eyes closed, her breathing settled and her grip on his hand relaxed. 'I'm all out of talking. Now go.'

'Like hell. I'm staying all night.'

And then he'd broach the subject of the baby.

CHAPTER TWELVE

'THANK GOD FOR my own bed.' Gabby slunk further under her duvet and closed her eyes. Safe in her own space away from the prying eyes of the hospital staff. Without the cloying closeness of Max and his pitying looks. She needed space to grieve for the baby she hadn't even known had been growing inside her. To come to terms with it and, yes, to move on.

It felt like she'd be moving on forever. And yet she'd never escape.

She allowed herself a few moments to not think. To not do anything. The last hour had been so full of pain and arguments with the hospital staff. Now she just needed peace and quiet.

But half of her was on alert for the phone to ring. The doorbell. Her cellphone. Because as soon as Max found out he'd be on to her.

No matter.

He could go to hell like the rest of them.

Funny, though, there'd been no tears when the nurse had whispered to her in the middle of the night and told her the truth of her situation. No tears, but a numbness that had spread through her body, a reconciliation that finally, *finally* Nonna's promised punishment had come.

No more babies. Nonna would be pleased up there on

her fluffy perfect cloud—she'd warned something bad would happen. Now it had.

No babies.

For so long Gabby hadn't even wanted any more. Hadn't allowed herself to think of more. But now the ache in her stomach was nothing compared to the sharp hurt in her heart. Just like the first loss, this was devastating.

She did want children. She wanted to be a mother some-time. Somehow.

Each breath came coated with a stuttered pant. Every-thing she touched shook in her trembling hands. And yet there were no tears.

'Gabby. Gabriella!' A loud hammering on the front door jolted her upright.

Max.

She held her breath and waited for him to lose inter-est. Fat chance. The man was nothing if not determined. 'Gabby. Let me in. I know you're there.'

Pulling the curtains tight, she closed her eyes, wishing to hell she hadn't chosen a ground-floor bedroom.

'Gabby.' He'd moved now and was hammering on the French doors to her room. 'I'm going to break the glass if you don't answer.'

Protecting her abdominal wound with her arm, she dragged herself up and leaned back on her pillows. 'Go away, Max. Please.'

'I will not go away. Either you let me in or I break the glass. You want that to happen?'

No. She didn't want anything to happen. She wanted the world to stop. In fact, to rewind to that first night when she'd taken courage in both hands and walked back to his apartment. She liked that brave Gabby. She wanted to be her again.

Then she could change everything that had happened

afterwards. Particularly the falling-for-him bit. And falling pregnant.

But there was no getting away from it, she had to face him. Face the world. She'd have to go back to work and he'd be there, too. At some point she'd need to look him in the eye and explain.

Because even though she'd long since reconciled the choice she'd made ten years ago, it was definitely the right one for them all. But she'd be taking a chance on Max believing her.

She edged carefully out of bed, opened the curtains and unlocked the latch. Might as well do it now. Be damned once and for all.

'Gabby, what the hell is going on? I leave the ward for an hour. One damned hour, and you discharge yourself. Are you okay?' His fierce gaze bored into her as he strode into the room. He scrutinised her, checked her, assessed her all in one look. And, yes, for the record, she felt wanting. Seemed her mojo these days was sneaking away.

She owed him an explanation, that much she knew. But did he have to break her heart all over again just by being so damned impassioned? And angry? And here?

He didn't deserve the pain he'd gone through, keeping vigil at her bedside. Or the inevitable pain she was storing up for him.

What she wanted was for him to climb right into bed next to her. What she wanted was to cling to him and never let go.

The right thing, however, was to be honest. And she was hardwired to do the right thing, no matter how much it hurt.

His lips formed a thin line and he looked utterly stunned. 'Are you barking mad?'

'No.' She eased back into bed. 'I just needed to get away.'

'How the hell are you going to look after yourself? What about your four-hourly obs, your medications?'

'I'm a nurse. I know what to do. I'll cope.' It wasn't the physical pain she was worried about.

He lifted the duvet and tucked her legs underneath it. Covered her up and took her pulse. Sat on the bed next to her. Only then did he lower his voice to somewhere around seething point. 'You want to tell me what's going on?'

She offered him a smile. 'Hospital food really sucks. I'm definitely going to have a meeting about that when I get back.'

'Food? Is that it? Really? You're crazier than I thought. I could have got you something, a takeaway. You should have said.' The concern on his face almost overwhelmed her. 'You look terrible.'

'Thanks. I feel like crap.'

'I wonder why? You are unbelievable.' She could see he was trying damned hard to be restrained when every impulse was to cart her back to the ward. The mad ward, probably. His breathing caught, and finally he snapped. 'Maybe if you'd stuck to doctor's orders, like any sensible person, you'd feel a little better. Maybe if you'd tried to talk to me instead of bottling it all up… What is it with you? When will you learn to talk to me? Tell me how you feel? When the hell will you trust me?'

I can't.

He started to gather up clothes from her armchair and stuff them into a backpack.

Jerking up, she tried to stop him. 'What are you doing?'

'I'm taking you back to the hospital until you're well enough for discharge. I will bring food in. Caviar, lobster or whatever the hell *Madame* requires. But you're going in.'

'No way. Put that down. Do not dare root through my stuff.' The pain finally winning, she sagged back against her pillow. 'We both know how desperate they are for beds. I'd be discharged tomorrow or the next day, anyway. I just need sleep.'

'And regular meds, and someone to cook for you.' He counted on his fingers before shaking his head in dismay. 'And someone to help you. To care for you. That anaesthetic has done weird things to your brain.'

'I'm fine, but you're not listening. I want to stay here.'

'Okay, then, you win. I'll move in here and look after you.' He threw the bag to the floor. 'Do not argue about this.'

'No, Max, you can't move in, and I'm not going anywhere.'

'So I have to stand back and let you put yourself at risk? I'm your.. what am I exactly? Your boyfriend? No. Your lover? Your confidant? I don't think so, because that would involve talking to me about things. You're clearly not safe to make any kind of rational decisions.' His face closed in and he stared at her. Then he actually laughed, deflating the tension. 'Unless it's to kiss me, of course. In which case I'd say you were very sane indeed.'

She turned her head away. 'No, Max. Please. Don't.'

The laugh turned bitter. 'I need to hold you, Gabby. I need to feel you in my arms. We both lost that baby. I know you're hurting. Hell, I'm hurting too.'

She knew that.

He'd come a long way. He could admit that he hurt. But she was still back in the emotional dark ages.

He hurt. For himself. For her. For what they'd lost.

Her throat clogged with thick emotion. She'd been thinking purely about herself and not how he felt about losing a baby, too.

What had happened to her? Had she always been so selfish? For so long she'd learnt to keep her emotions tightly locked away. Refused to discuss how she felt. Refused, even, to acknowledge that she felt anything at all. But now it wasn't just about her, it was about Max, too.

Her hand found his. 'I'm so sorry, Max. I know you'll make a great dad one day.'

'And you'll be a fabulous mum, somehow. But don't beat yourself up about it now. We can talk about all that another time. Just work on getting better.' His arm slid under her back and he pulled her to him. She knew he needed her comfort as much as she needed his. But she couldn't do this anymore.

'I can't hold you, Max. Not now.' Because if she did, she might never let go. 'Please, don't.'

Confusion shimmered in his eyes. 'When you're ready, let me know.'

He pulled his arm away but stayed on the bed next to her. A gap of a few inches separated them. Judging by the frustration emanating from him, it might as well have been a mile. An ocean. A continent.

Minutes ticked by. His breathing settled but he wasn't relaxed, not by a long shot. His thigh muscles remained tight under his jeans, his fists clenched at his sides.

It took all her strength not to reach for him.

Eventually he shifted from the bed. 'I'm going to get some food for you. Don't you dare move before I get back—I can't keep chasing you across the city. Besides, I want you strong and well for that dinner next week. I want to show you off.'

She knew he meant well and was trying to give her a focus to distract her. A reason to heal. Well, she didn't want one. She didn't want to be looked at and pitied. And she didn't want to string him along anymore. She needed to set him free. 'I'm not going to the dinner.'

'But you said—'

'I know what I said. But I have to tell you something.' She drew in a breath and readied herself for the most painful conversation of her life. 'I can't go—'

'Of course you can.' He spoke over her. Goddamn him. 'You'll be fine by then. You need something to look forward to. Is it because you have nothing to wear?' He'd jumped off the bed and walked across the room towards her closet. 'Let's see what you have in here.'

'No! Max, stop. Listen to me.' She leaped forward but a sharp sting across her incision scars whipped her breath away.

Before she could stop him he'd opened the closet door. He reeled back. 'Oh, okay. Wow. You have a lot of shoes. And so neatly stacked. You have OCD, too?'

No. No. No. Everything was unravelling exactly the way she didn't want.

She wanted to scream. To run.

'Don't...touch the boxes.' *Please, don't. Please, don't. Please, don't.* 'Max, come away from there.'

'Hey, silly. It's just shoes.' He picked up box three and examined it. His forehead furrowed as he took in the childish train stickers. The blue balloons. The number three in navy and silver glitter. 'What are the numbers for? You rating your shoes now, too?'

'Max—no.'

His hands were opening the lid. Her heart thumped and pounded and rattled. Her shoulders hunched up and squeezed against her neck. *Don't. Don't. Don't.* She closed her eyes. Opened them again to see the nightmare had become a reality.

He would ask. She would have to tell him. It would be over.

'What's all this, Gabby? I don't understand.' His voice was hollow as he showed her the contents of the box. Contents she'd painstakingly put there. The birthday card so lovingly written, that one day she hoped she'd be able to give. The carefully selected presents. The letters. 'What's this about?'

Her hand found her mouth and stopped the wobbling lip. But she couldn't stop the tears that threatened and yet never fell. Somehow she forced the words out through her burning throat. 'They are for my baby.'

Pain crawled across her stomach, up her spine, reached out to her fingertips, down her legs to her toes. Every part of her burned with the loss.

'Your what?' His focus was back on the boxes, his voice empty.

'There are ten of them. One for each year he's been alive. One for every birthday I've missed.'

Again he shook the box towards her. 'I don't understand. What are you telling me?'

'You'll get the chance to be a father again and again, Max. But I won't ever be a mother. Not again. I was once, though.' Now her heart shattered into a million tiny jagged pieces that would never fit back together again. She'd lost everything. She'd lost her babies. She watched as he recoiled, his face a grim mask of disgust. And now she was losing him, too. She was utterly broken. 'I gave my baby away.'

He couldn't believe what he was hearing. What did she mean? Gave it away? 'I don't understand.'

Didn't want to comprehend what she'd done. He gazed at the neatly stacked numbered boxes. One to ten. Covered in a pathetic collection of stickers that were aged appropriately. From teddy bears, bubbles and balloons to music players and groovy cartoon kids on skateboards. They looked like collages done by a child. The sense of hopelessness that accompanied them was almost palpable. And mirrored the same feeling he had in his soul.

Her eyes were dead. Her face a mask. How she held herself together to say those words he'd never know. But he needed to hear the rest. To discover what kind of person he'd lost his heart to. Because, God knew, she wasn't the woman he'd believed her to be. 'Go on, Gabby. I'm listening.'

Her voice, in contrast to his hoarseness and harshness, was shallow and soft. He had to strain to hear her. And yet he couldn't bring himself to move closer.

She gripped the necklace at her throat. 'I fell pregnant when I was fifteen. First time lucky.' The smile was false. 'First and only time. Until you.'

He supposed that should mean something. She'd waited how long to put her faith in someone? And she'd chosen him. But it didn't change anything. Couldn't change what she'd done. She'd given a baby away...for adoption? Foster care?

The same kind of life he'd had.

But it wasn't the same, he tried to rationalize. This was his Gabby, beautiful, kind Gabby who wanted every baby to be loved and looked after. She'd drilled that into him enough already. He couldn't imagine her doing such a thing.

So why? Why had she given a baby away?

Had she no idea how that kind of stuff messed with your head? How it always felt like rejection? At least, that's what he'd always felt. Like he was something nobody had wanted. Not his parents. Not his brother. Certainly not his uncle.

Rational thoughts twisted and screwed in his head. God, he was all kinds of confused.

He watched her throat rise and fall against the diamond heart as she picked her words. He couldn't find any words of his own so he let her purge herself.

She didn't look at him. Instead, she spoke to the space between them, her gaze directed somewhere around his chest. 'I didn't realise I was pregnant until I was quite far along. Twenty weeks. I've always had irregular periods and everything seemed normal, until they stopped altogether. My mum went hysterical when I told her. We had no money, nothing, no way of bringing up another child. Eventually Nonna found out. She was furious. She'd spent her life bringing up my mum then me. She had no intention of doing it again, and definitely no inclination to help me. "Get rid of it," she said. "Otherwise everyone will look down on us even more. You don't bring dishonour on your family."'

His laugh was filled with scorn but he couldn't hold it back. 'What? In twenty-first-century New Zealand?'

'You know what it's like to be a pregnant schoolgirl, do you? How it is to be under the thumb of an über-strict family who are old-fashioned and proud, who would never ask for handouts. Nonna dictated everything. What I did, who with. She had control down to a T. She'd always said my mum had been out of control and that's why my father had left, so she wasn't going to risk it with me. Short of locking me in the house, she had a hand in everything I did, who I saw, where I went. Monitoring calls, checking my texts. It was worse than prison.'

And worse, then, than his uncle. Who hadn't cared what

Max had done, as long as he'd excelled at it. Or had taken a beating.

'So this was the ultimate disgrace. Nonna threatened me. Told me I'd let the family down, that they'd disown me. Told me I was stupid and that I'd fail. That I'd be a useless parent, like my mum. That I would condemn my child to a life of poverty and misery, like mine.'

'And you believed her?'

'Truthfully? I was frightened to death of Nonna. She never hurt me physically, although she threatened it enough, but she was scathing with her tongue. She could twist anything to make you feel guilty and useless. "You'll ruin us, Gabriella. It's your fault we live like this, with next to nothing. Your fault we have no money. Do you know how much school costs? Food? Clothes? Bus fares? And for what? A stupid, selfish, hateful child who brings shame on us. You have the devil in you, Gabriella."'

Gabby dragged in a breath, shoulders slumped forward, as if she still believed every word her grandmother had said. '*Hateful. Stupid. Selfish.* Emotional scars aren't so easy to see, right?'

'Right.' If what he was hearing was true, her scars ran as deeply as his. He knew exactly how she felt. But still… Giving a child away? Max tried hard to understand what she'd been through, but how to do that with a series of disconnected thoughts running through your brain?

Social workers. Screaming. *Dip dip dip.* Choices made, so much lost to him. And now his pain was heightened by the crushingly sad look in her eyes.

She sighed. 'I was naive, God knows. I wouldn't have got pregnant if I hadn't been. But I believed Nonna. Believed I was stupid. I believed I'd fail.'

But there had been two people responsible for this baby. It wasn't just about how well Gabby would have coped.

'What about the father? Didn't he care that you gave his baby away?' Because *he* would have cared. He'd have fought for his child, whatever feelings he'd had for the mother. He wouldn't have given it away as if it were unwanted trash.

Gabby hauled in air. Just looking at Max's dark eyes destroyed her. She'd already lost him, that was obvious. Lost him because of something he'd never understand. But now that she'd started, she had to tell him the utter, absolute truth.

'Isaac was the only thing that made me feel I was lovable, desirable. Worth something. He was my guilty secret. In a family where I wasn't allowed any kind of normal social life, sneaking out to see him was my bliss.'

How naive and stupid she'd been. She'd truly believed the local college boy had been as committed as she had been. Blindsided by immature infatuation she'd thought was love, she'd been crushed when he'd rejected her. Risking that kind of betrayal again had been something she'd avoided for ten years. It hurt too much. Now, seeing the incomprehension in Max's eyes, the disgust and the anger, she decided she'd been right. 'When I told him we were having a baby he disowned me. He told me I was nothing to him. *Nothing.*'

Just like Max had. Nothing important.

The dark look she knew she threw at Max was jumbled with the mixed-up emotions of now and the past. She'd been so alone and scared, and rejected by everyone. But had made the very best decision she could at the time.

'Isaac didn't want a baby and told me to get rid of it. No one cared what I wanted, they just wanted the problem gone. Nonna arranged for me to move across Wellington to stay with a distant cousin until I gave birth. I was fifteen, Max, still a child myself. I couldn't imagine looking after a baby on my own, with no support. I couldn't do it.'

'There are social services. They'd have set you up in a flat.'

Oh, yes, he had all the answers. 'Easy in hindsight when you're a smart, rich doctor, but not when you're a scared teenager. Where would I have found out about that stuff? I was terrified. Terrified of giving birth, of being a mum, of being on my own. One night I was in the kitchen fighting with Nonna, and I suddenly saw everything clearly. I loved my baby so much I wouldn't let it eke out an existence like I had, where there was little love and too much control. My child deserved better than I could give him. I had nothing to offer. Certainly not a good life with a loving family. The kind of family I'd always dreamed of having.'

She nodded at Max as he dropped the box onto the floor and walked to the other side of the room. 'The kind you dreamed of too, eh? I didn't know what to do with a baby.'

'You can learn. There are books.' His jaw tensed and his lip curled. God, he really did hate her.

But she actually felt lighter by telling him. She was utterly broken but open. She'd never ever told anyone else about this.

'Nonna arranged a meeting with a private adoption agency who gave me files on couples who wanted a baby of their own. I chose one couple who sounded nice. But they were celebrities, the document said. They were desperate and they wanted a closed adoption to keep things from getting to the press. I realised, in the end, that was probably my best option. I wouldn't be able to watch someone else love him. It would break my heart to visit but not be able to have him with me. And I would never take him away from them, so they convinced me to give him up as quickly as possible, as it was best for all concerned.'

He leaned on the back of a chair, watched her from a distance, his gaze damning. And said nothing. She looked for a glimmer of understanding, but there was nothing but a taut stance and tight fists.

'In the hospital I held him for a few lovely hours. It was just me and him. I held him tight and told him over and over how much I loved him, how I wanted him to be strong and kind and happy. How proud I was of him already.' *How I was so, so sorry, but it truly was for the best. That I loved him so much I had to give him away.* There had simply been no other choice. The only way to be the best mum had been to give him to someone who could provide more than she ever could have.

Her lips wouldn't stop trembling. She bit them together. Tried to control herself. Relaxed her shoulders and finally let out the pain that had haunted her for a decade, and that she knew she would never shake.

'He was perfect, Max. So tiny. So beautiful. I gave him his own name, his name for a day: Joseph. My baby, Joe. I sang him a lullaby. Wrapped him in a blanket I'd bought—it's in box zero if you really need to know—just so I could have his smell with me for a bit longer. I spent those last minutes with him looking over his features, his tiny body, his little snub nose, at those teeny little fingernails. So I would never forget how he looked, what he felt like. So I would have something of his to remember him always. Just a snapshot in my head, but it's as clear today as it was then.'

How she would say the next words she didn't know. But she had to. She inhaled deeply and stilled the shaking in her voice. The bright ball of pain in her throat burned and prickled and throbbed. 'I pressed my lips to his perfect mouth and kissed him, and he gurgled. His baby voice was like sunshine, I didn't know he would sound so beautiful. I didn't know it was possible to feel so much love for someone I'd only just met.

'But then they came, and I told him again over and over how much I loved him. I loved him, Max. I hadn't got to know him, but it was there already, this immense and overpowering feeling for him. I loved him so much. That was all there was for me—my love for him. There was nothing else. Nothing. And then they came, and I handed him over. It was like a light going out in my soul.'

Just like that. Hers for a few moments, then gone. She hadn't known how she'd be able to live without him. How she could get up each morning and face a less bright day. But she had, believing he deserved better than what she'd had to give. Believing he was in a happier place.

But even then she'd wavered. Wondered if he was happy. Wondered if his new family burned with the same fervent love she did.

Wished she could turn the clock back.

And now she had nothing to look forward to. No child to hold in her arms. She ached as much for the baby she'd just lost as for the one she'd given away.

Tears pricked at her eyes but still none fell. Her throat was hoarse with an ache that she didn't think would ever heal, and the hole in her heart gaped wide.

'It was like a tight fist of pain that gets bigger and bigger until you think you're going to die because of it. For a long, long time afterwards I didn't get out of bed. I couldn't face each day. I wanted him back so much. I knew I'd made the right choice, but it was so hard to deal with. I loved him. I always will. And one day I'm going to see him again. Somehow.'

Max couldn't get past 'handed him over'. Handed him over like an unwanted Christmas gift.

He knew he should feel sorry for her, knew she couldn't have made any decision like that easily—but, damn, he couldn't stop his anger pouring out.

'If I ever had a child I'd keep it so close, treasure it. I wouldn't trade it away for a better future.' Or leave it behind like his parents had. He felt the rage spread across his chest. Rage for what? Now? Then?

He didn't know. But he heard it in his voice. Raw. Loud. 'You could have tried, Gabby, but instead you just took the easy route so you could carry on your life and be a success in your cosy nursing career. You are not the woman I thought you were.'

'Shut up. Just shut the hell up.' Her face darkened as she held up her shaking palm. Her voice rose a notch, coated with anger that matched his. 'You have no idea what I went through. You won't even listen, you're too caught up in your own drama. You make Joe sound like an inconvenience, not a baby.'

'Wasn't he?' Hadn't *he* been? He and Mitchell?

'No. No. No. And you make me sound uncaring and unloving, and I'm far from that.' Her finger pointed at him accusingly. 'I honestly thought you knew me better.'

'So did I, Gabby. So did I.'

'Seems we were both wrong, then. This is exactly what I didn't want from you. I thought, hoped, you might understand. I work hard every day so that when I do meet him, he'll be proud of what I've achieved. And I'll be able to hold my head up high and be someone he can respect. He might understand—more than you, it seems—why I did what I did.

'My life has never been "cosy". Everywhere I went in Wellington I bumped into people who knew me when I was pregnant and who asked what had happened to my child. You can't live four months in a place and not make some contacts. Sometimes they'd come into the ward. They'd ask difficult questions and then everyone I worked with wanted to know about it. And then there was the constant nagging from Nonna, and my mum. "Don't get into more trouble. You've ruined our lives".'

'Because you didn't become a doctor after that, and save their precious skins. I get it now.' The missing pieces slotted into place, making up an ugly whole.

Her voice rose even more. 'I couldn't eat or study for a long time. It was intolerable being around them, but they made me stay and make it up to them. I couldn't get away from it. And then—worse, much worse—every baby I saw, every child I looked after at work, I thought it might be him. My baby.'

'Not *your* baby. You gave up that right when you gave him away.'

She glared at him, eyes sparking with defiance. 'How dare you?'

'Don't like the truth?' He walked towards the door, but she was already out of bed and hobbling towards him, holding her side as she covered the distance. Her flimsy pyjamas barely covered the curves he loved. Her eyes sparked as anger took her too. Now he saw what had kept her going, what had been her salvation. She had spirit and hope and fight. She truly believed what she'd done had been for the best.

And, goddamn him, that was when he realised Mitch was right. He did love her.

Had loved her.

It was like a swift low blow to his chest. Something he had been avoiding all his life—giving his heart to someone else. But it had happened. He'd given it to the one person he should never have fallen in love with, but he'd done it anyway. And he'd been right, all along, too—the truth hurt, but love hurt more.

Right now he didn't know what to feel. He didn't want the kind of bleak future it would be without her. But he couldn't see a future that involved someone so careless about life, about a baby—no matter how much she told him she'd given her child up in an act of love.

And he'd had to wring it out of her. 'What kind of a relationship is built on silences and lies? Would you ever have told me this if you hadn't had the pregnancy?'

At the word 'pregnancy' she flinched. He felt the sudden stab in his heart, too. Truth was, it all hurt much more than he cared to admit.

'We didn't *have* a relationship, Max. To be honest, we don't know how. We're both too damned scared.' She stopped short in front of him, huge, furious eyes boring into his soul.

Although he was tempted to fling everything he had at her, he would never tell her how much he had grown to like her. To love her. And how much her story mingled with his hurt and made everything sour.

She shook her head, her eyes glistening with unshed tears. It damn near broke his heart. But he couldn't touch her now, not after this.

'I don't know if I'd ever have told you. I wanted to but I didn't know how. Seems I was right—just look at your reaction.'

'Did you ever trust me?'

She blinked then turned away. 'I don't know that either.'

'Did you even try?'

'I don't—'

'You don't know. You don't know. Yeah, I get it.' He huffed out an angry breath. 'Seems to me you don't know a great deal, Gabby. Except, of course, about hiding the truth.'

'Yes, and opening up has done me a fat lot of good.' She pushed her fists into his chest. 'In an act of love I gave him a better chance at life. But you just don't want to understand.'

'Oh, I do, Gabby. I understand entirely.' He lifted her hands away from his body and dropped them by her sides, didn't want her touch on his skin. 'I think your baby was inconvenient. I know all about that because that's what we were to my parents. That's why they dumped us with a nanny while they went off on their nice little sailing trip. I know what it's like to play dip, dip, bloody dip, too. And to lose. To be given to people who turn out not to be the loving family you deserve. I know exactly what it's like to be unwanted.'

'Oh, I wanted him, Max. More than anything. But you don't always get what you want, right? Like this. Us. I wanted you. For the first time in forever I thought I'd found someone I could fall in love with. I wanted us to make a go of things. But not now. Not when you won't even try to put yourself in my shoes. You're just like Nonna and Mum, you think I'm completely selfish too.' He saw the torrent of fury swell through her, watched her try to stay in control but fail. She jabbed her finger into his chest. 'You are way out of line, mate. The far bloody side. Don't dare judge me. Don't. Ever. Judge. Me.'

He held her gaze, saw the tumult of emotions there, the rage, the sadness simmering through her. The dying hope. Felt it reverberate through him. A black mist coated everything he saw—hopeless and livid.

Shoulders lifting, she shook her head and stalked to the door. 'Now, I've got a lot to work through, and you're not helping at all. In fact, you're making things a whole lot worse. So you'd better go.' She waved her hand as if he was some insignificant interference. 'Just go. And don't even think about coming back.'

In truth, he knew it was for the best. It was over. Messy and painful. But over. 'Don't worry, Gabby. I'm out of here.'

And with that he turned around and walked out of her life.

CHAPTER THIRTEEN

THERE WAS NO getting back from this, Gabby knew.

Max had gone because of decisions she'd made when she'd been a child. But she understood how he'd see her now—as a woman who had committed the most heinous sin in his book.

So she couldn't blame him. She could run after him, try to explain, pound her fists against that bruised heart of his. But it would do no good. She knew enough from the bleak expression on his face that there truly was no going back.

Great, Nonna. Happy now? The punishment was cruel but deserved. She'd lost two babies, her fertility, and the man she loved.

Her breath stuttered as she scraped in air. Yes.

The man she loved.

From the first moment he'd offered her those cheesy chat-up lines she'd fallen for him, too fast. Gabby, who shunned any contact with men, who focused entirely on her career, who never allowed so much as a flutter of her heart, had given him a huge piece of it that she would never get back.

Could it get any worse?

Oh, yes. Even more cruel, she'd have to face Max every day at work. Stand next to him as they worked on a patient together. Offer him a confident smile during a ward round. Be the ultimate efficient nurse she'd trained herself to be. Not wince at the rumours or the reality of him seeing someone else, settling down. Because he deserved that, at the very least. After what he'd been through he deserved a chance to be happy.

She'd made a huge decision to give up her baby, but seeing how damaged Max had been, being brought up by people who hadn't wanted him, she was doubly glad she'd given Joe to a family who *had* desperately wanted him.

She instinctively knew her son was safe and happy. Without her.

Now she had to prove she could still live without him. And without Max. No matter how hard it was, no matter how much hurt and pain she suffered.

But she would manage that, too. The one thing Max had given her was faith in herself, a renewed vision of life as something to celebrate, not hide behind.

Jumping off that tower had been the beginning, and now she would take every moment and grasp it. So she could show them all, show Max, show Joe, show Nonna—*show herself*—that she would never be beaten. She would fall, sure, but she would get up and keep going.

The ache in Gabby's throat burned fiercely as she replaced the lids on the boxes and stacked them in order back in her closet. Tempted for a moment to haul out Joe's blanket and press her face into it in search of a smell long lost, she instead found the steel in her back and fitted the lid tightly.

Pressing a kiss on her fingertips, she placed them on top of the box and then closed the cupboard door. She would continue to buy gifts for her precious boy, would write him those letters, but she would now reassert her own future. After all, that was why she'd come to Auckland in the first place.

She would not have a family, the one thing she'd wanted most but had been too afraid to admit. She would never hold her own baby in her arms again. She would never curl into Max's heat and let him soothe away the stress of the day. Or share a smile with him. A meal. A bed. But she would survive. Just. She had before.

Even though her heart was breaking all over again.

She looked over to where Max had tried to hold her in bed. To the door still swinging on its hinges with the force of his exit. Breathed in the last remnants of his smell.

He was gone. The sad story of her life.

Her bottom lip wobbled and she could feel her renewed determination wavering. She would allow herself one day to grieve, then she would forge forward.

Crossing the bedroom floor, the pain in her abdomen returned, accompanied by the familiar dull throb of regret. She climbed back into bed and pulled the duvet up to her chin.

Only then did she feel the dampness on her cheeks. When she glanced down she saw the droplets on her top.

And at last let the tears flow.

'A load of fuss over nothing. It's just a pompous dinner.' Max flicked Jodi's hand away as she fiddled with his bow tie. After his heart to heart with Mitchell, everyone had relaxed. Even Jodi. Gone was the nervousness, the awkward glances, and into their place had slipped a gentle burgeoning friendship.

The rest of the guests had started to filter into the opulent Heritage Grand Tearoom. Jodi tutted. 'And it's an award. For you. You've at least got to have a straight bow tie in the photos.' She shook her head. 'You're like a bear with a sore head these days, Max.'

'I'm busy. Too busy for this kind of thing.' And he was.

Since they'd lost their baby, and Gabby had dropped the adoption bombshell, he'd buried himself in work, too numb to contemplate a next step.

'Max, really?' Jodi's eyebrows raised. 'For as long as I've known you, you've never been too busy for praise. In an ego contest, you and Mitch would tie for first place. And then coerce the poor judges to decide on an overall winner. Then you'd argue about that, too.'

'So we've come a long way.'

'Yes, yes, you have.' She stepped back and admired her handiwork. 'I'm proud of you both.'

Mitch appeared and stuck out his hand. 'Hey. Time to go in? You ready?'

Max took his brother's offered hand and shook it warmly. 'Looks like I've been placed at your table. Is that okay?'

'No problem. Shame you couldn't have found a plus-one, though.' Mitch's voice was playful with gentle teasing, not the goading of the past. 'I mean, Max Maitland without a date? My, my! What is the world coming to?'

'Flying solo feels good right now.' Who knew? If he said it enough he might actually believe it. A part of him was missing. The best part.

'You mean she turned you down, right?' Mitchell laughed. 'What happened? You stuffed up again?'

'Yeah, well, with you all happied up, someone has to keep the family tradition going.' They shared a knowing smile. At least some things were improving, his family life if not his love life. That he could even be here with these two meant they'd made huge strides.

But Jodi wouldn't let it drop, even when they took their places at the plushly decorated table. She leaned across the crystal and glass and whispered, 'It's not healthy to work so hard, Max. You need some down-time. Get out there and play the field like you used to. God help me for saying this, but meet a girl, a different girl, have sex.' She patted Mitch's arm and smiled. 'Have some fun. It works wonders.'

'I don't want sex,' Max whispered in a gruff voice. At least, not random sex. He wanted sex with Gabby. And that was not going to happen anytime soon. Or ever. He'd drawn the line under that disaster and moved on.

He had.

If only he could stop stupid things reminding him of her. Like the ridiculous Sky Tower that invaded his vision every time he opened his curtains. The Shed. Mojitos. His bedroom. His damned annoying migraine-inducing scarlet sky-garden.

And right now the empty chair to his left was the most stark reminder of all that was missing from his life.

One week and it wasn't getting any easier. Yeah, he missed her.

Plain and simple. And way too complicated, just like everything that made up Gabby.

But he missed her.

Missed her sarcastic comments. The frowns. Her cute laugh. The feel of her. The tight press of her body against his.

Work had been almost intolerable. At first he'd missed her not being there. But, then, when she'd returned, he'd just ached to touch her.

But she'd broken his trust and he couldn't get past what she'd done. Couldn't fathom it. Given a child away. Hell, was there any worse thing to do?

She'd dented his stupid fragile heart. And he hated it.

He glanced around the room at the female guests swishing around in taffeta and silk. Once he'd have welcomed this kind of affair as a challenge: so many women, so little time. But tonight he just wanted to be on his own.

No matter. It was a temporary blip. In a few weeks or months he'd get back on the dating scene, wouldn't he? Go back to how things had been before he'd met her.

Was that possible? He couldn't remember the person he had been before Gabby had come into his life. He certainly didn't much like the man he'd been: an empty shell not prepared to feel anything. She'd made him want things: a commitment; a family; to finally fix things with his brother. And had given him the tools and courage to make them happen.

And now he'd let her go. But it had been the only sane thing to do. He just had to believe it.

After a passable dinner and a couple glasses of red wine, Max stretched his legs under the table and watched his brother and Jodi chat together.

The Jodi thing was definitely a pale memory. Just seeing them finish each other's sentences, the genuine warmth between them convinced him that what they had was forever. With Jamie well on the way to recovery and their relationship on track, he couldn't help admit that he was jealous. But, then, they'd gone through hell to get here, and Mitch had fought for his family every step of the way. Max didn't know if he'd have the strength to do that.

The MC called for silence and a few awards were dished out. Hating the phoney reverence and the limelight, Max cringed at the prospect of having to receive his. Was it too late to leave?

He didn't deserve an award for doing a job he loved. He just liked being able to give patients a second chance—surely everyone deserved one of those. He liked the satisfaction from a good day's work and coming home to... Damn, there was that reminder again. An empty flat.

'I'd now like to call upon the nominator of the award for delivering excellence, Mitchell Maitland, to say a few words.'

'What?' Max stared at his brother. 'You nominated me? What the hell?'

'You saved my boy's life. Got to get my own back somehow.' Mitch stood and squeezed past, his grin broadening.

'God, no, Mitch—don't you say anything. They'll throw rotten tomatoes at me.'

'Ach, so you see through my dastardly plan.' Mitchell took to the stage, his tie perfectly straight, courtesy of his girlfriend. He cleared his throat and began his speech, his eyes fixed on Max.

'Max Maitland has brought many changes to the transplant service over the years. He's shaken it up, modernised it and even ruffled a few beaurocratic feathers, in true Maitland style. But now we have a service second to none in the OCD. Full credit to him. And, yes, I admit, we've had a few professional differences in our lives and a few personal ones, so some of you may be surprised I'm up here at all.'

He paused until the laughter died down. Looking around the room, Max realised how much their feuding had resonated across the hospital as a few of his colleagues nodded, but raised their glasses to Max and smiled. Seemed the whole staff body felt the effects of this Maitland thaw.

Mitch continued, 'As most of you are aware, things haven't been easy between us. But despite personal setbacks and challenges, Max has never been afraid to chase a dream, however hard it may seem, to do the right thing, to make countless people's lives better. Including my son's. And mine. And for that I can't thank him enough. In all my life I've never known a better man. So there is no more deserving recipient of this award, and I'm proud to call him my brother. I give you Max Maitland, recipient of the Auckland Hospital Delivering Excellence Award.'

After collecting the award, Max returned to the table and sat next to Mitchell. 'Whoa. That was unexpected. Thanks. Nice speech—if you can see through the bull.'

'Yeah, well, don't let it go to your head. And I expect at least three nominations in return from you next year. Between the two of us we could take this whole awards dinner out. What do you think—a Maitland coup?'

Max laughed. 'Think big, my boy. Next stop world domination. But we won't achieve that without working together. So how about we finally put the past behind us and look forward?'

Mitchell's jaw tightened as he thought about it, running his hand across his chin. 'We've been through a lot, you and me. What they did was wrong. No one asked us what we wanted, no one thought about what was best for us. We were too young to be heard.'

And neither of them had really recovered. At least, Max knew he hadn't. He was still stuck in the emotional wringer. Hence his accusations of selfishness and God knew what to Gabby. It suddenly became clear. He'd seen her actions through the tarnished lens of his own experiences, mixed up his issues with hers, and had come out of it the poorer. Judged her. Lost her. 'How did you get over it?'

Mitchell breathed out and shook his head. 'You can't hate everyone forever. People make mistakes, that's human nature. But you have to let go and try make a good life for yourself or you'll die lost and lonely. It's taken way too long already. Now it's time we tried to build on the good things.' Those cool Maitland eyes zeroed in. 'Are you in?'

'Yes. Absolutely.' Max bumped shoulders with his brother and chinked his glass with Mitch's. 'To the Maitlands. A force to be reckoned with.'

'Hell, yeah. To us.'

Jodi looked across at them and winked. 'Whoa! Brotherly love overkill.'

Knowing that there was a future for them all sent a hot buzz through him. There was still a long way to go and a lot to work through. But he had a family. Okay. Wow. Who would have known how good that would actually feel?

Gabby would be proud.

Gabby wouldn't be proud of this, though. Much, much later, Max sat on his deck in the cool night air, his head in his hands, and stared at the decimated garden. So his attention had been temporarily distracted. He hadn't watered or fed the plants for a while—he'd been busy. And, yeah, okay, he'd kept the curtains closed so he wouldn't have to see them and the bright colour that reminded him of what he'd walked away from.

But did they all have to die?

Of course they did. Just his luck. He tipped his head back and let the emotion spring free from his lungs in a long, cold laugh. Typical that not all the happy cards could be stacked in his favour. He had a family, sure, but no one to share that amazing feeling with.

No *Gabby* to share it with.

Slowly he picked off brown leaves and let them drop to the deck. Maybe it was a sign. He should throw them all in the bin and retreat to the barren landscape of his pre-Gabby life. It was colourless but ordered. Dull but predictable. Most of all it was pain-free.

He looked across the tops of the city buildings to the Sky Tower. Remembered the bravery she'd found to jump off. The risks she'd started to take for both of them. The pain she'd endured for almost half of her life. The loss.

But she'd still taken her courage in both hands and followed her heart.

Maybe the dead plants weren't a sign at all. Maybe they had absolutely nothing to do with his failed relationships and everything to do with the fact that he buried himself in his job to avoid taking real risks. With his heart, and his life.

His twin was right—people made the best decisions they could at the time, and lived with the consequences.

Gabby had at least found the courage to tell him, and to make such an admission would have cost her. And yet he'd failed to even try to understand. Instead, he'd taken the route he'd always taken, judged and blamed. Refused to think things through beyond his own experience. He'd seen everything through the jaundiced eyes of his past.

Mitchell's words came back to him. Maybe he needed to stop blaming everyone else and take a chance on what he wanted. On what could actually, finally, make him happy.

He was, after all, the doctor of second chances. But was it too late even for him?

He shifted his gaze over the Auckland landscape towards the sun rising over Rangitoto. A glow of muted oranges and yellows infused the air, casting pale light over the lush green of the island. Above, the dark shroud of night gave way to a dazzling blue sky. There it was, just out of reach, waiting for him to grab it.

Damn it, it was definitely time to add more colour to his life.

What the hell? Persistent thumping on the French windows jolted Gabby from her sleep. Mad axeman? Police?

As she dragged open the curtain her anxiety hit a record high. A mad axeman might have been preferable. At least she'd have known how to react.

Her silly shaking hands refused to work and her pulse jigged along at such an erratic rate she couldn't think straight. 'Max? What the heck…?'

'Good morning, Charge Nurse Radley. I need to talk to you.' He stood in the doorway wearing a crumpled tuxedo with his black tie hanging loosely around his neck. Crisp white dress-shirt tails poked out from under his jacket. Creased, slim-fitting trousers emphasised his divine body. He looked like he hadn't slept for days. He looked ruffled and edgy. He looked…simply stunning.

Or perhaps that was just the stars in her peripheral vision. But good looks were no excuse for barging into her space.

Hell, she'd come to terms with him leaving her, and what he thought of her. She didn't like it but it had happened. And, as always, she was dealing with the fallout. Work helped. Mojitos helped more. But she was still raw. He hadn't given them time to talk things through more. He hadn't even given her the time of day.

It was bad enough that she bumped into him at work, but having him in her room again? Cruel. 'It's six-thirty in the morning on my day off. So this had better be important.'

'It is. It's a matter of life and death.' He bent down and produced a cardboard box containing the most pathetic collection of droopy geraniums she'd ever seen. 'We need help.'

'You can say that again. It's about time you realised.' Examining the state of the plants, she moved sideways and let him in, taking care not to inhale too closely. Lord only knew what would happen if she breathed in that smell of his too. It was intoxicating. Lethal.

But he'd come here at the crack of dawn because of plants? He'd clearly joined her in the crazy stakes.

She carried the geraniums through to the kitchen and

placed them in the sink. Then turned on the cold tap in an attempt at resuscitation. 'You need intensive care. Or at least they do. I don't know what I was thinking, giving you sole care of these.'

'I neglected them.' He studied her and gave her a nervous smile. 'Look, Gabby, I neglected a lot of things.'

'Oh?' Now this was getting interesting. Her heart restarted its weird axe-murderer lumpy rhythm. 'Like what?'

'Like telling you how very sorry I am that we lost our baby.' *And that you can't have any more.*

He didn't have to say it, but it was there in the silence and in those startling Maitland eyes. She pressed her lips together to hold the hurt inside. They'd never had a chance to grieve together and come to terms with the pregnancy and the loss. Everything had happened so quickly. Including falling in love with him. 'Me too.'

He took a deep breath. 'And I neglected to tell you I understand about Joe.'

'Oh.' Her hand instinctively went to her necklace. 'Max, I don't need—'

He gently placed his finger on her lips. 'I said I understand. I really do. I've thought about the hell you must have gone through so young. I couldn't see that. I just judged you because of what happened to me. The words "adoption" and "fostering" left me cold, and I couldn't see past that. I'm so sorry. I was a jerk.'

She shrugged, trying to find words, but nothing seemed adequate. So she smiled instead. 'Yes, you were. A capital jerk.'

He smiled too. 'Gee, thanks.'

'I was only agreeing with you.'

His smile grew serious. 'I do know how much you're hurting. Losing someone is tragic. I know.' His fingers went to the diamond. 'This is something to do with Joe, isn't it?'

'Yes, it's his birthstone. I never take it off.'

'I noticed.' His eyebrows rose and she saw his eyes were warm, sparking with a gentleness that melted that hardened corner of her heart. 'That first night in the bar?'

'Was his birthday.' The day she celebrated and regretted in equal measure every year. Now the hurt meshed with the love she felt for her child and for Max. She didn't know if she was strong enough to take any more.

Then his palm caressed the necklace, stroked her throat. Heat zipped between them. 'It's beautiful. Like you.'

Her need for him was shooting off the scale. Being so close to him was torment. She stepped away. 'Max, please, don't do this. I can't take these games.'

'Will you ever stop interrupting?' He laughed and filled the space she'd left. Kissing distance. That's all. 'Hear me out, Gabby. I neglected to tell you that I'm crazy mixed-up and only just beginning to get sorted out. I'm trying, I honestly am. I wasn't looking to fall in love with you, but it just happened, and I didn't know how to deal with it. And then the ectopic pregnancy clouded everything and I was scared for you... Eugh— What the hell?'

He tapped his foot and made a splashing sound.

Together they looked down at the lake of water lapping towards their feet.

'Shoot! The tap!' Gabby jumped to the sink, where the plants bobbed forlornly. 'Great. That's all I need. You causing chaos. A plant graveyard. And now a flood. It's Armageddon. Save me from the plague of...' She paused. 'Oh, yes. Of course, I know...' Arms dripping with water, she shook her fist skywards, tipped her head back and giggled. 'Nonna! That's enough now. Stop it. Leave me alone.'

'You don't believe all that, do you? She's not really got it in for you.'

Gabby smiled. For some reason, even though he was causing chaos in her home and her heart, she felt freer than she'd ever been in her life. So phooey to Nonna. 'No. But it's always good to have someone else to blame, right?' Shoving a towel at him, she said, 'Now, give me a hand clearing up.'

Starting at the edge of the room she knelt and pressed a towel into the water, then squeezed it out into the kitchen bowl. Max knelt next to her and together they worked through to the middle of the room. Every time he dragged the towel back towards him his arm brushed against hers. Every time their skin touched she felt the same jolt of electricity she'd had the first day they'd met. Seemed nothing had changed, certainly hadn't dimmed. If anything, her feelings for him had deepened.

When he caught her eye she captured his gaze. *I love you*.

The words were there, threatening to trip off her tongue, but then his little speech before the flood began to sink in. She knelt up and pulled him round to face her, the tight knot in her throat threatening to choke her. 'Hold on. Hey, Maitland One. You love me?'

'Finally. Yes, Gabby. I love you.'

'Well, wow. That's a surprise.' She balled the towel into her fist and screwed it tighter, not knowing how to deal with the sudden lightness in her chest. And trying at the same time to be strong when tears were springing in her eyes.

'Yeah, well, it was news to me too.' He took the towel from her hands and dropped it to the floor. Then took her hands in his and held them against his chest. Water seeped up through her pyjamas. But she didn't care. All she wanted to do was look into those eyes and listen to his voice. Soft and gentle, yet solid and strong.

'But it's the best kind of news. I'm not good at this, Gabby. You make me happy. That's all. From the minute I saw you in the pub I've been lost. In you. You've shaken me up, changed my life and I didn't want you to do that at first. I fought against it, I didn't want to love you. I lost my parents and Mitchell and I've been too afraid I'd lose you too. But now I have the love thing cooking well. And I'm working on the trust.'

Was this what she thought it was? Was this what she even wanted? This could be a chance for them both, a second chance at grasping the life they both wanted. 'What are you saying? The commitment-phobe wants to commit now? Somehow?'

He grinned. 'Yes. Yes, I do, Gabby. I know I have a long way to go, but I reckon that together we can put the hard times behind us.'

She'd never believed it could be possible. But seeing the devotion on Max's face challenged her beliefs. She could be loved. She was lovable. She could love. She just needed to let it in, and allow herself to give love too. To Max.

Just one thing stood in the way. 'But what about babies? You know I can't have any now, and I don't want you to hold that against me sometime in the future. You have to be honest with me. And I understand if you want to walk away.' She held her breath, her pulse racing as he looked deep into her eyes.

'I know, Gabby, and I'm so very sorry. You'd make a wonderful mum. Maybe we can get help, and we can certainly look at options. Whatever you want. And if it doesn't happen for us then we'll be stronger for it.' Cupping her chin, he tilted her face to his. 'Trust me, there are enough Maitlands in the world.'

How could there ever be? She laughed. 'But I want you to have everything you deserve, and that includes a family.'

'I have one right here. That's enough for me.' At her frown he pressed a kiss on her forehead. 'Honestly.'

'Are you sure? Because I don't want you to regret—'

His mouth pressed against hers and stopped her words. Stopped any kind of rational thought. All she knew was that he was there, with her, and that was all that mattered. Anything else could be talked about and worked on. Now that they both knew how.

His kiss intensified as he meshed his fingers in her hair, crushed his body against hers. And she crushed him right back, clinging to him because this time she would never let him go. His arms held her so tightly she knew he felt the same.

He tasted sweet and dark, promising a day of sinful pleasure. And another, and another. A lifetime.

After yet another mind-numbing kiss he drew back a little and traced his thumb along her bottom lip. She caught it between her teeth, mesmerised by the heat and the love blazing in his gaze. His words came out in a whisper. 'So how about we work on it together? Slowly.'

'How slowly?' She wriggled her hips against him and nodded towards the bedroom. 'Not too slowly, I hope?'

His hands ran down her back and cupped her bottom as a dangerous glint infiltrated those Maitland eyes. 'Well, we could start with the physical…see how we go. Give me a score and we'll work on improving it. Every day. I can work very hard and I'm a fast learner.'

As he picked her up and walked through to the bedroom she leaned her head against his chest, felt the regular solid thud of his heart. And hers jumped in sync. Whatever the future held for them now, they'd face it together. 'Sounds like a plan, Maitland One, a very good plan.'

Just like always.
A perfect ten.

Two years later...

'So Mister Five, happy birthday. How was your first day of school?' Gabby stepped into Mitch and Jodi's lounge, handed over the birthday present to her eager nephew, and couldn't hold back a smile. It was so great to see him tearing around without a care in the world.

He ripped off the wrapping paper and dithered, one eye on the playroom, clearly uninterested in the adult small talk when there was fun to be had with a new fire engine and lots of friends. 'Cool, Auntie Gabby. We had story time and a birthday cake for me.'

'Cool indeed. Now, go play with your party guests.' Gabby ruffled Jamie's hair until he dodged out of her grip. Then she went to help Jodi in the kitchen, preparing sandwiches for the hyped-up five-year-olds.

Two years had seen her and Jodi becoming fast friends, and the chances to meet up and grow into each other's life had become more and more frequent. 'He's growing up fast.'

'Way too fast. But healthy, thank goodness. There were times I didn't dare imagine he could even make five. But he's like a whirlwind. I wish I had half his energy.' Jodi stopped cutting and looked up, tired shadows lining her eyes. But they were happy shadows and for good reason. Gabby's heart did a little dance as she watched the soon-to-be mum press her hand to her bulging tummy. 'And how I'm going to manage with a baby and a five-year-old demon, I don't know.'

'Just so long as you take care and get lots of rest. And we'll be there to help.'

As Gabby spoke she heard the door latch drop, felt the familiar flicker of heat and her body's immediate response. Max was here. She wandered through to the front room, trying to keep her excitement in check. 'Hey, husband.'

'Hi, Charge Nurse Maitland. Sorry I'm late. You know what it's like. Things don't always go as planned.'

'You're here now and that's all that matters.' She curled into his waiting arms, pressed a kiss on his cheek. Then, leaning her head against his chest, she took a breath. 'I have news.'

'We got the house?' He drew back a little. 'I thought we were exchanging contracts tomorrow.'

'Yes. Tomorrow, and as far as I know that's all going well.' She bit her bottom lip, weighing up the words. For over ten years she'd shunned this—then struggled to believe it could be possible. 'Phillipe rang.'

'And?' Max's face clouded. Their journey had not been easy. Two rounds of assisted fertility had been testing on both of them, but they'd stuck through it, holding each other up when it had seemed impossible. He'd been there for her throughout, solid and determined and reliable. And had infused it all with his sense of fun and his love. Anything seemed possible with him around.

Her heart almost beat out of her chest. 'And it worked. I'm pregnant.'

'Okay. Sit down.' He steered her to a chair as if she would break at the tiniest touch. His mouth twitched into a slow smile that spread and lit up his face. 'How many eggs took?'

They both knew they had a long way to go. But she knew—felt deep in her soul—that this time it was going to be all right. This time it would work. She played with the necklace at her throat, knowing that no child could ever take the place of her firstborn, but would equally fill her heart. 'Just the one.'

'One. A baby. Our baby.' His hand tenderly touched her stomach and he gazed at her with such love she wondered how it was possible she could be so lucky. 'So definitely no multiples in there?'

'Two? Are you completely mad?' She smiled over at Jodi who nodded in agreement. 'One set of Maitland twins is enough for anyone to handle.'

* * * * *

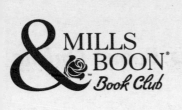

Join the Mills & Boon Book Club

Subscribe to **Medical** today for 3, 6 or 12 months and you could **save over £40!**

We'll also treat you to these fabulous extras:

- FREE L'Occitane gift set worth £10
- FREE home delivery
- Rewards scheme, exclusive offers...and much more!

Subscribe now and save over £40
www.millsandboon.co.uk/subscribeme